YANKEE DORIC

AMERICA BEFORE THE CIVIL WAR

A NOVEL BY BURTON RAFFEL

moon city press
springfield missouri
2010

www.mooncitypress.com

Text edited by Tita French Baumlin
Text layout by Angelia Northrip-Rivera
Cover design by Rebecca J. Sloane
Seating diagram by Jesse Nickles

Front cover photography: detail of Doric column at Yorkshire
    Museum Gardens (1827-1829), by William Wilkins
    Photograph © 2009 by Andy Marshall

Library of Congress Cataloging-in-Publication Data

Raffel, Burton.
    Yankee Doric / by Burton Raffel.
        p. cm.
    Includes bibliographical references and index.
    ISBN 978-0-913785-22-5 (alk. paper)
    1. Families—Fiction. 2. New York (N.Y.)—Social life and cus-
toms—19th century—Fiction. 3. United States—History—19th
century—Fiction. I. Title.
    PS3568.A37Y36 2010
    813'.54—dc22
                                              2010011619

"We have many dialects in our buildings, but no language . . . .
[W]e have developed in our ships, our carriages and engines a
new style . . . which I call the Yankee Doric . . . ."

—Horatio Greenough to William Cullen Bryant
27 Dec. 1851

Doric: "plain, rustic . . . the simplest of the three Greek orders
of architecture"

—*Penguin English Dictionary*

PART ONE

Doctor Bingham's house was not the biggest in Poughkeepsie.
It was plain . . . . But it was also nicely proportioned.

O
N
E

"I thank you for your receipt for greasing boots. Have the after noon to ride to the South road, and in truth my boots admit not only water, but peas and gravel stones."

— Daniel Webster, to his friend James Hervey Bingham
26 October 1801

Doctor Bingham's house was not the biggest in Poughkeepsie. Until relatively late in his career he was known as "the new doctor"—Doctors Bennett, Parvos, and Van Houten all having preceded him—but his house had preceded even old Doctor Van Houten, whose great-grandparents had migrated upstream from Nieuw Amsterdam. Bingham had bought his practice in 1814, from a doctor so nebulous in people's minds that he came to be known as "that fellow who sold out to Bingham," but he had bought his house from Cornelius Grandvoort. And as everyone in Poughkeepsie well knew, the Grandvoorts had been merchants for centuries, had been prosperous for almost as long, and they built to last. Cornelius had built his house in 1799, the very year young Frederick Bingham graduated from Columbia College—which Cornelius and other older residents found it difficult not to call Kings College. "It's all very well," Cornelius once responded to a patriot, who was scolding him for employing the royalist name of the state's prime institution of learning, "all this independence. The king was wrong and we had to be rid of him. But do we have to give up everything we ever had, names and all?" No Grandvoort liked to give up anything, either in name or in substance. The family did not have a motto—that would have been frippery and foolishness—but if they had it might have read, Change Nothing, Keep Everything.

The Grandvoort house, as it was known for its first fifteen years (and even after), was framed in solid brick, with a steep slate roof topped by two dormer windows. It had two storeys of equal size, and a basement below. It was plain—even the six steps leading to the front entrance were bare, and there was no overhanging roof to keep the rain and snow off the hats of anyone entering or leaving—and the bricks were kept whitewashed. But it was also nicely proportioned, with neat blue shutters that Doctor Bingham preserved in their original hue.

Nor had Grandvoort prevented his craftsmen from outlining the chaste front entrance in a kind of subdued bas-relief, two statuesque half-columns and a rigidly horizontal lintel above. There was a fan-shaped half-moon of leaded glass just over the door: the effect was subdued, but it was also distinctly elegant.

The house looked, as indeed it was, both substantial and costly. Cornelius would not have given it up, except that two of his children had died there, in 1809 and 1811, and then in 1814 his wife too had died, lingeringly and in great pain. And all this seemed to him to stick to the house, to coat the papered walls and line the neat rooms. The new doctor, who came with a young wife and no children and, it was reliably reported, a good deal of New York mercantile money behind him, appeared in Poughkeepsie barely a month after Mrs. Grandvoort's funeral; the house changed hands only a month after that. Cornelius Grandvoort took his surviving children and moved to New York City, where most of his clan had already dug deep roots, and spent the rest of his life adding to an already substantial fortune. He did not remarry, and he never revisited Poughkeepsie.

He would have had no trouble recognizing the house: the blue shutters—a kind of creamy light blue, carefully reproduced from painting season to painting season—were not the only things Doctor Bingham kept unchanged. The fruit trees out back, and the small urban stable, even the slatted chicken house, stayed as and where Grandvoort had created them. They were maintained, but they were not changed. Flowering bulbs set in the earth by Grandvoort hands, or Grandvoort servants' hands, went on pushing their bloom, year after year. Some of the same four-footed residents lived out their lives in and behind Doctor Bingham's house. It may even have been that some of the same vegetables grew and were seeded and were eaten and planted and then seeded and eaten and planted again. For the truth was that Doctor Bingham, though liking his comfort, had no interest in either architecture or landscaping, or indeed in altering anything about the shape of the earth he had inherited from his ancestors. He was a reasonably good doctor, and a reasonably good man, but he was considerably more passionate about his scientific correspondence, and the experiments that underlay it, than about either his house or any of the people who shared it with him.

His wife, Marie, mother of six children—three of whom survived to maturity—had more than enough to occupy her, without having to worry about the size, shape, or outer appearance of her house and the grounds around it. She kept the house in order, or tried to, and she steered food onto tables, clothing onto backs, and servants into doing more or less what they were expected to do. She worked hard at all these tasks, almost too hard: there were secrets to household regulation she could never master, methods she could never keep fully in mind. Everyone ate, everyone was clothed; the doctor had about as many hours in his laboratory, and in his study, as he required. But it all came hard, and she fretted and fussed, and sometimes, even in the presence of the children, and frequently in the presence of the servants, she wept.

The deaths of three children had aggravated a deep sense of the world's inadequacy. The first had been stillborn, and that was even before the first anniversary of her marriage to Doctor Bingham. He had come to her an elegant European-trained savant, of excellent birth and connections. She had expected she hardly knew what. But after a relatively brief honeymoon she had been carted off to Poughkeepsie, a thriving but provincial place miles and miles from any center of civilization, and her new husband had gotten terribly busy with his new practice, and she had gotten pregnant. The stillbirth, which had gone to full term, had been a shock from which she did not think she could recover. Her second child had followed without delay, and he had been healthy. And so had the third, another boy. But when the fourth arrived, in 1819, all her children had come down with an infectious disease that even her medical husband was not sure of, and the second boy had died. That had shaken Marie Bingham very badly indeed, and for some years there had been no further offspring. But in 1825 she had borne yet another son, and after another long interval a final son, Jonathan, in 1830.

She refused to have any more: her last pregnancy had been disastrously febrile and several times, in a state of desperation, she had begged to be relieved of her burden, of all her burdens. The sudden violent death of her fifth child, thrown from a horse and killed instantly, had not shaken that resolve. She was still only thirty-seven, more children were a plain possibility, but she would not budge. Her life had been quite sufficiently ruined by child-bearing, and child-rearing, and that was all there was to it. It was all very well for Doctor Bingham to talk: he could retire into his professional chambers; he could sit and boil ugly smelling vapors in glass jars, but she had to carry the children, and tend them, and raise them, and she had had enough. More than enough. And so the Bingham family, counting both adults and children, remained at five: Theodore, the oldest survivor, born in 1816; Anne-Marie, the only daughter, born in 1819; and the youngest of all, Jonathan, born in 1830.

Doctor Bingham was fifty when his final child appeared. He had not changed a great deal in thirty years. His moustache and trimmed beard showed some white; his stomach had rounded a bit, under his well-tailored vests (he wore a cravat every day of his life); but his skin was pink and unchangingly smooth, his eyes had not dimmed, nor had he lost either his hair or the erect, authoritative carriage the children unthinkingly assumed he had been born with. There was a permanent trace of British in his speech—his family connections included some very high gentry and even, if rumor was accurate, an earl—and no one in Poughkeepsie could wear white gloves with the same casual grace. His voice was deep and moderate, his vocabulary good, his manners as immaculate as his finger nails. His practice and his scientific labors kept him extremely busy; his practice was, in fact, somewhat the more successful of the two, though as a scientist he was known in the inner councils of the Royal Society, and also on the continent. Some correlation had been noted between Doctor Bingham's longish visits to New York City and his larger expenditures; it was said that his wife's wealthy merchant family kept the Binghams from being totally dependent on his medical practice. That seemed likely: her two brothers, Peter and Karl Andrée, had inherited their father's shipping business, and their mother, who had been born Maria Theresa Goldstock, had inherited a good deal from her father, a Hamburg-born merchant of very great connections in the European mercantile world.

Jonathan grew up, though he did not know it, with a distinctly unusual sense of there being worlds outside of his immediate one, worlds with which he and his betters—that is, his parents and all other adults—were intimately and naturally connected. Doctor Bingham might bring to the dinner table a large, stuffed envelope covered with strange-looking stamps, and announce that Peterson had made significant progress on the tubercule bacillus, and he might read them some of the closely written, incomprehensible pages. It was expected that they be attentive, comprehending or not. When they were older, like the oldest child, Theodore, who was virtually a man by the time Jonathan came to conscious awareness of him or of anything else, they were expected to ask questions. And their father answered them carefully, attentively.

Or his mother and father would exchange quite casual remarks about the *Amsterdam,* or the *Good Hope*—it was some years before Jonathan understood that these were the names of ships; initially he took them to be mysterious deities—and comment that brother Karl, or brother Peter, had said—Jonathan did not know what it was they had said, the words turned all jumbled and queer. "The c.i.f. dates turned out to be quite fortunate." "Really? Brother Karl had been worried on just that point." "The market's turn was unexpected, but he tells me prudence has been rewarded." Jonathan went to school with a girl named Prudence, and what *her* connection was with these mysterious dates—did you eat them? Or mark them off on a calendar hung on the wall?—he had no idea. But prudence was well rewarded, over and over, so he assumed that she, too, had linkages to the outside world, linkages of which he was as yet ignorant. He would know, in time, when it was appropriate that he know. In the meantime, children were here to be seen and not heard, and he was not heard; he took parental and indeed all adult incomprehensibilities as further manifestations of the divine order of things. It was an elaborate arrangement that long predated his appearance, and he well understood that it had been made without specific reference to him. It was his responsibility to learn: the divine order owed him no explanations, nor did it depend on his concurrence for its continued operation.

There were visits, too, both visits from some of those outer worlds and, as Jonathan grew older, visits to them. Uncle Peter was rather stiff—he was the oldest and always wore black and a sober frown—but Uncle Karl carried candies in his pockets and told stories and jokes, and his laugh was a great deal heartier even than Papa's. Uncle Karl teased Mother, too, which was something even Doctor Bingham did not dare: it was bewildering and yet delicious to see Mother's face turning red and to hear her stammering. Uncle Karl was a lively presence. Papa's relatives did not make visits: it was a Rule of some sort, but Jonathan could not decipher its underlying nature. There was one Long Visit to the elder Binghams, who lived north of Boston, but the children were not invited—and judging from their parents' grim expressions, both when they left and when they returned, the children were just as glad to be left behind. Theodore liked supervising his younger brother and sister, and Anne-Marie—herself eleven years Jonathan's senior—liked playing mother, with him as a flesh-and-blood doll. And Jonathan was too awed by his parents to feel left out.

It was not until many years later that he learned, from a passing remark of Theodore's, that his parents had not really visited the elder Binghams, but instead had gone to their funeral. And also that the will had revealed something of a shambles: no one inherited very much; almost everything had been consumed, which had been a distinct and unpleasant shock. The American Binghams were rarely mentioned, at the inner table or on other occasions. The Andrées, however, were discussed all the time; they visited, and they were visited.

Jonathan was seven, the first time he got to join an expedition to New York City. His sister, of course, was interested in finery and, since she had just turned eighteen, in young men. Theodore did not make the trip: he spent relatively little time in Poughkeepsie, having by 1837 graduated from Princeton and then apprenticed himself in the legal chambers of a family friend in New York. They saw him in the city, along with the rest of their relatives, but he was a young man on his own, independent and living in rooms very much of his own. Jonathan was dazzled by Theodore's stunning clothes, his sweeping speech, and all the names he could exchange with anyone who liked name-exchanging games. It was the clearest sign possible of full adult status; Jonathan knew that his brother was crossing the Bar in more ways than one. He knew, too, that he himself had a long way to go, and though he was envious he was not jealous: everything took time, and he could wait. His turn would come, exactly when it was supposed to come.

"Grandvoort hopes you still like the old house," Uncle Karl said to his father and mother, at dinner around the huge dining room table. There were more than two dozen of them, feasting and gossiping.

"I hope he doesn't want it back," Doctor Bingham laughed.

"No, but he envies you, he really does. Poor fellow."

"Has he remarried?"

"No, and he won't." Karl lifted his wine glass. "And you, Frederick, have the joyful possession of the old house, and the young Marie Andrée, and the esteem of half Europe."

Glasses clinked.

"And some day, who knows," said Uncle Peter in his usual measured way, "there'll be a Bingham in a still larger and better known house, also painted white."

Jonathan knew the remark concerned Theodore—he saw his brother blush and pretend to be busy brushing his lips with a large napkin—but had no idea what this meant.

For him, the important aspects of the visit, as of subsequent ones, were to be sure not the adult conversation, or the big houses they drove to, or even the immense meals they consumed, but the acquaintance with his own contemporaries, his cousins and his cousins' cousins, who spoke with effortless ease of things Jonathan knew nothing about. They prattled about hotels and parks and above all of names that no one in Poughkeepsie knew; he'd never heard even his mother and father discussing Astors and Vanderbilts and Roosevelts. But his cousin would run them up and down the scale, loading in dollops of financial news and commercial speculation that left Jonathan scrambling for the ends of all the different strings. When it seemed safe, or when they paused for breath, he tried to pin down a strand or two. And sometimes they untangled things for him, a little impatiently. But they also accepted him—blood was emphatically thicker than base metal, no matter how negotiable the latter—and they played with him, and taught him new games, and took him rambling.

There was a great deal to see, all over Manhattan island: tight little farms uptown, heavy carriages tearing up and down Broadway, and the hectic docks, noisy and cluttered and perpetually repopulated. It was nothing to his cousins to see men in turbans, men of assorted different colors, men in long dresses and men, even, with rings in their nose. It was not until Jonathan's second visit, the next year, that he got to see the *Sirius*, a British steamboat—and only the second ship in history ever to cross the Atlantic without using sailpower. But even in 1837, on that first occasion, there were ships up and down the harbor, both in the water and at the docks: New York was growing by leaps and bounds. One of his cousins told him—though neither believed it—that his father reported more than five hundred new business establishments being opened, each and every year. He could have added, truthfully, that almost two thousand new buildings went up every year—some so shoddily built that they collapsed only days after being finished. One brick building actually blew down in a thundershower. But though there were fires and accidents all the time, the city was growing: this was all that mattered.

There was more to see than boats. His cousins were not old enough to take him across the Hudson, to the Elysian Fields amusement center. (It was one of the few things about the city that pleased Mrs. Trollope.) But they could show him Fulton Market, a sprawling building with huge awnings and men swarming in and out of it, wheeling kegs or pushing wheelbarrows or even, two abreast, hauling off large handcarts of produce. The roar of vehicles, and the rush of peddling cries, were dazzling. Jonathan was also deeply impressed by New York's omnibus coaches, built like big closed carriages. They had entrances in the rear and the seats ran in two rows along the sides. They had schedules and pretty much kept to them: Poughkeepsie had nothing to match that. Nor did Poughkeepsie have gas lights, which already lined whole streets in the business districts. Night or day, you could make your way safely, in spite

of horses and dogs and carriages and more people pushing along in one
street than Poughkeepsie could even dream possible. Jonathan did not
get to go to the Park Theatre (neither did his parents: sober business
families did not have time for such frippery), but there were shipyards
to see, and factories sprouting all over, foundries and locomotive engine
shops and even a rotary windmill, like some huge circular kite planted
on top of a brick building. It worked, though what it ran was hidden
inside and Jonathan and his cousins could not get close enough to learn
what it was. But they stood out in the street and stared and his cousins
pretended not to be awed, since they after all lived in New York and
saw things like this all the time. There were railroads, with new tracks
almost every time he visited. The great Croton Aqueduct was being
dug, in 1837, and though his cousins had little to say about it, his aunts
in particular talked of it a great deal. Jonathan was impressed with their
fervor, if not with the subject: Poughkeepsie had no problem, so far as
he knew, with its water supply. He enjoyed oysters, from street vendors
and small shops: they were everywhere, oysters were consumed by the
barrelful, all over New York.

He enjoyed New York, the vigorous bustle, the noise and the lights
and the games, the chatter and the gossip. He went on enjoying it, and
got to know it well. But he liked coming home, too, and in many ways
he preferred Poughkeepsie, duller and in all ways quieter though it was.
It was insular—he knew neither the word nor the idea—but news fil-
tered in from outside. There was a local weekly, it printed accounts
of things national and even international. But that was not important
either, in his early years. What did matter was the regularity, the warm
predictability of Poughkeepsie events. In the winter the children would
sled and skate and (if they were boys) throw snowballs. In the spring
they would fish. In the summer they would swim and play ball games. In
the autumn they would ramble: all town children, girls included, spent
most of their autumnal free time in the woods and along the river. Not
that there was a vast amount of free time, when school was in session.
There were household chores, as well as school ones, for both boys and
girls; social class and economic standing were no barriers to housework.
Jonathan had a special pleasure, denied to most other children: in the
afternoons his father drove about in a neat chaise, visiting the sick,
and when Jonathan was available he would be brought along—not to
help medically, but to stand outside and hold the horse. These quick
gallops around the town were important occasions, as indeed his father was visibly an important local personage. And his father would tell

him snippets of medical history: it was astonishing to learn that Peter Miller's father suffered from perpetual hernia, or that Margaret Smith's mother seemed likely to turn downward into tuberculosis—after which medicine would be helpless. Doctor Bingham remained relatively calm, no matter how desperate the medical emergency. This rather astonished his son, but he also saw that his father was concerned and worked as hard as he knew how to keep his patients alive and well. Nature was the unpredictable factor: the weather, the particular physical and psychological makeup of the sick person, and of the sick person's mate, and much more. What helped Jones might not help Smith; what injured Smith might be good for Jones. Patience and stamina and good-humor all around were essential ingredients, plus a reasonable cheerful fatalism: in the end it was out of all their hands, doctors and patients and everyone else. It was important never to forget that.

And living in Poughkeepsie, more even than living in a growing metropolis like New York, they lived—each and all—in a *house*. The word is the same; the reality has utterly changed. There were shops, in Poughkeepsie as well as in New York, but they were used only when necessary. Pots and pans had to be acquired from a shop, if they had not been passed down with a family. China and silver had to be acquired outside the household, as did more elegant furniture. (Jonathan had a vivid memory of the opulent abundance at Duncan Phyfe's furniture shop, on Fulton Street in New York. So much carving, so much velvet: it had seemed to him like a museum of extravagance, and he had been awed and thoroughly silenced.)

But everything that could be made at home was in fact made in home, even in prosperous households like Doctor Bingham's. There was no such thing as a shop for cleaning clothes, or washing them; there were no greengrocers in Poughkeepsie, nor were there any butchers. There were wheelwrights, but basic carriage maintenance and repair was done, as it had always been, by stablemen. There were no machines to break down; most other repairs were too simple, too basic, to require outside help. You ate what you grew, and what you grew you prepared under your own roof, if not necessarily with your own hands. (It was a shock to Jonathan when he learned that the first year and a half of his existence had not been spent in the family, nor even under the family roof: he had been literally farmed out to a nurse, and only reclaimed when no longer a suckling.)

Every house had its own character; far more than now, the tastes and habits of the proprietors were immediately apparent to eye and ear.

And to the children who grew up in each house: families have never been alike, but the differences were considerably clearer, a hundred and fifty years ago. Doctor Bingham would sometimes read, at table: it was Jonathan's clear impression that no one else in all of Poughkeepsie, at least no one who had a family, ever dined with a book. That was a small matter. But how children were disciplined, from house to house—that was no small matter at all. Canes and reeds were most common, in the houses of Jonathan's friends. There were strap users, too, and palm fanciers. Doctor Bingham relied almost exclusively on his tongue.

"I am informed that a jar of apples, meant for Mrs. Michaelson, and to be delivered by you, Jonathan, was in fact not so delivered. Is this accurate?"

Or:

"You were visibly smudgy, at dinner, Jonathan. And if I am not mistaken you, at one point during the evening meal, allowed your nose to come into snuffling contact with your shirt sleeve."

Or:

"Your sister informs me that, when you were civilly requested to bring in some wood, you stuck out your tongue, and further that when pressed to perform this necessary chore, you said several things of a distinctly impolite nature. Is the report correct?" These queries were as mildly spoken as they must seem here, lying quietly on the page. But this was only the beginning: the procedure was both ineluctable and horrific. Jonathan was permitted to answer only monosyllabically, in the negative or in the affirmative. It was dangerous, he quickly learned, to answer in the negative, for that stance pitted him against his elders, and *that* was a struggle in which a child could not hope to prevail. So he came to see the wisdom of confession and regularly answered, "Yes, Father." He was then required to stand (his father would be comfortably seated, but Jonathan would stand, hands at his sides, face forward, eyes open and attentive) while the disciplinary proceeding went slowly and carefully forward.

"You are aware, of course, of the necessity / utility / advisability of prior instruction (and so on)?"

Jonathan was permitted (and required) to agree.

"Have you anything to offer in extenuation?"

Jonathan came to understand the question; he rarely attempted any sort of extenuation, for it invariably prolonged matters, and duration was basic to the punishment.

"I need hardly tell you," his father would proceed, sometimes quietly lighting a pipe to carry him through the rigors to come, "how essential is the cooperation of each and every member of a household, if that household is to continue to function. Nor need I remind you, I am sure, of the duties and responsibilities of the junior members of any household. I will not speak of these matters in a sacramental connection, though you are more than old enough to understand how seriously important that connection is. That, however, is a matter for your individual immortal soul, and you will be well advised to wrestle, in private, with the blemishes placed upon your own soul by this sort of conduct. You are a child. It is your social obligation to understand your place in the particular social microcosm in which you happen to find yourself—never minding the obvious fact that you did not choose to so embody yourself. We must each of us, child and also adult, learn a necessary tolerance for the rights and the obligations of others, both those placed above and those placed below us." (Here might follow, on occasion, a discursion on the immortal souls and the earthly social standing of servants; this was much more likely, of course, when an offense against a servant was being dealt with.) "The world is not an inherently orderly place. It maintains what order it has, indeed, only because of the unremitting struggle of the higher classes of human being to enforce an idea of order, a concept of values and priorities of which the lower classes are by and large ignorant. Now you, Jonathan, are not, as it happens, badly placed on this scale of understanding. This placement, though you did not earn it and may in the end turn out not to deserve it—that will be strictly for you to determine—carries with it an even higher set of responsibilities. It is distressing to find that, once again, you do not seem entirely aware of this important fact."

Etc.

What hurt was the duration, in part, and the rigid posture of attentive acceptance. But it was also the manifold demonstrations of something close to contempt—it might have been indifference, but Jonathan was too young to see the distinction, if there was one—which caused the intense pain the boy felt, enduring a lecture which sometimes lasted more than an hour. This was his father, not a hired schoolteacher, not a dependent preacher. This was the man who had given him birth, who had given him everything he had or might hope to have, to whom he owed debts greater than mortal man ought to be expected to repay. This was the ruler and model of his world; this was the man above all men whose love and approval he wanted and needed. This was hard enough to obtain, under the best of circumstances: his father tended not to notice him when all was functioning as it was supposed to. But when he had misbehaved, and when his father had either observed or been made aware of that misconduct, approval was about as obtainable as a mountain of snow in mid-July. His father did not often raise his well-tuned voice. The occasions of physical reprisal, throughout Jonathan's entire childhood, could be counted on fewer than the fingers of a single hand. But the articulate, almost dispassionate disappointment that was rolled out against him, like the verbal armies of some dark night of the soul, was withering. Not that he saw it as unjust: children did not judge parents, not even when worse things than scolding were involved. But it hurt, it hurt deeply and painfully and enduringly, and Jonathan tried as hard as he could to keep it from happening again.

It was also distinctly like cutting the anchor line on a small skiff, just before or even smack in the middle of a large storm. Jonathan's sense of differentness, his sense of how little he in fact belonged anywhere, was perhaps born in the lee of his father's temperate scourging—and then watered and sunned in the tepid blast of the next scourging, and the next, and the next. For he did not succeed in avoiding displeasure: it did not seem to matter how hard he tried, or how cleverly he plotted his own goodness, or on whom he tried to rely for help. There was neither success nor help, on this quest: the grail of perfection was perpetually, and repeatedly, denied him. And a part of him withered each time.

His mother's role in fostering his dis-ease, his growing sense of apartness—it seemed almost to grow as he grew, stronger and more powerful as he passed from weak dependence to greater capability— was a much more complex affair. Jonathan was able to see his father's role, later on, with a certain clarity. But his mother was almost as shadowy to his own understanding as she sometimes seemed to the townsfolk—for whom she remained a misty figure of badly defined outlines. It was not as if she were a recluse, seen only on the lawn after dark, or as if she skulked about in a long black cloak, hovering over smoking fires or investigating chicken entrails. Marie Bingham raised her children and ran her house, both as well as she was able. She dealt with tradesmen openly and fairly; her servants worked hard, often with insufficient direction, but no one was ever abused in Mrs. Bingham's household: no one lost any wages; no one had to deal with screaming fits or drunken incompetence. Doctor Bingham's wife even appeared at her husband's side, on the few social occasions when that was required, and she wore decent clothing and behaved unexceptionably.

But no one in Poughkeepsie could have said that they knew her. She had no friends: no one was admitted to her house who did not come for the doctor or on impersonal business. She discussed her private affairs, whatever they might be, with no one. She did not express opinions on social issues; she smiled when the subject of politics was talked in her presence, and even religion—though her family were regular church-goers, and Doctor Bingham's contributions to theological conversation could be counted on pretty much like the sun and the rain—did not stir her to personal utterance. She seemed, in fact, not to have any particular likes or dislikes; she almost seemed not to have any particular personality. Caleb Miller, the shoemaker who had the Binghams' custom, once told his wife, after visiting the Grandvoort house to deliver some work and take home some more, that Mrs. Bingham was like a night-time shadow when the moon wasn't shining. "There aren't no shadows when the moon's not shining," she replied with vexation. He nodded: "No, but suppose there were, eh?"

For Jonathan, who saw his mother every day of his life, she was just as elusive, and the frustration—though as a child he neither knew it existed nor could have acknowledged it if he had known—was a great deal more painful. When he was barely six, a dispute with another boy had driven him home, fuming. He had marched into his mother's presence and requested a hearing. She was sitting near a window, sew-ing. (Marie Bingham tried always to be in the right stances, the correct postures, even though her maids could have explained that every seam she put in had to be ripped out and done over, and every repair she at-tempted had to be patched and reinforced.)

"I can't help you with your little friends, Jonathan."

His anger kept him at it.

"I know, Mother. I don't want you to do anything. I just want you to listen."

She was not looking at him; her attention seemed centered just above her sewing basket.

"Why, if there isn't anything I can do?"

"Because," he insisted, clenching his hands in frustration. "Just be-cause."

She lowered her hands and sat silently for a moment.

"Run along and play, Jonathan. I'm sure everything will be all right."

She did not pick up her sewing; she simply sat motionless, wrapped in an aura of distance he knew could not be penetrated without making a fuss that would bring down still worse storms. He stood for a mo-ment, hoping something would change, but nothing did.

Back outside, he chased a cat up a tree, threw stones at it, then tried to kick his favorite dog, and finally sat just under the sewing room window, his back up against the wall of the house, and cried. No one heard him.

When he was nine his father went on a voyage to England—to deliver a paper (whatever that meant) before the Royal Society. Theodore, just admitted to the Bar of the State of New York, went along as his father's secretary, and as a kind of reward for his legal persistence. Anne-Marie, married only a month earlier, also went along, with her husband, a young doctor anxious to try *his* wings, too, in the scientific air of Europe. There were steamboats—crossing the Atlantic was faster every year, and less dangerous every year—but the trip was for all that not a casual affair. Solemn preparations were made, including a long visit from the family lawyer and an up-dating of Doctor Bingham's will. Jonathan was carefully assured that he would be, as the oldest male on the premises, the man of the house.

"But why can't I come?"

His brother chuckled, even his father smiled.

"Later. You'll have your time too, Jonathan."

Jonathan did not inquire how he could be the man of the house and yet be too young to travel to England. He thought it was strange, but it was not his place to ask such questions.

And then they all left, driving off in a rented carriage (so his mother would still have the family vehicle at hand). It was June; school was out. In three days they would be on board their ship, and then they would be on the vast ocean, and then they would be in England. And Jonathan had to stay at home, no longer even at school. He was, they had said, left in charge of his mother. That was a polite fiction, as he well knew; it was even a joke. But it was also true. His mother was unnaturally gay, for a short while: Jonathan had never known her ever to be gay, and at first the change was exhilarating. He thought they would certainly have a jolly time, alone together. But even at age nine it was hard to miss the extravagance of her gaiety, the high strain in her sudden laughter, the tension in her sweeping gestures and too-rapid walk. It was scary, and it was almost a relief when, the third day, she broke down in the middle of dinner and wept, her face lying flat on the table. The maid had to take her to her room—Jonathan rose and demanded the task, but the servants quietly, efficiently restrained him—and he had to eat the rest of his dinner alone. The big dining room turned tomblike, but he was stolidly determined and finished his meal, doggedly stuffing food from plate into mouth, bite by bite conquering the silence and the excitement and the trauma of his mother's instability.

He saw it even more clearly, in the weeks that followed. The gaiety did not often return—it flitted in and out, occasionally, like an indecisive butterfly—but the fits of weeping did. Yet extreme states were easier to deal with. It was when she was in the gray middle distance, neither exhilarated nor vastly depressed, that she was the most difficult. Silence was bad; silence was always bad. She could sit for hours, even walk for hours, without saying a thing. But there were even ways of handling that. He could take a book and read; he could draw; he could excuse himself and go outside, where he could run and be refreshed. Silence was not pleasant, but it could be endured. It was her snippets of conversation, when she was lost in those gray states that were the worst.

"You've been eating elderberries again, Jonathan."

"No, Mother."

"You never admit it. If I've told you once I've told you a dozen times, they make you ill."

"I haven't been eating them, Mother."

Her eyes turned hard.

"You're just like your father."

There was no response, and no escape. He did not know what it was he was being accused of—to be like his father was both impossible and glorious, beyond even his dreams—and he could not say to her, as suddenly he wanted to say, Oh be quiet.

He tried to get her to walk, and one day she went with him, briefly. They went out the back way, at her insistence, but she permitted him to offer her his arm, like a real gentleman, and he was pleased and proud. It was a cloudy, hot day, but she'd wrapped a heavy shawl around her shoulders. Nor would she change to walking shoes.

"I know what I'm doing," she snapped, and he stopped arguing.

They went down the lane and he turned toward the river.

"No," she objected, stopping. "Not that way."

"It'll be lots cooler. Besides—"

She turned away.

"I don't want to walk that way, Jonathan. Try to be a gentleman and don't dispute with me."

They turned into a thoroughfare, and she flinched every time a large wagon rumbled by, every time a horse clattered along.

"It's so dusty," she murmured, holding her long skirt closely around her.

"There's Mister Miller," he exclaimed, nodding to the shoemaker. His mother looked down, and did not raise her head until Miller had passed. "He's a nice man," Jonathan said lamely. He glanced at his boots. "He fixed that torn seam just dandy."

Her sigh was heavy. She walked slower and slower.

"So stuffy," she murmured.

"I'll carry your shawl, Mother."

He could not tell whether the sound she made was a reply or simply the clearing of dust from her throat. There was perspiration on her forehead. He wished she'd be sensible. If she were a child, he'd drag her down to the river and make her swim: *that* would cheer her up, even though she wouldn't believe it if he told her. She'd never believe him, no matter what he said. And she wasn't a child, and he was.

"I've walked enough, Jonathan," she announced, and turned swiftly around. He did not protest. "It was not an intelligent idea," she informed him. "I'm sorry you suggested it."

"Yes, Mother."

She pulled ferociously at his arm.

"The least you might do, young man, is apologize for the unpleasantness you've caused me."

"I'm sorry, Mother."

She sniffed, and they walked rapidly back to the house, after which she disappeared and he went out to the stable and helped groom the horse, and polish the carriage, and tried hard not to remember their abortive walk.

Toward the end of the second week, as they were leaving the dinner table, she touched his arm and asked him to sit with her. He was delighted.

"I feel mopey tonight," she explained, after he had settled her in a favorite chair, a small afghan over her legs. Fires never warmed his mother, no matter how hotly they blazed. "I do wish your father were here."

"Or we were there!"

She grimaced.

"I've no urge to see England. Such a tired old country, and such stuffy people."

Jonathan gaped.

"I'm sure father knows very lively people. And Martial's pretty lively himself." Martial—named by a Latinate father—was Anne-Marie's young doctor husband. "And Theodore always finds whatever's going on, you know he does."

She retucked the afghan.

"I wish they hadn't gone," she repeated. "Your father can be an exceedingly selfish man, Jonathan. And," she raised a hand warningly, "I dare say you'll grow up to be just like him. All men are selfish." She stared into the bright fire and Jonathan sneaked a look, wondering if it needed tending. It did not. She finally turned back to him. "And after all, what has all his European training brought him? Has it made him a better doctor? Has it brought him a better practice, has it enabled him to lead the life he would have liked to lead, has it made him truly independent of his wife's family? What *has* it brought him, indeed, except a restless dissatisfaction with everything he has, and a need to prove himself something he neither is nor ever can be?"

Her eyes wandered past Jonathan but she seemed, still, to be speaking directly to him.

"Why else has he gone, knowing how much he is needed here? But he doesn't care, he never did care. Never." She shook her head slowly from side to side. "If some fairy creature came down the chimney, right now, and granted me three wishes, do you know what I'd be tempted to ask for? That all of this might be cancelled out, vanished from the face of the earth as if it had never existed—oh, I'd like to see your father's face, when he returned and found nothing here! I should dearly like to see that. And then," she continued thoughtfully, "I think I'd wish that I were a princess, or a queen, and exceedingly young, and exceedingly beautiful, with chests full of diamonds and a heart like flint. And then I'd ask to be young forever, and never to be married, and never to have children, and never to grow old, and never to know illness and pain and all the things I've lived with these many years." She pursed her lips, then nodded vigorously. "That's what I'd ask for. Yes. Exactly that."

She let her head droop; he could not tell if she was asleep, but asleep or awake, she did not seem aware of his presence. And after a while he tiptoed out of the room—the servants would take care of getting her to bed, they always did, it was what servants were for—and went very quietly to his room, and undressed and got into bed. But it was extremely hard to sleep. He kept hearing his mother's voice, and the strange things she'd said. He could not understand it all, but he understood a lot. Too much.

He finally fell asleep. And for the first time in years he had a desperate nightmare, and woke screaming. And alone: no one came. His mother had not heard, or if she had heard she did not choose to come.

It was not the servants' business: he was no longer an infant; he was no longer a suckling farmed out in some strange woman's house. (He could never find out who the woman had been. They told him she had left Poughkeepsie, they told him she had died, they told him to be still.) It was a hot, dark night, with no moon and no air. He threw the bed-clothes to the floor and lay rigidly on his back, staring at the ceiling, determined not to cry. He did not cry, though his eyes several times turned damp. The dark silence was more threatening than he could remember. He stared hard at the ceiling, and in the end he fell asleep. But when he woke up, the next morning, he remembered it all—and then it was harder not to cry. He threw his bed together, flung on his clothes, and ran down the stairs, hunting a day in which to involve himself, a world in which to submerge himself.

T W O

". . . a lawyer, who preserved his integrity unspotted, deserves a place in the calendar of saints."

—Daniel Webster, to his friend Thomas Abbott Merrill
4 January 1803

"The usual, doc?"

"The usual."

The white-faced man dug slowly in his vest pocket; he piled the coins in a careful heap on the table.

"Six bits. Count 'em."

Doctor Bingham neither counted the money nor picked it up.

"Your pulse is troublesome, Michael."

The patient's laugh was feeble, but genuine.

"Trouble's me a lot more'n it troubles you, doc!"

Doctor Bingham shook his head.

"There isn't a great deal more I can do for you, Michael. You're like a clock with a tired spring."

There was an immediate pretense, deliberate and good-humored, of reclaiming the small heap of coins.

"Do I got to pay you six bits to tell me that? Seems like there never was much you could do for me—with all respect. I ain't being critical, you understand. But I've known since this thing started there wasn't much left. It don't matter. The farm ain't much, but the boy's doing right well with it—well as I ever did. The girls is all married. What the hell else—pardon the expression—could I do that I ain't already done? Why should I give a damn if I'm going to peter out?"

Doctor Bingham smiled.

"Your soul, I take it, is all prepared for its journey?"

The hand trembled as the coins were swept up and dropped into Bingham's lap.

"I ain't got no soul, doc. Here, take your money and go worry about someone else. You been here almost thirty years now, and you just can't understand. I got two hands and two legs, and I used to have a good strong back. That's as close to a soul as I'm ever going to get.

And I don't worry none: I been doing what I was supposed to be doing; I been working and raising kids. I done all right."

Doctor Bingham rose.

"You've even found your way to church, now and then."

"Now and then. That don't do no harm neither, if you don't take too much of it. Like whiskey, eh?"

Doctor Bingham touched him on the shoulder.

"Take care of yourself, Michael."

"Long as *you* can't, doc, I might as well try for myself, eh?"

The ride home—this had been the last patient of the afternoon—was slow and thoughtful. It was Jonathan who spoke first.

"He's dying, isn't he?"

Bingham rubbed his chin.

"So are we all, each in our own time. He'll die when he's ready, I dare say." He turned to his son, now twelve and gangly. "He's done what he can and I've done what I can—which isn't much. But I'd rather, at least, that I didn't help push him into his grave. What could I do for a diseased heart that's worth doing? Nothing, in truth. I suppose, when you come down to it, I don't really believe in what's called doctoring. I wonder why I do it, sometimes. I do indeed."

"You'd rather have worked in the laboratory, wouldn't you?"

"That's an odd way to put it, my son. I was not really consulted about my preferences, as in your time you will find that you are not consulted about yours. Life has a way of settling these things for you. And how could I have supported my family, closeting myself in the laboratory? I do like puttering, and pretending to be on the verge of large discoveries. But I've never thought it was what I was meant to do. That's the great thing, Jonathan: you'll learn it in time. Doing what you were put here to do."

The boy wanted to ask, "And have you?" But that would have been too much, he could not say it. It was better to saying nothing—and they rode the rest of the way with only a few monosyllables exchanged. But as his father pulled the horse to, and the stableman came out to take charge, Doctor Bingham picked up the thread himself.

"You're wondering if I've done what I ought to do, aren't you?" It was not a question and he did not wait for an answer. "I hope so; I trust so." The stableman waited; Doctor Bingham had not relinquished the reins. "I wondered the same thing about my father, you know. Your sons will wonder the same about you. It doesn't change a great deal,

Jonathan. It hasn't changed a great deal in thousands of years, I suspect. Only the Good Lord knows for sure, and He doesn't speak to the likes of us." They climbed down; the horse was led off, the carriage would be pushed into its shed once the animal was properly taken care of. "My father was a doctor, until he inherited his father's money. Which he spent the rest of his life squandering. I've always known I would practice medicine, Jonathan. So I made up my mind, very early on, that I would train myself as well as I knew how, and do the job as well as I was capable of doing it. Which is what I have done."

They stopped just in front of the six front steps that old Grand-voort had built for very different feet.

"It's the same with everything we do, here on earth. I may not be the best husband your mother could have had, or perhaps the best father to you and to the other children, but I have tried, I've done my best, such as it is. I rather doubt, you know, that one can ask more of oneself than that." He smiled a bit thinly. "Of course, that's not to say, not at all, that what one does will necessarily please others. My best may even be your worst, and you may sometimes be quite sure it is indeed that. But ask yourself this: how much responsibility for others can we safely assume? Realistically, that is. And are we entitled to worry more than a certain amount about what effect we are having on others?"

He raised a meditative finger.

"*That's* the question, you know. Can we be so arrogant as to assume that we really understand the effect of our actions? I don't think so. I think, and I have always thought, that it was a great deal safer, and therefore a great deal kinder, too, if we each stayed in our chosen sphere, like the planets in their predetermined orbits, and let all other men do the same. A great deal safer," he affirmed again, and then they went into the house, where the smells of dinner were already in the air.

But why is safety so important? Jonathan wanted to ask.

And why *can't* we know more about others? Why can't we at least try?

They were not questions he could ask of his father. If Doctor Bingham attempted to answer them, as he would not, the responses would not be illuminating: even at twelve years of age Jonathan knew that. His father did not think the earth had moved, that things had changed. But Jonathan also knew that his father lived in one world and his son in another—and if that had not changed, if all sons from the beginning of time had been born into worlds their fathers never made, well, whatever it meant it certainly meant working things out for yourself.

And why was his father so philosophical—openly so? Jonathan thought he knew that, too. It was because Jonathan's older brother, now three years an active lawyer in New York City, had decided to run for Congress. At age twenty-six. It was not hard to understand the retrospective light that shed for his father. Even if Theodore lost, as it seemed very likely he would, the attempt would be repeated, and sooner or later he would be successful, and Doctor Bingham would be the father of a public figure, a representative of the people, a man in his own right and a power in the councils of state. It was one thing to be a father, to see your children grow up. It was startlingly different to see them ascend—in his father's metaphor—into a different sphere, and one they had chosen for themselves. The laws of predetermination did not seem so sure, once that began to happen.

Theodore had always seemed a born politician. He possessed a very special sort of confidence, the kind of ease that permits someone to listen to and encourage others, wearing a smile, and leaving the impression of both seriousness and optimism. And conveying the all-important sense that what matters in the whole process is the person doing the speaking. The listener does not fade into the background, but he assumes a responsive aura, a sense of "Why-if-I-can-Billy-I'll-surely-get-something-done-about-that." The aura, to be sure, is not enough. There has to be something behind it—and Theodore had that, too. He'd become active in politics within a year of being called to the Bar. He was by nature a Whig: that is, he had a qualified faith in democracy, and felt majority rule had to be tempered by a variety of controls. He believed in getting rich; he believed in the chance to get rich; he believed in a government that delivered the mail and kept its nose out of things. A lot of Jeffersonians and Jacksonians doubted the good sense or the political appeal of such sentiments, but for a lot of years the Whigs proved them wrong, especially in the older and more settled areas of the country.

And Theodore, on the stump or in one-to-one laying on of flesh, was not so much an ideologue as a strong, persuasive *man*—an individual who could be trusted, who could be counted on, who would do things, for others and for himself. Jonathan had been convinced of that, as a small child. Some of his earliest memories involved his older brother, and his placing himself in Theodore's hands with a confidence he could not extend to either of his parents. It was Theodore who gave him his first riding lessons: no one else had been able to talk him onto the back of the wiry black pony Doctor Bingham bought for his younger son. Jonathan had been distinctly timid, in those days, and inclined to fragility. The pony frankly scared the daylights out of him. It was too big, too alive, its eyes were too large, its teeth too white, its hooves too hard and swift. But Theodore had smiled and stroked the pony's neck until it was very still, and then—talking quietly the whole time—he had taken Jonathan's hand and, before he knew it, the little boy was riding, his big brother walking beside him, guarantor and ensurer of all things good and safe. And by the second lesson he was riding with Theodore still there but not holding the pony. And then he was riding on his own, and that was the end of it, he could hardly be kept off the pony's back. Even his first spill did not frighten him, once Theodore had gotten him so well started.

It was the same when they went fishing together, and Theodore knew all there was to know about baits and lines and hooks, or when they skated together, and Theodore knew which was the good ice and how to keep the wind from eating you alive and which arm to extend for a spinning turn. Perhaps the earliest memory Jonathan carried with him was being in a garden, and trying to dig usefully, and finding it impossible until Theodore's strong hands began to guide his spade.

Theodore had joined a political club in Manhattan. The sitting congressman, well-entrenched and very adept at rough-and-tumble, was a Jacksonian named Michael Cleary; he had been elected four times running, and it was getting difficult to find Whigs to declare against him. Theodore had no secret information, no inkling that Cleary was vulnerable. He had an itch, and he had a yen, and since there was no one in his way and his Andrée connections explicitly promised campaign funding, he got the nomination, accepting it with a brilliant speech that made front pages and worried Cleary into a fast series of announcements, speeches, personal appearances, and the like, well calculated to remind the voters of his district what he had meant to them, each and all, and what he could mean to them in the future. It seemed to be more than sufficient.

"We don't expect you to win, Theodore," Karl Andrée had informed him.

"I don't expect I will."

They were in Karl's vaguely shabby office. There was dust on the ancient prints along one wall; there was even dust on the battered chair in which Theodore was sitting. But Theodore, like Karl's customers, knew better than to judge a book by its cover.

"We see it, your Uncle Peter and I, as an investment. We are not political people ourselves, but we care about the way things are done, we want to see good principles rather than bad ones prevail, if that is still possible in this country. We know your principles, Nephew; we know they are sound ones. And we have spoken to people, we also know that your talents *are* political. Yes. You are talked of in very encouraging terms, they praise your ability with words, and your vigor and your honesty, but also your attention to detail and your concern with seeing things through. Admirable," Uncle Karl murmured. "You ought perhaps to be in business with us. But since you so obviously fill the political bill, we are prepared to make this modest investment in your future success." He contemplated his nephew, nodding with approval at the young man's neat attire, his singularly erect stature, his sharp, alert eyes. "Is there any chance that you might win, do you suppose?"

"Not much, I'm afraid."

"A pity. Mr. Cleary does not strike me as the right sort, not at all. But you will do your best, and before too long you *will* win."

They shook hands on it, as indeed Karl Andrée always shook hands on concluding any investment. He was not known to make many bad ones.

It was not that 1842 was a good year for Whiggery. Tippecanoe and Tyler too had swept into the White House, but old Harrison had lasted only a matter of weeks and then taken to his bed and died, and Tyler, a safe, innocuous Virginian, had turned out badly, re-establishing links with the Democrats (whose ranks he had left when Jackson took over that party) and publicly subverting Whig principles. The Whigs in turn expelled him from membership and, in considerable disarray, struggled toward the presidential election of 1844.

And Theodore Bingham, twenty-six years of age, transplanted from his native Poughkeepsie to New York City only five years before, a very junior member of the Bar, in embryo but only in embryo a successful politician, struggled to overcome Michael Cleary's built-in strengths. Cleary was an immigrant's son; New York City was full of immigrants and their sons. Cleary was a Catholic, in a district where Catholics outnumbered Protestants two to one, and regularly outvoted them

three and four to one. (One of Cleary's lieutenants had been heard, on
an alcoholic election-night binge, to declare that the Catholic *gravestones*
had risen up in a mass and voted for his party.) Cleary was an incumbent
of some seniority; he had links with the powerful and the sub-powerful.
He knew where the jobs were located and the bodies were buried—and
no matter how gracefully Theodore spoke, no matter how long into the
night he toiled, no matter how many hands he shook or promises he
made, how was young Bingham to triumph in the face of such odds?

The answer, plainly, was that he could not. Cleary would have to
fall on his face in public—"and even that might not mean much, in
our district!"—or the heavens would have to open and the awful finger
of God point out Theodore Bingham as His anointed. Neither Whig
nor Democrat worried about the latter eventuality. And Cleary did not
worry about producing his own disaster, just as Theodore did not imagine any such development was even possible—until early in September.
Then, as an attorney, still as much in practice as he could find the time
to be, the apple fell into his lap. And he saw the Law of Gravity proclaimed in fiery gold letters.

He had dashed into his small office—actually a room in another attorney's larger office—to catch his breath and jot down some notes for
a speech to be given; he could not at the moment recall precisely where
or before whom, but certainly later that same afternoon. There was a
shabby looking woman, young but not really young, waiting for him. He
did not recognize her; she was not a client, not a friend to be sure, and
there was nothing about her that promised either money or success. She
looked up at him as he started to hurry past.

"Mr. Bingham?"

He cleared his throat, acknowledged his identity, tipped his hat and
started to excuse himself.

"I've got something very important to talk to you about," she said,
and it was impossible not to admit her, seat her in a vacant chair, and
ask if she desired a cup of tea.

"I'd rather some gin, but I won't have neither."

He sat down behind his desk and tried to seem attentive, though
his mind was still on his speech, phrases from which kept forming and
reforming. ("What does Mr. Cleary tell you, on the subject of the tariff?
It's very easy to tell you what he tells you. Nothing. He doesn't understand it, for one thing. But just as important, and maybe even a little
more important to you, my friends, since you have elected him and he

is supposed to represent you, he's never happened to be there when the tariff was being discussed. Or voted on. Or when much of anything else was being discussed. Or voted on. In fact, my friends, it is a melancholy truth that Congressman Cleary has almost never . . .")

But then he became attentive in fact.

". . . and now he won't give me the money he promised me. And I've got the baby to feed. And I happen to know—"

Theodore reached for a pen.

"How do you spell your name?"

She squinted at him.

"I haven't told you my name."

He smiled.

"It's hard to proceed without knowing your name."

She lifted her jaw faintly and continued to stare.

"And where was you planning to proceed, Mr. Bingham?"

"Wherever you instructed me to, Miss . . .? Or is it Mrs.?"

"It ain't neither. Listen, I know how you lawyers talk. I ain't here to proceed nowhere. Cleary knocked me up a year ago, and he's been supporting me, and then the baby. Now he won't pay me nothing. And like I started to say, I happen to know I'm not the only one. He's been making little Clearies all over New York. I can prove it, too."

Theodore put down his pen. She seemed singularly calm, singularly sure of herself. He did not doubt that she was telling the truth. Did she not want to sue Cleary? Did she, instead, want to blackmail him?

"How can I help you?"

"My name's Ella and you can't help me. See?"

Theodore's smile broadened. He spread his hands and shrugged.

"Then why—"

"Because I don't want him winning no more elections. Because I don't want him going around banging all the girls he meets. Because he's a no good son of a bitch, and I'll see him in hell before I'll let him get back to that congress. See? He's a liar, and he's a bastard, and I hate his guts. That's why. See? All right, I'm Ella, and then there's Jane, she lives over on Smith Street, and there's Gina I think her name is, she's Italian and I don't know where she lives, but he's had two bambinos with her. And there's more. You know what I'd really like to do?"

Theodore shook his head. Even as a lawyer he had never met a woman like her, never heard a female voice say the things she had been saying. He was not so much uncomfortable as slightly dazed.

"Yeah. Well, I'd like to cut his balls off, and if I knew a way to do it I would, let me tell you. But I can't, so I'm going to get him any way I can."

Theodore was neither naïve nor stupid. He was, however, very much what was called, at the time, a man of honor.

"I'm afraid I can't—"

"Yeah. Listen, I don't want you to do nothing for me. I think maybe if he walked in here right this minute and handed me a pile of bills, I'd just spit on them. And maybe on him, too. I don't want his money. I don't want him, neither. I don't want you writing him no notes, or threatening him, or nothing like that."

"Then—"

"Jesus. You're running against him, ain't you? In the election?"

"Yes."

"Well, for God's sake. You ain't got a chance, right? Mike's in with all the right people, he's got you beat six ways come Sunday—unless he blows it, right? So you make him blow it. You get the story spread around—there's lots of ways of doing it, I don't have to tell you that; you're a lawyer. He denies everything. So you drop some name, you scare him. He's got a temper, Mike has. I don't know just what he'll do, but when he's mad it's going to be something stupid. And he talks too much, when he's mad. So he'll dig his own grave, if you just give him a decent chance. That's all I want you to do. See?"

It might work. It wasn't decent, but it might work. Could he bring himself to do it?

"I don't know what to say."

She stood up.

"Then don't say nothing. See? I know you don't want to do it this way, you'd rather beat him fair and square and all that. Sure. But you can't, he's got you tied in a sack like a kitten, and he's sure as hell going to drown you. So it's up to you, see? If you want to win, that's how you can do it. I know Mike Cleary. Jesus, do I ever know him! I wish I'd never met the baboon."

She gave him her address, though still not her full name, and she left the office. He was too dazzled to escort her to the door, and she was too quick.

For more than a week he did exactly nothing, talked to no one about his visitor, did not even check on her or on her story. Then, persuading himself that it was more curiosity than anything else, he hired one of his regular "fact-finders" to look into the situation. It cost him only twenty-five dollars to learn that her full name was Ella Green, that she had been employed in a shirt-waist shop, that she had been taken up by Congressman Cleary, that she had had a baby, and that Cleary had been seen any number of times stopping off at her room. She had a straightforward reputation: "fast," to be sure, but honest. She did not drink to excess and had never so much as been suspected of thievery.

"Just another one of Cleary's girls, I take it?" Theodore smiled.

His fact-finder winked.

"Who could count 'em all, eh? With all due respect, Mr. Bingham, old Mike is quite a man."

Spreading Cleary's reputation far and wide, plainly, would do him no harm whatever. The voters would chuckle and vote as usual. Ella was quite right: there had to be something more, there had to be something to set Cleary into motion in the cause of his own destruction. It would take careful consideration; it would take delicate execution—and how could he, as a man of honor, bring himself to do it?

The lawyer from whom he rented his office space, a man three or four years older than himself, questioned him about his campaign.

"Fine," Theodore assured him. "Very much as expected, all in all."

"You mean, you're going through the motions in approved style, eh?"

"My dear fellow, it's not impossible that I should win."

"No, no, of course not. Nor is it impossible that I should have a letter from Messrs. Baring, this afternoon, telling me they had deposited a million pounds to my account, from a mysterious benefactor who wished me well and wanted me to enjoy this brief stay on earth."

Theodore made a face.

"To listen to you, you know, this is not so much an election as an execution."

"Thou sayest it, Bingham, old boy."

Theodore lifted a warning finger.

"Remember the old chestnut, my friend. Until the votes are counted, all counted, no election is ever assured."

The other man clapped him on the back.

"That chestnut, suitably roasted, is likely to be your only reward in this contest, Bingham. Unless, that is, there's to be some appropriate return on your investment?"

Theodore's scowl was not playful.

"I should like to think you know me better than that."

"No offense meant, no offense."

There were a number of other and painfully similar conversations. Even the party regulars who assisted him at meetings and open-air occasions had an air of accompanying the fatted calf to its slaughter.

"You think I might win this?" he asked one of them, as casually as he could.

The response was a shrug, a puff of voiceless sir, and then a brief comment:

"Why not? And supposing Cleary drops dead before they count the votes, eh?"

Even his Uncle Karl pushed him, unwittingly, toward the efficacious and dishonorable pathway.

"A fine speech," Karl said one night, as they sat at his uncle's table. Supper had been long and satisfying. The other members of the family had vanished, some to other duties, some in deference to the higher concerns of their father and cousin.

"Which one, Uncle? I've made so many, in the last while, that I sometimes find them running together on me. I rather doubt that I have anything of value left to say. Indeed, I wonder how people can stand there and listen to me, when I almost cannot listen to myself any longer. I suspect I could speechify in my sleep—and perhaps I do!"

"You've conducted yourself very well. We're proud of the effort you're making."

Theodore helped himself to the wine, hearing the unspoken afterword: *If only you could win.* Not that his uncle worried about the sums of money involved, all of which added together were trivial to him. It was in fact the principle that pushed at Karl Andrée: anyone who could address himself thus cogently to the public issues involved, by God, ought to be in Congress. Michael Cleary was as unfit to represent his district as the Emperor of Russia was to rule over that vast land. And since Theodore was in addition working hard at his campaign . . .

He sat at his small desk, in his rooms, later that night, unable to sleep. He did not write, nor did he read. There was one small candle; he did not need more. He sat staring at nothing, while the darkness hung quietly outside his window, and he did not lie down until faint streaks of light were showing in the East.

The next morning he was at the desk of Gordon Taylor, junior editor of the New York *Star*, barely five minutes after Taylor himself had arrived.

"Giving it up, Bingham?"

Which was how it came to be done—how Cleary read, in the next morning's *Star*, of his personal malefactions, and thereupon threatened to beat Gordon Taylor to death with a cane, and how from that point things went from bad to worse for Honest Mike (a name he had coined for himself), until by mid-October he was so entangled in conflicting statements, public and private (but mostly private), that people began to feel sorry for him, then to laugh at him, and then to heckle him, and how he began to respond angrily, and offensively, and how in the end his feet were so twisted together in his own large, active mouth that there was no hope for him.

"He's hung himself!" Theodore exclaimed, at a large meeting in which Cleary flailed out at his opponent as an anti-Catholic bigot, a Protestant Christ-baiter, a despiser of everything Irish, an enemy of the people, and very probably a seducer of chambermaids, too.

The judgment was only slightly premature. By election night, some ten days later, Cleary had indeed hung himself. Theodore's margin of victory was not immense, but it was incontestable. Congressman Cleary was Congressman no more; Doctor Bingham did not have to wait, in order to have a son in the public light; and Jonathan tasted the first wine of his life, toasting his brother's new-won fame.

It had been dirtily done, in a way, but satisfactorily done—and that was more important. Who would have heard of my name, thought Theodore fleetingly, if scruple had prevailed? And would Cleary have hesitated even a moment, had he been possessed of such an opportunity? Who knew, indeed, how Cleary had in fact risen to the prominence from which Theodore had tumbled him? And who cared, on either side, now that up was down and down was up and—from the Bingham and Andrée perspective—Right and Good had won?

"I'm not sure I like having a brother in Congress," said young Mrs. Martial Johnson to her still younger brother. She had just seated herself at the piano—her two children having been put down for afternoon naps—but instead of playing she sat with her hands in her lap and frowned at the keyboard.

Jonathan smiled.

"Don't fret, Anne-Marie. When you're in a room together, people will still notice you and ignore him."

She began to play, a graceful Haydn piece he liked, but broke off.

"It's enough to make me glad I'm not a Bingham anymore."

"It makes me very glad to be a Bingham!"

"Why? Pride? Vanity?"

Jonathan found it hard to be sympathetic; he much preferred her music to her philosophy. Anne-Marie played extremely well, more than well enough to have become a professional had there been any possibility of abandoning more important things, like husband and home and children, for the concert stage. No lady could have chosen such a career. But he was glad she played, because he had had endless private concerts, better than virtually any he had ever heard in public.

"Because he'll be doing an important job, and I know he'll do it well!"

She waved his response away.

"Of course he'll do it well. Theodore is a fine man; he could do anything well if he chose to. But why is it important to speechify, to stand up in public and trade insults with some mulatto horse-trader, to pontificate about the tariff or the state of the Union? What Uncle Peter and Uncle Karl are doing—that's important."

He reminded her that Uncle Peter and Uncle Karl had actively supported Theodore's campaign and declared it a matter of importance—and as if to get back at him she played a long, metronomic piece of counterpoint that nearly put him to sleep. He endured, and then tea was served, and first a gentleman and then a lady of Anne-Marie's acquaintance appeared, both young and voluble, and after a snatch of gossip she asked them how they viewed her brother's so-called triumph.

"Jonathan here thinks it's just dandy!"

The gentleman nodded and flatly agreed with Jonathan.

The lady—who was unmarried—giggled and said that whatever Theodore did was just fine with her.

Anne-Marie put down her cup with a startling clatter.

"Would Theodore like it, I wonder, if I had notices printed in all the papers that I was exhibiting myself in public? That I would perform Mozart and Beethoven for anyone with fifty cents to pay for the privilege?"

"It would be a privilege, I have no doubt," said the gentleman.

"You wouldn't!" exclaimed the lady.

"No, I wouldn't—but suppose I did. How would your precious Theodore like it then?"

The lady blushed and indicated it was not for her to say.

"He'll still be in the practice of law," the gentleman added, "if you're worried that he won't be up to anything useful."

Anne-Marie flung up her hands and marched to the keyboard, where for a quarter of an hour she banged out noisy marches, relieving her own vexation and leading the others to much tapping of toes.

And that night, after dinner, when her husband was puffing a cigar and reading a fat medical tome, she again reproached her brother.

"Why?" Martial wondered, lowering the book and looking over at her.

"Would you understand if I said it was a vulgar display?"

"No." He glanced down, sighed faintly, and closed his book. "I would have thought it was an honorable extension of his legal activities. There *are* gentlemen in Congress, you know. Even Mr. Tyler, whatever his other deficiencies, is distinctly a man of propriety and honor."

It was harder to argue with Martial. He was, as always, singularly calm. He was magisterial, and fair, and withal warm. He was also her husband.

"I know that. I don't know why I feel so strongly."

He came and knelt beside her; his hand rested on her knee.

"I have a suspicion you may be jealous of him," he said quietly.

She blushed. But there was nothing to say.

"A good politician is a kind of artist. And Theodore is clearly a good politician: he has won a notable victory, God only knows how. You are an artist, too: I've always known that, Anne-Marie. I think you'd like to be able to perform in public, as he can. Not for the applause and the noise: no, you're too genuine for that. But for the indefinable and very real value that public performance has for the artist." She squeezed his hand. "What would a doctor be, if all he had to work on were straw-stuffed models and wooden corpses?"

"It isn't possible," she murmured, looking straight down into her lap.

"Do you want it to be possible?" She did not reply. "We might be able to do something, if you wanted it badly enough."

She tried to keep from crying.

"That's part of it," she confessed, her voice breaking. "I don't know how much I want it. I have artistic leanings, yes. But would I want to leave this, the house, you, the children?"

"Would you have to?"

She leaned forward and rested her head on his shoulder.

"It doesn't matter," she almost whispered. "I don't want to. And I won't."

His arms were around her:

"You don't have to."

She pulled back, abruptly, half-crying and half-laughing at the same time.

"I never knew you were so—advanced!"

He smiled, rose, and offered her his hand. She rose, too.

"Am I?"

"If you're that understanding of your patients, we'll be rich in no time at all. And I'll really be jealous!"

"Shall we walk about for a little?"

Their garden was not extensive, but it was sufficient.

THREE

"If you were to walk every day from Andover to Reading, and from Reading back to Andover, you would know the road very well from Andover to Reading; but this daily itineration over the same ground would never bring you to Boston."

—Daniel Webster, to his nephew Charles Haddock
21 June 1817

Jonathan knew that his maternal grandmother, Maria Theresa Goldstock, had been a soprano of some distinction in Europe before her marriage, and even after both marriage and removal to the United States she had occasionally sung in public—if church performance was really performance. He knew, too, that his grandmother had given Anne-Marie the splendid piano she had been playing on, now, for more than a decade. It sat in the Johnson living room, having followed its owner from house to house like a superbly faithful dog. He had some notion of his sister's talent, though he did not think of Anne-Marie as a "musician." Talent was one thing, professionalism something utterly different. Even William Cullen Bryant, as near to a poet laureate as the young Republic had, neither expected to nor did in fact make a living from his art. Jonathan was immensely admiring of Bryant, as both poet and newspaper editor, and frequently produced imitations of both his crafts. But he did not know how he would have felt, had Bryant come before the public like the beggars professional artists always seemed to be.

And then there was his mother. In 1840, when he was ten years old, she had discovered the therapeutic value of painting. How it had come about was a mystery: there was no display of visual art on any Bingham walls; there were no known collections of art to inspire her, and there certainly were no painters or other artists among their acquaintance. Marie Bingham had from time to time attempted visual representations, in sewn form. They had been tepid at best. And then, at age forty-five, she had taken to disappearing into her dressing room for hours at a time, finally emerging with a veritable painting in her hands. It was roughly executed on a sheet of stiff paper; the coloring was a bit unsteady (her pigments were improvised affairs), but it was not at all tepid. It was, in fact, shockingly good. Jonathan had experienced a kind of thrill, seeing it: his own mother had produced that, had begun with a blank sheet and some fumbled-together colors, and an idea somewhere in her own head, and had turned out a fine little landscape, bright with houses and small people and even animals. It was gay, it was charming, and it drew much praise; even Doctor Bingham was impressed.

"Remarkable, my dear. Remarkable. What gave you the idea for that?"

Marie stood by, fussing with her nervous fingers, twisting a cloth of some sort.

"I'm sure I don't know."

Doctor Bingham's smile was indulgent—and pleased. He could see at once the soothing promise of this new occupation.

"It would seem to me that anyone capable of this much might well be capable of more."

"I don't know," she repeated. "I don't really recall what that stiff paper was doing here, but I kept walking past it, not thinking about it, and then one day, as if it were some sort of vision, I could see the painting on it—I mean really on it, as if it were there." She gestured anxiously toward her picture. "That painting. Just the way it is. I could see the whole thing, plain as day. So then I had to try to put it back."

"It's marvelous, Mother," Jonathan said.

"Well, I didn't know if I could get that feeling back. And it wasn't easy, believe me."

"Of course not," Doctor Bingham agreed, though he did not much like the talk about visions. His wife ought to be encouraged to paint, but not to see things that weren't there. Her tendencies in the nervous direction were already distinctly too pronounced; she needed no further encouragement.

"I had to do a lot of it several times; I'd put it on the paper and it wouldn't look right, so I'd scrape it off and start again. It always came out the way it was supposed to, sooner or later. That took a long time."

"Time well spent," Doctor Bingham confirmed, and that settled the matter. Marie converted one side of her dressing room into a kind of small studio. She had a crude easel made for her; she sent to New York for some brushes and some real paints, and for hours virtually every day she shut herself away and painted. In a sense, all her pictures were variants of the first: country scenes filled with familiar objects. But they were also landscapes of her own lunar interior, scenes she constructed out of the lights and darks of her own needs. Her pictures were intensely, almost supernaturally visual, but it was not the vision of a recording lens. It was, as she had recognized for herself, an inner vision, making use of the furniture and arrangements of an external world that mattered less, in the end, than the one inside her.

Jonathan did not, of course, see all this, when he looked at his mother's paintings. But he saw some of it. He understood that his mother was not painting out of self-indulgence, or out of any direct impulse toward recreation or indeed even of pleasure. Doctor Bingham did not see it at all, but as long as his wife's painting drained out some of the secret pus, eased the deep inner sources of her psychological edema, he did not care to question matters further. Etiology was less important to him, and to his profession generally, than relief. Marie's painting was a relief to her and therefore a relief to him. He welcomed it and did not pay any attention to the rest. Jonathan could not take so aloof a stance—not only because Marie was his mother, and because his daily contacts with her were far more intimate than were his father's, but also because he responded to her painting; he was moved by her painting, as his father was not.

Some of his mother's work—and he pretty much understood that it was work, not play—was distinctly disturbing to him. Especially when she handled scenes he knew as well as she did, scenes from directly and immediately around them, the transformations she engendered gave him disquieting insights he did not want. The world was intended to be square and solid: it had been designed and erected in exactly that way, intended to last forever. That was his father's view, and the view of most people. But his mother's paintings did not reconstruct that palpable world, did not even treat solidities as solid, or enduring things as enduring. A mountain would not exactly float, in one of her landscapes, but neither would it sit proclaiming its own eternal immutability. It might crouch, for all the world like some living beast, or it might seem to fold into itself, collapsible, like some paper creature wrought for a day and gone the next. Tree branches did not slide off into faces, in his mother's pictures, but neither were leaves as simple, for her, as to the ordinary eye. The patterns of leaves, in fact, were one of her major achievements: she worked them into glowing filigrees that set Jonathan's mind spinning somewhere distant, he did not know where. One could fall into his mother's pictures: he often did. That was obviously neither pleasant nor recreational.

It was not that she was a great painter, or even most of the time a thoroughly good one. Her range was extremely small; her technical competence quickly reached its outer limits, as when she experimented with portraits and found that she had serious problems with noses and even with lips. Jonathan did not have any true standard of comparison, but he did not think she was a rural Rembrandt, toiling in obscurity. He knew that to be moved by art did not mean much more than not being moved by it: there were stages along the way; there were levels, and he knew he was pretty near the starting point. But all the same, whether it was because he shared her blood or not, whether it was because he lived under the same roof or not, he responded to her work; he was excited by it, and it set him quivering in ways he could not hope to understand or control.

He tried painting: it was painfully difficult, and he was even more painfully inept. Whatever else he might have inherited from his mother, visual talent was not included. Not only did nothing look like what it was, in his attempts, but nothing looked like anything at all. There were blobs and other blobs; none of it cohered, the colors sank back into the paper.

Then he took one of his mother's largest paintings, as usual a landscape but for her a rather singular one. The time depicted was toward evening; the shadows were deep and prominent, the colors muted. There was a somberness over the whole picture that was marked and affecting. He sat cross-legged beneath the painting, trying to absorb whatever he could of its essence, and then he put pencil on paper and tried to recreate, in verbal form, what he had garnered. The result was a great deal more pleasing than his own attempts at painting, both to him and to others. It began:

> *These heavy shadows press from somewhere. Where?*
> *I see the darkness coming, feel the clouds*
> *Fade black above those hills, sense the storm*
> *That lurks beyond—how distant, who can tell?—*
> *And yet the scene bewitches, darkness and all.*

"But there isn't a storm," his mother exclaimed.

"There might be. I think there will be."

She was deeply puzzled.

"How can you possibly know that?"

"I don't, Mother. But it's as the poem says, I feel it, I sense it, I suspect it."

She read the lines over and over, then handed the sheets back to him.

"It's very fine, my son, but it's not my picture." She shook her head firmly. "But whatever it is, you've done it very well."

His father was blunter.

"Good Lord," he said, looking up almost at once. "You really know how to do this sort of thing, Jonathan." And he held the slim sheaf quite a while, reading it over. "I had no idea. Am I to be the father of a politician and a poet?"

"Even a musician," Jonathan laughed, then regretted saying it. His father was at first puzzled.

"Ah, Anne-Marie, yes."

The conversation ended.

The remark had of course been a joke, but his father at his best had a dim sense of humor, and on the subject of his daughter he had none at all. Jonathan was aware, ashamed, that he should certainly have known better. One did not jest about such things.

Martial read the poem with great pleasure, then queried its author about the meter of the fifth line.

"A bit lumpy there, isn't it?"

"Is it?"

Martial pointed.

"Shouldn't it be, oh I don't know, you're the poet, but perhaps something more like 'And yet the scene bewitches, darkness comes'?"

"You're thinking about Pope, and *The Dunciad*!"

"I am? I didn't know I was that erudite. Well, let it pass. The poem is splendid, you know. I'd like to see you doing a lot more. Perhaps, if you did something more topical, we could persuade one of our learned friends to have it inserted in a newspaper or a magazine."

Jonathan blushed.

Theodore rather surprisingly did not think Martial's suggestion a particularly useful one, though he liked the poem.

"It *is* a tradition in this country, I'll grant you that, but not for successful politicians—and not really for individual politicians. I care about the Whig cause, you see, but if I'm to engage a publicist it will have to be on my own particular behalf. By God, Jonathan, having gotten myself into Congress, I propose to do a bang-up job and I don't propose to see myself ushered back out again. Not until I'm ready to leave.

Anyway, what have poetry and politics to do with one another? I shall be good at the one, and you show signs of being good at the other, and between us we will transport the Bingham name into posterity. I can see the entry in some future guidebook: Bingham, Doctor Frederick, father of Theodore, the famous politician, and also of Jonathan, America's poet laureate."

Jonathan felt himself gaping under the swirl of his brother's rhetoric. Not yet sworn in, not yet functionally congressional, Theodore was already gearing his psyche to the brave new world to come.

"I'll vote for you," he promised; then they both laughed themselves into fits of coughing and collapsed into their chairs.

At school, literature played neither a large nor a small part. Poughkeepsie offered adequate facilities: when he was fourteen or fifteen, it was expected, Jonathan would go off to Princeton, as his brother had. He was already facile in Latin and fair in Greek. He could calculate with high accuracy. He knew the Bible, Old and New Testaments both, with easy familiarity, and he knew Shakespeare and Milton, Pope and Dryden, Edward Young and Erasmus Darwin. His father's medical practice, and scientific correspondence, had made him aware of at least the currents of thought in biology and chemistry: those currents were not yet in rapid motion, and he did not find them exciting. He had the average boy's understanding of agriculture, weapons, and machinery, in descending order of importance. He could, that is, prune a fruit tree and load a shotgun and fix a fishing line and stack hay and repair a leaking roof. He could swim, since he lived near a river, but he could also ride a horse and tend a cow and pretty much tame a mule. He knew nothing whatever of females his own age: his mother, his older sister, and a few assorted aunts and distant cousins were the sum of his knowledge on those scores. He did know grammar, such as it was, and he sang passably well (though he played no musical instrument and could not read music), and though he could not know what he was destined to be, he did know a lot of things he was destined not to be, from painter to doctor and lawyer. For he had a growing sense that it was downright silly to do what others before him in the family had done. His own father's father had been a doctor: how absurd, then, for his father too to have taken up that profession. It had been *done*; it was time to do something new, something different. As he passed relatively quietly into adolescence, in the early 1840s, Jonathan Bingham was something not even his brother Theodore (born, after all, just after the second war with the British, the so-called War of 1812) could quite claim to be: he was, in a word, an American.

There was some sense of that in his own mind, too, especially when he was away from quiet Poughkeepsie and visiting in noisy New York. His uncle Peter, though never particularly communicative, told him when he was fourteen that in the previous year there had been one thousand eight hundred and eight ships making port in New York, landing very nearly fifty thousand passengers. More important, both to Uncle Peter and to the city, was the over eleven million dollars in duties collected by New York Customs. (By the time Jonathan was eighteen, over three thousand ships made port in New York, landing close to two hundred thousand people, and bringing in customs receipts very nearly of twenty million dollars.) When he was fifteen a telegraph line was strung from New York all the way to Philadelphia (passing under the Hudson River at old Fort Washington, above Harlem).When he was seventeen, indeed, one of the ships making port in New York was the *Keying*, a Chinese junk—and probably the first vessel from China ever to visit the United States of America. But the more usual trip was across the Atlantic, and that could already be accomplished in ten days, by a good fast steamboat. Ten days from New York to Europe, from Europe to New York: that made the head spin, and made the heart beat. Boys and young men might still be seen, perhaps, playing cricket at places like St. George's, near the Red House tavern in Harlem, but it was most emphatically a new world. The main post office in Manhattan handled roughly forty thousand letters—and a hundred and twenty thousand newspapers—each and every day. As one merchant summed it up, writing a potential retail customer in the provinces (this customer was in New Hampshire), "With regards to New York, all are aware that any kind of Manufactures and Imports may be bought at a lower price than any City in the Union, and far larger stocks to select from." That, to be sure, was the name of the game.

Jonathan's uncles, and their families, and their associates and their families, gave him that very American sense of Ultimate Possibility— the conviction that, no matter how outlandish or unlikely a notion might seem, if it had good sense and sound practice on its side it would have at least a chance to succeed. Uncle Karl, for example, had been approached by a young man named Horatio Allen. Working out of the West Point Foundry, on Beach Street, Allen had built the *Best Friend of Charleston*—the first American-built locomotive, designed for and then used on American railroads. Working with one Stillman, an iron specialist known to him but unknown to Karl Andrée, he now wanted to go into machine-making in a larger way. The locomotive had been built in 1830; by 1835 he felt ready to turn to a Hudson River steamer, and to cotton presses, sugar mills, hulls for ironclads, and a variety of heavy machinery. Uncle Karl had helped fund the enterprise. And by 1850 Stillman and Allen had a substantial operation, set alongside the East River at Twelfth Street, with eighteen departments and a total work force of over a thousand men. (The employees were specialists, and so worked only an eleven hour day and were paid, some of them, over two dollars a day, with an average wage that in 1850 reached the singularly high rate, for those times, of a dollar fifty a day.)

One of Karl Andrée's friends was in the mortuary business—and Karl liked to cite him as living proof of the fact that in America you could sell anything to anyone, if you played your cards right. Steamboats would sometimes race each other down the river, both for the fun of it and also because the boat that could advertise the fastest trip would thereafter get the lion's share of the passengers and could also charge higher rates. Once in a while both boats would be losers, as overworked, overheated machinery broke down. More usually, one boat would win or one, breaking down, would lose. And rarely enough to make it notable, a fire would break out in the losing boat; even more rarely, as happened to *The Henry Clay*, the fire would go out of control, the boat would have to be beached (or even worse would explode), and dozens of passengers (and occasionally bystanders, too) would die. Karl's mortuary friend raced up the river, shiny fresh coffins on the back of a fast wagon, and flogged them at fine prices.

"Now in Europe," Karl moralized, "they might call that gruesome. In the old country they don't go rushing up to a disaster like that. They do everything politely. So the corpses lie out in the sun and turn truly disgusting. Is that more civilized? I'd say, frankly, it was a good deal harder on everyone concerned. If coffins are needed, there's nothing gruesome about supplying them. And if they have to be supplied, why not have good ones? And as long as someone is going to have to make a profit, why not whoever is the first to get there? We're going to build this country on principles like that: the race is to the best, and the fastest, and the smartest. And so it should be!"

If Jonathan did not know exactly what he thought of arguments like that, it was pretty much because he did not think about them at all. He heard them; he saw them in operation, and what was there to think about? (He was, once again, an American.) That was reality—and who was he to question it? His task, as he began to perceive it, was to find his own place in the reality others, and Nature, and God Himself, had created. That was the new American version of the Quest for the Holy Grail: Who am I and where do I belong?

His sister was of the view that things would take care of themselves.

"They always do, for men!"

"And then the men take care of the women. But really, Anne-Marie, it *is* easier for you. You always knew you would marry, and have children. You always knew you would play the piano."

"And Father always knew he would be a doctor."

Jonathan frowned.

"He was wrong."

"You don't say so?"

"He should have been—I don't know, perhaps a diplomat of some sort, perhaps someone who invents things. No, he wouldn't be good at that. He's really not a scientist, you know. He admires it, and he has in fact done some good work. But secretly, somewhere deep inside him, he's meant for something else. Who knows anymore? It isn't exactly that he's buried himself: I think he enjoys what he does. He's just, well, closed off certain things."

"Do you know what I used to secretly wish?"

"What?"

"I wanted to be a sea captain."

"Because you could be your own master?"

"Because I could be away from everything, and be by myself . . ."

"I thought you liked us!"

She ruffled his hair.

"You're a good enough sort, little brother. So is everyone. But just think how glorious it would be to stand on a deck and hear only the wind and the water, and sometimes a few birds—"

"And the sailors cursing."

She laughed.

"I'd whip them until they were still. On my ship, sailors would wear stockings over their bare feet, so their steps would be as silent as a cat's, and when they talked it would only be in whispers—and *below* decks, where the fierce captain could not hear."

"Were you intending to be a pirate, Anne-Marie?"

She stretched slowly, then adjusted the lace on one sleeve.

"I don't know. Perhaps. I dare say I would have been a singularly fierce one, if I'd cared to be. But it might have been nice to be Queen Elizabeth."

"Oh yes."

"Or even Cleopatra."

"The trouble is, you know, there are more Jane Seymours and Mary Queen of Scots and Didos . . ."

"Oh well, if you let yourself be led to the guillotine. I wouldn't. Jane Seymour was too gentle, too ladylike. *I* would have worn pantaloons and painted a moustache on my face, and I would have strutted about with a hooked sword at my side—a very sharp sword."

"Elizabeth didn't need one."

"But I would have been even fiercer than Elizabeth. And I would have taken no chances. Essex would never have gotten anywhere with *me*."

"How about Sir Walter Raleigh?"

The clock in the hallway chimed and she rose slowly from her chair.

"That would be a more difficult case, though I have always wondered about his faithfulness. But a good man is indeed useful, at times. Like Martial."

As Jonathan worked his way toward manhood it was his mother, surprisingly, who developed (or had perhaps always held) strong and severe notions about his future.

"You should of course indulge your talents, my son. You will always scribble, as I will always draw and Anne-Marie will always play. As my mother, indeed, still sings, though only to herself in the privacy of her own drawing room. But that is not enough, and you ought to be shaping your course toward some definite objective."

"Have you one in mind, Mother?"

"Yes, in fact I do. I believe you ought to do as your father has done."

"Become a doctor?"

"Is it so ignoble an idea?"

"No, of course not."

"Do you suppose you would make less satisfactory an accounting of yourself than your father has?"

"I hope not."

"Then what might be wrong with such a choice? A man ought to be both precise and realistic, and assume that stance as early in his life as he is capable of so doing. You would not be a satisfactory minister, I think, and I do not believe you would care for the law. Your brother has chosen the government—"

"And one is enough?"

"Not at all. He is older than you—"

"And has precedence?"

"Pray do not interrupt me, Jonathan. I meant no such thing. His talents are different from yours. You have never been alike, you know, not from a very early age. You are a clever boy and I have no doubt you could manage at any profession you set your hand to, including government or the law, but one can—and I think you should—aim at a higher standard."

"But I have no interest in medicine."

"That is almost beside the point. You have, if I am not mistaken, no very decided leaning toward any profession, except perhaps that of poet, if there is any such thing as a professional in that calling. The great advantage of medicine, for someone like you, my son, is that it is honorable, and sufficiently remunerative, at the same time as it is not either intellectually draining or indeed overly burdensome in other ways. Much of your time is your own. If you choose to dream, you can afford to indulge yourself."

"Or to do scientific experiments."

"Exactly."

Jonathan was impressed by her ability to focus, to concentrate, and to be realistic. She was seldom so earthy and almost sensible. But then, she was after all descended on both sides from families of merchants. He smiled at her.

"I shall consider it, Mother."

"I should hope, in all filial propriety, Jonathan, that you would do rather more than that."

"Mother."

"I am not speaking lightly, nor am I speaking without premeditation, my son. I have given a great deal of thought to this matter. And I am, need I remind you, your mother?"

"I shall take what you say very, very seriously, Mother."

"I would prefer that you took it dispositively."

He hesitated, not wanting to anger her. Realism balked could readily turn, for her, into furious fanaticism. He had seen it happen.

"The subject is new to me," he hedged.

"All the more reason to be guided by someone to whom it is not new, and someone a great deal more experienced in the ways of the world than anyone of your tender years could possibly be."

"I concede your priority, Mother."

"And you will go into the study of medicine?"

"I don't know."

Her eyes tightened.

"You will let me know when you do know, young man. And in the meantime, you may do precisely as you have obviously decided to do, keep your own counsel and keep it entirely to yourself. I do not wish to speak to you, or to be spoken to by you, until you have determined to be obedient."

She flounced out of the room. All was normal, of course, in less than a day; she spoke to him, and he spoke to her, and nothing was said of her pledge of silence. But he also knew she had not forgotten. And as he turned her proposal over in his mind he also knew, regretfully, that he could not do it. He did not know what he was or where he belonged: that was perfectly true. But medicine was not the pathway. He would not tell her if he did not have to, but if he had to he would.

He did not have to; the subject was never again broached between them. He was uneasy about her forbearance, and extremely careful about his own, but however forcefully she had thrown down the gauntlet she did not press the challenge. And he muddled along, growing slowly into early manhood, and wondering all the time how it would turn out, which way he would bend.

"And why not Princeton?" his father inquired.

Jonathan wished he did not have to explain, even as he had known all along he would have to.

"I shall defer to your wishes, Father, of course. If you desire me to matriculate at Princeton, I shall do exactly that, unquestioningly."

His father nodded, pleased.

"But you would prefer Columbia, even though I do not think it has improved a great deal since my time there, and even though your brother informs us that Princeton has become a veritable citadel of learning?"

Jonathan collected his thoughts. He was sitting in his father's consulting room; his father was seated behind his large desk.

"It isn't that."

He hesitated, leaning forward and entwining his hands.

"Pray sit straight, Jonathan. And attend to the matter at hand."

"Learning is to be sure important, Father. But Princeton is off in the countryside and Columbia is in New York City. I have always felt the city as a kind of magnet, from the time I was a very small child, visiting our connections there."

"Are you contemplating a commercial career?"

"I wish I knew, Father."

Doctor Bingham rubbed his chin. Then he rubbed the edge of his desk. Then he moved an ink well, and a pen, and rather aimlessly moved that again.

"Perhaps," he said slowly. "Perhaps." They sat in silence for some moments. "Your Uncle Karl, and your Uncle Peter, would be pleased to have you in the vicinity—if, that is, you were not to be more trouble than you're worth!"

"I would not be trouble!" He felt his hands quiver. "I could well be useful, I really could."

"I do not contemplate anything quite so unusual. It would conceivably be better to have you, unformed as you obviously are, in the neighborhood of steadier folk who had your best interests in mind. I suppose, all in all, that this rearrangement might well be possible."

"Thank you, Father."

"I have not decided, Jonathan. Let me write to your uncles, to determine their views. And let me—let me write also to some old acquaintances of mine. I should like to learn, if I can, precisely how things stand at Columbia at this moment. If it is not too much inferior to Princeton . . . well, let me try to find out, and we shall discuss it again at some later point. There is I believe no very great rush?"

"None whatever, Father."

"Then leave it at this, shall we?"

Jonathan rose, knowing himself dismissed.

"I'm very grateful to you, Father."

"You may not be, when all is determined. I suggest you save your gratitude; it may be more sensibly lodged elsewhere."

"All the same, thank you very much, Father!"

Which was, in the end, how Jonathan Bingham came to leave Poughkeepsie for New York City, and for Columbia College, and how he came to live in his Uncle Karl's house. And how, really, it all began.

"If any great scenes are to be acted in this country within the next twenty years, New York is the place in which those scenes are to be viewed."

—Daniel Webster, to his brother Ezekiel
26 March 1816

It was 1847. Theodore Bingham had been in the House of Representatives for five years, defeating ex-Congressman Michael Cleary in a brisk re-match, in 1844, and then running essentially unopposed in 1846. He was a good Congressman—eloquent, of course, but agile and amiable and hard-working. He had found, also, that not only was it unnecessary to give up his law practice, to do so would have been positively unusual. Daniel Webster, in the Senate, was only the foremost among congressional lawyers, drawing down large fees for appearances before both state and federal courts, notably the Supreme Court of the United States. Congressional salaries were not large, congressional perquisites were virtually nonexistent (by comparison with later times of high largesse), and no one talked about conflict of interest. A man had to live, and to live by politics alone was thought somewhat demeaning, perhaps positively dishonorable. Theodore was possibly Webster's equal in forensic debate (they had not yet met, and were indeed not likely to be on opposite sides of many questions, both being firm Whigs), and was at least his equal in political maneuver, but was not anything like the lawyer Webster could be when he took the trouble. Theodore was never indolent, as Webster frequently was, but neither did he have Webster's exemplary dispassionateness, his careful adherence to lawyerly calm and tact. In his appearances at the Bar, Theodore was much more of a partisan, and thus much less of a lawyer. Still, his practice inevitably swelled, both in New York and in Washington, and—especially since he did not have to compete with Webster either in politics or for the most part in business either—he had begun to do very well for himself. He was only thirty-one, but he was already well on the way to the considerable fortune he later accumulated—honestly.

At thirty-one, too, Theodore had now passed an extremely important constitutional milestone: in order to be a senator, one had to be thirty. He had come to Congress a very junior twenty-six; he was now lodged in the public eye, a man of obvious and well-known experience and maturity, and he was legally of an age to graduate into the upper chamber. And he not only wanted it, he thought he saw his opportunity glittering on the horizon: the incumbent was retiring, as inconspicuous in his leaving as he had been in his Washington career; the state legislature was extremely likely to go sharply Whig, in the next election, and of course it was the state legislature that elected the State's Senators; and despite the fact that the Senate was largely a body of well-ripened politicians, there was no need so to keep it. There was a growing sense all across the growing nation that new voices, new ideas, new judgments were needed. Theodore was not a visionary, though he had high standards and was a dedicated man: he saw his opportunity, he knew how he could go about taking it, and he set himself in motion, in quiet pursuit of the surprisingly realizable.

Thurlow Weed was the key. Theodore of course knew him: any Whig Congressman from New York who did not know, and to some extent cultivate, the undisputed leader of the Whig party in that state would have been a fool. Weed had helped swing the 1840 Presidential nomination to General Harrison, and like all good Whigs had been outraged when his successor, the perpetually safe John Tyler, had reverted, treacherously, to the ways of Jacksonian Democrats. Tippecanoe being dead, Tyler too had his chance—and the betrayed Whigs had suffered, loudly and painfully. In 1844 party sentiment dictated a return to fundamental principles, and they had nominated Henry Clay. And they had lost. There would be a great deal of sentiment for Clay once again, in 1848, but Theodore knew someone else was needed—and he knew that Thurlow Weed knew it, too.

He made it his business to be invited where Weed could be met, and he made it his business to drop into a vacant chair and chat.

"I've always admired that dodge you and Greeley thought up."

Weed was big and hearty; he'd begun as a newspaper editor, and he remained an editor to the end.

"Which one?"

"Calling the party paper *The Jeffersonian*."

"Greeley's idea. Crazy fellow, sometimes, but damn it all, he knows what he's up to."

"Rather like that whole campaign," Theodore added. "The American people aren't much interested in ideas: it's people they vote for. One Tippecanoe is worth a dozen good speeches."

"Then the canoe tips, and look what happened to us!"

"To be sure. But once bitten, twice shy. And the early supporters of the next Whig President might be able to make certain of the
next Whig Vice President, too. Might even be able to make him a New
Yorker, you know."

Weed turned and peered at him for a moment.

"You're too young, Bingham," he said flatly.

"Oh, not me. Good Lord!"

"Well not your father either—whoever he might be."

"I was thinking, the other night, that really, George Washington
wasn't much of a President. Oh, that's heresy, I know, but he was a
clumsy politician."

"He wasn't no politician at all!"

"Exactly. He was elected, as was General Harrison, because of his
military exploits. As was Jackson. As was Monroe, when you come right
down to it. Hamilton was thinking along those lines, poor fellow, when
he got himself commissioned, during Shay's Rebellion."

"And what lines are you thinking along, young fellow?"

"Zachary Taylor." He said nothing more; he could see from Weed's
face that he'd guessed right. There had been talk of running Taylor for
the Presidency as early as 1846; it hadn't gotten anywhere as yet. But it
could.

"Oh?"

"In my opinion, Polk has done a very stupid thing in openly quarreling with General Taylor. Not only has he alienated followers of our
current military hero, he has also politicized Taylor himself."

"And how do you know that, Mister Congressman?"

Theodore only smiled.

"How do you know he's even a Whig?" Weed demanded.

"He isn't much of anything, it seems to me, but if he's anything
he's a Whig. He'll stand, and he'll win."

"He might at that. I've been thinking along the same lines myself.
You've hit the nail right on the button, seems to me. We ought to be
up and doing, if we want to be the early bird that swallows the worm."

"Exactly. And with Taylor to carry the ticket, we have some interesting possibilities open to us." Weed stayed silent and Theodore went
on. "The Vice Presidential candidate need not in any case be a powerful
figure. He should however be a safe figure—and with an amateur politician at the head of the ticket . . . "

Weed broke in with a guffaw.

"You weren't thinking of me, were you? Or old Greeley, now?"

"Millard Fillmore. He has the additional advantage of being a bit of a maverick. And from our point of view, of course, he has the immense advantage of being a New Yorker. It's hardly a powerful post, but those who can control its awarding, well, they will have substantial influence in the next government in Washington."

"You've been reading my mind!"

"Just thinking."

"Blast it, I wonder if the other side can think as well as that!"

"What was it Mr. Emerson said the other day? The Democrats clearly have the best principles, but the Whigs clearly have the best men? If they could think so clearly, Mr. Weed, they would be Whigs."

"Right you are. And come out with it, now, you must be thinking of something for yourself. You can't have done all that good thinking without some damned good reason!"

"To be sure. With Taylor and Fillmore, we're offering the electorate new faces, fresh faces. We can't afford to go against that, even in the appearance, at other points in our ticket. This has to be made clear to the Whigs nationally. In New York, it seems to me, we can do just that by nominating for Senator a man who represents the interesting combination of youth and experience, someone with a strong political reputation and yet with a solid and respectable public stance."

"You wouldn't be thinking of Congressman Bingham, now, would you?"

"I'm afraid I would be."

"He'd certainly be an unexpected choice."

"But as I've just demonstrated, I believe, distinctly a rational one."

"Argued like a lawyer. That's what you are, ain't you?"

"Indeed."

"Well, no matter how this turns out, you can count on some useful business coming your way. Any man your age who can figure things out so neatly, he deserves his day in court, doing for a client what you've just been doing for the Whig Party—and for yourself."

"Thank you. I see nothing wrong with intelligent self-interest."

"Neither do I!" Weed thundered, starting to rise. He patted Theodore on the shoulder. "And if that self-interest is as intelligent as you've just been, my friend, there's enough to spread around and do good to more than just one man. There is indeed."

Weed wasn't enough, of course. Theodore knew he had to build himself a lot of bridges: as an incumbent Congressman that was not difficult, given the energy to tackle the task in the first place. There were helpful things to be done, useful calls to make, encouraging offers to extend. It was, in that time, much more of a seeking than a selling operation: the idea had to be implanted, before the reality could even be contemplated. And there was still more that had to be done. A Congressman operated on the national scene, but he operated relatively narrowly. There were not quite sixty Senators in all; it was both a more restricted club than the House and at the same time a less parochial one. Senators were expected to be men of larger vision, not unpartisan but not party zealots, either. They were expected to be, as indeed the framers of the Constitution had envisaged them, a body of wiser men, somewhat above the temporal brawls of their lower-browed colleagues in the House of Representatives. Statesmen: that was what they were expected to be.

Theodore made the necessary approaches, quietly and efficiently. He made the necessary speeches—far-ranging, carefully edited into publishable shape, and then, in fact, published in selected New York newspapers—Mr. Greeley's *Tribune* among them. Though Mr. Greeley had as yet shown no great enthusiasm for the hero of the Mexican War, General Taylor, as a candidate for the President of the United States, he remained a good Whig. Theodore's campaign had gotten off to a good start: the trick was to keep it rolling gently while at the same time walking tall and staying as free as possible of entanglements—anything which could lower the tone of his appearance, in the eyes of the narrowly based electorate that controlled his chances. He cultivated the friends of General Taylor—and of Mr. Weed. He remained a sedulously active Congressman. And he waited, largely keeping his own counsel.

"It's the only time I'll ever represent myself," he told his younger brother, as they sat over a broiled chop and a tankard of fresh ale.

"Do you have a fool for a client?" Jonathan inquired.

"I won't know, will I, until the thing is settled? But do you know, I think I may have been, briefly, a small force in national affairs. Weed had been thinking of Taylor; that was plain. But he'd also been hesitating. I suspect my conversation with him, that night, may have helped decide him—and I'm sure you have noticed how cleverly he's been maneuvering to bring Taylor to the fore."

"My dear brother, haven't you been informed? I am a college student. What has General Taylor to do with Cicero, or with the niceties of quadratic equations?"

"Bosh. You stay abreast quite as well as the next man, and indeed somewhat better."

"Indeed, and rather better than I stay abreast of my studies."

"Dry stuff."

"Were you addressing yourself to the chop, the ale, or to the matter of higher education in this Union?"

"An interesting question. Let us first consider it from the procedural and then the substantive side, and then as a matter of either common law or of equity—"

"Good Lord! I shall never be a lawyer, brother. I could not stand it."

"What will you be?"

"Dear brother, we shall have to wait and see. One thing is clear, however."

"Which is?"

"I shall never be a force in national affairs, not even briefly."

Theodore almost choked on his ale; Jonathan had to rise and pound him on the shoulders before the fit subsided.

"Yes," Theodore said, clearing his throat, "very well said. Now if I were a Roman senator, brother, I would at this point stretch out my neck for you to slit."

"You may have read that at Princeton, but at Columbia, these days, we avoid all the nasty parts."

It *was* dry. Columbia College did not move uptown (to the old Deaf and Dumb building on Fiftieth Street) until ten years after Jonathan's arrival, and did not complete the migration to its uptown campus until forty years later. When Jonathan matriculated, the college sat almost cheek to jowl with the old Park Place Hotel, on Broadway facing City Hall Park. Not only was the center of official city politics thus within a stone's throw reach, but just the other side of the park, on Park Row, stood Tammany Hall. The college was a single three-storey building, with a modest lawn and a fenced yard in front. It was neither a luxurious nor even a commodious site. Students joked that the small observatory, perched on the roof, was always trained north toward City Hall and Tammany Hall, where all the really interesting activity took place. Students also joked that the venerable professor of moral philosophy and political economy, the Reverend John McVickar, M.A.—who taught everything from grammar and rhetoric to political economy and the evidences of natural revealed religion—should have been mounted on the roof, too, to frighten away students not prepared for the rigors of Columbia College.

Jonathan much preferred the rigors of the German Winter-Garden, an immense and elaborately gotten up beer hall, filled with fashionably dressed men and women (and children, too, running from group to group, tugging away at their parents' hands)—almost a kind of promenade-ground, criss-crossed by attentive waiters with trays and bottles of good cold beer and ale. You could walk about on the main floor, watching or chatting; you could sit at tables, perhaps with your feet up and a beer in front of you. You could also circle about on the narrow balcony ringing the entire huge place, staring down at the Lilliputians below, or else staring up at the steel and glass latticed ceiling, rising into a crowning glass cupola that in the late afternoon sun gleamed and glowed. It did not matter if you knew no one, or if no one knew you. But any reasonably well-connected New Yorker was bound to find someone of his acquaintance. It was a great deal more entertaining than Professor McVickar.

"We took the wrong things from the Germans," was a common saying among the students, as they strolled in the Winter-Garden. "We should have left them their educational system and taken all their beer halls!"

Jonathan had no need to visit Dr. Rich's Institute for Physical Education, one of the many gymnasiums established during the thirties and forties to counteract the tendency of city life to produce flabby muscles and short wind. But among his college friends there were some, native to New York City, who did need to visit such healthful places. He watched them run and leap and swing, cavorting on the standing horse, crawling on nets across the ceiling, lifting and dropping weights and dumb-bells. He very seldom joined in, but even watching was vastly more fun than listening to Professor McVickar.

"And how is Columbia College?" asked his Uncle Karl, that first undergraduate autumn.

Jonathan had a room on the second floor of his uncle's house and of course ate with the family.

"It may improve."

"I have heard that Professor McVickar is a remarkably intelligent man."

Jonathan became occupied with his napkin, and succeeded in covering over his choking laugh.

"I assume he certainly must be intelligent," he answered at last, his face again composed. "He would not otherwise be entrusted with our education, in so many of its various forms."

"I had not considered you disrespectful, Nephew."

"I trust I am not, sir—certainly not to you."

"I was referring to your learned instructor."

"You must admit, Uncle Karl, that it is difficult. We humans are of a wide variety of sorts and natures."

"But you, Jonathan, are of the younger variety and Professor McVickar is of the older."

"Indeed, sir, and I try my very best to keep that well in mind. So too, I'm sure, do my classmates. But as I said, it is difficult. Professor McVickar's mind travels in channels very unlike my own."

"Isn't the point of education, however, to learn the channels he so tirelessly pursues, and in the end to adapt your as yet unformed mind to his—as best you are able?"

"That may be. But it is still difficult. I do not find myself remarkably occupied with many of the things that occupy him. It may be that I am young, but might it not also be that I am meant to occupy myself differently?"

"You are not yet in a position to make that decision."

"Indeed, and that is why I am at Columbia College in the first place."

"I take it Professor McVickar is what we used to call, in my time, a crashing bore?"

"The phrase is still employed, sir. And it is still, I'm afraid, quite remarkably apt."

The younger children having left the table, Jonathan's aunt came and stood beside him.

"What might you find more interesting?" she asked.

He smiled gratefully. Aunt Sophia said very little, but rarely spoke off the point. And he knew, too, that when necessary she was a useful adjunct to his uncle's commercial affairs. He had seen her dispose of columns of figures faster than a seamstress could dispose of buttons.

"I'm afraid I am too young, Aunt, to really know. I may perhaps have some talent with words, whatever that may be worth."

"Have you any talent for business?" his uncle asked.

"I don't know. If I have, I have had no opportunity to know that. I have no inclination to follow my father in his, and in his father's profession. *That* I do know."

"Nor Theodore in his?"

Jonathan smiled. The dinner table at his uncle's house was one of the jolliest he had ever encountered. Talk had seemed just as serious, he supposed, at his father's table, but there was a gallop and a glow to things, here, that he'd never found in Poughkeepsie. People were somehow more direct; they spoke for themselves, not for some intellectual community, not out of some fairly abstract artistic concern. And there was more laughter here, though it was not levity.

"Isn't one statesman sufficient?"

"Ah?" said his uncle. "Is that what Theodore has become, these days? We shall have to be more respectful, the next time he comes to our house, Mrs. Andrée. I had not been aware that we were entertaining a veritable statesman."

"Husband," she wondered, preparing to leave the room for duties elsewhere, "why don't you introduce our nephew to something of what takes place in your offices downtown?"

"He has never invited such an introduction."

His aunt turned to Jonathan, smiling.

"It might be of profit to you."

"I'm sure it would. I am grateful indeed for the suggestion—which proves, Uncle, as you will have noted, the callowness of my mind and the limited extent of my experience. Had I been so attuned to the world as the learned Reverend McVickar . . ."

His aunt left the room.

"If your scholarly duties do not entirely preoccupy you," Uncle Karl proceeded, "perhaps we might trouble you to attend during the day tomorrow? There might conceivably be something of interest and utility with which to occupy your attention."

"I shall come directly after lunch."

Uncle Karl rose.

"I shall be delighted to receive you."

The countinghouse was on South Street, which of course meant that ships docked directly across the street from the windows of Andrée Bros. Just as Wall Street was already the great center of finance and exchange, and Peal Street was the nation's emporium, so South Street was where the merchant fleets of the world converged, edging past Sandy Hook and through the Narrows or, sometimes, in truly foul weather, down rather than up the East River to the wharves where merchants like Uncle Karl and Uncle Peter plucked them clean and proceeded to grow fat on what they plucked. The largest commercial houses, and Andrée Bros. was among them, took most of their wares out of bottoms they owned and operated themselves: if you had enough capital to cut yourself into the share of the pie earned by the shipping end of things, why hold back? There were other benefits, too, like rapid marine and commercial intelligence, and reliability of deliveries, and thorough control of shipping conditions. It was one thing to know that a captain was a first-rate sailor and a careful custodian of the goods entrusted to his care; it was still better to have that same captain in your own pay, and directly under your supervision, and even, at best, himself entitled to a percentage of the profits of a voyage.

"The harder you work, the faster you think, the more you know, the closer you watch—the more you earn." Uncle Karl had laid that down as his credo, and he and his dour, swift, perceptive older brother practiced what they preached, and prospered accordingly. There was not much to be seen of Uncle Peter, at the countinghouse: he was the outdoor partner. His responsibilities were ships and shipping and longshoremen and drays and all the rest of the work of keeping vessels in service and loaded and unloaded. He worked like a black-coated fury, almost never speaking but on target when he did.

There was a great deal to be seen in front of the countinghouse, even so late in the day as when Jonathan strolled up. The clerks had been at it since seven in the morning; the sailors had been at it even longer. Everyone was busy, but on the other hand nothing could ever be finished, there was always more, and more, and more. It was, to be sure, the sign of a flourishing enterprise: a motionless countinghouse was nine-tenths of the way into bankruptcy.

Jonathan stood on the pavement, watching. People were friendly enough, they smiled and nodded to him, but no one stopped to speak. There was a handcart going by, just to his left; two large drays were coming down the street toward a ship docked not forty feet distant; there were gangs of men alongside the ship, surrounding piles of merchandise, he could not tell of what nature; barrels seemed to be heaped everywhere; and high-hatted men in long frock coats came and went, often walking slowly, engrossed in sober conversation clearly of a high commercial sort. There was a lot of noise: the pavement was cobblestoned, and horses' hooves and cart wheels and barrel staves scraped and banged and pounded away. And people constantly shouted to be heard, so others tried to shout more loudly still. Jonathan was not struck, as men of a later time might have been, by the virtually total absence of women: men and boys, men and boys, everywhere.

Andrée Bros. was housed in a squat four-storyed brick structure, plainly designed with function rather than esthetics in mind. He turned and entered.

A clerk slipped off a high stool and intercepted him.

"Might you be Mister Jonathan?"

He was conducted through a dim chamber that seemed to be lined with pried-open barrels and peeled-back bales. There were shelves and some counters, but he could not tell anything from anything else. They went through a narrow doorway, into a still larger and considerably brighter room, warehouse-sized, and filled with stools and tables, all dominated by a singularly large oaken desk mounted on a raised platform, and strategically placed to the center rear, from where it served as well as a crow's nest perched high on a mast. And behind the large desk, head buried in papers as Jonathan approached, was his Uncle Karl.

"A moment," said his uncle, not looking up.

The clerk went back to his stool; Jonathan stood to one side, concerned that he might be obstructing his uncle's managerial view. Jacketless, sleeves tucked back, Karl was apparently toting up a column of figures. There were papers all across his desk, some stacked high, all visibly in order, neat at the edges. Jonathan did not smile: it might have been some school exercise, for all he understood, but he knew perfectly well how much depended on his uncle's quiet concentration. It was fairly quiet in this back chamber. The scratching of pens was audible, even the rustling of sheaves of documents. Men came and went, with measured step; boys darted in and out, and sometimes from station to station within the room. Some were very young, thirteen or so at the outside.

"There," said his uncle. "Grandvoort never makes a mistake, you know, but there's always a first time.

"The same Grandvoort?"

"The same. He's getting on, the business will be passing to his boys before too long—they're already taking hold nicely. Good fellows, both of them. Now: what can I show you, Nephew?"

"I scarcely know."

"Haven't we had you down here before?"

"Never. I'm afraid I'm an utter innocent."

Karl rose and hopped down from the platform.

"Well then, suppose I introduce you to the premises, and to some of the good people who keep us in running order, and then perhaps we can stop back here and talk a bit about you taking some part."

The operation, at least to hear Uncle Karl tell it, was simple. Peter took exclusive charge of the ships and everything connected with them. The inside work was Karl's. Most of their activity was importing, though their export trade was not negligible. Many houses focused heavily on one or another commodity, increasingly so as the volume of trade swelled. But Andrée Bros. were general merchandisers, which meant they handled incoming textiles above all else, but also sugar and coffee, largely from the Indies, and iron from Great Britain, and tea from China, and hides from all over the globe (including Russia), and laces and dried fruit and clocks and pot ash and copper and even rags.

"Rags?"

"What did you think your daily newspaper was made of, eh?"

Cotton was their biggest export commodity, but they shipped a good deal of flour, and were beginning to ship more and more cotton goods. A lot of foodstuffs went to South America—butter, cheese, grain—and also whale oil. There were miscellaneous items by the score, from unassembled barrel staves to live cattle.

"We do a fair business in provisioning ships. And things being what they are, we handle a good trade in what we don't make in this country."

"I beg your pardon?"

"We bring things in, from England say, and then we re-export them. There's no reason for you to know it, Nephew, not at your age, but this city is the gateway to the whole country. Would you believe it? Goods for Boston often come to us first, and we send them on to our northern cousins."

"For a fee."

"For a fee, to be sure. That's what business is all about, my boy. Do you think the insurers over on Wall Street would insure our boats and our cargoes for the sake of friendship? When I bring a draft across to the bank, do you suppose they give me every penny that's written on it? You can be sure they don't. They live off their discounts, and the insurers live off *their* percentages, and we live off ours."

They had toured rapidly through the warehouses on the upper storeys, crammed full of goods, some identifiable, some mysterious. They had walked around in the front rooms on the lower storey, which it turned out were more or less showrooms—through Karl was of the view that those who had to look were not the sort he much relied on.

"You learn pretty quick which are the men you can trust and which are the men you can't. If you trust 'em, by God, a shake of the hand is good enough. If you don't trust 'em, don't deal with 'em, I say. The best-drawn set of papers in the world aren't proof against a scoundrel." They turned in the narrow door and proceeded back to Karl's desk. "If they know me, they ought to know my goods. I'd no more sell 'em watered sugar or sour molasses than I'd serve such things at my own table. But things are growing so fast, you know, that I suppose it's necessary, all in all. Too many new people in the business, and at both ends of it, too. There are thieves and slovens in every land, Nephew, our own included. It's better to keep your feet dry, even when you're not sure it's raining."

Jonathan was invited to perch on a stool, alongside his uncle's solid chair. The whole working mass was spread in front of him.

"What do you think of it?"

"Incomprehensible."

"Nonsense!"

"Shouldn't it be called handling rather than *trading?*"

Karl put a finger to his nose.

"You can call it what you like, Nephew, so long as it turns a fair profit. We're not as particular about words, down here, as you fellows are in college. Though we watch our words pretty carefully, in truth."

"Who does it all go to?"

"Anyone who wants it—who can pay for it. We deal with all sorts, as long as their credit's good. And ours." Karl patted a stack of paper. "This is quite a few dresses for the ladies, at least in embryo." He touched a series of sheaves. "That one came from Liverpool. This one's going up the Erie, in a day or two, and from Cleveland who knows where it'll head? Small stores all over the prairies, and some peddlers' backs, too. That one came in from Jamaica. Don't do as much with them as we used to, but some of their people know us pretty well, and we know them, and we still do a bit of business. Been doing it since before I came in here, do you know that? Your grandfather, now, he started in with ships—Peter's the spit 'n image of him. He used to trade with Jamaica more than anywhere in the world. Fact. But we've gotten away from that—not entirely, mind you. Old things don't necessarily have to pass away; some of them are worth keeping. This lot, not much to it, but we've got our eye on some interesting things we can maybe bring through, if we handle it right. *That's* British bone china: good stuff, and pretty expensive to deal in—all that packing, and then the insurance, and we have to inspect every piece of it, every piece, mind you—but the profit's good. People need to eat, and they need to have dishes to eat out of, and some people know good china when they see it. We don't handle all the British lines, but we can get 'em, and for a good customer we do, we get anything, even it if costs us more than we sell it for. Fact."

"I thought you were never philanthropic, Uncle."

"I never said that, and I'm sure neither did your Uncle Peter. It's a hard world, down here. Nine of every ten go to the wall. Fine merchant, what's his name, Lord, Lord, how quickly we forget —." He pondered. "Well, he ended up a common sailor, and a gale caught him out at the end of a yard, and washed him to a watery grave. We all know that, we could any one of us end the same way, tomorrow morning. So we pull together. And we try, most of us, to be as decent as we can. We do as much for the city as any group of men you'll find. Karl slapped his knee and smiled. "But you're too young to worry about philanthropy, Jonathan Bingham. Unless you're heading for the pulpit?"

"No. Except, perhaps, to shake hands with the minister after a good sermon."

"Exactly. So we don't need to be solemn. How would you like to learn a bit about us, first hand?"

"Is it possible to begin so late?" Jonathan nodded at a thin boy. "That fellow there can't be more than twelve."

"He's fourteen."

"He'll learn a great deal in the next three years."

Karl grinned and patted Jonathan's arm.

"He'd better, or he'll be chasing his bread somewhere else. But you, Nephew, have certain advantages. And who knows? The teaching may be so much better, down here than up at Columbia College, that you'll come to us as much for recreation as for knowledge."

"Register me as a pupil, Uncle—the rankest beginner of them all."

"Now?"

"Why not? I believe it is written somewhere, Uncle, in some very wise man's learned book, that the best place to begin is, in fact, the beginning."

"Roll up your sleeves, my boy, and we'll start to make the mysteries less mysterious. It's not too late for you: I'll warrant that, I will!"

Jonathan rolled up his sleeves, first of course removing his jacket, and his uncle put him directly and immediately to work. South Street merchants were indeed as good as their word; nor did they let opportunity slip by. It did not seem to Jonathan that he had very much to offer his uncle, but that was not for him to decide. And Uncle Karl had long since learned to look out for his own interests. Jonathan sat at a small desk, on a high stool, for all the world like any of the clerks all around him—and what, in fact, was the difference, except that they knew what they were doing and he did not? But he would learn: Uncle Karl was surely right. It was not, perhaps, what he would want to spend the rest of his life doing, but he would learn and then decide. It could not be too late. And neither could it be as boring, as useless, as what he occupied his hours with at the college. What would Professor McVickar have done with this bill of lading, now? For all his talk of political economy, could the very learned professor have negotiated this bill on change, or indeed have deciphered its arcane language in the first instance? Jonathan was very determined not to imitate his academic mentors: that much he understood considerably better than he did the bill of lading. But unlike Professor McVickar, he would learn.

F
I
V
E

"The tendencies of a college life are doubtless drowsy; and you deserve therefore the more praise for showing signs of life."

—Daniel Webster, to his nephew Charles Haddock
13 October 1825

"She's been exceedingly pale."

"Since?"

"Off and on, really, ever since we came back from England."

"I hadn't noticed."

"It hasn't been consistent. If anyone should have remarked it, it should have been myself. I attributed it to excitement, and to moving about—and then, to the children."

"Of course."

"But I'm afraid it goes much beyond that."

"Has there been sputum?"

"And blood, yes."

The two physicians sat quietly; the thing had been said, and they each of them knew very clearly what would happen. The younger would lose his wife; the older would lose his only daughter. There would be four small children motherless. Not the next day or the next week or even perhaps the next year. But inevitably: there was nothing either of them could do, anyone could do.

"The Lord giveth, and the Lord taketh away."

"Doctor Bingham," his son-in-law replied, "I don't mean to be offensive, believe me I don't, but it seems to me that sometimes He takes without rhyme or reason."

"Mrs. Bingham and I have already lost three children, Martial."

"I know. I'm sorry." The younger man covered his face for a moment, holding back tears. "I can't accept it."

"You'll have to."

Martial bit at his lip.

"I could take her to the West. There are regimens that are said to help."

"Once there has been blood?"

Martial sat staring at the floor. Outside he could hear a whippoor-will in the cool night air. There was a mild breeze; leaves shook audibly.

"No."

"No one in our family has ever contracted tuberculosis. There is no familial pattern. I find it hard to understand."

"Does it matter how she contracted it?"

Doctor Bingham sat silently, then shook his head.

"I suppose not. Perhaps I seek a kind of refuge, Martial, in trying to approach it scientifically, or at least as scientifically as I know how. It is very hard to face, for me as well as for you. To lose your wife, on the threshold of your best years together, is very difficult. But Anne-Marie is my only daughter, and she will be the fourth of my children to pre-cede me. I'm afraid that is hard, too. Not that I intend comparisons: I do not. Mrs. Bingham and I have been married for thirty-three years; we have seen a great deal together, for better and for worse. She is herself not a well woman."

"I know."

Anyone peering through the open window would have taken Doc-tor Bingham for a relaxed old practitioner, calmly discussing some moderately interesting medical case with a younger colleague. His voice was audible but not loud.

"I have wondered, at times, what it would have been like, had one of the children been spared and she been taken instead."

"You'd have married again."

"I dare say I would have. So too will you, Martial."

"Good Lord! Anne-Marie is still alive!"

"That is how the world is, Martial. We did not make it, nor were we consulted. It does no good, I'm afraid, to reject the inevitable. The temptation is great, but I have found that only increases the pain. It is better, so long as we must come to that in any case, to bow our heads and try to make the best of things."

"And if there is no best?"

"Your bitterness is natural; I have felt it myself. One learns to curb it."

"Damn!"

Martial strode to the window and stood there. It was obvious that he was not seeing anything.

"I think I ought not to trouble you any more, this evening," Doctor Bingham began, rising slowly. But before he could complete his leave-taking Martial turned from the window, his face convulsed, and threw himself blindly into the older man's arms. Doctor Bingham patted the weeping man's back and said nothing. There was nothing to say.

"It has been very damp lately, Frederick. Should we start lighting a fire after supper?"

Marie Bingham was sitting with a book on her lap; it was, however, closed and she was not pretending to read. Her husband had no book; his hands were slightly raised, the fingertips of one hand resting against the fingertips of the other.

"If you like."

"Actually it's not myself but my pigments I'm concerned about."

He gave her a quizzical glance, then realized she was referring to her paint colors.

"By all means, do light a fire, my dear."

"You don't care, do you? I wonder if you ever did care, Frederick. I'm like a piece of furniture, as far as you're concerned."

"I'm sixty-seven years of age, Marie. You are fifty-two."

"I am not!"

"This is eighteen and forty-seven, my dear. You were born in ninety and five.

"I am *not* fifty-two!"

"Very well. However old you may be, my dear, why cannot we try, to the best of our ability, to live our last years on earth in peace?"

"I don't think talk of 'last years' is particularly useful, Frederick. Or particularly pleasant. I would think good cheer is an important part of the peace you so often prate about. It would be more appropriate if you shed some cheer, instead of always carping at me. Could I have been a better wife to you, or a better mother to the children?"

"No, my dear."

"Now, I had six, and Anne-Marie, she only has four, and it does seem to me that she neglects them fearfully."

"I don't think she does, no."

"And what do you know of the subject, pray? Did you ever spend a quarter of an hour here at home, tending to your family? You're always out and about, tending to every Tom and Harry in the State of New York, or else you're locked up in your so-called laboratory"—she pronounced it, scornfully, in her husband's British style, with the second rather than the first syllable accented: laBORatry—"and the one who's been at home, day in and day out, never with a single day to herself, has been me. What do you know of raising a family, indeed?"

"Anne-Marie strikes me as a very capable young woman."

"Capable! She'd rather be tinkling at the piano than tending to a baby. I'm sorry Mother ever thought of giving her that piano, and even sorrier we didn't think to send it right back, the moment it came. If it weren't for that piano, she would have had to face life directly, as I had to, so young as I was then. She always runs to that piano for comfort, rather than to me, or to her lawful wedded husband. She can sit there for hours, and not remember there's a world anywhere but in her addled head."

"You're not being fair, Marie."

"Fair!" She made a noise expressive of a very singular disgust. "I like to hear you talking about what's fair, Frederick Bingham. You don't have any right to use words the meaning of which you don't understand, and especially not with me. Mind you, there'll be no good that will come of Anne-Marie's hanging her flag to the keyboard. It will serve her ill, and serve Martial ill, though he deserves better. And the poor little children, they'll suffer, too." She sobbed abruptly, and stopped to dry her eyes.

Doctor Bingham rose.

"I will be in the laboratory, my dear," he said quietly, carefully pronouncing the word American style—LABratory. It was as close to ironical as he ever permitted himself, with her.

"To be sure you will. If *I* want you, you're always occupied somewhere else. Oh, it's different if some lazy ploughman thinks he requires purging, you're always ready to drop everything and rush to *their* help. But that's the way you're made, isn't it? Selfish and boorish from the beginning, that was your great secret, Frederick, and how you hid it from me so well, before I made the mistake of marrying you, I will never know."

Frederick did not hear her last words; he had turned and left the room as soon as her complaint began. He could however hear, fading quickly, the sharp clamor of her voice—and he had heard all the words before, he had no need to hear them again. But he would, he knew he would: over and over and over.

"Anne-Marie! What's wrong with your hands?"

Martial stopped a few feet from her. She was sitting at the piano, playing furiously, and her hands were as white as her face was red. He thought he did not know what, and sweat came to his face.

"Nothing!" she laughed, swinging away from the keyboard, and then rising and throwing her arms around him. "Don't be such a goose, Martial." She leaned back and stared up at him. "Besides, women are supposed to have exceedingly white skins, aren't they? It's a sign of beauty, as well as of good breeding. And I'm exceedingly beautiful, don't you think?" She laughed. "I'll not say I'm of good breeding, because that would prove the contrary." She released him and whirled in a double circle, then fell back toward the keyboard, slightly dizzy. Her hands shook. "Oh, you *are* a goose. Men are so silly." She lifted her hands and waved them at him. "I was making you some pastry, and that Haydn sonata came into my head—you know, the one I was working on last week—and I had to run and catch it before I lost the sense. Phrasing is the key, you know."

He muttered something.

"Did you think I was ill?"

He shook his head.

"I may not look terribly horse-like, Doctor Johnson, but I am healthier than any horses in your stable. No—any horse in the State of New York. There are only two horses in your stable, after all, and I shall surely see them and their children's children into the grave." She turned back to the piano. "Listen to how nicely I have solved the phrasing. Mind: if you don't praise me extravagantly, I shall run away and spend the rest of my life performing on the stage, in a *very* low-cut gown, while dashing men throw me money and children bring me large bouquets of flowers." She glanced at him; he was standing like some sort of statue. "And you, sir, have forgotten to bring me flowers for almost a week. Is it so difficult to wield a scissors in the garden as well as in your examining room? I ask you now!"

She played the Haydn beautifully. There were tears in his eyes, and when she turned she saw them and ran to him again, her arms even more tightly around him.

"What a goose you are, and how nice to have you!"

He stroked her hair and could not say anything. When she pulled back, twisting her head from side to side to restore her hairdo, he had his tears under control.

"Aren't you even going to ask me what sort of pastry I'm making for you, you silly?"

"No. I trust you implicitly, Anne-Marie. You'd never make something I didn't like."

"Nor will I, ever. You may trust me for, oh, the next fifty or sixty years, young Doctor Johnson." She peered at her hands. "Permit me to continue with my pastry, and absent myself from your charming company."

"Please."

When she had gone he found himself standing next to the piano, looking down at the keys for the traces of her hands. There were only a few crumbs of damp flour. That was exactly how it would be: a few crumbs, a mark here, a mark there. And she would be gone. She felt enormously healthy, and that was itself a sign of the disease. He would care for her as no tubercular patient had ever been cared for since the beginning of time. He would keep her alive, and he would keep her from knowing, for as long as he could. There might be a remission, there might be a miracle. While there was life, there was hope. But he did not hope. He simply determined that while he had her, while she still had life, he would care for her as never before, and love her so tenderly that when she left him she would go with a smile on her face. He let his fingers touch a small crumb, and the motion produced a faint twinkle from the piano. He pulled back his hand, as if it had been burned. When she was dead, no one would ever play this piano again. He would burn it, rather than have anyone touch it. It was Anne-Marie's, and Anne-Marie's only: no one else would ever have it.

Uncle Peter stood in the driving rain, the long spy-glass to his face. If there had been much of a wind he could not have hoped to see anything. Theodore, who could scarcely see his hands in front of him, did not in fact believe the other man could see anything anyway. But it was not a cold rain, and the counting house stood just behind them, dry and warm, whenever Peter should give up looking, so he stood and waited. And waited.

"Do you see anything, Uncle?" he finally inquired.

Peter did not answer, did not so much as grunt. Theodore was not surprised. It was not rudeness, not in Peter.

"It is not, I think, a dangerous storm," he ventured. Peter grunted but did not turn around. They had been standing out on the wharf for a quarter of an hour. Peter's slicker kept him reasonably dry, but Theodore's light coat was soaked.

"Captain Smith would have put up, surely, had things been worse out there than they seem from where we stand."

"Harkness," Peter snapped.

"One of your own captains?" But Peter did not reply. "In any event, Uncle, any sober sailor . . ."

"Sailors ain't sober."

Peter smiled and shook his head, amused in spite of himself.

"I meant, dear Uncle, any responsible captain, who would surely know how to handle the craft in his charge in even so light a storm as this."

Peter turned to him, scowling.

"Nephew, if you are determined to interrupt our business here, at least have the sense to do it indoors where you can be dry." Peter collapsed his telescope with a swift motion and grasped Theodore's arm in a tight grip. "Come. I see you are determined, and since I cannot spy my ship, or any sign of her, I will give over and let you say your piece."

A clerk brought Theodore a towel and he wiped his streaming head. Peter sent for two mugs of hot toddy.

"Now, young Congressman Bingham, I dare say you came looking for my brother."

"For either, or better still, for both of you, Uncle."

"Deftly spoken, Nephew. I wonder you don't turn your talents to the making of money, instead of to the spending of it."

Theodore understood the reference.

"Congress does other things than spend public funds, Uncle Peter."

"I hadn't noticed. Oh, you jaw a good deal, and when we make the mistake of not properly electing ourselves a president, you kindly do that for us. How much have you spent, do you suppose, to chase a bunch of bob-tail Mexicans out of their own lands and claim them for yourselves?"

"Barely as much as was necessary, Uncle."

"Necessary!"

"And also useful—not just to you, here in New York, but to the whole country."

"I'll bet you've spent millions."

"Indeed."

"And some good part of that was mine, let me tell you. I pay it into that old Customs House Building, down there, by the bushel-full. Nor will I ever see a red cent of it back again, after you've finished whipping the Mexicans and taking a quitclaim deed to their property."

"The whole country, as I said, will benefit, not only because we have shown the world that we can stand up for ourselves, and that we will not hesitate to shed blood if we need to, but also, let me remind you, Uncle Peter, because any territorial accessions will—"

"Territorial accessions my foot!"

The toddy arrived; they sipped quietly for a moment.

"Well, now, Nephew, apart from a good toddy on a wet day, what can I do for you?"

"Let me reassure you, Uncle, that I've not come after money."

"Just as well: it's been a bad year. But let *me* reassure *you*, young Theodore. I give you the rough side of my tongue, but from all accounts you're doing well down there in Washington, and if it would be going a mite far to say that we were proud of any politician in this country, still we're pleased to have a few sane ones, and you among that few."

"Thank you." Uncle Peter had not changed, to his memory, had always looked and dressed and thought and talked the same. But Peter Andrée was some years his own father's senior, and Doctor Bingham was now over sixty. He had been born in the prior century, and the current century was nearly half gone. "I enjoy Congress, Uncle. It's the instrument I play the best in the whole world—as the man with the jew's harp said to the man with the one-string fiddle."

"I can't say that it keeps you out of mischief, Nephew. But I'd be surprised if it doesn't help your law business."

"It does. But I'd do it anyway."

"The more fool you, then."

"No, Uncle: there have to be people helping to run the country, and if I'm good at it, and I do not think I boast when I admit that I am, why should I abstain?" There was no response, audible or visual. "And I have the feeling, too, that as I go along I get better at it. I learn how to get things unstuck, to whom to address certain kinds of communications, when to hold back, when to move forward as rapidly as possible."

"You sound for all the world like your sister. I've heard her prate very similarly, describing music to the rest of us benighted heathens."

"It *is* a kind of art, Uncle. But no, I make no claim to be an artist, only a fair-to-middling lawyer and, I think, a better–than-average politician. I've an itch to be a better politician still."

"And?"

"And I've about decided I'll make the attempt."

"Who'll have you? Old Zach's the man—"

"No, I don't propose to challenge that heroic general, who in any event will probably run on our own Whig ticket. I'm aiming at the Senate seat, about to be vacated."

"Does it pay better?"

"A little, but not a great deal. Money's not the point."

"Ain't it?" Peter Andrée threw up his hands. "Well then, sir, I have wasted this long life of mine."

"Do you think me too young, Uncle?"

"I know more about your judgment, Nephew, than I do about questions such as that."

"And you think me deficient?"

Peter Andrée leaned forward, and suddenly clapped his nephew on the knee. His broad hand stung, the sound was like a small rifle being fired.

"I say more power to you, boy! Go out and take the Senate, and don't stop until you're in the White House itself! If you can do it, Nephew, and I'm prepared to bet you haven't been sitting idly by. No, I'm sure as I sit here you've been out beating the bushes and testing the waters, so why not? Indeed, why not? Have we better men for the post?"

"Some hundreds, I dare say."

"No, no—not so! Politeness is all very well, Nephew, but not in matters as serious as this. Can you convince the Legislature?"

"With luck, and hard work, I think they can be persuaded that I am a serious candidate, and that I could be a useful senator."

"Who are the key men? Or is there a single key man?"

"Weed, Thurlow Weed."

"The editor?"

Theodore nodded.

"And have you approached him in some appropriate way?"

"Yes."

"What then is lacking?"

"Uncle, it's not really that anything is lacking. I'm not anxious to involve the family, or indeed to impose on any member of it."

"Nonsense."

"I can't have been much of a politician, if in these past five years I haven't learned how to manage these things. No, I'd like something else from you, Uncle Peter. And from my Uncle Karl, too, when I have the chance to discuss matters with him. I can't go to my father, you see: he doesn't understand, and I think he cannot understand."

"A harsh judgment for a son to pass on his father."

"I think not, Uncle. You're perhaps a few years older than my father, but your life has been spent out in the world. Oh, he's a doctor, to be sure, but he's not fundamentally a worldly man. I don't mean that as criticism. It's simple fact. I would not come to you, Uncle, if I had a severe intestinal flux. My father is a professional man and I think rather good at his profession. He is a competent man of science. But he is neither a politician nor a businessman, and what is more, he lacks any feeling for the impulses and strictures of those professions." Theodore hesitated. "You see, I don't want help, in the usual sense. I want advice. And I don't want it on a familial basis. Think of me, perhaps, as a cargo destined for Liverpool, and your position that of a potential investor in the merchandise I represent."

"I deal in more solid goods, Nephew."

"Is that your judgment, then?"

"Not a bit of it. I meant only that your analogy is fundamentally defective."

"Think of it, then, if you will, as—"

"Theodore," his uncle interrupted, "I can only think of it as I think of it. I suspect you of sophistry, and I suspect your sophistry stems from some sense that you would not be doing the right thing. I do not of course know what is involved, nor do I know the full process of your reasoning. But I would recommend that if you are to approach the matter in this spirit, it is better left alone."

Theodore could see, through the narrow pane behind them, high on the bare wall, that the rain had stopped. But Peter made no move to return to the wharf. Unlike the members of Congress, his uncle confined himself to one activity at a time. Whatever he was doing, he did it as fully as he knew how. Peter had challenged him, simply and directly, and this was indeed a serious business.

"I may well be sophistical, Uncle. I certainly do have doubts. I would be distinctly wonderful, I think, if I did not. I may fail, and it would be very bad to fall. Politics is not like business, where you can fall and rise again. A fall in politics is like the fall as Milton describes it, 'hurled headlong flaming.' A failed merchant may become wealthy; a failed politician will not rise again. But even failure is not, I admit, the main concern. The principal difficulty I would have in winning election is my comparative youth—and might that be, in fact, a genuine deficiency in me, a failing of maturity and knowledge, not to speak of wisdom? But there is even more that troubles me." He took a deep breath. His uncle had not moved in some minutes, but there was small doubt he was following. "I came to you, and to Uncle Karl, before I challenged my predecessor for the seat I now hold. I came for support, and as you well know I came for fiscal help. But I came, too, for some sense of how others in the family might feel about my plunging into public life—for the public light that shines on one, tends to shine on all. As a congressman I am not unknown, I am mentioned here and there. But there are many congressmen and, assuming I obtain the post, not many senators. My name would become a great deal more public. The whole sphere of international activities is peculiarly within the province of the Senate. My speeches and my votes and even the people with whom I broke bread would become, ineluctably, a matter of public note. All of which would mean, Uncle, that no one closely connected with me, and even some not at all closely connected, would be obliged to bear a considerable and perhaps unpleasant public scrutiny—and an unrelenting one."

"You could not damage our business affairs."

"But I might trouble your tea-parties. And those of my aunt's, and those of my excellent cousins. Public figures attract gossip; all the trivia of our democratic existence are likely to be magnified, and broadcast far and wide. If my uncle drinks, or deals in, port rather than Madeira, why, it may well be asked, does not this portend a tariff change, or a treaty with the Bey of Bumble-Bumble?"

"You are a man, Nephew. A youngish sort, but plainly a man. What a man does, provided he does it decently and properly, is subject to whatever inconveniences may attend on his chosen line. His family, it seems to me, has nothing very much to say about it."

"But Uncle, I would like to give you that opportunity—I would like you to be able to speak your mind in advance, before it becomes too late."

"But it is you, Theodore, not I, who is considering a run for office."

"Will you at least, dear Uncle Peter, discuss this with your brother, and with your good wives, and with your sons and, yes, your daughters too? I have had an exaggerated sense of familial propriety, but I do feel deeply how large a step I may be taking, and not for myself alone."

"It will be discussed."

"Do you recall how Anne-Marie felt about my becoming a Congressman, five years ago? The race, so long as it seemed quixotic, rather appealed to her. She found something gallant about it, and was all for my doing it. She felt rather differently once I had actually won."

"A man cannot permit women to make his decisions for him."

"Indeed. But a man also has an obligation to ensure the happiness of those women who are directly dependent on him."

"Your sister's husband has that responsibility, Theodore. And that privilege. I believe he is capable of exercising it."

Theodore rose.

"Uncle, I wish men of your stripe could still be in manufacture! We are become a lesser breed: there seems to me no doubt of that."

Peter did not rise.

"Nonsense."

Theodore laughed vigorously and straightened his damp coat as best he could.

"I wish it were. If my children's children are as much less direct and forceful as I am less direct and forceful than you are, our country will have deeper problems to contend with than the questions of my running for the Senate!"

"If so, Nephew, it will be their problem. I shall not live to see it, and neither, I dare say, shall you. But I trust," he affirmed, finally rising, "that you will come as safely into port as that delinquent schooner of mine. If I don't spy at least her top's'l, well, Captain Harkness may find himself aback out on a yard arm, reefing sails at someone else's direction. I wish you well, Theodore, I would be much surprised if my brother's mind was any different, on this whole subject. But as I said, I will indeed broach it to him. And though you are not in need of funds, I would be pleased to offer whatever you might need if you later on discover such a need."

Theodore took his arm and squeezed it gently.

"I don't know why I worried about your being offended, Uncle."

"Nor do I, my dear Nephew." Peter pulled out a well-polished chronometer and studied it for a moment. "If either you or I charged for our time, by the hour, this conversation would probably have beggared the two of us. I earnestly hope it has not, at least, beggared me."

He was smiling so very broadly that Theodore wondered, in a startled new awareness, why he had not seen, all these long years, what a jolly character this stiff old uncle truly was. But the smile vanished quickly. Peter's shoulders drew tighter, and as he ushered Theodore back through his counting-house and left him in front of it, striding off down the wharf, his pocket glass emerged from his jacket pocket and extended as if by itself as he walked. Theodore remembered how many other occasions had ended in essentially the same way, and he realized, both fondly and sadly, how rare an occasion this had been. Deservedly, to be sure: these were not boyish matters he had come to discuss. But all the same, he left South Street, walking much less rapidly than his uncle, filled with a strange, only partly understood sense of a very different world, abutting on his own, in intermittent communication, but in the end spun along a different axis, pursuing a different orbit, perhaps even wound into motion by different hands. Once again he smiled to himself: *that* might be religion, it might be philosophy, and whatever it might be, he was clearly better off leaving it alone.

Jonathan did not know that his sister was mortally ill, nor did anyone else in the family, other than her husband and her father. Everyone would know, in time: the symptoms of tuberculosis were nothing mysterious; almost everyone had a relative or friend who had died of it. But neither Doctor Bingham nor Doctor Johnson wanted the appearance of the sick room. Whatever honest glow might be left to Anne-Marie, they wanted her to have it, undampened, unhindered. There would be time enough for the inevitable "last moments."

Columbia College was supposed to be occupying Jonathan's time, as well as his thoughts. It was incapable of either. He did not tell his father, in any of his regular letters, about either his dissatisfaction with the school or about the time he was spending on South Street, puzzling over arcane documents and copying them in a clear, clean hand suitable for sea captains and merchants and other quasi-literates. He did enough college work to keep himself in good standing: that was all he thought necessary. He did not have to like Columbia, so long as Columbia did not expel him from its ranks.

"Cousin, you seem remarkably uninterested in whatever it is you are reading."

He was sitting in his Uncle Karl's drawing room, with his aunt and several of her children.

"Books by boring people are apt to be boring books," Jonathan smiled.

"It must be by Professor McVickar!" exclaimed the youngest of the children.

"We do hear a lot of him," their mother noted.

"Not half so much as *we* are obliged to hear of him, Aunt!"

"I wonder," she mused, not looking up from her sewing, "if you find your uncle's counting-house more stimulating?"

"*Much* more."

"Oh, that's all money, money, and then more money," a cousin objected.

"It's a great deal more than that, Susie," Jonathan assured her.

"And you ought not bite the hand that feeds you, young lady," said Susie's mother. "Might you be considering some further exploration of trade and commerce, Jonathan?"

"I don't know. I've not quite turned eighteen. I dare say I'm supposed to understand a great deal more than I do, but the fact is I know quite stunningly little about what I ought to be doing." He hesitated. "I have thought about shipping out as a supercargo—if my uncle thinks I know enough to handle the task."

"You might ask him."

"I might. But I've also thought about—oh, a host of other things."

"I'd love to sail to China!" a cousin exulted.

"Lordy, so would I."

"But not to Africa."

"Or the Indies. Ugh."

"Children." Their mother called them to order. "What other things, Jonathan?"

"Some of them quite silly, I dare say. It's the vice of my age, I know that perfectly well." She lowered her sewing and looked across at him; he blushed. "Well, I've thought about writing a monstrously fine epic poem, and I've thought about founding either a magazine or a newspaper, I haven't decided which. And I've thought about going to Theodore, to see if he could find me a place in one of our European embassies. Paris would be very nice. Or London. I've always liked water, so I've thought about the navy, too. Not the army: it wouldn't be the fighting part which interested me."

"And the other things you've thought of?"

He opened and closed his book and looked away.

"I can't remember them all, Aunt."

She did not press him.

But half an hour later, when she had sent the children off to bed, she asked if he had any interest in writing for a newspaper.

"Oh yes—if I write well enough."

"Is it that difficult?"

"No. I dare say any of my classmates at Columbia could manage it at least as well as most of those doing it right now."

"Shall I say something to Mr. Greeley?"

It had never occurred to him.

"Do you know him, Aunt?"

"He has been here. I believe your brother Theodore knows him. And knows Mr. Weed, who is also an editor of some renown."

"I should be very grateful, Aunt. I really should be."

She simply nodded and resumed her sewing.

He sat a while longer, making no further pretense of reading his book, then excused himself and went out for a bit of air. There was a faint anticipatory tang: winter was not right around the corner, but the soft summer was fading. Since the city had installed gaslights, more people trusted themselves in the streets after dark. It was not crowded, but neither was New York empty, even at something later than ten at night.

Walking kept him warm. He was not aware of rambling in any particular direction; neither did his mind follow any track. His head and feet simply followed themselves—but he was not surprised when he found himself on South Street, standing in front of his uncle's shuttered place of business.

One was not supposed to visit South Street late at night, he knew, but it was not yet really late. And there were other people about, some of them unloading a medium-sized vessel, some of them working with a large pile of merchandise. There was a horse and wagon, waiting nearby, the horse stomping rather amiably, tethered to a post, the driver sitting almost motionless, reins slack in his hand. Pitch flares were burning, both on the vessel being unloaded and on the wharf alongside: it was not so much an eerie as a strangely romantic light. Shadows flickered long and wispy, down the cobblestones and along the planks. The sounds were disjointed, but somehow very cheerful.

Images and then lines began to take shape in his head: by God, he was at it again, standing in the middle of New York's mercantile district and composing poetry. He felt a fool—Uncle Karl had found him, once, editing a sonnet on a discarded envelope, and smiled indulgently—but he felt too moved to check himself. What harm did it do, after all? Poetry had meant a great deal to a great many people better than himself—and if his poetry meant nothing to anyone but himself, well, it was still no despicable thing. And this scene, it was in its way noble; it was bold, and yes, it had a heroic side, too.

The arm that touched his own startled and at first frightened him.

"Do you often walk the streets at night, Jonathan, talking to yourself?"

It was his Uncle Peter, dressed in his usual black coat and tall hat.

"Was I talking to myself?"

"Unless you have a companion I cannot see."

Jonathan tried to think of a decent excuse.

"I'm afraid I was composing verses, Uncle."

There was no response; he wished himself five miles distant. Even Uncle Karl barely tolerated his versifying. Uncle Peter, so much grimmer and duller, must indeed think him a fool.

"About some young lady, I presume?"

The tone was neutral, but the purport was unmistakable.

"Not a bit of it!" He waved at the flares and the wharf activity. "About that, the sense of wonder in goods coming from all across the seven seas and ending up here, right in front of us." Silence: he took a breath and went on, resolved not to go down without a struggle. "It's commonplace to you—I know that. You see it every day, Uncle; you've been seeing it for years. But it's new to me, and I see it, perhaps not so much fresher as certainly differently. You'll think me quite addled—I know you will—but I find it as romantic as ancient castles and magic lakes."

"No," said Uncle Peter calmly. "No, I still see it that way, myself, at times. It *is* a wonder, and I find it wonderful, Jonathan, even after all these years."

Jonathan could find nothing to say.

His uncle released his arm and they stood in silence.

"I walk this way often, at night," Peter went on slowly. "So much of my life is here, during the day, that it's hard to cut it off. Your aunt never understood that, and neither, I think, do your cousins. Perhaps you have some sense of it, Jonathan. I guess you might, from what you said just now."

Jonathan could not answer. He did not know whether he understood anything at all, not any more.

"Would you let me hear what you've composed, Nephew?"

Jonathan took a couple of long breaths.

> *"The earth disgorges, the sea swells and carries*
> *Scents and flavors, bark and gutta percha,*
> *Hides and ambergris, here to us.*
> *Sailors and merchants, captains of land and wave,*
> *Work these ropes, these crowded wharves, as men*
> *Till fields."*

He stopped and his sigh was very audible.

"That's as far as I'd gotten."

Peter stood with his arms folded across his chest.

"That about 'captains of land and waves,' now, that isn't far from the mark, is it?"

Jonathan did not correct him, too pleased to have escaped without either censure or satire.

"And I can tell you've been reading what you've been copying in the countinghouse, Nephew. I don't wonder that you've got all those nice names in your head: gutta percha, now, just think of that! I don't think I've ever heard of that making its way into a poem. But why not, eh?"

"Indeed," Jonathan said, weakly.

Peter clapped him on the back.

"You finish that, my boy, and let me see how it comes out." Peter lifted his hat. "I'll wish you goodnight, Jonathan. Don't stay for the winter air that's coming. It brings you a cold if you let it."

Peter walked rapidly off.

The world contained wonders within wonders; Jonathan had not known it was so rich and various. It felt extraordinarily good to be alive, and to be young, and to live in the wonderful place, and in the wonderful time, in which he was fortunate enough to be unrolling his life.

Uncle Peter praising a poem, a poem composed on the spot by none other than his own blood nephew!

Jonathan glanced up, half expecting to see a bloody comet or some other sign of civil madness. The stars were all in their places; the heavens were at peace. He looked down the wharf. The flares were still guttering; the men were still at work.

He rocked on his heels, and returned to the making of his poem. The trick would be to go from the image of agriculture into a comparison, perhaps even an extended comparison, between that traditional and well-accepted way of life and this new, bold, and infinitely more exciting path. The horse would do very well as a kind of bridge: after all, he pulled the plow and he also drew the wagon. He sat heroes, too, and warriors, and even princesses. . . .

A tremendous tapestry began to open out in his mind; his breath came faster and instead of rocking he began to walk, almost to pace. His hands went behind his back and clasped together. He stared down into the cobblestones, not seeing them, lost in the images washing through his head.

S
I
X

*"I never heard what particular substance Archimedes wished his
desired fulcrum to be, resting on which, he was going to move the
world; but if his design had been to move everything in it, he would
have wished it cash . . ."*

—Daniel Webster to his brother Ezekiel
5 May 1804

"Mr. Andrée?"

Jonathan was seated not far from his Uncle Karl's high desk. He
could see the nervous man, in early middle age, who was standing just
below the platform. Karl had been working through a sheaf of documents: Jonathan had long since realized that his uncle's desk would
never be clear. This was a Monday afternoon, neither a particularly slow
nor a particularly busy day.

"Mr. Schimmel? How do you do?" said Uncle Karl.

"Thank you." The visitor did not walk up on the platform, and
Karl did not indicate that he was to mount. "About my draft."

"Yes. Four thousand, three hundred and eighty-two dollars, due
Wednesday next, promptly at nine in the morning. To cover, as I recall,
a shipment of hides."

"Yes."

"Your troubles are not unknown to me, Mr. Schimmel."

"I did not think they were, Mr. Andrée."

"But I trust you will indeed be able to make prompt and full payment?"

"I very much doubt it."

"I see."

"My former partner, George Wilson, has defalcated, as you know,
carrying off certain funds necessary for the continuance of our business."

"Has he been apprehended?"

"Not yet. I have hopes that he may be."

"I join you."

"But for the moment, at least, the obligations of our firm will be
more than I alone will be able to meet."

"I see."

"I came to ask for whatever extension of time you might be willing to grant. Under all the circumstances—"

"I'm afraid," Karl interrupted him, "that under all the circumstances, Mr. Schimmel, I shall have to insist on prompt payment."

Jonathan had not expected that response. His heart quickened, he felt impelled to intervene—and did not move.

"I have some excellent arrangements in progress, Mr. Andrée. If we are permitted to continue in business, I have no doubt that even George's defalcations can be fairly readily made up."

"That may be."

"I should be glad to make you acquainted with the details, Mr. Andrée."

"Thank you, but I will have to decline the opportunity. The running of one business is almost more than I am able to manage, as it is."

"We will go under."

"I am sorry to hear it. Is there no one to extend you further credit, Mr. Schimmel?"

"I think not."

"I doubt, then, that I can reasonably be expected to be more generous than your own bankers."

"Thank you for your time, Mr. Andrée. I bid you good day."

"A good day to you, Mr. Schimmel, and I will continue to hope your expectations will be disappointed and the draft will be paid as promised."

There was no further conversation. Schimmel did not weep, did not beg; he remained erect and went walking out of the counting-house calmly and at much the same pace as when he had walked in. No one spoke to him, and he spoke to no one. It was extremely likely, Jonathan knew, that every clerk, every runner, every casual passerby even, was fully aware of Schimmel's plight, and could have predicted the result of his visit to the inside partner of Andrée Bros. "We will go under," he had said, precisely and probably accurately.

Schimmel and Wilson was not one of the great South Street firms, but even a newcomer like Jonathan could have identified it as a flourishing business. What would happen if indeed it went under? What would happen to Schimmel's family, to his employees, to his creditors—like his two uncles? Jonathan badly wanted to corner his Uncle Karl and obtain answers to such questions, but that was plainly impossible. Even had he been older and wiser and more important than he was, he would have hesitated to interfere, thus publicly, with Karl Andrée.

He had difficulty concentrating on his work. The steady yet
somehow not quite firm tread of Mr. Schimmel kept intruding on his
thoughts. The courage of the man had impressed him: Mr. Schimmel
would be going down like a gentleman. But why would Uncle Karl
make him go down? If there were profitable ventures underway, if the
debts caused by forces beyond the man's control could in fact be paid
off, why not exercise some degree of mercy? Would Andrée Bros. do
any better by forcing a bankruptcy? Why could not Mr. Schimmel and
his "excellent arrangements" be yet another investment for the Andrées? Jonathan had admired much in this busy South Street hive. Its
owners and proprietors had revealed themselves, he fancied, as rather
purer and loftier men than his preceptors at Columbia College. But for
all his tiresome windiness, would even Professor McVickar have said no
to a plea so cogently, so manfully, so quietly and decently made? And
if this was the true underside of Andrée Bros., did he want to stay any
longer under its roof?

"You are wondering about Mr. Schimmel," said Uncle Karl, when
the evening meal had been concluded, the dishes cleared, and the
younger children excused.

"Has he failed?" inquired Aunt Sophia.

"No, but he will."

"Need he fall?" Jonathan said, as calmly as he knew how.

Karl poured wine into all their glasses, then sipped at his.

"Did you know, Nephew, that something like nine out of every ten
merchants in this city do exactly that—fail?"

"He seems a singularly courageous man."

"He will need to be."

"But let me ask once again. Need he fall? He spoke of profitable
arrangements, matters which would permit him to pay his—and his
absconding partner's—debts."

"Jonathan, no one ever goes down gladly, or without a struggle. Mr.
Schimmel has been in business in this city for years. He is known to be
in many ways an admirable man, certainly an honest man. He has sufficient knowledge, I believe, to conduct a successful firm."

"Given a fair chance."

"He has had a fair chance."

"Is it his fault that his partner has absconded?"

"If it is anyone's fault, Jonathan, who else would be to blame? It
was Mr. Schimmel who agreed to go into business with George Wilson,
was it not? That was an entirely voluntary act. And such choices go, I'm

afraid, directly to the heart of the matter. Mr. Schimmel is if anything too trusting. He has extended credit where credit should not have been extended. His own bankers have warned him; in point of fact, Jonathan, I have warned him. I have been one of his creditors, and I do not like to see any man with whom I choose to do business fail. There is a softness to Mr. Schimmel's judgment, an inability or an unwillingness to face hard facts. He is as you say a courageous man, but he does not much like to see things as they are. He wishes they were otherwise."

"So do we all, at times."

"Indeed. I could wish that a merchant could extend infinite credit, could handle only such merchandise as he himself personally favored, could exist by dealing only with men he liked. I could wish that capital were not necessary—I could even wish that employees did not have to be paid, but labored for the joy of contributing to a successful enterprise. But as the old proverb has it, Nephew, wishing does not make it so."

"But you could help him, Uncle, if you chose to."

"For how long, Jonathan? Let us say I extended the date of payment on his draft. Let us say he somehow managed to meet the next due date. What would happen to the drafts to which he afterwards signed his name? What would happen in his dealings with my fellow merchants, and with his bankers—who are bound to keep him on a very short rein, if indeed they are prepared to keep him at all."

"No one can really say, can they?"

"Arguably, yes, you're right, Nephew. But when a wolf, for instance, finds himself in a steel trap, does he sit debating whether his broken leg will heal, if ever he gets it free? No, he gnaws it off, knowing full well that he cannot repair it, and that to try to keep it will result in certain death."

Jonathan was sitting toward the front of his chair, his legs apart, his hands supporting his chin. He tried to seem as unconcerned, as calm, as his uncle.

"Aren't you rich enough—forgive me, Uncle, if I trespass—to support a man like Mr. Schimmel for a small while? Does he not deserve such assistance?"

"He is a religious man, and I think he will have all the support he is entitled to from his faith. I do not owe Mr. Schimmel his opportunities, and I certainly do not think I owe him any part of what I have been able to earn for myself and for my family."

"That seems somehow not quite right. I must say that to you, Uncle. It does not seem right that a man of Mr. Schimmel's qualities should be discarded in this way."

"Is he being discarded, Jonathan?" put in his aunt. "I do not know a great deal about these things, but I have some slight awareness and I have seen for some time that Mr. Schimmel was engaged in dealings at best risky, at worst careless and heedless. One cannot be reckless and have any claim on others."

"I must concede that, Aunt. But I have seen the man, and he seems to me of sterling mettle."

"He is that, in many ways," Karl responded. "Perhaps what it comes down to is simply this: By what standard are we to measure a man's true worth? There are intangibles, to be sure. You might purchase a business, let us say, with a stock of fifty thousand dollars, and capital of twice that, for as much as another twenty-five or fifty thousand dollars, allowing thereby for the good business relationships established, for the existing credit arrangements, for the stability and the continuity created by years of hard work. These are intangibles, but they have value, and they should be counted. But would you pay two hundred thousand dollars for them, instead of twenty-five or fifty? Would you purchase a business with no stock and no capital for the same sums, because the man who wanted to sell it to you was a good man and well liked? Take yourself, Jonathan. You are young but by no means devoid of talent. I cannot say that you would necessarily do well in business, should you choose to engage in it, but you plainly have some of the necessary attributes. I have seen that for myself. There is nothing wrong with being somewhat romantic about one's activities, as I think your Uncle Peter has long since proved. He mentioned his meeting with you, by the way, and I see clearly that you and your uncle have a great deal in common, more perhaps than do you and I. But be that as it may, suppose I had the disposal of some publishing venture. Would I be justified in handing it over to you, your talents and capabilities not withstanding?"

"I'm sure you would do nothing so foolish, Uncle!"

"To be sure. But don't you have a right to exercise your talents? Don't you have a right to be successful in your own way?"

"I suspect I do. But as you carefully point out, I am still very young. I need to prove those talents, whatever they may be."

"Exactly. Why should the same not apply to Mr. Schimmel?"

"But hasn't he proved that he has abilities considerably greater than mine? He's kept a business afloat for some years now."

"Afloat, but leaking steadily, so that its grounding, not to say its sinking, was inevitable."

"And yet, you did business with him yourself, Uncle. You extended him credit: he would not owe you four thousand and some dollars, to be paid Wednesday morning, if you had not advanced him the use of that sum."

"He is a good man, Nephew. He is an honest man. He has tried hard, and we have tried hard to help him. It is time to cut all our losses: it will not work; it is plain that it will not work. He will do something else, and I pray he will do it better."

"I'm glad you did try, Uncle."

"I don't regret it. Mistakes are inevitable, in business just as elsewhere. We are solvent, thank the Lord: losses of this sort will cause us no trouble—and Mr. Schimmel will pay us something, as much as he can, perhaps even fifty cents or more on the dollar. *He* will try, too."

"I think," said Aunt Sophia, "that what your uncle wants to say to you, Jonathan, is both that he has a conscience and that, in this case, it is a clear conscience. He is not a ruthless businessman, though he may be a reasonably successful one."

"I am persuaded of that, my dear Aunt. I only wish that Mr. Schimmel, from what little I know of him, had been better equipped for my uncle's world."

"The young are frequently rational, while their elders are simply experienced. There's no use in rationality, Nephew. The world has no place for it, except in monasteries, perhaps, or in old books. It's a fatal credo to try to live by."

"I suspect my father would be amused, Uncle, to hear me being described as rational. And by you, of all men."

Karl emptied his glass and poured more, this time only for himself.

"I have always been able to amuse your father, Jonathan. He laughs unusually well at my jokes. I have always wondered if that indicates some fundamental virtue in me, or some fundamental defect in him. Not that I mean to insult your father, please understand." He rose suddenly, slightly unsteady on his feet, and drained his glass in a long swallow. "It is just, Nephew, that it has been a singularly long day, and I find myself a bit flown on this excellent wine. If I have misspoken myself, do please forgive me. I had no such intention."

He bowed awkwardly, then left the room, walking slowly and balancing on his wife's arm.

Jonathan was smiling to himself. He had never before seen either of his uncles tipsy: he wondered if Mr. Schimmel's impending bankruptcy had anything to do with it? The faint slur on his own father, if that was in fact what it was, did not disturb him. He had come to understand the relation between Doctor Bingham and Doctor Bingham's Andrée connections. Particularly since he had begun to spend several afternoons each week in the counting-house of Andrée Bros, the relationships between aspiration and economics were becoming clearer. It now seemed to him that he had grown up on a pretty heavy diet of the former, and it was just as well that he was finding himself introduced to the latter. No matter what sort of existence he ultimately chose—a decision that still seemed as much in the future as it had ever been—it would do him no harm to know from whence came the butter which, until now, had abundantly coated his bread.

He remembered Mr. Schimmel, and was immediately sorry—but not quite so sorry as he had been before. The hall clock struck; he listened, then rose. It was time for the minimal duties he owed the College. He would parse, and he would construe, and then he would sleep. And in the morning—well, who could tell what the morning would bring?

He had never thought of her as a nervous person. It occurred to him, suddenly, that the faint tapping of her fingers on the table cloth was not some newly developing tic, but the unconscious working out of a musical passage. There was a faintly faraway look in her eyes—and was it surprising that, as the disease progressed, as her imagination grew gradually more heated, more fervid, her attention focused more and more on music? Did even their children mean more to her?

"Anne-Marie."

It took her a moment to realize he was speaking to her.

"Martial. I'm sorry, my dear. What did you say?"

"Nothing, yet. I was waiting for you to come back from that far-off land."

"It was Mozart, this time. Do you know, the older I get, the more irresistible he becomes?" She leaned toward him, her face faintly flushed and very lovely. "That unearthly combination of sweetness and strength—there's really nothing like it. I don't think anyone will ever bring all of it to the surface. I don't think it's possible, though I propose to keep trying. Perhaps, in another fifty years . . ." She smiled at him. "Do you think I'm dithering?"

"I think you're very beautiful."

"And I think you must want something of me, to flatter me so outrageously."

"Nothing. Except you, that is."

She bent so far forward that her face almost touched the cloth, and her outstretched hand caught his.

"Can you doubt that you have me?"

He pressed his lips to the back of her hand.

"No." He released her; it was a long slow gliding withdrawal, as she straightened. He had a quick vision of a coffin on slowly descending ropes, and tried not to think of it. "But I doubt that you're spending enough time on your music, if it so obsesses you even at the dinner table."

"You're keeping something from me. Something must have gone wrong, for you to say that."

"Isn't it true?"

"You're evading me, Martial." She wagged a finger at him. "You have always tolerated the piano, but just barely. Do you remember what you actually said, once?"

"What?"

"It was before we were married, but just after we were engaged. You stood looking at the poor piano, which was wondering if I would be permitted to take it to my new home with me, and you said, briskly and really rather sternly—you succeeded in frightening me for a moment, you really did—'Which one of you musical sisters am I to be married to?' My heart sank, I confess it."

"My musical taste is much improved. How could it not be? And I have improved my knowledge of you, too. I know much better than ever I did how much music means to you, Anne-Marie. It isn't easy for a nonmusicial person like myself to truly appreciate that. I don't think there's ever been anything in my life—excepting always you, my dear—that goes through and through me, as music does you."

Her eyes were moist.

"Do you mean that?"

"About your music? I certainly do, though it has taken me years to fully realize it."

"About me, Martial."

He could not smile and he refused to permit himself tears.

"Profoundly, my love. I could not mean it more." She had no hesitation about weeping with pleasure, and he rose and stood behind her chair, his hands on her shoulders. She was not sobbing, her body was not racked. How emotional the disease makes them, he thought for a moment, and then pulled himself back from this objective, medical stance. "Which is why I have engaged another maid, to free you for the piano. Will you fit me into your schedule, too?"

Her hand covered his and pressed it gently. Her hand seemed unusually warm, and it was some seconds before he could respond to her tenderness.

"Will you be after taking my advice, Mr. Congressman?"

They were sitting in the yard of Theodore's boarding house in Washington. Not very many men sent to Washington by their constituencies bothered to purchase houses and set up even semi-permanent residence in the national capital. Even as late as 1847, Washington was a raw and unpleasant city. Many in Congress, indeed, never took their wives or their families with them; virtually all lived in boarding houses, and only when Congress was in session were they to be found anywhere in Washington.

It was a brisk day; autumn was turning cold. But there was not room enough to walk, and they did not want to risk being overheard, either on the street or indoors. So they sat on a plain wooden bench, their coats drawn around them, and endured the modest chill.

"I'll gladly accept any advice that promises to work. I'm not so foolish, Mr. Brady, that I imagine myself able to manage these things on my own, or out of my own wisdom and experience. I need older and wiser heads, and I know I need them."

Morris Brady had begun life as a commission man. He was one of the first of what was about to turn into a vast influx of immigrants from Ireland—and then, as the century went on, immigrants from Germany, and from Italy, and from Poland and Russia. Irishmen would build the railroads; most Irishmen seemed to congregate in cities, perhaps because they had tried the farms of the old country and found them desperately wanting. He had landed as Maurice Brady, his mother having turned to the hated English for her children's names, perhaps hoping a British forename would eliminate the stigma of a Celtic surname. Americans tended to call him "mawrEES," and he had gotten tired of correcting them. A clothing store owned by one Morris Fishbein had caught his eye, and from that point onward he was Morris, too. (Nor was he above claiming to be half-Irish and half-Jewish, when the occasion seemed to make that advisable.)

Brady was still a commission man, and most of his living was earned, still, by the placing and handling of other people's goods. It took a quick tongue, and a fast pair of feet, and knowledge of a lot of people as well as the brass of an entrepreneurial Theseus. He fell on his face, from time to time: there were some Gordian knots which would not be untied, neither for words nor for money. But he was essentially honest, he worked immensely hard, and those who lacked his knowledge, his brass, and his energy had learned to rely on him. It was his proud and accurate boast that he might have failed himself, from time to time, but he had never once let down a client. His world was built on his word, and he kept the one in order to keep the other. He was small, spare, with remarkable clean hands and small bright eyes.

"I'll tell you, then. A legislature is a wonderful thing, it is. Like a church organ, I'm telling you: when you can keep your feet on the right pedals, and your hands on the right keys, you can sound like Our Holy Father in Heaven. But one key out of joint, one pedal loose, and you'll be sounding like there was a rat in the bellows."

"To be sure," agreed Theodore Bingham, having spent the last five and a half years in a national legislature. He did not condescend to Brady's homily.

"The trick, as I see it, is to claim nothing until you've got everything. You fellows in Congress are a cut above, it seems to me, but down in Albany they run like sheep. The ring has to be on the bellwether, and the heads have to be turned in the right direction, before you can slap them on the rump and yell them home."

"Agreed."

"So what's after being done, as Brady sees it, is getting them one at a time and talking them around. You can't use the same tack on them all, you can't. And you can't talk them around and then leave them alone, thinking they're talked around for good and all. That's why a good shepherd keeps a couple of yapping sheep dogs, with good legs and lungs, and good teeth too, when it comes to it. You've got to stay at it, or the flock ends up in someone else's barn, it does."

"Have you some suitable canine friends?"

"That I do. And I'm not a bad yapper myself, when it comes to that." He pushed his hands deeper into his coat pockets. "It's not as if we'd be buying them, you understand. But you have to pay for things some way, in this world. Maybe not in the next: it's not a prophet I am. A couple of good men, and myself, and something to drink now and then, and something to eat maybe. Them is the needful, as you might say."

"It shouldn't be a great deal."

"Not a great deal, no. But that all depends on where you might be coming from, Mr. Congressman. When I was first off the boat, well, it would have been a fortune, that it would. It would still be a sum I'd want to reckon over, before I saw my own self paying it out. It all depends, you see."

"Something like five thousand dollars?"

"Hard to say. I'm not trying to bamboozle you, mind. It might be less, it might be more. Depending."

"In for a penny, in for a pound. I know you for a reasonable man, Mr. Brady, and I don't expect you to run me into the ground. Win or lose, I'll find the money."

Brady pulled out his right hand and stuck it out. They shook on it.

"You've got yourself a deal, Mr. Congressman. This time next year, if all goes well, I'll have to be calling you Mr. Senator." He scratched his head. "It has a nice ring to it, now, don't it?"

Theodore could only agree. It had a very nice ring, indeed.

My dear Mr. D'Urbeville,

Your letter of 14 July is before me. My gardener made trial of the seeds you kindly sent, and several of them have done extremely well. Whether they will prove as satisfactory as simples as they have as simple growing plants, I cannot yet tell. I will be diligent for opportunity, however, to put them to the test.

The kind of igneous rock you request is not, alas, available to me here. I have written to several of my correspondents in other portions of this country, to see what can be had. You may be sure that anything sent to me, on your behalf, will be promptly forwarded to you.

You remind me that it has been eight years since we met in London. Your calculation is beyond dispute, alas! And I do not think the defect—namely your presence on the one side of the ocean, and mine on the other—is likely to be remedied in our lifetimes. You are, I believe, some years my junior, though probably not very many, but the course of your affairs does not seem destined to bring you across that vast body of water. It has of course become a more rapid and a much more luxurious trip, with each passing year. Even now, after but eight short years, it seems somewhat wonderful to me that my family and I traveled by clipper—excellent vessels, and as fast and commodious as one could expect from any boat driven by the power of the wind only—but how dim and unlikely they strike us, today, now that steam vessels have to all intents and purposes replaced them. There is now a telegraph line, in this country, reaching between New York and Philadelphia. Other such lines have been placed or are in the process of being thus created. And now there is talk, which I have reason to believe is not mere words, of laying a telegraph cable underneath the very sea itself, so that even if we cannot look across its thousands of miles we can travel, at virtually the speed of light, beneath it, and speak to one another, and reply to one another, to all intents and purposes as if we stood together on the same shore.

These are marvels indeed, and marvelous, and I stand in awe of what we humans have done and are doing. And yet I feel, both as a physician and as a man, more deeply convinced than ever of our fundamental incapacity and weakness, our eternal dependence on a Power greater than ourselves. There is so much we can do, traversing the sea, transmitting electrical impulses across it, and yet we stand eternally in His hands, He disposes of us as He pleases, and it is both our duty and our inevitable need to obey. No physician, indeed no scientist of any description, can ignore the limits to his merely human powers, or His ineluctable submission to that greater Power which arranges and disposes of us all.

I am moved to these reflections, which I trust are not an infringement on our more strictly utilitarian exchanges, by the fate of one of my three surviving children, my daughter Anne-Marie. She is married, as you may recall, to that excellent young physician, Dr. Martial Johnson, who accompanied us to England. She is the mother of four small children, and an admirable wife and mother; she is also, in this limited circle of things, something of a musical figure, having inherited, through her mother, no small share of ability in that sphere. Her playing of the pianoforte has been pronounced, by experts, to be of expert quality. She is still with us, but the signs of tuberculosis have become unmistakable, and we are helpless to stop its ravages. She will have perhaps a year or two of uncertain health and intermittent happiness, and then all will fairly rapidly be over. Her mother, poor woman, does not yet know, and no more do her brothers and the other members of our various families. Nor does my daughter herself yet know; I do not think she will suspect for a very long time. It is a blessed fact that the mortally ill seem always to be the last to understand their situations. May she remain ignorant for as long as possible!

So we are able to circumnavigate the globe without relying on the capricious force of the wind, and we are able to do a great deal more, and are able each year to do still more and more. But what can we do when our Lord in Heaven beckons with one finger and says, simply and powerfully, "Come"? I wonder that any man thinks to become anything but a student of God's Word. These last months, when my family has thought me shut in my small laboratory and hard at work on my little scientific tasks, I have in fact done nothing but read and re-read the Holy Writ. I have tried, though I know I will not succeed, to understand. We are exceedingly helpless, and never more than when we think ourselves huge and powerful. I feel this most keenly. Whether I will be able to return to my scientific work, such as it is, I cannot now say. I hope I can be preserved a little longer, and in such health and state of mind that I can go on. For the moment, however, it does not seem possible. In truth, it does not seem important. When eternity beckons, of what significance are everyday trivia?

I will try to persuade my good wife of the need to peruse and to submit to the guidance of God's truth. It would be, in truth, easier if she would join with me. I do not think she will, nor do I think that others in my family will be able to fathom what they would surely see as a turn in my own direction. Perhaps it is; I no longer know. But however it may be, I am resolved to go on as, now, I have begun. Forgive me for preaching at you, my dear sir, but let me record for you what I cannot say to anyone on this side of the ocean: as I have been sitting here, these months, in my silent laboratory, I have learned that there is a peace in the shadow of the Lord, a calm and a quiet in His shade, that does not exist in the bright sun of the world outside. Your own great Isaac Newton knew that, for sure. One does not need to be a cleric to search after and to find it, nor does the fact that one is a scientist inhibit that search.

Well, well. This is not such a letter as you are used to receive from me, I have no doubt, and I have more than a suspicion that it is not such a letter as you will cheerfully receive a second time. It is no justification for a man to say, as I might say to you, that it could not be helped. But that is all I am able to say to you, and if I have trespassed on our epistolary friendship I am sorry. May that not be the case. And however it may be, my dear sir, do not think me anything but,

> *Your devoted and obedient, etc.,*
> *Frederick Bingham.*

> *"I have persuaded myself that I have been very busy; a point in which indolence is apt to succeed, when it solicits belief."*
>
> —Daniel Webster to Mrs. E. B. Lee
> 12 March 1834

Mr. Greeley's head seemed larger than all the rest of him. It gleamed, it swayed atop his narrow shoulders like some huge egg. He was thin, his eyes were pale blue, his hair sandy. Nor did he dress like an Important Figure, A Personage. But he was. Jonathan knew it, all of New York and most of the rest of the country knew it, and it was distinctly possible that Mr. Greeley himself knew it. His head was naturally large, however; it was not swollen. He held out his hand in a most unaffected manner, and bade Jonathan enter his chamber.

"I'm very grateful to you for seeing me," said Jonathan.

Mr. Greeley deposited himself behind his desk, which was surprisingly small and astoundingly clean, and motioned his visitor to a hard-backed chair. It was a medium-sized chamber, almost without decoration, and fastidiously neat—and though Jonathan was to see it many times, thereafter, he never again saw it in anything but a state of profound disorder, papers hanging and spilling off the desk, papers spread out everywhere and anywhere, and frequently Greeley himself writing furiously, spattering ink as he went, and dropping each finished sheet unto the floor, for a copy boy to rescue and deliver to the one typesetter at the *Tribune* who had been set the task of mastering the editor's chicken scrawl. Jonathan did not of course know that Mr. Greeley had just two hours earlier returned from a long lecture tour, during which time no papers had entered his office and all the papers he had left there had been carefully exhumed and deposited each in its proper niche elsewhere. Jonathan thought that so famous and energetic a man as Mr. Greeley must surely owe his fame and his success to habits of an unusual orderliness. He at once vowed to correct his own mild slovenliness.

"I'd much rather see *you*, Mr. Bingham, than one of my own employees. They would be sure to find immense amounts of work for me to do, and as I am newly returned to this office, and still in the throes of exercising voice and brain together, in lyceums and halls across this great country. I welcome any excuse for postponing a full return to harness." His voice was high and rather squeaky; it did not seem to fit the rhetorical torrents that poured rapidly forth on its uncertain tide. "In addition, to be perfectly truthful, I do not happen to agree with the common view that a man of affairs is as likely to enter the kingdom of heaven as a woman of ill reputation. We are a moral people, but we are also an enterprising people, and I incline to the view that our enterprise would not soar if it had feet of such heavy clay as are often assigned to it. Our morality, indeed, frequently fails to soar . . . but tell me, Mr. Bingham, for I have forgotten, why your good aunt, Mrs. Andrée, requested this interview for you? You are, I believe, a student at Columbia College? Do you know my good friend Professor McVickar?"

Jonathan took a deep breath, but there was no need for hesitation. Mr. Greeley had asked his questions and was now awaiting whatever might be the answers.

"My father, sir, is a physician, as was his father before him, but though I am determined not to be medical I have not been able to find what I should be."

"What sort of physician?"

After a brief discussion of homeopathic medicine, which obviously much interested Mr. Greeley, but about which Jonathan knew essentially nothing, the editor nodded and terminated the digression.

"You are matriculated at Columbia, are you not?"

"I am, sir and like every student in the college I of course know Professor McVickar, though I doubt he knows me. And I am troubling you, today, because I seem to have some aptitude for written expression and should like to determine—"

"I am a vegetarian, Mr. Bingham, and despite my reputation I do not dine on college students. But I must frankly tell you that a mere literary fancy will not do, in this business. We are not in the newspaper line in order to turn out pale verses on Mistress Tyler's latest ballgown." Greeley thumped his desk with a bony fist. "No! We do not run the United States of America, and we do not aspire to. But without us the United States would cease to function. The people of this country have more than a right to information, they have an absolute need for it. Every man who comes to the *Tribune* is working for me only in the first instance: the higher power for which he labors is the cause of democracy, for which a free and an active press is the single most necessary ingredient. It don't matter if the railroads stop for a week, or if the ships can't sail, but if the voters of this country fail to read their newspapers, morning and evening, the wheels of democracy grind to a stop, by God! My paper—it's not my paper, Mr. Bingham, it belongs to my readers, and my readers are Everyman: they're in every state in this Union, they're of every social class. Men who can barely sign their names sit and spell out what we have to tell them! Men out on the frontiers returning to their log cabins and hunting up a month-old copy of the *Tribune*, then sitting by firelight and learning what we have to tell them! We are writers, by God, and we are readers, too, but we are not practicing our trades in some polite literary *salon*, we are right out in the market place of life, we are smack dab in the middle of things, and we're going to stay there, we're afraid of no one and we have no intentions of budging, now or ever." He wagged a thin finger in Jonathan's face. "Do I make myself clear, young man?"

"Indeed you do, sir."

Mr. Greeley half rose from his chair, then fell back again. He looked down at his bare desk, with distinct puzzlement on his face, then re-addressed himself to Jonathan.

"We have no need for a reporter, I'm afraid, but we always need reporting. You might be interested in stringing, if there's a place. You look bright enough. Tell me the truth, young fellow. Can you write? Can you *really* write? Do you weigh every word, do you polish away the fat and try to make the bones glisten? Do you hear words in the wind, and do you have your eyes open, do you let your eyes see what's presented to you?" He banged the desk again, though more softly this time. "Are you *alive?*"

"Mr. Greeley, if you died tomorrow I couldn't take your place. Nobody could. But I'd certainly like to help, and I'd like to learn—and yes, yes, I don't think there's anything in my life I care about so much as I care about words. Am I alive?" He laughed. "I'm an American, Mr. Greeley, and I was born in a great time, I'm growing up in a great time. How could I be anything but alive?"

A boy entered, bearing a sheaf of printed paper. He deposited it hurriedly on the editor's desk, just before the editor's long thin arms reached up and pulled it down. In an instant Greeley was reading, fiercely attentive. Jonathan sat for a moment. Then a bony arm waved vaguely in his direction, though the reading was not interrupted.

"Go see Taylor."

Silence. After a moment Jonathan got up and walked quietly out, asking the first man he saw where he could find Taylor, to whom Mr. Greeley had sent him. He got directions, and he followed them.

"We seem to have done rather well, this time around."

"We don't have the Senate."

Theodore laughed at his colleague's sour view of things.

"To be sure. Nor do we have the Presidency—yet. Mr. Polk can poke along a bit, still. But one hundred and fifteen to a hundred and eight—that strikes my non-mathematical mind as what might be called a majority."

"You forget, my dear Bingham, that there are also four Do-Gooders, or Do-Nothings, or whatever they're called these days."

"And you forget, my dear sir, that four and eight make twelve, and that no matter how you count, fifteen is always going to be a larger cipher than twelve. No, I would say we have done quite respectably well for a party supposed to be moribund. Do you know? We have carried—mind this well, if you please—New York, New Jersey, Ohio, Maryland, Georgia, and Florida. And very nearly Pennsylvania as well."

"It is an off-year, may I remind you."

"It was an election, let *me* remind *you.* Those one hundred and fifteen Whigs will shortly be seated here in Washington, and it is they, representing the Whig voters of this country, who will organize and who will run this House."

"Bosh. Whigs have shown themselves unable to govern anything, even themselves."

"Wait. A sheep who smells fresh grass can run like a deer."

"The sheep analogy, unfortunately, is singularly well-chosen . . . ."

Theodore had any number of similar conversations, in the last weeks of 1847. Whig prospects looked even stronger than he had contemplated. He was deeply convinced that his own move had to be made soon, or such a chance might be slower coming around for a second such venture.

"Scott has taken Mexico City," he kept telling his colleagues, "and our campaign is not nearly so arduous, nor so dangerous. And he fought, do note, on enemy soil. Here in these United States, the Democrats must fight us on our own soil. And we shall trounce them!"

Theodore Bingham, Representative from New York, had been for two years one of only seventy-seven Whigs in the twenty-ninth Congress. There were almost a hundred and fifty Democrats. There was (just barely) a Democratic Senate and a very Democratic President: power and prestige and headlines necessarily flowed where power and prestige already were. It was Theodore's task, if he were to exercise any leverage on the legislature of his state, to make himself felt right here in Washington. If he could not at a blow transform himself into a Big Gun, or overturn governmental policies, or get himself made a general and fight some sterling battles (besides, the war with Mexico was essentially over), there were nevertheless things he could do. He was after all one of only two hundred and twenty-nine men elected to the federal House of Representatives. There were something over twenty-one million people in the country, so it was a very good start on public attention, being an elected, and a twice re-elected, Congressman, in the face of such odds. It would be very strange had he been unable to help himself, given that sort of positioning.

Plainly, there were debts to incur, and debts to collect on. Every Congressman, from the days of Washington and Jefferson, has known, or has quickly learned, how to provide aid and assistance and, above all, jobs to the needy and desirous in his home state, and especially in his home district. Congressmen do not come to Washington in order to be sent away at the next polling time, and Theodore Bingham had most emphatically not come as a transient, or as a man unconcerned with the retention of his House seat.

But now he was after something more than mere retention, and though he did not give up his maintenance activities he also pushed himself into larger matters. He did his best not to alienate those of his own way of thinking; he had made his quiet campaign for the Senate known to the Whig leadership, so it was expected that his would be a voice a good deal more heard from, now, than it had been at the start. New York being his base, he chose as his central issue the continuing debate over the tariff. It was in some ways a dry affair, and he had a good deal to learn before he rose for his first major speech on this subject. But he knew that, dry as it might be, it was also a bread-and-butter issue, the kind of thing that voters remembered because, simply enough, it touched their purses and their stomachs. He also knew that his constituency, as he appealed to the Whig legislature of New York, included even more men of standing and wealth than when he had addressed himself only to the voters of his Congressional district. It was no use speaking to the slavery issue, well-heated by the Wilmot debates earlier in the year. What was slavery, one way or the other, to the legislature of New York? Nor did the late war with Mexico have any charm. So too Oregon, settled as an issue by the treaty of 1846, was totally dead as a political tool. Judicial reform could be whipped for some few drops of notoriety. So too could bankruptcy, a perpetual Congressional quagmire. But Theodore needed more juice than could be squeezed out of anything available to him, so far as he could see, except the tariff issue. So to that issue he rose, a Don Quijote from New York, tilting at the windmills of national concern with free trade and most especially of free trade with England.

"Mr. Speaker," he began, holding his notes as far down as he could manage, so the gallery would think him entirely extemporaneous, "there have been voices heard, of late, arguing here in this House that this is a settled issue, that the schedules elaborated in last year's tariff legislation have made any consideration of tariffs, their rates and their imposition, a dead letter. I do not so understand the workings of democracy. It seems to me, as I examine our heritage and the evolution of our federal government, that there is only one theoretical moment when a substantive issue, an issue felt deeply and perceived as important by any significant segment of our population, could possibly be a dead issue. That theoretical moment, to be sure, is not a practical one, for it would involve the most basic of changes in our government. We would have to cease being a democracy, in order for a substantive issue to thus become a dead issue. I do not think there is a gentleman here who thinks *that* a lively possibility. We are founded on change, but not on that sort of change: it is the destiny of this nation to move forward, inexorably, powerfully. I do not think it possible for us to move, as admittedly other nations have done, retrogressively, to turn back the hands of time—or of progress. It is our very capacity for change, indeed, our capacity for growth and adaptation, which has turned us in less than a century—much less than a century—into a large and, may I remind you, a powerful nation, one carefully noticed in all the councils of all the governments of Europe.

"Mr. Speaker: it may well be that, in any one session of this Congress, conflicting views cannot be fully resolved, and legislation on any and all subjects cannot be enacted. But the existence of conflicting views is not erased by comparative inaction—nor should it be. We are, in this House and in our sister body, considerably more than a machine for cranking out pieces of statutory governance. We are, to be sure, the legislative organ of this government, but we are, I submit, far more than that. We are a national forum, gentlemen, the leading and the most important gathering place for all the differing voices heard in all the differing parts of this land. We cannot resolve all differences, and we must not pretend to such perfection. But we must air these differences, we must expose them to public concern, or we will have failed more drastically than if we simply fail to pass this bill or that one. It is sometimes said, Mr. Speaker, that our many grand and glorious newspapers are the nation's forum. They perform nobly, on the whole—but who has elected them, who has signaled them out, who has chosen them to speak for many of our citizens?

"The tariff legislation now before us, gentlemen, proposes what any tariff legislation must propose, namely a change in national tariffs. That we must have tariffs, as for years now we have had, is I assume not an arguable proposition. The call for so-called 'free trade,' after all, is as senseless as the cry of a spoiled child in its nurse's arms, reaching out for the moon or for the stars shining high above. There is no such thing as free trade, and never has been. The proponents of 'free trade' have admitted, publicly, that it is an ideological device, a mere fiction invented for the express purpose of bamboozling and humbuggery. Those who call for 'free trade' call only for a strengthening of their own hand, for the addition of yet another weapon to their mercantile arsenals. 'Free traders' want to trade as they please: that is the entire sum of the freedom they plead for.

"We are a federal union, and we are barely three-quarters of a century old. We are not so compact and stationary as the British union, nor so vast and static as the Russian one. We recognize, freely and openly, that we have differences, that in many particulars we *are* different. This is inevitable and natural and it is healthy to admit it. Just as this House is not a machine for stamping out bits and pieces of standardized legislation, so too this country is not some new social machine for rendering its inhabitants uniform. Or its lands uniform. Or the crops grown on those lands. Or the products fabricated in our shops and mills, wherever they may happen to be located. We *are* a union. We *are* a democracy. But we are not all alike, and we do not stem from identical soils, and we are not motivated by the same concerns. You who grow cotton, your urgencies are not those of your cousin who spins it. The farmer who ploughs his wheat is concerned that his crop grow; the miller who grinds it is concerned that it become flour; the baker, that it becomes bread; and the men and women who break that bread, that they be permitted to eat it in peace. We are all united under the one roof, set fortunately in place by our ancestors, and we are as we well know justly the pride and the envy of the entire civilized world. But for all that we are not all the same, we cannot be all of us the same, and any attempt to render us thus identical is bound to fail. Our federal union depends for its vitality and endurance on our diversity and our energy. In our unlikeness, Mr. Speaker, lies our strength. We must cherish our differences.

We must not exaggerate them, but neither must we suppress them. It is in politics as it is in stock breeding: the best bull has a mixed pedigree.

"The proposed legislation seeks to change our national tariffs. Why? For the sake of change itself? I trust no member of this House would believe any such accusation, if there be any to make it. Is it then a factional proposal, or a merely sectional one? Mr. Speaker: this is national legislation that we propose, the other sponsors of this bill and I, but it is necessarily local as well. It stems from our concerns, our needs. We seek to impress those upon our colleagues here in this House, and on both our friends and those who may frown upon us, elsewhere in the nation. . . ."

The orators of Congress spoke, at times, for three and four days running. The galleries would crowd up in advance, people pressing and pushing for admission, for the right to say to their grandchildren that they heard Henry Clay or John Calhoun or Daniel Webster rise and declaim. Theodore Bingham did not command such loyalties, nor did he venture to speak for quite so long. But he had a large fish to fry, and he spoke at some length.

"Bingham doesn't think he has the votes, does he?" remarked a Democrat from Kentucky to a Whig from Pennsylvania.

"He knows he don't."

The Kentuckian looked at the gallery, which was half filled but unusually attentive for an off-day audience. The unusualness of the proceeding was apparent even to the public at large.

"Ain't got his wife up there, has he?"

"Not married, that I know of."

The Kentuckian spat into the nearest spittoon, then dabbed his lips with a kerchief.

"It's not a bad speech. Leastways the way you fellows set up for these things. What's he up to?"

"Don't know. Maybe the folks in his district—he's from the City, you know—have been riling him up."

"Good speech," agreed the Whigs. "Didn't know he had it in him."

"Sensible fellow, for a northerner. And a Whig. And a city man. We done some business, me and Bingham. Looks to me like he's aiming at bigger business."

"Could be. Could very well be."

One of Theodore's New York colleagues, not from the City but well connected to Thurlow Weed's Albany machine, and on distinctly cordial terms with Weed—Weed being known pleasantly as "The Dictator"—knew rather more about what Congressman Bingham had in mind.

"Well, he might do." The Whig alongside him, from Connecticut, agreed.

"He's young, though."

"Ain't a handicap, these days. Do you see what he's doing? Setting up as a statesman, that's what. The Union forever, but New York, too. Help for everyone, as much as everyone deserves it and can bargain to get it. It's almost a platform for next November."

"Depending on who's going to stand on it."

The Whig from New York did not reply, but only nodded. He had begun to understand who was the likely occupant of the party's candidacy, and did not want to discuss ideational notions in so unideational a context. The Whigs of the Northeast leaned quite naturally to Henry Clay, but he had lost—a squeaker, but he had lost—in 1844, and it did not seem to make sense to give either him or any of the other old faithful of the party another chance to adulterate success with principle. Better a general, old Zack or Winfield Scott, who could ape old General Harrison and stand on his name and his fame rather than on anything more specific. Harrison had stood firmly for nothing, and had won. Clay had been very specific, but Polk was now in the White House. With a general to lead the way, the party could offer statesmen at its lower levels; with new faces in prospect, it could reasonably offer still other new faces.

"He might do. He just might."

"How does he stand up in Albany?"

"Let's see how he winds up," suggested the Whig from New York. "Let's see if he can cut it right down to the end."

The gallery was three-quarters full; word had gotten around, as it seems always to do on such occasions, that one of the younger Congressmen had risen to do heroic battle, and was conquering dragons and saving maidens right and left. Dragon-slayers are never in long supply, and people like to watch them charge. Theodore had a very respectable audience for his final remarks—he had spoken for almost three hours—and he knew it.

"Mr. Speaker, I shall trouble your patience only a moment longer. I have not spoken emotionally, because this is not to my mind an emotional issue. I have not sought to appeal to prejudice, or to narrow interest, because this is a national issue. I think bread-and-butter is of concern to us all. It sits on all our tables, East and West, North and South. Let me urge my colleagues, from no matter what region of this union they come, to chew on the facts, to digest the reasoning, to understand as well as they can our situation in New York. It will be our turn, inevitably, to try to understand their situations: this is what we have come here to Washington to do, to preserve this imperfect but glorious union. We of New York are prepared to share our bread-and-butter: every American is entitled to a share; we recognize our responsibility to the country as a whole. But we must ask of those who share with us, to share in turn. It is no longer a question of staying together, so we may not hang separately. We *are* together, we are one people, we are already a great nation and we are growing rapidly greater. To join hands, to march steadfastly into that opening future, calls for a courage and a certainty and a willingness to share. We have demonstrated, as a people, that we have an ample stock of those traits. We have made that demonstration over and over again. We need not be anything other than what we have been, than what at our best we already are. I suggest, Mr. Speaker, to you and to all the gentlemen here assembled, that the legislation now before us seeks out the best in us. We ought to respond in that same spirit, exactly as we have so many times before. I do not seek to sway my colleagues, or indeed to change the interests which they represent. I seek only to persuade them of the legitimacy of our interests, and of our importance to them. That is, I think, a much larger issue even than the question of the tariff, important though the tariff may be. I am proud to be a New Yorker, Mr. Speaker, but I trust it will do me no harm in my home state if I assert that I am still prouder to be an American."

With which he sat down. There was applause, including some from the gallery, before the Speaker gaveled the House into adjournment. There were mostly favorable comments, on the floor. Theodore had some fervid compliments, and some unusually warm handshakes.

And the next day he had more newspaper attention, in New York and elsewhere, than ever before in his career. Was a new light shining, a new star a-borning? Theodore was inclined to answer positively: he was becoming convinced not only that he would do, but that he might well get the chance.

"The older she grows, the more fond I am of her name. The more *fitting* it becomes," she smiled.

The two youngest children were asleep; the two oldest were running in the garden. Some rational whim of providence had arranged that the first two would be girls, the second pair boys.

"I assume you are not speaking of Alice, who seems every day less certainly female."

"Do not be less fair to your own children, Martial, than to the children of others. She's only five years old. A girl can hardly be expected to have the graces of a lady, at that point in her life."

"Exactly: but Grace at not quite seven does have them. You were saying so yourself, not a moment ago."

They watched the game. Alice ran like a steam locomotive. Grace seemed almost to float across the grass—and the younger child could never catch up.

"She moves like an angel," Martial said softly. "Were you thinking that of her, when you insisted on the name?"

"Did I really insist?"

"Shall I tell you the truth? Yes, you did. You did not make a scene; that is not your habit, Anne-Marie. But I had leanings in other directions, and you were terribly firm. You were right, of course."

He smiled and she sat, staring directly at him. He held the smile as long as he could, then grew a bit uncomfortable. Her look was unusually probing.

"Martial," she said musingly, then bent over and coughed. It was only mildly wrenching, more a shallow tic than a deep lung-convulsing eruption, but he leaned toward her and tucked the lap robe carefully into place. She straightened slowly. "Martial," she said again, and her eyes seemed deep, her voice lower in pitch than he could recall hearing it. "Do tell me the truth."

He tried not to show the sweep of fear that passed through him.

"When have I not told you the truth, my dear? And about what?"

She was looking down at the lap robe. One hand smoothed it, resting especially long at the fold he had tucked. It was a bright fall afternoon, late, with a full sun. Sitting near the back of their house, at the edge of the garden, they were almost as warm as they would have been inside. The air made her eyes sparkle.

"Are you warm enough?" he asked after a moment.

"Perfectly," she said, still looking down. "Am I ill?" Her eyes did not meet his until after she had spoken. Then she looked at him longingly. "Please do tell me. I'm not a child, Martial. I'm the mother of four children."

"Do you feel ill?"

"I've not been feeling myself: you know that. There have been signs, I've not wanted to recognize them. That time there was blood from my lungs . . . oh, I know it could be anything, and there are hemorrhages for all sorts of reasons. It could have been simply a strain, as you said. But is that what you really thought? Is that what you think now? My father has been dismally silent, when he's been here. And you, Martial, you've been as attentive as a mother hen."

"I'm a singularly appreciative husband, my dear."

"And those strange fevers, coming and going. That odd flush in my cheeks, some days." She reached over and took his hand. "Please tell me. I have a right to know. It's consumption, isn't it?"

He could not lie to her; neither could he squeeze her hand and assure her it would be all right, there were no problems, everything was under control, the two medical men understood and would take charge of everything.

"Yes."

She did not take her hand away.

"I did know it, you know. I didn't want to know it, but I knew. It wasn't your attentiveness, Martial. You *are* a good husband. And a good father, a very good father. What have I done to cause it, Doctor Johnson?"

Her face wore an expression of immense good humor. He realized, shocked and at the same time relieved, that she was glad to know, eased, soothed.

"I don't know."

"And what is the prognosis?"

He cleared his throat and did not try to meet her glance.

"I don't know."

She tugged at his hand.

"Please. Tell me, Martial."

Her fingers pressed on his. He wanted to put his head in her lap and cry.

"It depends." He managed to look at her: there was no disapproval, and almost no pain in her face. She was totally attentive to what he was saying. "We understand so very little."

"Will I die?"

He would have pulled his hand free, had he dared. He did not want to touch her as this was being said.

"We all die—"

"But I will die somewhat earlier?" she interrupted, her voice for the first time taking on a slight edge. He did not blame her. He had been hedging, sliding, trying to dig in his heels, going down the slope an inch at a time. She needed to know, not to be dissembled to any longer. And yet it was terribly hard for him, so hard that he could not actually speak the words. He only nodded, and then he sat, her hand on his, trying to push his feet flat against the ground, trying to do he did not know what. He stared straight down.

"I feel as if I ought to comfort *you*, Martial."

"I'm sorry," he mumbled.

She covered her eyes with her free hand, then let it fall into her lap.

"Oh, it's going to be hard," she said slowly. Her voice grated, as if she had to push at herself to make the words come out at all. "I don't want to die, Martial. Not now."

He tried to put his arm around her, but she did not bend to him, she sat inflexible.

"We'll be together," he said lamely. "I'll help, Anne-Marie. I'll help."

"But then I'll be dead, and you won't be. The children will need me, and I won't be there. Grace will grow up, and she'll be beautiful, and I'll never see her. And how will you raise them?" She turned and looked at him: her face was drawn and severe, her eyes were piercing. "You'll have to marry again. I know that's how it will have to be. I'm right, aren't I?"

He did not answer.

"But you'll have to," she repeated, and her voice had softened. "How could you manage otherwise? I'll be leaving you with four children, and the two boys are so small. How long will it be, Martial? Just tell me that."

"I can't."

"Do you mean that you won't, that you don't want me to know?"

"Anne-Marie!" He spoke loudly enough so that the girls looked over at them, for a moment deflected from their game. "I mean that I can't," he said more carefully. "Your father and I have conferred."

"I knew you had."

"Not that there was anything to be said. We know nothing, really. We can guess: that's about it."

The children laughed and she stared quietly at them.

"A year?"

He looked down and tried to stay calm.

"Perhaps two."

"But not more?"

"Not likely."

She surprised him by once again taking his hand. Her touch was not different, if anything it was softer.

"So now I know everything there is to know. That's the worst of it, Martial. Now that I know, it won't be so terrible. You'll see. There are worse things, my dear. And there are worse ways to die—I need hardly tell *you* that."

He did not reply.

"But it will be hard for you, I do understand that. I'll have the certainty, and you'll have the never knowing, and the sense that it's you that's being left behind."

In spite of himself, despite the exertion of every bit of strength he possessed, and more, there were tears in his eyes.

"Do you know how much I love you?"

"I think I know. But you can tell me. As often as you like."

His throat thickened, words were impossible. But there was nowhere to go, there was nothing to do. So they sat in silence, until the sun began to dip and it was time for the children, and themselves, to go into the house. It was autumn; soon it would be winter, and then spring. How many more springs would she be allowed to see? How many more summers? How soon would it be before he was sitting alone, he and the children?

"Why don't we take them inside?" he suggested, amazed that he could speak, that his voice was normal again, and that when he did speak it was to say such everyday things.

They rose, she leaning only lightly on his arm.

"I'll be as strong as I can."

He pulled her against him, and this time she bent and she came.

"You're likely to be stronger than me," he replied—and then realized, a bit dazed, that he was smiling. What in the name of all that was holy did he have to smile about? And yet there he was, smiling. He looked down. She was smiling too.

"We must learn to count our blessings, Martial."

He nodded seriously, then burst into laughter.

"Why don't we become the children, and let them be the grown-ups?"

They marched sturdily into the house, and the children followed.

EIGHT

"You have a foolish notion that one should not write unless he has something to say. That is nonsense. If he has nothing to say, let him say so, and that is something."

—Daniel Webster, to his son Fletcher
11 January 1846

Mr. Taylor was Bayard Taylor, only five years older than Jonathan, but already famous for his travel writing, and even for his poetry. He held no executive post at the *Tribune*, but he was Greeley's friend, he was deft and knowing, and he had no objection to being troubled. He was a singularly good-looking man, with a rich, carefully modulated voice.

"Horace told you to look me up?"

Jonathan did not think he looked like a newspaper reporter: more like one of the younger tutors at Columbia College, he would have guessed, or even a newly frocked minister.

"Aren't you the right man?"

"Oh, I'm the right man, all right. There are a lot of right men around here. Horace likes a paper with a lot of right men. That way he can sit in his office and throw a stone in just about any direction and still find someone to do his work for him."

Taylor did not have an office of his own. He had a desk, smack in the middle of a large and crowded, hectic room. He had been sitting on top of the desk when Jonathan approached, a book in his hands, reading. He still held the book and he still sat on top of his desk. Jonathan stood alongside: there wasn't an empty chair in sight except Taylor's own.

"Did Horace want me to give you advice? Or money? Or perhaps a copy of my own book, autographed in my best copperplate? Don't tell me: let me guess."

"I'd like to do some writing for the paper."

Taylor hefted the book experimentally and made a wry face.

"For pay, or for the love of letters?"

Jonathan suddenly found it easier to smile. This famous reporter, this fledgling young star among writers, was in fact only a little older than he was, and not at all stuffy.

"For pay, eventually. To get a crack at it, for now."

Taylor abruptly handed him the book.

"Here. Do you know anything about gardening?"

"Not a great deal."

"You'll be the ideal commentator, perhaps—free of bias." Taylor pointed at the book, which was visibly slim. "Shouldn't take you more than an hour to chew through that. Go off in the corner there," he waved vaguely, "read the thing, then write me an account of it. Horace wants it mentioned and you came along just in time. I don't know what I would have done, if I'd had to do it myself! You may not be able to write—though I'd guess you can—but you can at least comfort yourself that you've saved my life." Taylor sat down at his desk, picked up a document, then glanced at Jonathan, who had not moved. "Ready, get set, go!"

Jonathan could not find a chair, but there was a dusty window ledge, and he perched on it and quickly read the little book. It was raining, just outside the window, but the pane was almost too dirty to see through. Still, the sound was comforting, a hint of regularity in this strange, disordered place. The book, by one Adolf Burleson, was virtually devoid of substance. It had been written, in all probability, to satisfy the author's itch for fame, and perhaps also to scratch his wife's (or even his mother's) itch for proximity to fame. There were vapid hints on flower arrangement, endless effusions on color and scent, and some trite observations on the superiority of American to all other gardens, no matter where located. It was hard to tell if Mr. Burleson had actually seen any gardens elsewhere in the world: his prose was so imprecise that fantasy and sentiment thoroughly clogged observation. Why had Mr. Greeley wanted the book noticed? To damn it? Because the author had sent it to his attention? Because (but it could not be!) he thought it a work of native genius, of the sort the *Tribune* constantly called for and praised?

Jonathan sat on his window ledge for some while, musing. Then he borrowed several sheets of copy paper, turned his back to the desks and scurrying boys, to the noise and the bustle, and using the window ledge as a kind of writing desk, penned a brief notice.

> Mr. Adolf Burleson would like all of America to gar-
> den, and all the rest of the world to pay attention. He
> prefers flowers to fruits, apparently because he finds

more color in the former than in the latter. He dislikes weeds. He is unclear on the subject of tomatoes.

Mr. Burleson is a warm-hearted man, full of admiration for petals, overflowing with love for buds
and blossoms, and deeply passionate about grass. He
does not appear to believe in insects: none inhabit the
gardens where his feet have trod. He tolerates birds,
and also cats. I find no opinions on dogs, nor any on
the larger animals familiar to our landscape. There is
one sentence which might be derogatory of fish, but
I cannot be sure.

The sun is all a-wash in Mr. Burleson's soul. He
floats on a sea of gold and green. Gardening is a species of sculpture, to him—or a variety of portrait
modeling—or even an act of poetry. I do not know
who might find his book useful, but there are I am
sure kindred spirits who would find it uplifting.

Jonathan carefully considered this notice, which it did not give him any
great trouble to produce. Suppose the book were indeed meant to be
puffed? Suppose, God forbid, Mr. Burleson was personally known to
Mr. Greeley? That Mr. Greeley had a lively sense of good fun he of
course knew, as did all the many readers of the *Tribune*. It seemed obvious that Mr. Taylor had one. But for all that, was this the right tack to
take? He read it over three times, could not see any different way to get
the job done, and rose from his window ledge to hunt up Mr. Taylor.

It took half an hour: Mr. Taylor, as it turned out, was not always
to be found at his desk, any more than was anyone else at the *Tribune*.
It was in fact somewhat miraculous that Jonathan found him at all, and
it was not at his desk, or even near it, that he was finally found but on
the sidewalk just outside the *Tribune* offices. He was with an elegant lady
of about his own age and did not seem to be pleased with the meeting.
Jonathan pushed the sheet of copy paper at him; Mr. Taylor took it but
scowled. Then he glanced down.

"Ah! It's not a subpoena." Jonathan, who did not at that point know
what a subpoena might be, did not reply. "Yes, yes, I recall. The gardening book." Jonathan nodded. Mr. Taylor stuffed the sheet of copy
paper into his pocket. "I'll get to it first thing this afternoon. Thank
you very much." The smile flashed out, and Mr. Taylor, and the lady on
his arm, were off and away. It occurred to Jonathan only later that Mr.

Taylor had been ruffled, perhaps even worried. Nor had he introduced Jonathan to the lady. He had seemed extremely gentlemanly, earlier. It was odd for him to turn so impolite—unless the identity of the lady had created the problem. Probably it had: she was exceptionally pretty.

The rain had stopped. New York's streets were still glisteningly moist. Horses' hooves kicked up faint mists, half water, half dirt, and the clatter of hooves and wheels sounded different on cobblestones streaked with moisture. One or two parasols were still raised, but most people walked along, open to the elements. A church bell rang out: one o'clock. Jonathan reflected on the comparative urgencies of a scheduled class at Columbia and an unscheduled stroll. The stroll won out, in only seconds; it was hardly a contest.

Carefully choosing a direction different from that taken by Mr. Taylor, he moved through the crowded streets, already beginning to reflect the coming Christmas season. New York was not his city; he had not been born or raised here. As a child he had come as a transient, a visitor, agape at sights and marvels. Poughkeepsie was still his home, to be sure: wherever his father and mother dwelled was still his home. He was deeply fond of Poughkeepsie—he knew it thoroughly, and in a way that could never leave him. But New York was more than a stopping place, now. It might not be his city, but he felt special affection for it, special regard, special wonder.

He could not help fantasizing a bit, as he strolled. There was always the chance, to be sure, that Mr. Taylor, or Mr. Greeley, or someone or anyone at the *Tribune*, would look at his three-paragraph commentary on Mr. Adolf Burleson and chuck it into the wastebasket. And its writer along with the scribbling. That was a chance, but it did not seem a likelihood. Neither did it seem likely that he would be welcomed with passionate eagerness—"Oh do accept the editorship, Mr. Bingham; I shall soon be retiring and I need to know that a capable hand will be left at the help"—or even offered payment for anything he might write. (He did not know that Mr. Taylor himself was receiving twenty dollars a week—and Mr. Dana, with heavy executive responsibilities, only five dollars more.) For the moment at least he did not need payment. He was still at college; he was still wholly supported by his father's generosity. By his *family's*, he corrected himself: Uncle Karl and Aunt Sophia contributed board and room, and how much more had they contributed earlier? But eventually, when he was older, when he knew more and could do more, and especially when he understood the direction he was intended to take, he would need to strike out on his own.

A duke's son, now, back in old England: now, that was different. . . . No, being either a duke or a duke's son did not much appeal to Jonathan. Nobility had no interest for him, though it still charmed his father. And Jonathan meant to work. Whatever it was he was intended to do, he proposed to do it, and do it as well as he could. Why would anyone want to sit at home, feet up in front of a fire, when he could be out working?

The rain began to sprinkle down, suddenly, and quickly went from a fine spray to a fairly brisk shower. He had not been sightseeing, or even paying much attention to where his feet took him. He ducked toward a building and peered around. The neighborhood was not one he knew well. It was on the shabby side, though clean: a workingman's district. There was a saloon fifty feet down the street. He pulled his neck down into his coat and walked through the swinging doors.

He ordered a whiskey; the bartender squinted a bit but produced it. It was a generous drink, more probably than he had ever drunk before at a time. He looked for a table and found none. The interior was both dim and crowded. He sat on a stool, placed his drink solidly in front of him, and sat waiting out the rain.

"You're too young to be a lawyer."

The man on the stool next to him was gray and heavy; there was a touch of brogue in his voice.

"I'm not."

"A process server?"

Jonathan smiled: he must be wearing something particularly distinctive, or be carrying himself in some special way.

"No, I'm just a student."

The man put his drink down and stared at Jonathan.

"You're in school?" He shook his head, then emptied his drink at a gulp and ordered another. "Sure, and there's something wrong with the world, when young fellows your age are still sitting about in school."

"Columbia College, actually."

The man stretched his head. He did not seem to recognize the name, but "college" was plainly something different.

"Ah?" He belched, then covered his mouth. "Excuse me. A bad stomach, I can't keep anything down." He took half the next drink. "Been stevedoring all my life, you see, but I can't do a thing now."

Jonathan did not ask who or what was paying for his drinks.

"You just come in here out of the rain, right?"

Jonathan smiled and nodded.

"Quite."

The man snuffled, then wiped his hand across his face.

"You look familiar. You do."

Jonathan shrugged.

"I shouldn't wonder if I looked like a lot of people. You can't hang a man for it."

"No offense, no offense," the man said hurriedly. He squinted at Jonathan again. "Seen you somewhere, though."

"I come from Poughkeepsie."

"Pa . . . Don't know that."

"Up the Hudson a bit."

"Oh. Yeah. The river. Yeah." He finished the drink and ordered yet another. "Got to keep the pipes open, you see. Whiskey's the best thing for 'em. Cleans 'em, opens 'em up."

Jonathan wondered, silently, if either his medical father or his medical brother-in-law would subscribe to that opinion.

"If you're wondering who pays for my drinks, well, it ain't my family. I don't need to bother 'em, you see. Besides, this ain't permanent, this bad stomach of mine. Couple of weeks more, I'll be back lifting barrels and throwing bales with the best of 'em."

Jonathan nodded, sipped his own drink, almost choked on it, and quietly put it down. He would let it stay where he had put it, when the rain let up and he could leave.

"Down on South Street, that's where the money comes from." The man leaned toward Jonathan. "Seen you down there?"

"You might."

A large finger was pointed at him; a large smile broke across the heavy face.

"Right. You been doing some copying there, for old man Peter."

"My uncle, yes."

The man smiled with satisfaction.

"Never forget a face. Knew I'd seen you before. Old Peter's nephew, eh? You look more like Karl."

"My mother is sister to both of them."

"Right." He belched again; the odor was horrendous, but Jonathan kept himself from turning away. This was more than a bad stomach, though he did not know just how much more. His father would know, though. Or Martial. "Peter knows I'll be back, so he keeps me going. I worked for him and for his father before him, before the old man died and the business changed hands. I mean, before the brothers made it a partnership. Man and boy, I been stevedoring for the Andrée family over thirty years."

Jonathan only smiled. Did Peter have any idea how serious the man's illness was? Should he say something?

"Not many houses down there would have kept me on. The Andrées always do: you work for them you're all right, no matter what."

It would not be a long pensioning off, from the looks of it. But it was unusual, from all Jonathan knew. In most businesses a man who could not work did not eat. Or drink.

The doors swung open, and Jonathan could see the sun shining outside. He slipped off the stool, nodded to the man next to him, and walked quickly back into the open air. What could be growing in the man's body, to produce an odor so foul? Would there possibly be a cure? It was unlikely, as it was unlikely that the man had even bothered to consult a physician: workingmen in the cities did not indulge in formal medical care.

He paused at a corner, letting the carriages roll by. It would be marvelous to know what took place inside such diseased bodies, and even more marvelous to curb the illnesses, even cure them. A great physician was a great thing, a wondrous thing: if that was not precisely how his mother had presented it to him, nevertheless it was true.

He smiled and crossed to the next sidewalk. The sense of possibility, even that and no more, was itself a great thing. He could easily become a physician, if he so decided. There was plenty of time. If he got the chance to sample newspaper work, he could learn how that fitted him and still choose something different. He was as open as the country itself.

And Andrée Bros., his Uncles Peter and Karl, were worthy men of the sort who had opened the country, of the sort who would someday make it the greatest in all the councils of the great. What was England, after all, to these United States and what they could become, what they were every day becoming in fact?

And what did Mr. Taylor think of his book notice?

"Aren't you forgetting your usual evening's work, Mr. Bingham?"

Theodore sat quietly on the sofa and only smiled up at her.

"I *have* seen you performing at whist, have I not?"

"It is possible but not, I suspect, likely, Mrs. Davis."

"You are resting, then."

"To the extent possible, yes, I am."

"Ah," she observed, sitting down at the other end of the sofa. "I understand perfectly well. You are tired and wish to be left at peace. That is, inevitably, the moment when noisy people like myself come and trouble you with conversation."

"Je suis enchanté, chère madame, pas troublé."

"Gallant, but hardly truthful. Still, you confirmed bachelors cannot be permitted to have it all your own way."

"Is that what I am, a confirmed bachelor?"

"Any man who is old enough to have been in the public eye for perhaps half a dozen years, and who is still unmarried, ought to deserve some such appellation, don't you think?"

"No, I'm afraid I must disagree. I have been looking, you know."

"You can't have been looking very hard, Mr. Bingham."

"On the contrary. I have been looking in almost every spare moment."

"That is almost a definition of what is generally meant by not looking very hard."

"There are some subjects where a man may have a chance, in discussion with a woman. But this is not, I should think, one of them."

"A man of your oratorical skills, Mr. Bingham?"

"I have yet to meet a woman who could not tie spider webs around the deftest verbal maneuver I ever attempted."

"Nonsense—and exactly the kind of nonsense spoken by almost all confirmed bachelors. Do you know, Mr. Bingham, I have not realized how perfectly you fit the type? Your friends will have to stir themselves, or it will soon be too late for you. There is indeed a season in the affairs of men—as you well know."

"I abandon myself to your hands, Mrs. Davis."

"The neatest evasion of all. It is true, then, what they say of you, Mr. Bingham?"

"What do they say of me?"

"That you are practicing diplomacy, in preparation for an upward turn in your fortunes. Some say you are destined for an ambassadorship. But most say you first intend to spend some time in the Senate."

"I am flattered."

"On the contrary, Mr. Bingham. You are one of the most careful politicians I have known since my late husband brought me to Washington. I do not mean that you are a cold and calculating sort, mind you, but only that you are a man who thinks and who does not act until he has thought."

He made a sitting bow.

"As I say, I am flattered. I wish that my colleagues, and the newspaper editors, thought so well of me as you obviously do."

"A defect that may well be remedied, I am told, if you go on as you have lately begun."

"But how in the world can you pretend to think so well of me, my dear lady, if you find me so transparently duplicitous?"

"I think you are not quite so transparent, perhaps, to the rest of the world as you are to me. And in any event, you are very likely to be successful, and success cures a great many faults."

"Is that what they say of me?"

"Indeed. It is also what I think myself."

"I very much hope you prove to be right, Mrs. Davis."

She sat and watched him a moment. He was not usually made uncomfortable by women, but she was no inexperienced girl; she was the widow of a very well-connected banker from Virginia who had died not two years before, leaving her with more than enough money to sustain the social level to which marriage had brought her. She was, additionally, a singularly handsome woman: she did not pretend to be an innocent, but dressed and behaved with the full license of her position.

"So," she murmured, "it is true. I am glad to see you casting such cleverly molded bread on the waters, Mr. Bingham. And that was a fearfully good speech you made, on the tariff issue."

"Did you happen to hear it, then?"

"Are you surprised?"

"I am, once again, flattered."

She reached over and touched his hand reprovingly with her fan.

"That is not what I asked you, sir. Were you surprised?"

"Must I own it?"

"It does you honor, if not credit."

"I must strike my colors, Mrs. Davis. Your firepower is too hot for me, and the only course left me is surrender."

She leaned back and slowly folded her arms.

"Indeed?"

"An American legislator does not admit defeat lightly."

"And you admit it?"

"Have I a choice?"

She tapped her foot lightly, then briskly nodded.

"You may redeem yourself by fetching me a small dish of ices, Mr. Bingham. Wait," she directed, as he began to rise. "There is a condition to your ransom."

"There always is, I have noticed!"

"You must return, dish in hand, and sit yourself here once again, and you must thereafter permit me to divert myself with your conversation while I divert my palate with what you have carried here."

"I accede."

"The penalties are severe, for defalcation."

He rose.

"It would never have occurred to me, madame. If our fleet could so readily, and so pleasurably, redeem its errors, we would rapidly replace Her Britannic Majesty as the world's dominant sea power. I will be but a moment."

Her fan covered the lower part of her face, as he bowed, but he could see how carefully she surveyed him. A devilishly capable woman, he told himself as he went on his errand. Fearfully strong. And as rich as she was good to look at. He smiled: she plainly meant him to think exactly such thoughts, as he walked along. Well, he would think them, and the devil with it. A new young senator could do a good deal worse than . . . but it did not pay to have his left foot quite so far in front of his right one. One thing at a time.

The ochre was worse even than usual. It smeared, and it hung together in dusty globules. No amount of pasting, beating, or careful mixing and stirring could force it to blend as proper ochre was supposed to. She put down her brush and stared furiously at the stuff. It was always this way: nothing that was done for her was properly done. Any hack painter in New York City would have ochre that fairly melted. Except that if she were resident there and she sent her husband to fetch ochre for *her*, well, it would come back defective, rotten, half-usable at best. If not worse.

She felt an impulse to destroy the picture, to lift her palette and grind it against the thick paper. She was tempted to pick up her knife and shred the thing. Or to walk to the window with it and fling it to the winds—or to the cows, more likely. It was said that animals liked to eat fresh paint, before the flavor had utterly dried out. Well, they would be welcome. Except that she could not destroy it; she had already done so many hours' work that there was something of herself clamped onto the easel. It was already alive in something the same way a child is alive. She was not a murderess; she knew her frustration would not end in violence. Not, at least, violence of that sort.

What if she threw the ochre at her husband, when he next entered the room? Her smile widened into a silly grin. This would be both well deserved and delightful. He would look so silly, his stupid dignity would be so desperately affronted! She held back the giggles slipping from her throat. No, that would not do, either. Frederick would not be likely to protest; he would simply turn and clean himself off. Nor would he ever remind her, by express reference, of what she had done. But she would pay for it. Oh, yes, that was the guiding principle of her dear husband's life: people paid for what they got, and for what they got from him they were likely to pay double.

She had never had very much from him. She had paid, it was clear to her, distinctly more than double: she did not even want to compute in exact terms.

She sent a maid to her husband, at work in his laboratory, and was told by return message that the doctor was at work and would be with her as soon as he was able. As soon as he was able! Did he think she was a dog or a horse, to be held at a hitching post while waiting his convenience? She threw down her brushes, stamped out of the room and to the laboratory, where her knocking was brisk, peremptory, and remarkably loud for one so languishing.

There was a small silence. She was raising her hand to knock still more commandingly when the door clicked and her husband appeared, book in hand, his glasses perched on his nose, blinking at the light and the commotion. She glowered; he neither moved nor spoke.

"Frederick, it is cold here."

He blinked provokingly. Had the man lost what sense he possessed?

"Ah?" he murmured, seeming confused, but when the apparition of his wife did not fade he stepped back and admitted her. "Come in, my dear. I'm sorry I could not come when you—"

"Why couldn't you, I should like to know?"

He stood looking at her with a mild, almost cheerful countenance.

"I was occupied, my dear."

"And *I* needed to speak with you."

He shuffled toward a pair of chairs, waved her into one and then sat down himself. The book was still in his hand, clutched either absent-mindedly, or else, as a child seizes on a toy, as protection against imaginary evils. Was he turning senile?

"You do not seem to me to be at work," she declared, looking at his table of flasks and bottles. It seemed dusty, very much unused.

"I was."

"What sort of work?"

He peered across at her, apparently more near-sighted than ever.

"What did you need to discuss with me, my dear?"

She stamped her foot.

"What sort of work, Frederick?"

"We will discuss that later," he said carefully. "May I know what brings you to my place of study?"

She raised her hand accusingly, then dropped it. Why had she stormed into his laboratory? She searched her mind and could not recall. That, too, was his fault: he was always putting her off the track; he was always pretending that she raged without reason. Oh, she had reasons and to spare!

"Why do you distract me so, Frederick?"

He did not reply. Nor did he move. He waited. She stared at him, then at his laboratory materials, then back at him. She wished it were possible to cause the whole thing to blow itself sky high—preferably with him inside the room.

"You do not permit me to conduct a rational discussion, Frederick."

"I'm sorry, my dear."

"It's too late, I've been distracted. There was something terribly important I needed to broach with you—but I cannot recall it."

"I'm sorry," he repeated. The quiet benevolence of his voice irritated her, and she produced several high-pitched, stifled sounds that under other and more favorable circumstances might well have been screams.

"Why do you torment me so, Frederick?"

"I was not aware—"

"Aware! When were you ever aware of anyone but yourself, pray tell?"

"I shall endeavor to improve."

"Quite likely! They say that the worst sinners finally blanch at their reflection in the mirror, just before they reach their graves."

"Death is not to be contemplated—"

"Don't drivel at me, please. I came here to talk with you, not to be preached at."

He did not respond. She stared around her, unsure what direction to take. How, indeed, could she begin to breach the defenses of this impregnable man, this monster of selfish unconcern? She stood up and stalked to his work table.

"You can't have touched these, whatever they are," she exclaimed, touching one and then recoiling at the accumulated dust. "Not in months."

"No."

She turned on him, her back against the table. It felt better to be standing while he was seated.

"Why then have you continued to lock yourself away in here?" She leaned her face toward him. "Have you begun to go soft in the brain, Frederick?"

"I trust not, my dear."

"What have you done in here, all those hours and hours you've spent?" She rocked the table. The flasks and bottles rattled and shook. "I thought you were safely puttering. And now it turns out—what?" She laughed nastily. "Have you taken to conjuring, Frederick?"

He simply shook his head.

"We should have Doctor Parvos look at you, I think."

"If you like."

"Or Martial. He'll be more aware of the latest advances."

"I sha'n't trouble Martial, my dear."

"And why not? He's troubled us enough, I should think. And if you have a newer and better doctor than yourself so readily to hand, why shouldn't you make use of him, I'd like to know?" He did not respond. "I have never seen so perverse a man, Frederick."

"I'm sorry."

"Very likely. I can just see how sorry you truly are, Frederick, But *what* have you been up to, I want to know!"

"I have been laboring—"

She waved him silent.

"Oh, don't go repeating the same silly things over and over! You've *not* been laboring; you never did any honest labor in here in the first place. I can see from your bottles and what-not that you've not been at work. So what have you been doing? You've not been seeing patients."

"No."

"And you've not been at the housemaids. You're too old for that"— and seeing him recoil, she grimaced—"and you're not that sort. Yes, I know. And the maids would have told me at once—they know whose head is properly adjusted in this house."

"My dear."

"Oh, the holy Binghams, they never stoop to such things, of course, of course. They only squirrel away their money in rotten trees, and keep their children from having any of it. Nothing so open and honest as trifling with the female servants. Oh no."

"It may be difficult for you to comprehend, my dear, but—"

"It's not difficult, I assure you. It's as transparent as the best window glass."

"But I have been at work. The nature of my work," he continued, as though she had not interrupted, "as you have noted, is not the same. I shall be glad to make it known to you, when you're in a calmer mood."

"Calmer!" She crossed her arms and stared at him. "How can you sit there, Frederick, like some monstrous slug on a garden wall, and prate to me of calm and sanity? The next thing you know, you'll be telling me all about holiness and the little angels who've been visiting you." She stared hard. "Have they?"

"No."

"You wouldn't tell me, if they had. You've never told me anything, Frederick. You never told me we would come here to Poughkeepsie, this abandoned village in the middle of the wilderness, when we were married. Oh, you put a very different face on things! And when it came time to go to England, who was it who went? Not me, I can assure you."

"You refused to come."

"I was worn down with bearing your children and keeping your house and stuffing your belly!" She stamped her foot. "If it weren't for me, Frederick Bingham, you'd have perished years ago, in this godforsaken place you dragged me to! I was—oh, it doesn't matter, it doesn't matter anymore!" Her voice cracked. "Whatever I was, I am no longer. You've taken all of the good years, Frederick, and what have you given me?" Her voice rose again. "What have you ever given me, I'd like to know? Even your presents were paid for by my own brothers." She waved her arms around her, indicating the house and everything in and around it. "Even this house, which you like to call yours. Paid for by my brothers, every blessed cent of it. You've taken and taken and taken, Frederick—and if I have nothing left to take, now, you're still after me to bleed myself further, for your comfort. You'd like me to go quietly back into the house, wouldn't you, back to my woman's work, back to making your sanctified existence more comfortable! You'd like to go back to doing whatever silly, vicious nothingness you were 'occupied' with, when I came on the scene so unexpectedly. You didn't expect me to come, did you? You thought you could be rid of me, with just a word. Oh, that is the way it's been; I admit it. But no more. You'll not be rid of me so readily, from this point on, Frederick." She smiled fiercely, nodding with triumph. "You'll not find me so easy to handle, from this point on, do you hear? Patient Griselda doesn't exist any longer, not here in Poughkeepsie. You've taken my patience, too, along with everything else, and now that there's none left, it's you who'll have to bear the consequences. You, Frederick! Let's see how you like it. Let's just see."

She seemed to have planted herself. Her eyes were squinting, her mouth was taut. She might have been daring him to try to move her. Just try! He did not attempt it. He sat motionless, perhaps waiting. She waited with him, point for point, jot for jot. Whatever he was up to, whatever he did finally attempt, she would be equal to him. She had never felt so certain of herself, of her powers, of his contemptible weaknesses.

"Marie, it is difficult to change anything, at my time of life. And it is perhaps even more difficult to make any changes known to—to those who have known one."

"But you have decided to become a Catholic! You are entering a monastery, in Mother Italy! Well, you would fit very well in one, Frederick."

"Pray listen seriously, my dear."

"I've never been more serious—or, while I'm at it, less your *dear*. You have no right to such words, Frederick. I will thank you to stop using them with me."

"Very well."

"And take that butter-won't-melt-in-my-mouth look off your face."

"Marie, please listen to me."

She thumped her crossed arms against her chest.

"I'm listening."

"I have done much thinking, these past weeks and months. I have done much reading, and not in the books from which I am accustomed to draw sustenance."

"Trash!" she muttered, but that was all she said.

"I do not think it is given to us to say that we have wasted our lives: such determinations are made by a higher authority. But I think we can see, at least, how we may have taken wrong turnings, missed a better direction. I have been given such an opportunity."

Her lips moved, but she was so astonished that she could not immediately speak. She touched her cheek, her forehead, then tottered slightly. He did not move, and she fetched a chair for herself and sank into it.

"Do I hear you correctly?" she gasped. "Have you admitted to an error?"

He wondered if she were being ironic, or dramatic, and then decided that her astonishment was real, however unbalanced.

"To many errors."

"I can't believe it! This is too much. You, Frederick? You?"

He felt anger and suppressed it.

"May I tell you more?"

"Go on." And then a strange half-smile flittered across her face, and she almost cackled. "It's terribly strange. It's terribly funny, too. You have no idea how strange you seem to me right at this moment, Frederick, making amends for all the years of arrogance. No one who's not had to live with you could possibly imagine how I feel. *You* cannot possibly imagine it."

"*May* I go on, Marie?"

"Go on, yes. You'll have to excuse me if I seem impolite, Frederick." She tittered. "Just listen to me! Apologizing to *you*. As if you deserved my politeness. As if I were a girl again, and you a handsome young medical man, courting me. As you did, you know." Her eyes had slowly closed as she spoke. But she was not at all asleep. "Wasted lives: oh, I know all about that subject, I can tell you. I could have told you, all these years I could have told you. I tried, too, I really tried. But you would never listen to me, Frederick. You thought I was a peculiar woman. You thought sometimes I was out of my head. Could I have lived all these long years with you, Frederick, lived as I have had to live, and been unaffected? I *am* strange: do you suppose I don't know that? But I am as sane a woman as you will find, believe me. And I know what I speak of." Her eyes flung open; it was her turn to be angry. "You want to confess to me? To *me*? Why? What good do you imagine it can do you? None. I cannot forgive you, Frederick. How could I? You talk of wasted lives, of you wasting your own. But you have wasted mine. Do you have any understanding of that? Is that one of the errors you can now admit to?"

He had never felt more like striking her. Nor had he ever had less reason so to feel, if what he had been trying to tell her was truly real. Was it real? He tried to control his breathing, his heartbeat; he almost touched a hand to his wrist, to monitor his own pulse rate. But that, too, was not the way. If there was a way, and he had been granted a vision of it, even a limited and partial vision, he ought to be able to conquer both himself and her. He ought to be able, at the very least, to oblige her to listen. God would not do it for him. Nothing would be done for him, now or afterward. He had to throw up some sort of bridge, to open her ears, her mind, her soul.

"Do you know what book this is?" he asked, keeping his voice steady. He held it up; she did not look.

"I don't care, Frederick. Your books—"

"You *must* care."

Her mouth was half-open, whether in amusement or astonishment it was impossible to tell.

"I *must*?"

"Marie, look at what I have in my hand." She would not look; her eyes were on his face, though what she thought she saw he did not know. "Marie, please look."

Her smile was surprisingly youthful. She seemed for a moment a great deal younger, and very much prettier. She had not seemed pretty in more years than he could count.

"I can very nearly date the last time you said *please* to me, Frederick. I believe it was before Robert died. We never talk of him, do we? He was a dear little child; he was, indeed."

"We have endured many losses together," he began, but she did not hear him.

"I wonder if other women feel such things? I can still hear his voice, and there are days when I almost see him playing on the lawn. I've sometimes wanted to paint him, but I haven't dared. Not yet. Perhaps now I will." She stared directly at him. "If you will say that it is all right for me to paint him, I will do it. Will you?"

He tried to keep a handle on the conversation.

"Yes. Of course."

"Oh lovely, lovely!" Her eyes flickered shut again. "The dead are much more beautiful than the living. I've needed to paint him."

"Marie," he said decisively, as strongly as he dared, "do you believe in the Lord?"

Her closed eyes had a blank cast.

"Of course," she said dreamily. "Don't you?"

"I do!" he exclaimed, seeing his opportunity. "I have found him, Marie. In these last months, shut up in here; I have sought Him and I have found Him."

"What on earth are you talking about, Frederick?"

"Marie, do listen. Please. Nothing I have ever said to you has been as important as what I need to say to you now." He paused; she had not moved, still. But she might be listening, this time. "We are not sinners in the hands of an angry God, Marie. But we *are* as infants in His care, and His care is no more tender than we deserve. He does not spare us. But in the end He will protect us. He will raise us up."

"Frederick. You're raving, talking to me like that."

"I am *not* raving, Marie. I am simply trying to tell you—"

"I know raving when I hear it, doctor or no doctor. Physician, heal thyself. You can't expect people to let you heal them, if you're ill yourself. Have you taken your temperature?"

"Marie, I am not ill."

"No, you're just quietly out of your head, and raving."

"Will you listen to me, Marie?"

She stood up.

"Why ought I to? Do you ever listen to me? Are you listening to me now?" She dismissed him with a twist of the arm. "And what can you have to say to me, Frederick, that might be worth all this fuss? You must surely be the fussiest man alive. Always fussing about this and that and the next thing. I wish I had been able to ask your mother about that: I dare say you fussed in your cradle."

A good many of his patients would have pushed her bodily back into her chair. One or two would surely have tied her to the chair; there was one who might well have gagged her, to silence that infernally wagging tongue. It might have been better, had he been able to resort to such measures. He could not. Other aspects of himself could change, but never that.

"We will lose another one, Marie."

One hand was raised to her hair, a strand of which had come loose.

"Another what?"

There was no concern in her voice. She had barely made out his words, she had not troubled to understand them.

"Another child."

"What on earth are you talking about? More raving, is that what it is?"

"I'm talking about Anne-Marie. About our daughter."

Her hands fell to her sides.

"What? What?" She clapped both hands against her forehead. "What are you saying? What?" Her voice rose with each word. "What about Anne-Marie?"

"I did not mean to tell you. But how else can I make you listen?"

"What are you saying about Anne-Marie? Tell me."

"You must understand, Marie—"

"No! Tell me. What are you not telling me? Why must you always torture me?" She stamped her foot several times. "Tell me. Tell me."

He tried to seem self-possessed, even professional.

"She has a consumption."

"Anne-Marie? No, you're lying to me. She's as healthy as I am. Why do you want to lie to me?"

He started to rise, to go to her.

"It's the truth, Marie, the dreadful truth."

Her scream was piercingly loud. She rushed toward him, both hands raised, like some avenging fury. How it happened he did not know, but she fell against him with such force that he swung backward against his chair, and then he and the chair both fell to the floor, and she fell across them. But it was suddenly totally silent in the room. He could hear his own rapid breathing, and that was all he could hear. For a moment he wondered if her scream had deafened him. But she was not continuing her mad assault.

He pulled himself free. She rolled onto her back and lay motionless. He started to tidy his clothing, then noticed the strange texture of her skin.

Kneeling beside her, he touched her cheek. She did not respond.

"Marie."

She did not reply, she did not move.

He bent to her chest and put his ear against it. Nothing. He took her pulse, or tried to. There was no pulse to take. He remained kneeling, her hand limp in his. What had happened? Had she suffered a syncope? Had a blood vessel burst? Had he injured her, in the process of tumbling to the floor? He released her hand; it dropped with a faint thump. He shuddered. It did not matter how, but the event was clear enough. She was dead. Whether of shock or rage or some other cause, neither he nor anyone else would ever know. She had understood her daughter's illness. It had been the last thing she would ever understand, and she had been overcome by it. She had meant to attack him: she saw him as the instigator of all things, he had been demonic in her eyes, never human. The measure of her disappointment in him? The reflection of the love she had surely once felt for him, distorted insanely out of shape?

He would have to bear everything alone. She had not been a great deal of help, not for very many years. But to be alone was quite a different matter. He had not expected ever to be alone: he was many years her senior; by all rights, he should have been the first to die. He had never expected not to be.

But was he alone, was he really alone? Hadn't he found someone higher, someone nobler? Wasn't he blessed with a powerful new ally, an ally he should have known years before, but one he had definitely established firmly and securely in his heart and mind? He lifted his hands and prayed. Or tried to: no words came. There was no sense of connection, no sense of occurrence. It was a futile gesture, an empty stance. He lowered his hands, slowly, angrily. She had died, and in dying she had taken this from him. It could have saved them both; it could have spared them agonies past calculating. He had found it. But she had destroyed it. If God stood in his soul, before, his soul was now empty, a shrine of no significance, unpopulated, useless.

He climbed painfully to his feet. The corpse would have to be tended to. There would have to be a funeral. Children and other relatives would have to be notified. The household would have to be put into mourning—mourning! For her? It would have to be: how could he explain to anyone, least of all to her own children, what in dying she had done to him? For all he knew, they would in truth be on her side, they would be apt to think him the monster she had thought him. It would only confirm that, were he to condemn her as she should in all justice be condemned. Could God possibly admit the like of her to Heaven? Could that be possible? He quickly pushed the thought from his mind: blasphemy would not help. Neither would it help to drag her body into the yard and douse it with volatile spirits and ignite it, let it burn down to hell as it surely deserved. No. She would have to have a Christian burial, and he would have to participate, along with her children. And his. They were his children, too. Were they? Were they in truth? Were they in fact changelings, wished on the two of them by the devils of hell? How could he wear a black suit and a solemn face? How could he acknowledge funereal greetings and condolences; how could he keep a straight face?

He turned toward the door, trying to assume a reasonable stance. He did not feel in any way reasonable.

The first of the servants to see him gasped. He tried to act as if he had not noticed.

"Your mistress is dead," he said brusquely, and the woman reeled back. "Come, come. There is a great deal to be done. Hysterics are of no use. Do you want to lose your place?" He snapped his finger at her.

"Tell John I need to speak to him. And bring Jane to me. I will be in my consulting room. Hurry!"

She broke into a staggering run. He shook his head: servants! Then he stepped into his consulting room. He would need to do a great many things, before this was over and done with. He did not want to do any of them. But they were obligations, and he would conduct himself properly. They would be done, and as well as he was capable of doing them: this was not something about which there was any room for hesitation. He did not hesitate.

PART TWO

Horace Greeley (1811–1872)
"Go West, young man, and grow up with the country."

N
I
N
E

"If, on a given occasion, a man can, gracefully, and without the air of a pedant, show a little more knowledge than the occasion requires, the world will give him credit for eminent attainments. It is an honest quackery. I have practised it, and sometimes with success."

—Daniel Webster, to his son Fletcher
15 January 1836

The small wagon was waiting at the dock; Jonathan did not know the man holding the reins, but there was obviously no difficulty picking him out, as the indifferent group of passengers descended from the steamer at Poughkeepsie.

"Mr. Jonathan?"

Jonathan threw his grip into the wagon, and climbed in himself.

"I dare say my father won't be at home for some while yet."

"No, sir, he's there now."

Odd: his father was not in the habit of spending afternoons at home. Perhaps—though it hardly seemed like the Doctor Bingham he knew—the day of his son's homecoming had been set on the calendar like a holiday.

They drove at a familiar pace: slower than slow. He had been away less than a full year, but this sort of driving seemed better suited to snails than to humans. New York had spoiled him, obviously. He would have a summer's breath to recover in: not a whole summer, as he was afraid his father expected—but that would have to be dealt with later, face to face.

He made no conversation with the new servant. It was not snobbishness: he would not be at home long enough for any serious contact, and he wanted the time, as they ambled along, to survey his old stamping grounds. He had planned and anticipated nothing: after less than a year, how momentous an occasion could his homecoming be? But it seemed more significant, somehow, than he had believed possible. It wasn't that Poughkeepsie had necessarily changed—and it hadn't, he could document virtually every familiar landmark—as that he suddenly saw the town differently. The dockside area seemed impossibly tiny, almost toylike. It had been immense and thronging with activity, when he was a child. There was a sense of peaceful stagnation, now—or was that only in contrast with the furious bustle of South Street? The shops seemed shabby: had the paint always been peeling back, the walks rotting away, the glass dirty and the lettering half illegible? He was less than a hundred miles from New York, but the people strolling up and down were dressed differently, and they walked differently, too. In New York, he smiled to himself, these would either have been ancient millionaires, no longer concerned with making a living, or else some of the bewildered newcomers who were starting to pour off steamers and clippers, immigrants from Ireland and Germany, as well as from England, Scotland, and Wales. He actually knew most of these Poughkeepsie people, and a good many of them by name. He smiled and nodded, and they nodded back. A few called out his name in greeting, and he called back, naming each and all. The wagon did not stop, but it was not expected to. They had their business and he, now grown up, had his, too. But he knew them, and they knew him—and why did they seem so strange, not really like relics, more like stale projections out of a no longer vital past?

He did stop for one passerby, Caleb Miller, the Binghams' shoemaker for as long as he could remember. Jonathan jumped out of the wagon and they shook hands.

"Are you back, eh?"

"For a visit."

"Going to stay over there?"

"I don't know, Mr. Miller. I've got a lot of learning yet; I do know that."

"Your daddy could use you." Mr. Miller considered, his head bobbing slightly, his tongue pushed against the side of his cheek. Then he endorsed his formulation. "Yep, he could use you."

"I'm not studying medicine, you know—or farming!"

"I know. Seems like a long time since your mother died, though. A real long time." He touched his hat. "Good to see you, Jonathan."

"Good to see you, Mr. Miller."

The wagon rolled forward. It was no more than six months since his mother died, since they had buried her and gone about their business. His father's letters had not changed a great deal; they were perhaps shorter, flatter, but that was not surprising. There had been no reports of odd behavior, or of strangeness. Mr. Miller did not speak idly, however, nor did he ever speak without prior reflection. There must be something, and it must be visible. And it could not be good.

The house did not look different. Jonathan permitted his grip to be carried by the new servant, and followed quietly after. It was a bright June day, and he could not at first make out the interior with any clarity, but it too did not seem changed. As his eyes adjusted he could see some slight signs of poor housekeeping, but that did not surprise him. His Aunt Sophia did not tolerate any degree of disorder; even his vaguer and more distracted mother had kept things reasonably under control. For a male, living alone and supervising household matters himself, his father was not doing badly. That was encouraging. He did not think household matters had ever before engaged his father in any way.

Doctor Bingham was in the drawing room. He had a book in his lap and put it down to embrace his son.

"You look well, Father."

"For a man of sixty-eight, that may well be true, Jonathan." His father's glance had been wild and unfixed, at the time of the funeral. It was better focused, now, but still not so firm as it had been. There was a narrowness to his mouth, a kind of turned-down bitterness. "My only attention to myself is, however, professional. I am, I fancy, rather like the engineer of the steamboat you probably came on, today: as long as the boat moves forward, and at more or less the desired speed, the condition of its decks, or the paint on its bows, does not truly concern me." He motioned Jonathan to a chair. "If the boilers threaten to explode, I shall attend to them." He wandered to the window, then back, not really looking at anything. "Not that there is a great deal of vitality left in an engine so old as mine." He stood staring at his son, but did not seem to be seeing even him. "You too look well, Jonathan," he finished quietly, and resumed his own chair.

"For a man of eighteen . . ." Jonathan smiled. His father did not respond. "I would have expected to see you in your laboratory, Father. Your new man told me you were at home."

"Gerald: I believe he is Irish. The others left, the maids, too. It was just as well. I did not relish the sight of them."

"Of course."

"I'm at home a good deal, Jonathan."

It was not the sort of statement a son could pick at.

"I see."

"I've closed up my so-called laboratory. There was no scientific work worthy of the name to be done there, not by me, and the room was distasteful to me. Your mother's seizure took place there." Doctor Bingham's tone was almost disinterested. "My European correspondence has dried away, of late. The things I have to say to my distant friends do not much compel their attention, and the things they have to say to me do not much compel mine."

"I'm sorry to hear that."

"It hardly matters. A few less rocks and shells going this way and that, back and forth across the Atlantic: pish, it doesn't affect commerce and it never made any scientific stir. The doings of small men are of some importance to them, but only to them. Neither eternity nor even the rest of the world owes them any notice, though it may damage their pride to realize how insignificant they are. I do not seriously think it has damaged mine—but then, I never had much to begin with. I do not know if I have lived an unexceptionable life, Jonathan, but surely I have lived a tepid one."

"No, I hadn't noticed that, Father."

"You are, as you say, only eighteen. There is a great deal which will escape your attention until you are much older."

It was the same drawing room, the same house: he had grown up here. The furniture had not been changed. His father was barely a year older than when Jonathan had moved away, half a year older than when last seen. But he felt almost a stranger, more a guest than a resident. Was it his new status as an apprentice adult, was it the new non-parental stance his father seemed to assume in dealing with him? Or was it only his imagination, and the time he had been away? Had he forgotten?

"I trust your patients are well," he said at last, trying to turn the conversation.

"I see remarkably few patients. If they are well enough to come here, I do what I can for them. If they are not well enough to come here, it is better for them that they see one of the younger and at this point more capable physicians in the area."

"I suppose you've referred some to Martial?"

"I have referred no one to anyone. People are perfectly capable of making such decisions for themselves; there is nothing in any way technical about it. Nor is Martial within easy distance, for a sick person. His practice and mine have never interfered one with the other."

"Barely a dozen miles, if that."

Doctor Bingham's stiffness seemed to be increasing rather than waning.

"Quite long enough, on horseback, and still longer, in a carriage. Perhaps we shall one day be shot back and forth, from one end of the country to the other, like human cannonballs. But until that time, Jonathan, we must be content with what the Lord has seen fit to permit us."

Jonathan wished his father would send for something cool to drink. He wished they could take a turn in the garden. He wished they were not so starkly alone together.

"I trust Anne-Marie and my little nieces and nephews are well?"

Doctor Bingham looked at him severely.

"Have you any reason to suspect the contrary?"

"Of course not!"

"But you will have to speak to Martial about such matters. I think he is a great deal better at his trade than I am, or even than I have ever been. And in any case I now spend my days quite differently."

"You've certainly earned the right to—"

"To be entirely truthful, Jonathan, I question whether in all my life I have earned much that is worth earning, other than a modicum of earthly goods and possessions."

"Sure, Father, you are unfair to yourself! Just think of—"

"I think I am not unfair to myself, Jonathan. But if I am, better to be unfair to myself than to others. And what does any man earn, by being born onto this earth, other than the right to respect his Maker, and His Maker's laws? I have only just realized that, Jonathan. I trust that somehow it is not too late for me. Only in God's great mercy could it not be too late, after the life I have led. I must humble myself to His great will and to His purpose—not with the absurd notion of any reward, but only because I will be doing what in truth I should have been doing all along. What all men should be doing, if only they understood." His sigh was extremely long and deeply depressing. "If only they understood. But how few even try! I am not a trained ecclesiastic, Jonathan. God's will must be manifested to me in spite of my darkness of mind, in spite of my infirmity of will, in spite of all the wrong turnings and twistings I have made."

Jonathan rose; he could not sit any longer, listening to his father speak the language of mold and decay. He had begun to understand what Caleb Miller meant to tell him.

"You are perhaps too much alone, Father."

"I think I am the best judge of that, Jonathan."

It was like the silent slam of a door, thrown closed by a gust of wind.

"Well, then, I hope that at least I can cheer you a bit, while I'm here."

"I do not need cheering: again, I will thank you to leave such matters to me. Nor do I consider a summer to be a significantly abbreviated time."

The fat was in the fire.

"I don't think I shall be here for the entire summer, Father."

"Your presumption gains on you rapidly, Jonathan. I do not find it an endearing quality in a youth of your comparatively tender years. Was it for that sort of education, indeed, that I sent you to New York? Is your Uncle Karl aware of any of this?"

Jonathan sat down again.

"Let me try to explain, Father."

"Do."

"I have not found Columbia College an especially enjoyable experience."

"Did you think you would? Is enjoyment the reason for attendance at university? I confess that is an idea totally new to me."

"I mean, Columbia is not, I think, the place for me."

"You will recall, Jonathan, that it was your idea not to enter Princeton, and that I consented only after much discussion."

"I doubt that Princeton would be more appropriate."

"Well, then, I suppose we should apprentice you to a carpenter? Or did you plan to open a greengrocer's establishment?"

"Do let me explain, Father."

"I was under the impression that I was doing exactly that, Jonathan. You are not overly clear-headed, I'm afraid, nor are you more logical than one might expect of someone your age.

"With my Uncle Karl's permission, I have spent a good many hours working in his and my Uncle Peter's establishment. I cannot pretend to know very much of it, but I have, I trust, learned enough to understand at least the principal direction of the business."

"Which is, of course, to work hard and to make a living from your work. I dare say you find both of those principles objectionable, do you now, Jonathan?"

"On the contrary, Father. I believe I have worked hard, and though I have not sought to earn money for my work, I do not find the principle in any way objectionable."

"I'm sure your uncles would be delighted to have your approval. You have ventured to tell them, I assume?"

It was much like being a small boy and having his father shred his remarks, scattering pieces to this wind and that one. Except that he was aware of being no longer a small boy. His father had not been a patient man, and he had not improved in that respect. Nor had his son omitted to learn the lesson of impatience.

"Aunt Sophia is acquainted with Mr. Greeley."

"I wish her joy of the connection, Jonathan. But what, pray tell, has that to do with our conversation of the moment?"

"I was admitted to Mr. Greeley's office, he directed me to Mr. Bayard Taylor, and for the last half year, Father, I have been writing for the *Tribune*."

"Upon my word. Do you mean, Jonathan, that Mr. Greeley's newspaper cannot find, not anywhere in these United States, better things to put into print than the effusions of an adolescent?"

"You might address that query to Mr. Greeley, Father. I could not presume to answer for him."

"But you have no hesitation, so far as I can see, in presuming to me, young man. I am to be sure not a famous editor, and I do not live in the famous metropolis. I am an admittedly inconspicuous, not to say a deservedly inconsequential, provincial doctor. But for all that I am your father, and I do not care for your method of address to me. I will thank you to amend it, and at once."

"I'm sorry, Father. I had no intention of offending you."

"I should like to know what else you thought you might be doing— but let it pass. Pray continue."

"There is much political activity, right now, this being a presidential election year. The *Tribune* has invited me to spend the greater part of the summer working as a junior reporter."

"They propose to allow you to write about political matters? You, Jonathan?"

"Their regular men will be much occupied with politics, Father, and they wish me to fill the gap in a variety of ways."

"As my late father would have said, *mon dieu!* Do they also propose to remunerate you for this professional activity?"

"Yes."

"To what degree, may I inquire?"

"I've not discussed it, Father. My Uncle Karl has kindly offered me the use of the room I have occupied at his home, this past year—"

"Very decent of him. Very decent. Of course, he might have consulted your father and sole living parent, before extending such an offer."

"The offer is conditional upon your approval, Father."

"I see."

"As is my willingness to accept the *Tribune*'s invitation."

"But you have told them you would be overjoyed, have you not?"

"I have told them that I will and that I must defer to your wishes."

"How dutiful." Doctor Bingham rose, slowly, looking already pre-occupied. "You will excuse me, Jonathan, until dinner time. My business is not perhaps of this world, but it occupies me nevertheless. Shall we discuss these fascinating matters more fully, over dinner?"

"As you please, Father."

"Your room is as it was, Jonathan. Why don't you take possession of it once again? And then you might like to amuse yourself, surveying the old homesteads for signs of change and decay. You'll find a good bit of that, I'm sure. There is no escaping change and decay, you know. Nor have I tried."

His father started to the door.

"Perhaps I shall ride over to my sister's house."

His father turned sharply about.

"No, I don't want you doing that." There was a small pause: Jonathan could see words being shaped and discarded. "There will be time enough. You young people are always in an immense hurry."

His exceedingly dry laugh was not persuasive. "No, you will stay here, Jonathan. We'll dine a bit earlier than we used to. There won't be opportunity for a proper visit. Or even time. You should stay here."

Jonathan bowed, and his father left the room.

Did Theodore, too, experience trials of this sort? Did other fathers—but there was no point to idle debate with himself. He was here, as he was supposed to be, as in good conscience he was obliged to be. Whether his father needed him or not, as Mr. Miller seemed to think, was also beside the point. There was not very much he could do for his father: that struck him as abundantly clear. There was, however, a good deal that his father could do, still, to make life unpleasant for him. He was required to be patient—more patient, he knew, than he had so far succeeded in being. He might well need to enlist his sister's help. And Martial's. And any other help he could drum up: perhaps he should spend this first afternoon drafting a letter to Theodore? But his brother had, he was keenly aware, many other things pressing on him, things of considerably larger import than a summer post for an eighteen-year-old boy.

Was the relationship between his father and his sister strained? Or had Doctor Bingham perhaps quarreled with Doctor Johnson? It seemed unlikely, especially since his father had plainly withdrawn from active practice. And wouldn't his sister have said something, in one of her chatty letters? Perhaps not. He did not understand his father; he never had. It seemed quite probable that he never would. Sons were not in general well-placed for the understanding of their male parents: he had heard even Theodore, now and then, express some considerable irritation with their father's ways and views.

He would re-occupy his room. He would let the rest of the afternoon pass quietly by, while his father busied himself—with what? With things that were not of this world? Had the old man turned to necromancy, in his final days? Jonathan smiled to himself. Now there would be an interesting development! He could see his father with a tall, peaked cap, and a smoking flagon . . . . He laughed out loud, turned, and left the room.

"Well, we've gone and done it."

"That we have, Mr. Brady."

It was Philadelphia, and it was June, 1848. The Whig Party had just, in convention assembled, notified the world that its presidential nominee in the fall would be Zachary Taylor of Virginia, sixty-four years of age and the undoubted hero of the recently concluded war with Mexico. The Whigs had also notified the world that neither their old faithful, Henry Clay, an ideologue who had gone down to miserable defeat in the previous election, nor their prime orator, Daniel Webster, who never got the nomination but who ran for it year after year, was to be their candidate. Their platform, such as it was, consisted of a glorification of Old Zach, his exploits and his heroism. There was no talk of principle, this time: Clay had done enough of that. And though the country was beginning to split, and split badly, on the slavery issue, there was no talk of that in the platform or in any Whig speeches. Nor did they discuss Taylor's Virginian origins (it might have been predicted that Taylor's children would fight on the Confederate side, in the coming War Between the States—and in fact they did). Nor did they discuss Taylor's neophyte status as a politician. What the Whigs were notifying the world, in short, was that they proposed to win, principles be damned. They would win. It would also be both the last election they would win, nationally, and the party's last gasp, as a unified (or relatively unified) national force. In eight short years, when the new Republican Party broke through, the Whigs would have ceased to exist: the price of success would be a heavy one. And there were those among them, even in the euphoria of 1848, even in the certainty of an election triumph to come, who suspected at least some of the future. No one thought Taylor an ideal candidate: in finally endorsing him, early in September, Daniel Webster managed to condemn him roundly—but to condemn his opponent, Lewis Cass, rather more.

"Generals run well, Mr. Congressman. But what do you do with 'em after they've done running, eh?"

"It might have been Scott, if it hadn't been Taylor. I don't myself know much about either of them."

"Except that they're generals, right."

There was no need to talk about Millard Fillmore, of Buffalo, New York, who had won the vice-presidential nomination. Of what significance was a vice president, even once elected? John Tyler had succeeded to the presidency, to be sure, and he had run behind another Johnny-come-lately Whig general, Tippecanoe Harrison. But Tyler's situation had been highly novel, and there was some doubt in the country that he had in fact become president, that he was not simply a fill-in, an acting president, or at any rate something less than a fully and properly elected leader. And what chance was there of it ever happening again? Harrison had been feeble; Taylor was marvelously healthy, vigorous, forceful. There had been jockeying for the vice-presidency, of course. Abbott Lawrence of Massachusetts, a wealthy manufacturer and ambitious political boss, had wanted it badly. But Fillmore had it and that was that. In the final analysis, who cared?

But Taylor made a difference. He would run with broad coat-tails extended: there would be numbers of other candidates swept in behind him. And Taylor would have all the vast rewards of federal patronage to bestow. What would Fillmore have? A gavel to bang, as he sat wearily in front of the United States Senate. A desk. A title. A small line in the history books.

"Still, Mr. Brady, I suspect our own chances are better, with Taylor at the head of the ticket."

"No doubt of it. Mr. Weed, now, he's gotten what he wanted. He'll need you, Mr. Congressman. If we're going to carry New York, why, he'll need you in the worst way."

"Even if he gets as much help from Mr. Van Buren as he seems likely to receive?"

Brady spit loudly and took another bite of tobacco.

"Van Buren!"

"He'll take more votes from Cass than he will from Taylor, if they go ahead and run on their own ticket. And he'll run well in New York, you know he will."

"So will Fillmore, by God, and so will you, Mr. Bingham! And is Mr. Weed the sort of fool, now, who'd wait to let someone else—and the likes of Mr. Van Buren at that—do his work for him? Would he be the man he is, do you think, if he counted on has-beens and noise-makers . . . but he don't, and you know he don't. He don't count on nothing, in fact, until it's in the bag and sealed. You don't win by expecting to win and loafing to the polls: you know that, by God. You win by running hard from the minute you get out of bed in the morning until you finally lay yourself down to sleep at night—and pretty late at night, at that. Mr. Weed, damn it all, he's a *politician*. He ain't a bank clerk, toting up vouchers. He's going to win, that's what he is, and he's not going to take a decent night's sleep until he's done it."

"He'll win."

"And so will you, Mr. Congressman. And the same way. Your name won't be on the ballot this fall, but there's not going to be a man in New York who don't know you're running. So you'll be out there, all over the state, that's what you'll be doing, and you'll talk up old Zach and you'll hold hands with Fillmore and you'll cut Mr. Van Buren down to size and you'll whomp away at General Cass—by God, we'll be running you like a race horse." He dug out a small sheaf of letters. "I've got invitations for you, right here, for a dozen nights in September and October. And that ain't nothing, that's just the start of it. We're going to have more invitations than you've ever seen before. And you're going to make a speech for every damned one of 'em."

"Even if they're for the same night and a hundred miles apart?"

"We'll turn you into the flying cavalry, by God. And if you can't make it one night, we'll have you there another. And we'll have people talking about you, when you're not speechifying—we'll have you rising up from the ground like a flock of mosquitoes at nightfall."

"I'll be dead of exhaustion by the time the Legislature meets."

"You'll be dead sure of winning, that's what you'll be."

It was exhilarating.

It was also daunting.

And it was the way it would be.

"Grace will be almost as pretty as her mother," Jonathan noted, after the child had brought him a tray of party sandwiches and waited decorously while he chose what he wanted. "Not to slight Alice, of course."

Martial's enthusiasm seemly oddly dampened.

"A lovely girl. I'm almost as fortunate, having her, as I was to win her mother."

"Ah, from what I heard, Martial, it was no contest. You were the winner hands down and flags flying. You know, I think I do my sister no injustice by letting you know that, oh for perhaps a year, she seemed never to discuss anything else. It was Martial, Martial, for breakfast, lunch, and dinner. I don't know how she held out for as long as she did. Propriety, that must have been it. The well-bred woman does not readily admit to her passion."

"You were very young, Jonathan. Your memory probably plays you tricks."

"On the contrary: because I was so very young, my attention was absolutely riveted. I thought your courtship, you know, the most dramatic thing I'd ever seen." He tried a bit of Martial's wine, and nodded approvingly. "You see, *that's* what you learned in Europe, and what I never learned, not having had the opportunity to accompany you. That turned drama into tragedy, I can tell you. For me, it was a very unhappy moment."

"You've recovered nicely."

"How sage you are, Doctor Johnson!"

"Tragedy at age eleven? That is how old you were, is it not? How long ago it seems!"

"Only a Biblical seven years, I'm afraid. You've had four children and made a great deal of money, you've become a prominent senior practitioner. Who knows, perhaps when my brother ascends to the Senate, they may decide to put his brother-in-law in his Congressional seat."

"From here? No, I don't aspire to politics, or to fame. I'd like to stay just as I am, I'd like everything to stay just as it is. Everything."

Jonathan raised his glass.

"So be it."

"Not quite so easy, I'm afraid."

"Oh, I dare say nothing is easy. But the question is one of possibility, isn't it?"

Martial shook his head.

"You collegians. You can turn everything into an abstraction, and then find a rule to govern it."

"It *is* impractical as blazes, I can't deny it. You know, my father has more or less agreed to let me spend most of the summer doing cub work for the *Tribune*. I'm supposed to be swatting up my Greek, but I can't find it in my heart, somehow, to care particularly deeply about enclitics and postpositives. I'm not made to be a grammarian, even for only a few years of my life."

Martial seemed to return from a long internal journey.

"Indeed," he murmured.

"I don't expect my father will bring the subject up, but if he does—you take my meaning, I assume?"

"Hmm? Oh, certainly: I'll put in a good word for you. I'll assure him that your enclitics are in good hands. What by the way *is* an enclitic? It sounds as if I ought to prescribe for it."

"Never mind. I think I'd only display my ignorance if I attempted to explain what I understand so shakily. I may not live to accomplish my degree, you know."

"Nonsense."

"Quite seriously, I assure you. Suppose that Mr. Greeley is so enchanted with my performances, this summer, and with the manifold advantages of having me in his employ on a regular basis, that he decides to dispense with one of his less sparkling reporters and invite me to remain?"

"Is that likely?"

"Why not? I have been paid small sums, for most of this past year, to spin out deathless prose for the *Tribune*'s columns."

"I hadn't realized that."

"For shame. I've told you, myself, on at least three occasions. Perhaps four. And I've boasted shamelessly to my sister. Didn't I send you clippings, after a number of particularly notable coups?"

"You probably did. You must excuse me, Jonathan. If I seem inattentive, it's because I am."

"Worrying about a patient?"

Martial took a quick breath.

"Yes."

"Well, I'm used to it. My father may choose to disparage his attendance as a physician, but he would often be so preoccupied, thinking through a course of treatment—and so weary, maintaining it—that we in the family might well not have existed. Why, you could talk to him, at table, and he'd not so much as respond. You at least endeavor to keep up appearances." Jonathan rose. "But I sha'n't interfere with the progress of medicine." He motioned Martial to remain. "No, you ponder herbs and poultices, and I'll spend an hour or so with my sister. After all, it was she and her children I came to see, not the hum-drum husband and father of them all."

Martial smiled wryly, and Jonathan left him alone, walking past his father, two of his father's grandchildren and their nurse, and making his way into the house. It was in fact almost true: he had not realized, while he was in New York, how much his sister's presence meant to him. And her playing. He had heard some of the leading performers of the day, in the past year, and none seemed to him to excel, and very few to equal, his sister.

She was standing near a window, in an inner room that he might not have entered had the door not been wide open. Her back was to him, her shoulders were oddly hunched.

"You've slain the fatted calf, Anne-Marie, but left the rest of us to eat him unaided!"

She turned to him slowly. Her face was unusually pink, her eyes strained. He did not remember ever seeing her so worn, or for that matter quite so thin: the bones in her cheeks stood out in semi-relief.

"I'll be along very soon," she said evenly, but very softly, as if using as little breath as possible. He did not know what was wrong, though clearly something was. Had she quarreled with Martial? Had there been bad news, perhaps about one of the children? Had she been ill, perhaps with some sort of cough? He smiled nervously and left, as she had directed. He felt quite remarkably like an intruder, which was not an emotion he had felt, before, in his sister's house. The Johnson' had been virtually a second home for him, from the very beginning.

The two little boys, Mark (who was three) and Michael (who was barely two), were climbing on their grandfather's lap, when Jonathan returned. Martial had left; the children's nurse was with Grace and Alice, at the far end of the garden.

"Have they pummeled you into submission?" he smiled, sitting down near his father.

"It would take remarkably little skill. They are very dear to me." He righted Michael, the younger boy, just as he was about to topple head first onto the grass. "I'm not sure whether it was truly disadvantageous for you and Theodore and Anne-Marie to see so little of me, when you were children. But for better or worse, in my dotage I intend to be with these children as much as possible."

"It's obviously good for all parties concerned. It's good for you to be away from—from the Grandvoort house," he stumbled.

"I dare say."

"Might you want to dispose of it entirely, Father?"

"Are you in the market, Jonathan?"

"What an idea! But I'll bet there are a host of people who might be. Perhaps even Mr. Greeley. He's enormously fond of the country. He rather likes farming, too."

Doctor Bingham set both children on the grass, then dusted himself off.

"You've returned from New York a veritable cornucopia of ideas, I see." He rose and looked about. "I wonder where Martial has gotten to?" Then he nodded to his son. "It may also, to be sure, be a question simply of your age. I do not recall your brother being quite so fertile, at roughly the same period in his life, but there was a considerable quickening. Quite considerable. It may be, I see, that permitting you to spend the greater part of the summer in the city will have its disadvantages. You bring so much of it here with you, when you come. On the other hand, I must say that it is personally gratifying to me, to think of you igniting and flaring not in mine but in other people's company. I am decidedly too old for you, Jonathan. Some fathers and sons can grow to be friends, I know, but you and I are fifty years separated, and that, I begin to realize, is too large a gap to be surmounted. Well, that will be as it must." He pulled out a silver chronometer and checked the time. "I must say my farewells; my schedule does not permit more than this modicum of socialization." He turned toward the house. "You may stay, Jonathan. Martial can lend you a horse."

The two little boys ran after him, as best they could, but he walked rapidly and they stopped, discomfited.

"Mark and Michael," Jonathan called. "Let me show you something."

They pranced and tumbled toward him and he spent ten minutes entertaining them. But he was relieved when the nurse swept them up, wriggling and protesting.

"Nap time, young gentlemen!"

And away they went.

The garden was quite remarkably quiet. If it were my garden, he thought, and if it were ten years from now, I'd light up a cheroot, pour myself a glass of Madeira, and musingly compose an epic poem while

I digested my lunch. He smiled: provided I have by then developed a taste for cheroots, and provided I have it in me to compose anything, and provided I have done well enough to earn an establishment this spacious and secluded.

Had Martial gone to look after his bothersome patient?

Why had not his sister come out?

Why had his father talked of a schedule? He had no schedule, so far as Jonathan was aware. He had virtually no demands on his time other than ones he laid on for himself.

What had been wrong with Anne-Marie?

Why had Martial not identified his patient, even in passing? And why had he seemed so deeply depressed, despite the joyousness of the occasion—the return of the prodigal son, the family reunion of almost all who were left in the family? Other than Theodore, they were in fact all present, all well and at ease. But were they? His father had been singularly irritable, crabbed and sour beyond anything Jonathan had known or been able to predict. He had put it down to his mother's sudden death. He had put it down to age and to God only knew what. But perhaps there was a specific and more definable cause. Perhaps Martial's despondency was linked to his father-in-law's upset, and both were linked to those exposed, flushed cheek bones he had seen, abruptly, when Anne-Marie turned toward him.

He leaned forward and plucked some blades of grass, then stayed bent over, wanting to block things out, wanting to isolate himself for the moment. What if Martial's troublesome patient was Anne-Marie? What if his father—who would of course have been consulted, as both parent and medical authority—knew and had known for some time? A lingering illness, something that raided the color and wasted the flesh, something that would—it came to him swiftly—bend her into that strange hunched posture, as she fought off a spell of coughing. He did not need to name the disease, even to himself. It was more than familiar.

And what if even his mother's sudden death was linked to Anne-Marie's illness? What if—but his mind dithered into inconsequentiality, slithered and slipped and spun. Was it all true, he demanded? Was he spinning out morbid imaginings? Was he seeing—he couldn't remember who had put it this way, but did not try very hard to remember—the thing that was not?

He straightened, about to rise, then sat back. No, it would not do to go storming into the house, seeking to know what no one wanted him to know. Anne-Marie was his sister. But she was Martial's wife, and his father's daughter, and four children's mother. She and they had rights which took precedence over his, whatever his might be. However Anne-Marie wanted it to appear, that was how it ought to be. If she wanted him to know, it was not difficult to tell him. No, on the contrary: it was not an easy thing to say. What should she do? Come and sit down next to him and say, simply and plainly, "Brother, I am dying of a consumption?" Could he just up and say such a thing, if the condition were his? He rather doubted it.

Had his mother known? He did not think he would ever learn the answer, and he did not think he would ever ask the question.

Should he speak to Anne-Marie? Should he speak to Martial, first? Would it be better to talk to Anne-Marie? No, it was best to speak to Martial: he might be interfering medically, if he spoke to Anne-Marie without her doctor's approval. Shock and surprise were surely not what was indicated.

Had shock and surprise killed his mother? Had she suddenly, unexpectedly learned, and died of the knowledge?

Anne-Marie might well die, if he confronted her. It would be reckless and dangerous to do anything whatever, without some knowledgeable prior opinion. It would have to be Martial; he would have to speak to him. But what would that do to Martial, working as hard as obviously he was to encapsulate Anne-Marie's condition, to preserve for her, for as long as humanly possible, as normal an environment as he could sustain? What good would it do, to air his sudden suspicions to her husband?

And what if Martial denied it, what if he scoffed and said it was all humbug and nonsense? There could be no argument—and what would have been accomplished, then? Martial would have to redouble his vigilance, and doubly exhaust himself. And if Anne-Marie was indeed to die, Martial would need all the strength he could muster. He would have to be father and mother to their children, and just at the moment when he would feel irremediably weakened.

Plainly, it was better to say nothing.

It was a good thing he would not be in Poughkeepsie long. Work, and work that took him to New York, would be an excellent solution to at least his part of the problem. He was a very small part of it, he knew that perfectly well. And maybe he was wrong, maybe he was speculating stupidly, senselessly. He was seeing all sorts of connections, but what if they did not connect; what if what he feared was a chimera? It would not be the first time! His father had spoken, unpleasantly, of his presumption, and of his callowness. Well, he was callow, and how much more could he presume than he had been doing, the past few minutes? He might leave for the rest of the summer and find, when he returned in the fall, that the shadowy monster he had created had no substance at all, had vanished with the summer flowers and the bees and the long hot afternoons that fed stupid notions. Days like the one right now, notions like all that he had been thinking.

The hand on his seemed very warm.

"I'm sorry to be so long, Jonathan." He fetched her a chair and she sat near him.

"An only child develops all sorts of resources."

Her cheeks were in fact wasted. Her skin was in fact flushed, though clearly she had put something on her face to mask it.

"Is that how you think of yourself? We were all so very much older, were we not?"

"I made an eminently suitable stuffed doll. Would it were a lifetime profession."

"I'm sorry you'll be away in New York, these next months."

"Should I stay here instead? I could minister to the children, you know. I'm an expert nursemaid."

"I dare say."

He wanted to ask her to play something; he was afraid he would never get to hear her again. But how could he ask, when she had come to sit and chat, when she looked so worn that the thought of even musical exertion was fearsome?

"I might even learn to cook."

"I'm not sure we could survive the experiment! No, you'll do better to do exactly as you started out to do. We shall languish, here, for lack of your company. But you will return to us in the fall, covered with laurels."

"Or with newsprint."

"Theodore will be a Senator. And then you will be an editor, with your own paper, and you can write strong editorials to support him."

"And he can throw government printing business to me!"

She refocused; it was as if she had been looking into eternity and then forced herself to see less far.

"Is that how it works, indeed?"

"Ah, if you only knew."

"Tell me."

She sat back in her chair. And trying not to give himself away, trying not to give her away, trying to seem as gay as he desperately wanted her to think him, instead of as stricken as he in fact felt, he told her.

T
E
N

"The love of fame is extinguished; every ardent wish for knowledge repressed; conscience put in jeopardy and the best feelings of the heart indurated by . . . mean, money-catching, abominable practices . . . . The love of money is the ruling passion of this country. It has taken root deeply, and I fear never will be eradicated. While this holds everything in its grip, America will produce few great characters. We have no patronage for genius; no reward for merit. The liberal professions are resorted to, not to acquire reputation and consequence, but to get rich."

—Daniel Webster, to his friend James Hervey Bingham
19 January 1806

The lady was not pleased. She was not precisely angry; their relationship was not sufficiently intimate to justify anger. But without any doubt, she was not pleased.

"I had thought better of you, Mr. Bingham. I will confess it."

"I should like to think myself as deserving."

Her hand on his arm was stiff, almost hard. They had been walking barely five minutes. Once the obligatory trivia had been dispensed with, the initial, small chatter of weather and friends and the like, she had turned the conversation to his plans for the remainder of the summer. And at that point he had been obliged to say that he would not be in Washington for the rest of the summer, nor in all likelihood for the autumn. He had made a joke about the differing seasons around which they each revolved, she warming herself in the rays of the social season, he in the fitful glow of the political one. She had not so much as smiled.

"I did not for a long time think of you at all. You seemed a kind of northern counterpart of that bound race which toils for us in our part of the country. Except that your slavery, Mr. Bingham, was to the sessions of the national legislature. And to the sessions of the various courts."

"A man must labor for his bread, Mrs. Davis."

"Granted. But labor and toil are not perhaps the same thing. At any rate, by processes of which I ought not to speak, I had been brought to think of you as a friend, and even—well, you have ended that."

Her Washington home—there was a larger residence in Virginia, but she lived much more, these days, in the capitol—was no more than a quarter of an hour from the political center. But it was secluded by groves of trees, and surrounded by enough land to constitute something rather like what the British call a "park." Not the sort of estate that a duke might cultivate, but sufficiently spread-out for two strolling people to ramble in. The grass was well tended and the trees, if somewhat wild, were not overly natural: the grounds were meant for just such polite, leisurely walking and talking as he had thought they would be doing. He had been invited for lunch; it was not the first time, in the past weeks and months, that he had been to Whitetowers, as the house was known. But today things had not been going either casually or well.

"It is hard, very hard, Mrs. Davis, to serve two masters."

"I take it, Mr. Bingham, that your opinion is something like that of the British poet. A woman must 'stand and wait,' the masculine sphere being necessarily paramount."

Theodore took his time before replying. The woman was immensely attractive, and in a more or less desultory way he had in fact been courting her—or being courted by her: it was sometimes not clear to him who was the active and who the passive party. Her wealth was also attractive. But he had come to understand that these things, no more than any others, would come to him free of cost. Her mind, or more accurately her will, had an intensity, and a focus, to which he was not accustomed in a woman. They sparred, from time to time, but he always felt himself at a disadvantage. How indeed did one dispense with, or even disarm, the peculiar strategic stances from which a woman could rain down arrows and shot? He knew how to combat most masculine warriors. Nor had he encountered equivalent difficulties with other women. Damn it, there *were* no women like Arabella Davis! He did not know what to do with her, he did not know what he would be likely to want to do about her, but he did know that he did not want to lose her, and he wanted her to like him. Her friendship, or something more than friendship, was already important to him.

"My opinion, Mrs. Davis, is that a man, like a woman, must do as he must, but that matters of feeling are every bit as important as matters of state."

"But men and women have different seasons?"

"Inevitably. Do we eat oysters in months containing the letter 'r'?"

"No, and we do not pick roses in February, not even in Virginia. But nature and politics are not, I think, quite the same things, or subject to the same inexorable rules."

Her voice seemed to have eased a touch. Her hand had not; it touched his arm with the same degree of stiff cordiality.

"I wish that there were indeed more flexibility. But as yet another British poet once put it, 'there is a tide in the affairs of men' . . . . I think if I were to neglect this particular opportunity, it might well never come again."

"So you prefer to neglect me?"

"I would much prefer that you not so construe it."

"Is it not plain?"

He stopped on a small rise. To his right, through the foliage, he could make out the house, and especially the two slender gazebos, one rising from each wing, which gave it its name.

"You have two fine houses, and arguably the finest carriage in Washington. You have more friends than I have enemies—and a politician has more than a sufficiency of those, as you must know, even if he smiles at everyone and does nothing that he thinks may offend. This season, and that which follows it, are the most glorious of the whole year. You can be out and about, there is no need to be confined in stuffy drawing rooms or boudoirs. How much additional company could even the loneliest of women require, at such a time?"

Her smile was small, her glance was turned down.

"You will think me indecorous, if I reply."

"Indecorous? Never."

She looked straight at him, and his knees started to waver.

"You will think me odd, and certainly different, Mr. Bingham, but I find it impossible not to be frank with you."

"Please," he murmured, not quite the master of himself that he had been.

"And I *am* different, I know that. A widow of thirty-five cannot pretend to be a blushing virgin of seventeen." She watched very closely, but he did not flinch. She was in fact thirty-nine, but too scrupulous an adherence to the truth did not seem to her useful. She knew exactly how old Theodore Bingham was, and how he was regarded both at the Bar and in Congress, and she had formulated a very accurate notion of his chances for the Senate seat. She was prepared to bet on him—and it cheered her that he did not blanch at her age. "I am a woman, not a girl. I cannot ape what I was, when I am now something different."

He wanted to respond but could not trust his tongue.

"And you will surely think me forward, Mr. Bingham," she swept on, noting carefully the pink at the end of his nose and the sudden slackness at the corner of his mouth. "But I am too disappointed, I'm afraid, to care. I had counted on all the things you mention, I had very much looked forward to just those pleasures. But I had anticipated them as things to be shared, not savored entirely by myself."

It was necessary to speak. Silence was about to become unmanly. But words had become both dangerous and difficult.

"I would sever myself in two, if I could, in order to have whatever small part in that process of savoring might be open to me."

"Small part? Surely you do not so mistake me, Mr. Bingham. I may not be ladylike, but I like to think I am still articulate. I had hoped that your part would be a very substantial one—if you so desired it to be."

"Desire" was a risky verb, but she held it neatly to her bowstring, and the arrow went home.

"My dear Mrs. Davis," he began, feeling invisible hands at his shoulders, steering him forward, "I am not insensible of your situation, and I am not at all insensible of your person, and—I dearly wish I did not have to so utterly devote myself to what may well be no longer the first passion in my life!"

He was perspiring and more than a little dazed.

"My dear Mr. Bingham, do I understand you correctly?"

He held out not one but both of his hands, and she lightly deposited hers in them, making of it just such a symbolic transfer as might be taken to imply a transfer of affection, a deposit of trust.

"I hope you do! I should like to know that, when I am able to return to Washington, successful or not in what I am attempting, I will be able to have you to return to."

"I shall be here."

"But for me?"

She watched him, made a final appraisal, and on the whole approved. He would need some amending, but that would be distinctly possible; he was not too far gone along wrong roads.

"How would you have me?"

"For myself," he said a bit thickly. "At my side for the rest of my days."

"Is that a formal putting of the question, Mr. Bingham?"

He did bend forward, and she did not turn away, and for the first time in his life he kissed her lips. She kissed him back and he felt even dizzier. Releasing her hands, he grasped her by the shoulders. He was looking straight down into those lovely eyes, and from a fatally close angle.

"Will you marry me, Arabella?"

His answer was another kiss, more protracted than the first.

When they walked back to Whitetowers, their gait was considerably slower; they walked very much closer to one another, and instead of her hand resting on his arm it was firmly held in his. Except for the wedding date, their wedding was a settled matter.

He did not get to write about politics—though on occasion, when politicians were involved in less exalted activities, he did get to write about them. When Lewis Cass spoke to a group of "friends" in New York (he did not carry the state, in November), Jonathan was assigned to the hotel in which the candidate stayed. He wrote about the social goings on in the hotel lobbies, and the conversation on the stairwells, and relayed several raggle-taggle jokes current in back rooms. His job, of course, was to make Cass look, in the words of a Van Burenite song, like "a Cass without the C." Mr. Greeley had set the tone, declaring that "the country does not deserve a visitation of that pot-bellied, mutton-headed cucumber Cass!" The *Tribune* did not always speak with one voice, nor did Mr. Greeley so tightly control things that his ipse dixit necessarily required others to take the same view. There had been several interesting occasions, indeed, when his colleagues wrote replies to a Greeley essay, and published them on successive days. But on Mr. Cass there was total agreement.

Van Buren, of course, appeared in the pages of the *Tribune* as a Barnburner, and the retiring President, Mr. Polk, as a Hunker. Mr. Greeley also delighted in, and reprinted, young Congressman Abraham Lincoln's drawling explanation of Cass' 1812 War record: "He *in*vaded Canada without resistance, and he *out*vaded it without pursuit." Daniel Webster and many others might feel deeply that Zachary Taylor was "a swearing, fighting frontier colonel," and not much more—but all the same they knew, as Greeley did, that he was more, and, no matter how reluctantly, they campaigned for him. Cass was a "dough-face"—that is, a fraud, and specifically a northern fraud, because as a Senator he had not voted for the Wilmot Proviso and thus against slavery. A "frontier colonel," even one who hailed from Kentucky, would do better than that.

Mostly, Jonathan wrote about matters considerably less inspiring than campaigns and campaigners. He wrote, in truth, about anything and everything; sometimes he gathered material for others who wrote; on a few occasions, especially at the start of his summer tour of duty, he was used as a kind of glorified messenger boy. He did not mind, and he certainly did not object. It was all grist for the mill.

"Are you really a newspaperman, Cousin Jonathan?"

They were at dinner, at his Uncle Karl's, where of course he continued to reside.

"Maybe somewhere between a newspaperman and a newspaper-boy. It's a little like being on a seesaw with someone who's tons heavier. Maybe you can get them up in the air once, but can you do it again? and again? And what happens if you're stuck way up there, and you can't get down?"

"Is that indeed how it feels, Jonathan?" asked his aunt.

"I'm afraid it is. Oh, I know this is America, and if you give an American boy a jackknife, he'll carve his way around the world. To be sure. But what would not be surprising to my brother seems, still, very surprising to me. I wonder why Mr. Horace Greeley bothers to even talk to me. But he does. Or at least he has!"

"Does he talk to your brother?" asked Karl.

"I dare say he does, when the opportunity presents itself. Theodore is after all an established politician—and Mr. Greeley has a hankering, I think, to try his hand at running the country more directly than from the columns of a newspaper."

"Do they say anything about Theodore's run for the Senate?"

"Not a lot—at least, not directly. They're on the same side, so the *Tribune*'s people comment on Theodore's speeches. They even quote him."

"That will do him no harm."

"I suspect it will not. Bayard Taylor—for whom I have done quite a lot of leg-work—says that an author would rather be noticed badly than not noticed at all. I suppose the same applies to a politician."

Karl carefully dried his lips on a napkin.

"I think it does. But I wish it did not. I wonder if your brother will turn out as different from the others as your uncle and I have hoped?"

"He, and my sister, too, were almost more parents to me than they were sister and brother. Do you know, Uncle Karl, we have not yet talked politics, Theodore and I—though we have of late talked rather more as equals than ever before."

"Perhaps he has been sparing you, Jonathan."

Karl went off to his writing desk. Jonathan, his aunt, and several of the younger Andrée children remained at table.

"You do smile more, these days, Jonathan," his aunt declared.

"I hear more things that are only fit for laughter."

She offered him a plate of biscuits. He declined.

"I'm told, however," she said quietly, "that you sometimes seem to have been born in the top drawer of a city editor's desk."

"I could guess the origin of that remark, Aunt, if I wanted to! It bears an unmistakable flavor."

"And you do like the work."

"Immensely."

"Will you give it up, in the fall?"

He took a deep breath.

"I shall try."

"Think about it carefully, Jonathan. And if you decide to abandon Columbia, even for the time being—"

"I'd never be able to go back, if I ever permitted myself to escape!"

"Then think very carefully indeed. You will have to deal with your father."

"And my uncles?"

"Your uncles, young man, are not and have never pretended to be scholars. I believe my brother Peter has kept up his Latin. I do not think your Uncle Karl could construe a page of Caesar if his life depended on it."

"Do you read Latin, Aunt?"

She smiled at his discomfiture.

"Never you mind what I do and what I don't. I wanted to tell you that your uncles have no objections to a young man following his nose, especially if he's paid for doing it."

"But *do* you read Latin?"

She pushed back from the table.

"*Abyssus abyssum invocat*," she murmured ("The deep calls to the deep"), and left him trying not to gape. Lord: perhaps the most important thing he had been learning, since coming to New York less than a year earlier, was that you could not tell very much about people, really about them, until you began to know them well. The old maxim about books and covers was simple and literal truth. Aunt Sophia (an oddly pregnant name, that!) had just quoted Psalm 41 to him, David's remark about the abyss calling out to the abyss. More: she had dexterously combined sound religion and sound scholarship, and by wryly involving a condemnatory phrase, while acknowledging her own learning, she had made a keen observation about the place of book-learning in a modern woman's existence, namely, that it had no place. Samuel Johnson had said, of a female preacher, that it did not matter how she preached: the wonder was that she could preach at all! How things had changed, how obtuse old Johnson now seemed, less than a hundred years in his grave. How different would it be in 1948, a hundred years still farther on? And what *would* he do in the fall?

"Would you play a game of draughts with me?" one of his cousins asked.

He smiled: it was settled, for now, what he was supposed to be doing.

"Of course."

And then he was beaten, three games out of five. It was a useful touch: the would-be great writer was glad to have his balloon thus punctured, to have his feet dropped back onto solid ground. You never could tell what would happen, once you climbed up onto that see-saw: he had to keep such facts sharply in mind.

And for now he had to go to bed. Mr. Greeley liked to see his employees at work when he arrived—and he arrived precious early. It was said, and for all Jonathan knew it was true, that Greeley rarely bothered to go home at night, that he slept where he was and wrote where he found himself—and, in short, took nothing seriously, including his family, that did not absolutely require to be taken seriously.

Jonathan did not know if he wanted to be exactly like Mr. Greeley.

He did know that he wanted to stay in Mr. Greeley's world for as long as he could. How long that was to be—well, who could tell?

He fell asleep without difficulty, rose early, and in fact beat Mr. Greeley to the *Tribune* office by a good quarter of an hour. The day was off to a good start.

"It does not seem to affect my playing, at least."

He smiled and did not say anything.

"Except my stamina," she added.

She was at the keyboard, though not at the moment playing. He was as he so often had been, in all their time together, seated close by, silent, attentive. It was early evening, the children were asleep, the house was quiet. They did not have frequent visitors, now. Even her father appeared less often, and stayed for shorter period; he had several times taken the children, and their nurse, to stay at the Grandvoort house. They had taken to calling it that once again, since Mrs. Bingham's death.

"I'm already tired of being ill, Martial."

"I know."

"I'd like to die. I'd like to have it over with."

He started out of his chair, but she waved him back.

"No. I don't want to be comforted. I want to be healthy—or nothing."

"It isn't that simple."

She snatched a vase from a side table and threw it to the ground. It was a feeble motion, and the vase hit on a rug and did not smash.

"I'm going to lie out in the snow, this winter!" she exclaimed, her voice very shrill and high. "I'm going to take off all my clothes and lie out in the snow until I freeze to death!" She began to sob and Martial rose and went to her. She allowed him to hold her in his arms. "I can't go on, Martial. I can't. I can't."

"You must," he said softly, and she did not argue, did not reply, only went on sobbing.

"You are of course hoping that, in the fall, the legislature will make you our newest Senator."

Theodore had just finished an afternoon of campaigning—but campaigning seemed to run from sun to sun and did not stop even them. It seemed never to stop.

"It will be a Whig legislature."

"Spoken like a politician."

"I think I will have certain claims upon the members of that legislature." Theodore would have preferred to be standing up at the bar, where things were a good deal more public—and less intense. But he had been led to this distinctly secluded table, and there were only the two of them, and the subjects raised were as he had feared both intense and difficult. Nor was there any possibility of avoidance. "Claims, I might perhaps note, both public and private."

"But party claims, in either case."

Theodore cleared his throat. It would not do to remain passive, not with this man.

"No, Mr. Greeley. I am a New Yorker and an American, and not necessarily in that order, long before I am a Whig."

"I am glad to hear it."

"And I think I have amply demonstrated my loyalties and my concerns, as well as whatever abilities I may possess, in my several years in the Congress."

"I think you have been a good Congressman, Mr. Bingham."

"I think I would also be a good Senator."

Mr. Greeley's smile, if not exactly condescending, was somehow irritating.

"It is a somewhat different office. And you are rather a young man, Mr. Bingham. The Senate has tended to be a chamber of older, perhaps even of wiser heads than the House."

"The one, Mr. Greeley, does not require the other."

"True. But I rather think the Founders expected that age, which comes before wisdom in most cases, would be a helpful guarantee. It is not accidental, don't you think, that the age limitation is set distinctly higher for the Senate than for the House? And that popular election is prescribed for the lower chamber, but not for the upper?"

"Mr. Greeley, you are surely aware that I am past the age limit set by the Constitution?"

"I am. And are you aware, Mr. Bingham, that you would, if elected, be far and away the youngest member of that chamber?"

"Is there do you think some defect hidden in that fact?"

"Spoken, now, like a lawyer." Greeley leaned forward. "I happen to be neither a lawyer nor a politician, Mr. Bingham. Believe me, it is not mistrust of you which leads me to speak to you as I am doing. Nor am I disappointed with the representation you have given to this city, these past three or four years."

"Six."

"Six, then. We not only hear good things of you, at the *Tribune*, but we print them."

"I am grateful."

"We would not print good things of you, if you did not deserve them. But the Senate is a vitally important body, not only for New York but for the entire nation. We are entering on a singularly difficult period in our national existence, I am afraid. We will need the ripest, soundest judgment possible, in our primary leaders. You have spoken of General Taylor in remarkably high terms."

"Which, on the whole, I think he deserves."

"On the whole," he repeated. "Well. Certainly, in comparison to his mutton-headed opponent, yes, he deserves all our praise. Not, I may add, because he is or is not a Whig. I do not myself think Mr. Taylor is much of anything, along those lines. He is a strong horse, but an unshod one. I have seen, bye the bye, a letter from Mr. Webster, taking us all down a peg on this subject. His advocates, he says of General Taylor, tend to think him 'a miracle of a man, knowing everything, without having had the opportunity of learning it.' Mr. Webster speaks well, here, it seems to me."

"Mr. Webster always speaks well. He is a most eloquent man."

"To be sure. But perhaps too much of a party man, don't you think?" Mr. Greeley waited and got no response. "I am not myself a party man at all, Mr. Bingham. I would as soon vote for a hunker or a barnburner, if I thought right was on their side."

Theodore laughed, but wished he could escape. Greeley was after something, and it began to seem likely what that something was.

"Is that possible, now!"

"Possible, yes. Probable, no. But that is beside the point. Mr. Bingham, I think you, too, are perhaps too much of a party man, at least for the Senate, at least in these times."

"No one dictates my votes, Mr. Greeley."

"I did not say that." Mr. Greeley's arms and hands began to wave and swing as he spoke; his high voice grew higher and squeaked at intervals. "Pray, do not mistake me. I do not mean to even suggest that you are a venal man, Mr. Bingham. Not a bit of it. What concerns me, rather, is the perspective you will bring to the Senate, if you come there. Or, to speak a bit more plainly, the perspective you will *not* bring there."

"Are you planning to oppose my election, Mr. Greeley?"

"I do oppose it. Though not you: I do not oppose you, Mr. Bingham."

"I was referring to the columns of your excellent and influential newspaper, Mr. Greeley."

"I am one among many, at the *Tribune*. It is not an autocratic paper, you know."

"So I have heard, yes."

"Ah, your brother. I sometimes forget that Jonathan is in fact your brother. He is so very much younger."

"And not at all a party man—as yet."

"Yes," Greeley replied vaguely. "Do not think, Mr. Bingham, that I am seeking to force you from the field. Or that I have sought to create some sort of conspiracy against your candidacy. No, I am speaking to you as a private citizen, but a deeply concerned one."

"You've not spoken, I take it, to Mr. Weed."

"Ah, Mr. Weed."

Theodore took a long breath, then paused and wiped his forehead. He was tired. It had been a long day, and there were many more even longer days still to come. The election was two months off.

"Perhaps you *ought* to speak to Mr. Weed."

Greeley looked over Theodore's shoulder, almost as if there was someone standing just behind him.

"I thought it would be better, all in all, to speak directly to you. I am not interested, you see, in dividing up the spoils. I am not interested in spoils, in point of fact. I am interested only in protecting our nation. You seem to me a man who may well be fit for the Senate, in due time. I think you have mistaken your time, that you have put yourself forward a bit early, perhaps even a bit rashly. I wonder, that is, if you will find the Senate even congenial, a proper place for your talents and abilities? Have you considered such questions, Mr. Bingham?"

"Could I have entered my name without considering them?'

"You have earned your forensic reputation, I see. But what of that haunted and lonely damsel, the spirit of truth, the spirit of relentless inquiry, the spirit of fearless seeking out and speaking out?"

"Are we discussing the Senate, Mr. Greeley, or the editor's desk at the *Tribune*?"

Greeley was not put off.

"Don't you think, if it comes to it, Mr. Bingham, that indeed someone who qualifies to sit at that desk should also sit in the Senate? 'Should,' please understand, in the sense of fitness, rather than in the sense of obligation, and surely not in any party sense."

"I am not opposed to parties."

Greeley sipped at the water glass from which, a bit ostentatiously, he was drinking nothing stronger than water.

"Nor am I. They are undoubtedly useful institutions. But it is men who have principles, not parties."

"But a man must win, for his principles to be effective."

"Effective, perhaps—but meaningful?"

Theodore threw up his hands.

"I take it you are not interested in winning elections, Mr. Greeley?"

"On the contrary, I am very much interested in winning them. But I am still more interested in the principles for which one contests an election. The office is a great deal, I am not such a fool as to deny that. But the man is more, and the things for which the man stands—ah, that is the highest of all, to my mind."

Theodore rose.

"I will think of what you have said, Mr. Greeley. I cannot promise you more than that."

Greeley stood up, too. They shook hands.

"That is exactly what I hoped you would say, Mr. Bingham. It does you credit. You have listened, and you will think: no one could possibly ask more of you."

All the same, Theodore said to himself, a good deal more was being asked, and Mr. Greeley's face had looked much less happy than his words expressed. This had not been intended as a high-toned discussion of general principles. Greeley had action in mind, and swift action at that. What might he now do, if Theodore's answer, when it came, was not satisfactory to him? Or if the answer was too long delayed? Or if it never did come?

Mr. Greeley might not have spoken to Thurlow Weed—Theodore could not be sure whether that was or was not the case—but it was time for Weed to be spoken to.

ELEVEN

The house had burned; in fact, several houses had burned. But houses burned all the time, in New York as in Poughkeepsie, though rather more often in New York, where the buildings were so much more closely crowded together, and where also they were so much more rapidly, and shoddily, constructed. These things were inevitable. They were still, for all that, news. Not sensational news, not the stuff of which front pages were constructed, but still news. The trick, accordingly, was to write up the fire—and in not more than say three neatly turned paragraphs—in ways that would convey the news but would equally well create it. How much new was there left, after all, in the mere destruction of a few ramshackle buildings, in a not overly affluent part of town?

"Flames roared . . ."

No: flames always roared, in the pages of other newspapers. The *Tribune*'s readers wanted, and expected, and had a right to expect, something more from its reporting. What was the something more, in this particular instance, which would give readers—and his superiors at the paper, who would set to re-writing his story if it did not instantly prove itself on the correct tack—that slant, that bait, that target . . . He ran all the slogans through his mind, sifting for the one that might help. He consulted his notes.

"The two-story dwelling at Seventeen Water Street was gone in a matter of minutes."

That was better. He could get that lead past the editors, if what followed had the right ring. He spread out several sheets and studied them. Was there anyone in the buildings? Apparently not. A pity: human escapes, just as well as human tragedies, made excellent dramatic material. And the *Tribune* required drama. All newspapers required it. Readers ate it up, and came back for more if they found enough. Where then was the drama, here? The ownership? That seemed to be in dispute. The age of the buildings, then, or something about their location, or—he fumbled, considered, rejected. Damn.

"Will you be eating, young fellow? Or do you propose to become a journalistic anchorite?"

"Bayard, how do you make a hum-drum fire dramatic?"

The papers were taken from his hand and sifted into a neat pile.

"You don't. You eat a good lunch, and drink an extra glass or two, and hope that before you come back there'll be no room for the silly story. Or even that someone will have set fire to your notes. Hum-drumly, of course."

Jonathan pulled on his coat and hat and they left the building.

"I'll be going abroad again, shortly, youngster, and I wanted to say farewell."

"Am I leaving, too?"

"I beg your pardon?"

"I mean, won't I be here when you return?"

"Will you? Besides, who knows when or even if I will return? It has been the dream of my existence, you know, to find a princess in Turkey, or a queen in Ethiopia, or even a lowly countess in England or France, who will recognize both my great genius and my immense personal charms, and sweep me into her castle, there to feed, clothe, and otherwise entertain me, while I pour out immortal verses for the delectation of the entire civilized universe. You laugh. Do you think I jest? Come with me, youngster, and as the pen falls from my hands, in the depths of Siberian snow, you can be there to pick it up and return to tell of my fatal end. But not hum-drumly. Please: not that."

"Bayard, so help me, I would rather learn how to make a hum-drum fire dramatic. I'm not ready for Europe."

He was led swiftly around a corner.

"A new eating-house, and I suspect an even worse one. I am hunting for the archetypical awful table: we may find it today. And in any case, Jonathan, perhaps Europe is not ready for *you*. Your arrival might shake it ancient foundations, might even—but here we are."

The cloth was only faintly dirty, the food bad but not startlingly so.

"But the beer they have piped in for us is cold. That is something. I do not expect even that much, youngster, where I am going."

"I will keep watching. If I find that archetypical restaurant . . ."

"Don't tell me. The frustration will be too awful, at whatever distance I am. Besides, you know, you need to have tasted proper food to know what truly awful food is."

Bayard hunched over, suddenly. The newest patron of the eating house had not seen him; the danger passed.

"That's Newton, of the *Star.* I think he intends to challenge me to a duel. But just before I'm to sail? Was ever anything less gentlemanly? We on the *Tribune* would never stoop so low, I'm sure of that."

Jonathan picked at his food.

"You're terribly serious these days, youngster. I've noticed a sharp drop in laughs per square inch. You were hired to be amusing, didn't you know that? We thought you'd have them rolling in the aisles—or in the columns, at least. You've been altogether too solemn."

"My sister's dying. I'm not supposed to know. No one is supposed to know, and I think almost no one does."

"I'm sorry. She's older than you?"

"Isn't everyone? Yes, eleven years. She's married. To a doctor, as it happens."

"Children?"

"Four."

"Lord. How do you know? Did your brother-in-law tell you?"

"No one's told me. I can see it very plainly, in her looks, in her husband's behavior, in my father's behavior. It may even have been what killed my mother. She'd lost three children, earlier on. I think she guessed."

"Do I remember correctly, or did you once say your sister was a pianist, a very good pianist?"

"Indeed. Had she not been a woman, I think she might well have been internationally known. She really is that good. Or has been: I'm not sure she can still play. She's lost a great deal of weight, her bones seem to stick right out of her."

"Sad."

"Very. But I didn't mean to burden you with all this. These things do happen, even in the best regulated of families—and mine is not one of those." He wrinkled his nose. "We have a rather strange family, it sometimes seems to me."

"It's not something you can keep to yourself forever, youngster."

"Patently."

"I should perhaps tell Horace."

"Please don't. For one thing, he knows the relatives I live with, here in New York. And what good would it do, after all? I dare say I'm better off, you know, being taken for an idly happy young fellow. It probably does make me smile more, really it does."

"May I ask one question?"

"Please."

"If you're as close to your sister as I take it you are, if she's as important to you as plainly she is, shouldn't you start now to think about—well, how it will be, in the end?" He smacked one hand into the other. "That's not very tactfully put: forgive me. I'm trying to say the unsayable, I suppose. What I mean—Lord, do I mean anything at all? Tell me you understand, please!"

"You're a poet, Bayard. No one's supposed to understand you. You're supposed to charm flowers and hypnotize snakes."

"Nasty, nasty. For that, youngster, you should be condemned to read a hundred pages of Joel Barlow every night. And then on to Freneau. Not Bryant: he's too good for you. You deserve only—"

"I do understand, Bayard. I appreciate your trying to help. It's not that I'm beyond help, really—but what can I do, in fact, now or later on? I have to hold my tongue: that's perfectly clear. And I have to watch her wasting away, and Martial—that's her husband—dying a thousand deaths, and my old father . . . well, he seems worse than in many years. It's terribly hard on him, I know that. He's not a patient man—no, that's unfair. He's not—oh, I don't know what he is and what he's not. But I do know it's hard on him. Very, very hard. And I can't comfort him. Even if I tried, he wouldn't let me. It's just not his way."

"Bad. Are you sure you don't want to come with me? I'll get to England, and France, and maybe to Egypt. Have you an itch to climb the Pyramids? To take a ride on the Sphinx?"

"I thought poets were supposed to have their heads in the clouds. You're being most unpoetically kind, Bayard. But I really can't go. Maybe your second or third trip from now? I could help tidy up your rhymes, perhaps, or invent some suitable similes."

"Milton didn't like rhyme either," Taylor noted.

"*I* like it."

Taylor leaned forward suddenly, but this time it was an idea and not a hostile colleague that impelled him.

"And what's this about your brother?"

"Theodore? Nothing special, really. He proposes to ascend to the Senate, and what Theodore proposes, Theodore usually succeeds in doing."

Taylor pursed his lips.

"Do you know, Horace has suddenly realized that seat will be vacant?"

Jonathan gasped.

"Are you serious?"

"Perfectly."

"And is Mr. Greeley . . . ?"

Taylor shrugged.

"Horace is always serious, you know that. But he flits from one thing to the next. He's a marvelous fellow, I love him dearly. But I can't imagine him in the august Senate of these United States. Horace? Rising to contend with Daniel Webster, or with Calhoun, or with Henry Clay? Can you imagine it?" He snickered. "Pray, don't think me disloyal—but have you ever heard Horace lecture?"

"He lectures me all the time."

"Formally, I mean. No? Well, he's earnest, and he's well informed—the man's mind is a bear-trap of facts and notions—but he can no more debate with the likes of Webster than I can flap my arms and fly. No, he'd not do well, and I don't think anyone other than himself thinks he would." He nodded. "But he might make a bit of trouble for your brother, you know. Unless he's diverted. You never know when Horace is going to be diverted. He might receive a pamphlet in the mail tomorrow morning, advocating a new system for feeding horses on air, or for Christianizing the captive Mexicans by a process of inoculation. Or for improving the lot of factory workers. Or for giving women the vote. You never know, with Horace. That's what makes him a dangerous political influence, to be sure."

"I can't imagine his being dangerous to Theodore." Jonathan reflected. "I can't imagine anyone being dangerous to Theodore, when there's something he's decided to do."

"Is your brother so fearsome?"

"Fearsome? Oh no, I don't think he's fearsome at all. He's well organized, and he's very sharp, and he knows what he wants. I'd not like to be someone in his way. Do you remember Michael Cleary?"

Taylor thought a moment. "He was in Congress . . . ?"

Jonathan grinned.

"He was indeed, until Theodore put him out of Congress."

"Ah."

"I don't think Mr. Greeley will get too far."

"You may be right, youngster. But don't underestimate Horace, either. And look at all the clever men he has working with him! How would you, now, like to be told to lampoon Congressman Bingham in our sacred pages?"

It was a droll notion, but Horace Greeley was not the man to create such a situation for his young staff member: they both knew it with absolute certainty. Mr. Greeley was far too decent to be a politician.

It occurred to Jonathan, as they walked back to the *Tribune* offices: what did that realization also tell him about his brother? He smiled to himself. Not much: one man's meat, and all that. Theodore was not ruthless, not any more than Horace Greeley. Greeley was a successful editor. Theodore was a successful politician. What did the taste of apples tell you about pears?

"Do you know what you get," he asked Taylor as they turned in at the front door of the *Tribune*, "if you mix apples and pears?"

"Fruit salad, of course."

They went in laughing.

"Our nephew is too much occupied, Husband."

"Ah?"

Sophia stared down at her sewing, Karl sat with a decanter in front of him and a stogie moving slowly, even dreamily from hand to mouth and then back again. He puffed much more than he drank.

"Does he seem contented to you, as a lad of eighteen should?"

"Yes. A good lad. And almost nineteen."

Sophia laid her sewing aside.

"I could wish he were more carefree."

"I can't imagine why, Wife. What earthly good would it do him? He has a solid head on his shoulders, more Andrée than Bingham, if you ask me. Indeed, he could make a place for himself, in the business, if he chose to. And perhaps he may yet. I'd welcome him. So would Peter. But don't tell the lad I said so!"

"You know me better than that."

"The biggest problem young Jonathan has, it seems to me," he said ruminatively, "is Frederick. How does a young fellow come into his own, with a father like that? Did you know that Frederick has gone off the deep end?"

Sophia was too startled to reply.

"It's a fact. He's written me some of the ding-darndest stuff you've ever seen. Got religion, he says." He shook his head somberly. "Poor Marie. She's well out of it."

"May her soul rest in peace."

"It was never very peaceful while she lived."

"How good that you were able to help her, Husband!"

"What would our Doctor Frederick have done if I hadn't, eh? But I must say, the children have come along well. Theodore's fortunes are looking up, Jonathan has turned out to be a bright lad, and Anne-Marie is well married. I'd rather have Martial Johnson at my bedside than Frederick Bingham."

"Four strong children, and she's kept them all."

"God be praised. Her mother couldn't do as well."

They sat quietly for a moment.

"All the same, Husband, I'm worried about Jonathan."

"It'll do him no good, and you no good, and me no good."

"He ought to be more settled than he is. He'll be wanting to marry, some day. He'll be wanting a family. And how in the world is he going to manage it all? Not with his father's help."

"Or mine. We have children of our own. More than enough of them!"

"He's thinking too much. He's too much *inside* himself."

"Because of his mother's death?"

"Marie was your sister, Husband, but I must say the lad was never really close to her. She was a difficult woman."

"She was a difficult girl!"

Sophia picked up her sewing, examined it with a distant, unfocussed eye, then sat it down again.

"All the same, I wish he were settled! Or at least that he would kick up his heels and run a bit."

Karl offered her wine, and she shook her head. He poured a bit more for himself.

"Perhaps we'd better get to bed."

"Is there anything we can do for him?"

"Seems to me we've done more than our share already. Maybe, Wife, you're chasing a spider up a drain. Maybe young Jonathan isn't the sort to settle down. There are men like that, you know. Or maybe he'll settle down, bang, all of a sudden, when he meets the right girl. I'm surprised he hasn't shipped out to California, digging after all that gold."

"He's better off here."

"Then shall we stop worrying about him? Come: let's go to bed. The morning comes very early, these days, and I've a lot to do. Jonathan is a great deal younger than I am, and he's going to have to take care of himself. He will, too. He'll be all right."

She rose and followed. Would it do any good to speak to brother Peter? No, her husband was, as usual, realistic. How much could you do for another human soul? How much could you make bright, how much could you keep dark? She sighed and they went to bed.

"Old Horace is getting the itch, eh?"

"Palpably."

Mr. Weed hefted his belly and laughed.

"Well, then, let's scratch it for him?"

Theodore squinted at him.

"I beg your pardon?"

"Bingham, you're too good a politician not to see what I mean! Think, man. Here's a famous newspaper editor, with a powerful journal at his fingertips. Can we afford to antagonize him, especially just before an election as important as this one? Clearly, we cannot, and we must not, and so we will not. He wants to play at politician. Well, you know he's not fit for it, and I know he's not fit for it, but he don't know it— and neither do the people who might vote him into office. So we let him in—but just in the door and out."

"Ah," he said slowly. "If I were to resign now . . . ."

"You've got it!"

"He'd have no more than ninety days or so."

"How much does he need? You know enough of old Horace to know how light-footed he is. He's a Whig this time around. Maybe he'll be a teetotaler the next. He likes Van Buren, damn him, so maybe he'll be a Free Soiler. Horace does lean that way. But it don't matter: next time is next time, and this time is right now, when it counts. You can keep the future, Bingham. Just give me right now." He pointed at Theodore and wagged his finger enticingly. "Just think how we can dress it up, so it'll go down smooth. He talked to you, and you took his wise words to heart, and decided to give up your seat the next minute. And since he was so concerned, and so obviously fitter than you," Weed chuckled at his own cleverness, "why, you went to Boss Weed and you dropped Horace's name into the hat. Maybe we could tell him we went down on our knees . . . no, he's too smart to believe *that*."

"And what will he do after the legislature meets?"

"What *can* he do? Besides, he'll be in Washington when it meets, he'll barely know what his own name is, by then. He won't be paying any attention to you, Bingham. He'll be deep into serious national matters.

Don't worry: he'll find some. He's a ferret, old Horace. He'll be making noise, and making headlines—and is there anything he likes better? I wouldn't know what it is, and I've known him, and worked with him, a long time. He'll be so grateful to you, Bingham, for making it all possible, for letting him into the true seats of power—mark you, that's how he's going to describe it—that he'd lend you the money to buy the seat, if you asked. Not that he's hard to touch for money: do you happen to have an idea how much that man gives away, just pours into other people's pockets? Well, never mind. That's how Horace is, and there's no changing him now." Weed thumped on the desk. "Besides, who's interested in changing anything? We've got the election, we've got the presidency, we've got everything."

Theodore could not disagree. It was a marvelous stratagem. Nor did it hurt Greeley: all it did was sidetrack him, and in one of the nicest ways possible, letting him sit in Congress for a bit and be the Honorable Horace Greeley, member of the House of Representatives. It was all true.

And then, in late November, when the legislature met . . . what? Would he be assured of his own election? Would Weed lead *him* on, too? Thurlow Weed would lead anyone on, his own mother included. What guarantee did he have? None, none at all. If he stayed in the House, he would at least have that seat, safe and sound as he had had it now for half a dozen years. But if he stayed in the House, now, he would alienate both Horace Greeley and Thurlow Weed. Nothing ventured, nothing gained. In for a penny, in for a pound.

"I'll have more time for the campaign, too," he murmured.

"Precisely!" Weed chuckled with delight. "Oh, it's a beautiful little scheme, I love it when things are so neat, Bingham!"

"All's well that ends well," Theodore said quietly. "What date should I put on my letter of resignation, do you suppose?"

Weed was all business.

"Let's see now. What we need to consider . . . ."

"I thought you were newspapering, Nephew?"

"I am, Uncle. For all I'm worth."

Peter was not often found indoors. Jonathan had reached the counting-house just before a heavy rain, a late summer shower of drenching proportions, and found the outside hands battening down as if for a storm at sea. He had stood in front of Andrée Bros. for a moment, seen that neither of his uncles was visible, then stepped inside. And just inside the door, sitting on one bale and leaning against two others, had been Peter, his slicker laid out beside him, his arms crossed, his face calm. The light was poor in the front room, where wares were displayed: why waste good light on non-existent viewers of merchandise? When the customers came, so, too, would the lights.

"Just as I'm stevedoring for all I'm worth, eh?" He patted a bale. "Pull up some rags and sit down, Nephew."

The bales were heavy but Jonathan did not complain. There were no chairs in this outer chamber: did anyone need to recline as they examined the wares displayed for their greater enlightenment?

"It's almost the first time I've seen you sitting, Uncle Peter. At least, here on South Street."

"Work when you can work, I always say." Peter nodded toward the quay, out beyond the closed front door. "Any fool could see that was a nor'wester, and there wasn't going to be no work done for a spell. Even a ship sails herself, sometimes. You just batten down and reef up and let her go. It's a slow day, anyway; been a slow week. Happens. Why run for the sake of running?"

"You'd never be a politician, Uncle!"

"What're *you* going to be, Nephew?"

He was not surprised at the blunt question. But he was stimulated into a reply he hadn't premeditated.

"No scholar, I can tell you that much. If what's practiced at Columbia is scholarship, I'm not interested. I'm not going back, Uncle. I just can't."

"Have you told your father?"

"No, not yet. How could I? I just made my mind up half a minute ago, when you asked me that question!"

"I saw it coming. We all did. Karl says it's the Andrée in you working its way out."

"Indeed." Jonathan found himself grinning broadly. Was it so lighthearted a matter, after all? "Is it the Bingham in him that's propelling Theodore into the Senate?"

"Got some pretty high mucky-mucks on your Bingham side, don't you? Leastways, your father always said you did. Supposed to be a duke or an earl mixed in there, somewhere along the line."

"I never took any of that seriously, Uncle."

"Your father did. And maybe Theodore's the proof of it."

"Maybe I misremember my history, Uncle, but I've the distinct impression that dukes and earls are never elected. Not in England, anyway."

Peter smiled the quiet, half-furtive smile that, for him, passed for a huge grin.

"You going to Greeleyize us?"

"You mean, Uncle, am I going to stay in the newspaper business? I think the answer is yes, if that's the question."

"It isn't, though I'm pleased to hear it. I suspect you'll do well, Nephew. No, I was asking about your visit today, right now." He motioned with his chin at the bales and barrels around them. "Are you here to romanticize us, to make us interesting to the readers of the *Tribune*? If you are, let me tell you right now you're wasting your time. It can't be done. They're either interested already or they don't give two hoots and a holler. You watch people picking up a newspaper, now, any paper, not just yours and Mr. Greeley's. They go right for what they think is important, and they ignore everything else. The merchants look at the commodity notices. The politicians want to see who has been saying what about them. The lawyers want to see who's died and not left a will. The ladies want to see what's for sale at the fanciest prices. Nobody reads it all."

"Nobody could! We do half a million things at a time. I guess that's the difference between writing for a newspaper and writing for yourself. There's no time, when you're writing for a paper, and there's no room, and you never know if they're going to print it anyway. So we all just muddle along, Mr. Greeley included."

"Is that what you're doing, then? Muddling?"

Jonathan wanted to hug his uncle and knew it would not do.

"No. As usual, in fact, I don't know what I'm doing. It was lunchtime and I didn't much feel like eating. I bought a couple of rolls from a peddler and I munched them as I walked along—and my feet just took me here." He smiled cheerfully. "Maybe they were trying to tell me something, Uncle."

"You stop listening to your feet at my age, Jonathan. Mostly what they tell me, these days, is to sit down."

"As you never do!"

"Well, I've heard of countries where people listened to their stomachs, and maybe to other parts of their anatomies, but never to their feet. But I'm glad you wanted to ramble this way."

"I wasn't looking for anything in particular."

"Why, that might be the motto of Andrée Bros.! Don't look for anything in particular—but take anything you can get!"

"I won't put that into print."

"Oh, they'd believe it. They'll believe anything about us business-men, if they're not in trade themselves. Your own father would believe it. When will you tell him, Nephew?"

"Tonight, surely. I'll have to write to him tonight."

"You're fixed in your own mind?"

"I suspect I've been fixed for longer than I was willing to admit, even to myself. Did you know Aunt Sophia reads Latin?"

"We've read a page or two together, when there was time. We're no scholars, but there's a good sound to it. It's a tough language, it was a language for trade and war before it was a church language, you know."

"Uncle, you may be more of a scholar than my Latin tutor will ever be!"

"More's the pity, then, because I ain't no scholar. No more is your aunt. We just like it."

"I wish my tutor did. I wish—do you know, Uncle—I wish Colum-bia College had altogether more love and less learning? That may sound strange, especially from someone not quite nineteen, but I sometimes feel the whole college is nothing but a kind of mausoleum, a church of the dead!"

"Don't say that to your father."

"To be sure. I don't know what I'll say to him, to be perfectly hon-est."

"Tell him you like the *Tribune* better. Tell him how much money he'll save. Tell him you can stay on at my brother Karl's, or at my house if Karl won't have you. He will, I know that for a fact. Tell him," he went on in the same neutral tone, "that for the next ten years your crazy old Uncle Peter is giving you five hundred dollars a year."

"What?"

"I couldn't tell you before, Nephew, because I just made up my mind half a minute ago. Do you credit that?"

"No."

"Good. No, I thought of it some time ago—that night we met down here, and you were making up verses about what was happening out on our docks."

"Good Lord. Why?"

"You'll not have anything from your father. I suppose you know that?"

"I'd guessed. My father does not discuss money with me."

"That's because you haven't got any, and neither does he. But he's discussed it with me and with my brother Karl, I can tell you. But I don't mean to criticize him, Jonathan: he's a different breed from us. It seemed to me, thinking about it, that Theodore was well taken care of, and so was Anne-Marie, but that you, Nephew, well, you were a tasty pudding that hadn't had time to set. So I decided to stick in a handful of raisins, to help things along."

"I—I hadn't expected anything of the sort, Uncle."

"Do you think I didn't know that? I'm older than you, but not I trust much more foolish."

"I'm still taken aback, Uncle. I don't know how to thank you."

"Don't bother. I wouldn't be doing it if I didn't think it a useful notion. And if I couldn't afford it. I've got only the two children, as you know, and Karl has seven. He couldn't do it. If I didn't, who would?"

Jonathan wiped his forehead, which was suddenly damp.

"I had no idea anyone would."

"Use it wisely, that's all I ask of you, Nephew. You'll have enough from your newspaper work to keep yourself, I suppose?"

"Yes. I think so, at any rate."

"Have you told Mr. Greeley you'll be staying on?"

"No. I really couldn't have, Uncle. I did in fact just make up my mind, not ten minutes back."

"I should think he ought to be consulted. He might not want you."

"He'll be told this afternoon—but I think there's small danger of his not wanting me. Mr. Taylor's leaving for Europe and the Middle East, and there's no one who knows Taylor's work better than I do. I'm sure Mr. Greeley will be fair, when it comes to my stipend."

"What is it now, pray tell?"

"Five dollars a week."

"I suppose he can do better? Well, that's for you to settle. I don't mean to tell you how to conduct your affairs, Nephew."

"I wish you would. It's a subject you know a great deal better, I'm afraid, than I ever will."

"I trust that's your infernal politeness. You're sometimes a nuisance, with your polite talk. You might be a Frenchman. You speak French, I believe?"

"More or less."

"I'd rather you'd learned Dutch. Or even Spanish. There's more use to them than there is to all the polite French talk in all the books you've ever read."

Jonathan was tempted to ask what use there might be to Latin, so thoroughly dead a tongue—but decided it was better to hold *his* tongue.

"Well, all I wanted to say," Peter resumed after a bit, "was that you oughtn't to throw your money away. Save some of it, maybe, for when you need to do something substantial."

"I hope I have the opportunity."

"You will, by God! Don't be timorous, Nephew. I want you to have the help you need, so you won't have to be quaking in your boots. No Andrée I know of has ever been afraid of putting his shoulder down and shoving his way in."

Jonathan felt his strength returning. Five hundred a year?

"Believe me, Uncle, I will do my best."

"I think you always have. Nor would I invest in you—that's what I'm doing, you know: if I could invest in your brother, why not in you?—if I thought you'd waste what I've worked hard to get." He stood up, suddenly. "But not that hard. And back to work, speaking of it so closely as we are. That rain will have let up, if I calculate her right."

They opened the door. A faint drizzle was still falling, but off to the East the sun was breaking through.

"How did you know, Uncle? You couldn't have heard, from in here."

Peter tapped his head.

"It was raining in *here*, Nephew. That's how I can tell." He touched Jonathan's arm. "You write to your father, and I'll speak to my lawyer, and by tomorrow it will all be done. And a good piece of business for the both of us, to my mind. I'm pleased with us both, if you want to know."

Jonathan could only smile, and then his uncle stepped outside and was instantly at work. The door closed behind him—and when the darkness swung back with it, Jonathan realized that he was still inside, that the room was empty except for himself, and that he, too, ought to be getting back to work. He would look for a cab. No, he caught himself: frugality ought not to be abandoned. Uncle Peter would not approve, and he was right. The distance was hardly overwhelming; it could as readily be walked as it had been on the way down. New York was not yet London, or even Paris.

And even with five hundred a year, he was hardly a man of wealth.

But for ten years, at least, he would not have to worry about starving. He had not ever worried about starving, but now he never would. Or at least not for ten years. He laughed to himself and did not care that people turned to stare at him. How often does such news bolt out of heaven and strike you right between the eyes?

Would Peter have given him this annuity if he had stayed at Columbia?

No matter: he was not staying at Columbia; he had the annuity, and he felt better than in months. There were turnings and twistings in the road, all right, but they were not all bad, as he had been starting to fear. That had been silly of him, even wrong. Things were not like that. He felt distinctly good. He smiled at passersby and at shopmen, strangers all of them. And why not? It was his world just as much as it was theirs. He had started to disbelieve that, but he would never again be a disbeliever. By God, it was all right, all of it!

T
W
E
L
V
E

*"There is good angling of a morning for rock fish . . . . But I am
afraid of the sun."*

— Daniel Webster, to his friend Isaac P. Davis
26 June 1842

"My son speaks of marriage," Doctor Bingham said, holding up a letter.

"Jonathan?"

"I should hope not! I referred to Theodore."

"Of course, yes. How silly of me. I'm afraid I'm not as well focused as I ought to be, these days. I hope my patients haven't suffered.
I dread the day when my inattentiveness will damage some innocent
person, someone who deserved better of me." Martial shook his head.
"I don't need to tell you. It is hard."

Doctor Bingham glanced down at his letter.

"A Mrs. Davis, a widow. Wealthy, he says."

Martial smiled wanly.

"I don't imagine that's why Theodore is proposing to marry the
lady."

"No. He has done well for himself, as lawyer and as politician. He
says the Senate matter seems moderately likely."

"Have you seen him, of late?"

"It has been my experience that male children are considerably less
familial than females. Theodore is too well established, in both Washington and in New York, to think of Poughkeepsie as his true home.
And since his mother's death . . . ."

"Of course."

"The problem is, Martial, he knows nothing of Anne-Marie's illness." They were seated in the living room of the Grandvoort house.
Martial was completing his rounds; Doctor Bingham had asked him to
stop by for a moment. "He talks of a winter wedding—'after the election,' as he puts it. I imagine he means the Senatorial election."

"Probably, yes."

"But can we have a wedding, with Anne-Marie—dying?"

Martial smoothed the sleeve of his coat.

"Why not? I think she'd rather see her brother married than lose the opportunity. She's not the sort to begrudge others their happiness."

"You speak as if she were fully apprized of her situation."

"I'm sorry, I'd meant to speak to you of it. She guessed, some while back, and confronted me with her suspicions. I could not allay them."

"You told her."

It was distinctly accusatory.

"I had no choice. And in a way I did not tell her, she already knew. Your daughter is hardly a fool. And she did grow up in a medical household, she knows a good deal about basic symptomology."

Doctor Bingham's face was dark.

"Damnation!"

"'I'm sorry, truly I am. It couldn't be helped."

"Strictly speaking, Martial, you mean you were unable to help it."

"I don't think that was called for—but let us not quarrel." Doctor Bingham glowered and Martial felt barely able to deal with the old man's anger. He was too tired for this, he was more than tired. "We had agreed not to tell her, I know, and I still think it was the wisest course. I followed it for as long as I could. Anne-Marie made that impossible. She would not have believed me, had I attempted to deceive her."

"But you did not attempt it."

"My dear sir," said Martial carefully. "There are things between husband and wife, as surely you must know, that cannot be discussed outside the martial chamber. Not even, I'm afraid, with the parent of one of the parties. You will have to trust me, and to believe that I have done all I was able to do, and further that I have acted honorably, both as doctor and as husband. I do not see how we can proceed, otherwise."

Doctor Bingham did not speak.

"We must put this behind us," Martial went on, as warmly as he could manage. "Anne-Marie will need all the help we can each of us give her—she will need us increasingly, as you well know."

"Why couldn't you help her with a simple fiction, when the need arose?"

"Because I couldn't! That's why, and it's done, and I suggest once again that we forget what's past and done and concentrate as best we are able on the immediate future."

"I should like to forget, Doctor Johnson, that you married my daughter in the first place, and weakened her with incessant child-bearing."

Martial stood up quickly.

"Doctor Bingham, do you wish to precipitate a break between us?"

"You have already accomplished that, sir."

Martial turned away, then turned back at once. "We will do Anne-Marie no good by quarreling. Believe me, it will not help her. Nor will it help the children."

"They and we are in our Maker's hands."

Martial suppressed an exclamation.

"You are the children's grandfather, their only grandparent, now. I could not make them known to my own parents, and I do not want to cut them off from the only grandparent they have left in the world."

"I will grieve for them. And I will pray for them."

Martial stepped closer.

"If I have given any cause for offense, I am sorry, truly I am. Please extend to me the charity we are supposed to extend to all living souls, and think as tenderly as I do of your daughter." There was no response. "How would I explain to her that her father no longer wishes to see her, or her children? How can I possibly—"

"You seem to have been deft enough with explanations, on earlier occasions."

Martial bit at his tongue.

"Can I do anything to make you change your mind? Anything?"

Doctor Bingham's voice was heavy but firm.

"You have done enough already. I do not wish to prolong this conversation. You will oblige me by leaving my house."

There were a dozen imprecations in Martial's mouth, but he said nothing; he turned and strode out. The world was indeed made of sand, and it was crumbling in his hands, tumbling down like a castle built on a beach. This would kill Anne-Marie, it would torture her and shorten what little time she had left. The children would recover, but she would not. Her father surely knew that.

He stopped, on the walk just outside his father-in-law's front door, and turned back. But he did not go back in. It would do no good. Perhaps he could come another time, after the weight of this decision had had some chance to sink into the old fool's brain.

He was more than an old fool. He was half-mad. He was no longer in his right mind.

And could he tell Anne-Marie that?

What could he tell her? What? What?

New York, 3 September 1848

Dear Father,

    You will excuse me, I hope, for whatever impropriety there may be in communicating—to you of all people—important matters by the cold medium of pen and ink. The warmth of flesh and blood which lies between us is perhaps some justification, however. I would like to think too, that in our last interviews, at Poughkeepsie, you already saw much of what I have only subsequently realized. Again, do please excuse me for not returning to Poughkeepsie to convey all of this to you: my employment at the *Tribune*, unfortunately, does not permit me the leisure I would like.

    Mr. Greeley has done me the honor of offering a fulltime position with his distinguished newspaper. The offer presents a singularly attractive opportunity, and one which at my age I am most fortunate to have. You are aware that my experience with Columbia College has not been illuminating. It seems plain to me, Father, that I am not intended for any of the truly learned professions. My mother, as you are, I am sure, aware, urgently desired me to do as you had done, namely adhere to the profession of your father. But I have always been convinced I would be something less than a good physician—probably, indeed, very much less. I do not have the force of mind required for the law. Neither am I fit for the pulpit. I have no hankering for the glories of military existence, if there be any such in the modest army of our country.

    It is my feeling, accordingly, that there is no great gain to be expected from continuance at Columbia—or at any other university. And there is, I hope, something to be gained from educating myself in the world of letters, where, if anywhere, I more than likely belong. The experience I would gain from some years under Mr. Greeley's supervision, and the knowledge of his craft I would acquire, would be more valuable to me than any number of years spent studying moral philosophy or, in point of fact, the literatures of ancient Rome and Greece.

    Subject to your approval, then, I have notified Mr. Greeley that I am prepared to accept his kind offer. His suggested terms of employment have been, like the offer itself, generous. As a sometime employee I was paid five dollars a week, which is probably more than I have been worth of the *Tribune*, requiring as I have to be schooled before I could be fully useful. Mr. Greeley has offered to double that remuneration, for fulltime work. That is very good pay indeed, and will be more than sufficient to keep body and soul together, even fairly stylishly together.

    Forgive me for speaking about monetary matters. I know they have not entered into your own generous calculations: you have been kindness itself, in funding my education. But more does need to be said on this score. You will of course be spared the necessity of further expenditures on my behalf. You will also be reassured to learn that my Uncle Karl and my Aunt Sophia have indicated that, if the entire *plan meets with your approval, I may continue as a boarder in their house. I will of course remit to them some portion of my weekly stipend.*

And there is still more. When I had communicated my tentative decision to my Uncle Peter, indicating of course that it was subject to your confirmation, he infinitely surprised me with an offer of such a singular nature that it is hard to believe I heard him correctly. But I did, and I have since had a communication from his attorneys to confirm the fact. In a word, Uncle Peter has granted me a yearly annuity of five hundred dollars, for a period of ten years. There are no restrictions placed on the payment of this sum. It is not conditioned upon need and if I do not spend it in a given year, as indeed how could I, it remains mine to do with as I see fit, at any future time. I need hardly say that this totally unsolicited and immensely startling gift will make things still easier for me: whether I deserve such kindness or not, it has been visited unto me, and I am, and I have expressed myself to be, deeply and humbly grateful. Let me emphasize that, knowing to be sure of your paramount position, my uncle did not extend this offer until after I had told him I intended to seek your permission for the change in direction already outlined in this letter.

And this letter grows I am afraid overlong. I do not mean to weary you with my prolixity, Father. I will therefore close, having said all I know how to say. I hope and pray there is nothing to give you offense, here, and I hope I may hear from you before too very long, that you approve of what I have suggested. It is, may I repeat, in no way a settled affair: only your approval could make it that, and absent your approval it will not be a settled affair. I am, as I fondly hope you know, fully aware of how much I owe to you, and how carefully I need to obey your wishes in this as in other matters.

Your obedient son,
Jonathan Bingham

Poughkeepsie, 9 September 1848

My dear Jonathan,

Your letter does not of course surprise me. Neither does it please me: I had always hoped, though not of late very sanguinely, for better things of you. It is fair to say I think that you were born to better things than scribbling.

However, you have reached an age, and I have reached an age at the other end of the scale of things, where despite your protestations it is clear that I in truth have nothing decisive to say. I can continue to fund your education, if you desire to con-

tinue it. I cannot fund much of anything else, as surely you are aware. Your Uncle Peter's generosity, as you call it, is quite beyond my means. I am keenly aware of how well your uncle knows this.

I wish you, in short, to do as you plainly wish to do, namely, exactly as you please. It is neither filial nor unfilial of you: for whatever it may be worth, you seem to me, from my admittedly limited experience in these areas, to be distinctively of the younger generation of that race known as American. I find myself, though born and bred here, decreasingly American, so that the distance between myself and most of my compatriots grows each year almost palpably greater.

You have become accustomed, as your letter makes perfectly clear, to deciding for yourself what you will and will not do. I cannot in all candor say that you have reached an age, or a degree of understanding, which seem to me to merit that sense of self-regulation, but I recognize it, and as I say I also recognize it in others more or less of your generation, at least in this country. Whatever you may or may not owe me, therefore, you may consider discharged by the attempted obedience of your letter. You do not need, in the future, to refer your decisions to me for my pro forma stamp of approval, and I will indeed thank you not to so refer them. I have other and I am sorry to say more pressing matters to attend to.

I do not, finally, really see how a restless and overly juvenile character such as I take yours to be can properly find peace in any vocational decision. You have, however, made up your mind, for the time being, and I trust you will receive in due course whatever measure of satisfaction you may be capable of receiving.

We will probably continue to meet on such occasions as may attract the others of this fast-shrinking family. Do not consider it necessary to inform me of all the details of your diurnal existence. Nor shall I trouble you, as I have in the recent past, with news of

Your Father,
Frederick Bingham

"Would you be listening to me, Mr. Congressman?"

They were in a small hotel—hardly a hotel, hardly even an inn—in a town somewhere upstate, but exactly where Theodore had forgotten. There had not been a place for them, except in a tiny room outfitted with an even tinier bed that somehow seemed to stretch from wall to wall. There was no breathing space around the bed, nor was there much space left in it, with the two of them occupying it together. There had been a dinner, and two speeches—or had it been three? Theodore's tired mind could not bother with the details—and then there had been

some liquid refreshment and then they had been escorted to their resting place, where, in fact, even rest was difficult. Sleep had been totally
eluding them, fatigue notwithstanding. Sharp microscopic-sized teeth
had not been eluded, however: Theodore could not recall a bed that
itched so furiously. It was some while before he realized that it was
what was in the bed, rather than the bed itself, and by then he was too
exhausted to move, or even to care. Let the bed bugs bite: if they could
find anything much to sink their teeth into, so much the better for them.
He felt so like the board that the mattress was surely constructed from,
that he was faintly surprised they should bother with him at all. Perhaps
it was proof—he did not feel he had any other—that he was still alive.

"Mr. Congressman?"

Brady did not sound tired at all. He never did. Perhaps Brady should
run for the Senate, and Bingham should go home. Home would shortly
include Arabella, and Arabella's two lovely residences. Home would include starched sheets and a canopied bed, and all the peace and quiet
he needed, and all the isolation, all the freedom. There was nothing free
about campaigning for office, especially not on this statewide basis. He
was not formally campaigning; it was the legislature that voted and not
the legislators' constituents. But even with Thurlow Weed's blessing—
and he seemed to have that—he had too many handicaps simply to
let himself follow the usual electoral procedure, which involved a few
speeches and public meetings, and for the rest depended on friends and
prior reputation. That was the difficulty: he had too little prior reputation; he had too few friends; he was still too unripe a figure to allow
usual procedures to dominate. That was Mr. Brady's warning, and he
did as Mr. Brady told him.

"Are you awake, now, Mr. Congressman?"

"I am."

"Would you be after taking a bit of advice from the likes of me?"

Theodore sighed and rolled an inch to his left.

"Have I ever *not* taken your advice, Mr. Brady?"

"If it was me, well, frankly, I wouldn't be smiling quite so much."

Smiling? Had he been doing anything quite so ludicrous? What in
God's green earth did he have to smile about? And where would he find
the energy to so wastefully part his lips?

"Mr. Congressman?"

"I hear you, Mr. Brady."

"What you need," Brady explained, sitting bolt upright—the bed
clothes pulled sharply away from Theodore's side, and a blast of cold

air bit those parts of him from which the bugs had thus far abstained—
"what you need, you see, is consistency. Con-sis-ten-cy, Mr. Congressman. You ought to be seen, in all these heathen places, as a statesman,
you ought to be seen as larger than life, as someone gifted with—"

"The blarney stone, Brady, which obviously you have touched."

Theodore tried to cover his exposed side; this helped, but only
partially.

"Sure, and I don't mean to harass you, Mr. Congressman. You're
paying me good money to help, and I want to earn my daily bread."

Let him eat cake, Theodore said soundlessly, motionlessly.

"The average man, now, he don't know nothing about politics, nor
about Congress, neither. But this is a democracy, it is, and he has to feel
that you know everything there is to know, and at the same time—at the
same time, mind you—that he's as good as you, every bit of it."

Theodore managed to sneak barely enough covering over him to
keep off the cold. A delicious warmth rolled up and over him.

"People think that's an easy task. You and I, we know better than
that, Mr. Congressman. It ain't easy, and it ain't never going to be. But
the trick, it may be, the central trick . . . ."

The central trick: it was the last thing Theodore remembered, until
a pale, cold light bludgeoned him awake and he knew, trying desperately to close his eyes rightly enough so that nothing could penetrate,
another day had dawned. Another day, another speech. And another.
And another.

"Mr. Congressman?"

Brady had survived the night. Brady would survive even the Flood.

"Are you awake, now?"

Theodore grunted. It was the best he could do.

"I've been sitting here, thinking. It seems to me—"

He paused, as Theodore groaned.

"Is it all right you are, Mr. Congressman?"

Theodore squinted, to keep his eyes from opening. Do not open,
he commanded. Stay right where you are.

"I'm fine, Mr. Brady. Perfectly fine. What were you thinking?"

"Well, it's like this, Mr. Congressman . . . ."

"Grace, would you bring me my shawl—the one on the piano stool."

"Yes, Mother."

It was a Sunday. The sun was bright but not overly warm, and she was able to sit in the garden. They had been fairly regular church go-ers, until recently. The effort was beginning to be too much for her, and Martial had dissuaded her from making the attempt. He had also spoken to their pastor.

"Perhaps I should bring you inside? It's cooler than I'd thought."

"No, please. Autumn is a very special time of year for me; you know that. I'd like to relish it as much as I'm able."

"But not to the detriment of your health."

"Don't treat me like just another patient, Doctor Johnson! I am im-mune to even your best bedside manner." She laughed. The sound was thin: it sounded to him like a feather floating on the wind. "I know all your medical tricks, and don't you forget it."

Grace returned with the shawl and Martial helped cover her with it. Alice was trying to organize three-year old Mark and two-year old Michael in some sort of formation, as her older sister always organized her. It was difficult, and Grace went to her aid.

"She's growing up terribly fast," Anne-Marie said quietly.

"You used to say that was how all girls grew."

"I used to say a lot of things. You oughtn't to have listened to me. Why isn't my father here yet? He always ridden over on Sundays, imme-diately after church—and he goes to a very early service." She smiled. "I think, these days, he may well rouse the minister from his bed. He's become terribly zealous about it, since my mother died." She toyed with the fringe of her shawl. "That does happen a lot, doesn't it? Will you become terribly religious too, Martial?"

"Don't be a goose."

"But you don't know. Things will change for you, they'll be very different. You can't say now what you'll feel then."

"I'm not interested."

"But I am! You know you'll be here. Martial. It doesn't concern you terribly much, because whatever happens you'll be here, and you can always do what needs to be done, somehow. But I know I won't be here, I know you'll be alone and I won't be able to help you. So I want to help you now. I want to live on, you see, even after I've died. It will help me, too, to know that I've helped you in that way. Do you understand?"

It was difficult for him to reply.

"I always try to understand."

"I wonder if I would have been as nice to you, if you were the one who were dying?"

"Can you doubt it?"

"Oh yes. I'm not nearly as nice as you seem to think me, some-times. I'm not nearly as much of a lady, either. Being a lady is fearfully tiresome, much of the time. Did you know that?"

"I had guessed."

"It's not at all like being a gentleman. Being a gentleman requires you to *do* things. Being a lady requires you *not* to do them. That's all the difference in the world. I think my mother never came to terms with it. She was the only girl, and both her brothers were expected to be active. She had a good mind—and did you know that? it didn't always show— and she would have liked to be active, too."

"Did she say so?"

"No. She never talked about it. But I could tell. It wasn't like my grandmother, who sang in Europe. My mother never did anything."

"Except raise three children."

"More or less. It isn't much of an accomplishment, you know."

"On the contrary. It seems more than sufficiently difficult to me."

She reached out and touched his hand.

"I'm sorry, I wasn't thinking. Forgive me."

He managed a wide smile, but it did not convince her.

"For what? I wasn't thinking of *that* either!"

"Was that my father's horse?"

He pretended to listen.

"I think not."

"I wonder where he can be? Could he be ill, do you suppose?"

"He would have notified you."

"I suppose he would. He's never been this late, not in months." She stared into the threads of her shawl. "I'd really rather have been a man."

"I'm glad you did not get your wish!"

"Except for you, of course. But when you come to reckon it all up, Martial, I've not been very useful to you."

"What on earth—"

"I've lived with you a very short time, and I'll be leaving you with four small children and all sorts of problems. You'll really have to marry again. I know, I'm forbidden to talk about such things. But I *have* to talk about them, Martial. Can't you see how important it is to me? And the children, they're mine too, they'll always be mine, even when some other woman is raising them, even when they learn to call her Mother, too. They will, don't say they won't. And it's right that they should. She'll be doing all the things for them that I . . . ."

Her voice faded.

"You're being silly, Anne-Marie."

"If so, it's my right. But in fact I'm being perfectly sensible. You *will* have to marry again. How else could you manage? How else could the children hope to survive? And they will!" Her eyes shifted from him to the children and back. She seemed partially distracted. "I would pick your new wife for you, if I could."

He rose quickly.

"Anne-Marie."

"No, let me say it. It's important to me. I know I can't do it, I know it's impossible, but I wish it weren't. I'd like to pick her for you, and I'd even like to come to your wedding. It would make me happy, did you know that? It would be a great relief to me, really it would. I would know you were taken care of, and I wouldn't worry about you so much as I do. I worry about you a great deal. Did you know that? I lie in bed and I worry that you'll have such trouble, that it will be too hard for you."

He bent over her but she pushed his hands back.

"I ought to carry you in."

"No."

"You're tiring yourself."

"And what if I am? It doesn't make the slightest difference, now."

"Anne-Marie, you're the only wife I have, and the only one I want."

She banged feebly on the arm of her chaise.

"Don't talk nonsense, Martial! You make me desperately angry when you talk such idiocy. Ought I to lie in bed and worry about myself? What good would that do? I'm going to die, and fairly soon: what good would it do to worry about *me*? But I shall be leaving you behind, and the life we've had together, and the children we've created. I have to worry about you and about them. I *have* to. Don't you see? It would be inhuman to try to stop me. It would be cruel, and it would be foolish. You ought to help me, not hinder me."

He sat down again.

"Help you to worry?"

"Is that so strange?"

"It seems so to me, I must admit."

"Men. You're a vastly inferior species on the whole, did you know that?"

"I've never attempted to deny it."

"You're supposed to be so strong-minded and practical. And we are supposed to be light-headed and romantically impractical." She managed a faint laugh. "What a wicked fairy tale. The world is all upside down, in that case."

"It seems very probable."

"All the practical details of life are in women's hands—and so they ought to be. You men are such great babies: you'd perish from the earth in a year, if we left you to yourselves."

"Agreed."

"You're humoring me, Martial! Don't!"

"I happen to agree with you, my dear. Is that permitted?"

She pursed her lips.

"I'm sorry, I'm dreadfully cross. Is it the disease?" He did not reply. "I'm also worrying about my father—and don't tell me not to! He's not a young man, and he insists he won't ride in a carriage, just to come here. He thinks it's beneath his dignity—at his age!"

"He is, I believe, sixty-eight."

"He's not a young man. He might fall off his horse, he might right now be lying in a ditch somewhere, praying that someone would remember him and come to find him, before it was too late."

"Your father is an excellent horseman."

Her voice rose:

"But they are exactly the ones to whom accidents always happen!" He started to reassure her, but she went on. "Send someone to look for him, Martial. I'm terribly worried. I can see him all crumpled up in the muddy water. Oh, I know there's something wrong, I just know it!" She was sitting upright, her face was flushed, her eyes damp. "Do send someone, and quickly. Please!"

He took her hand in his and tried to soothe her. She was adamant and would not so much as lie back.

"I won't be put off, Martial. If you won't let someone else go, I'll have my horse saddled and look for him myself. I know something has happened, I can tell!"

"You don't need to worry so."

"Will *you* go? If you won't spare someone else, will you go yourself? For my sake, Martial? Please?" Her voice cracked and she began to weep. "Please?"

He was able, now, to ease her into a lying position. He knelt beside her, stroking her forehead. It was dry and hot.

"Won't you go? Please? Please?"

It was Scylla and Charybdis: what choice did he have? She would kill herself if he did not tell her; she would kill herself if he did. No, her father would kill her, in either case. He loathed the old man, now; he had tried to like him, and he had thought himself successful in the attempt, but it was plain to him that he never had been, never.

"Anne-Marie," he said softly, "Let me tell you something."

It was as if she did not fully near his words, but caught the tone of his voice. She stopped trying to expostulate with him, her body went limp.

"Is he dead? Is my father dead?"

"No. He's very much alive, and in as good health as I have ever seen him."

"Thank God. Oh, thank God!"

"But he won't be riding over this morning."

It was hard for her to follow; he could see her straining to understand.

"Has he gone somewhere? Is someone else ill? Is it Jonathan? Theodore?"

Lord: he felt that he could cheerfully have broiled Doctor Bingham on a spit.

"No one is ill, Anne-Marie. No one. And your father has not gone on a trip. He's in the Grandvoort house, just as always."

"But there is something wrong. Isn't that what you're trying to tell me, isn't it?"

"Yes. I'm afraid there is."

"Is he angry with you? Is my father angry with you about something? About me, about your treatment of my illness?"

Did it matter if he told her the precise truth? He had never lied to her, but did it matter, now? And could he tell her that her father was half out of his mind, perhaps more than half? It would kill her, it would be an incredibly risky thing to do.

"Yes."

She closed her eyes.

"Oh. Oh." She was silent for a moment. "He's so proud, and so silly. He hasn't been himself since my mother's death, he really hasn't." She looked up at him. "I'm sorry, Martial. I'm sorry you had to have this, too. It wasn't your fault, I'm sure it wasn't."

"I think not."

"But he'll get over it. He may not see that you're right; he's a very stubborn man. And no matter what you say, he is getting older; he's not easy to please any more."

"No."

She squeezed his hand, her grip astonishingly feeble. He wondered fleetingly if she knew how weak she had become.

"I'm sorry, Martial. It isn't my fault, I know that, but he is my father, and even if he won't apologize for himself, I will apologize for him. Will that do?"

"You don't need to—"

"I must. Don't you see? I want you to ride there, right now, and tell him—tell him anything. Tell him whatever he needs to be told. I need him to be here, Martial. I need to see him with the children. I need to know that it's all right, that I can leave them in both your charge. Yours and his, too."

He shook his head, slowly.

"Won't you go? Oh please!"

It was almost impossible to speak.

"I can't. I can't, Anne-Marie."

"You're not so proud, Martial. I know you're not! He can't have offended you so desperately as that. And even if he had, you'll go for me, not for yourself. You'll go for me, won't you?"

He felt faint and fought it back.

"I will go, if you want me to, but it won't help."

"Oh yes, it will, it will!"

"He won't see me."

"No," she said after a moment. "That's not possible. You know that's not possible. He may have *said* that, Martial, but he didn't mean it. He's even sillier than you are, I know that, I know he is, truly. But he won't turn you away from his door. You will go? Ride there and bring him back, Martial. Please." Her eyes closed. "Please."

It was a command he could not disobey.

"I'll go."

"I knew you would. I knew you would."

Her voice was barely audible.

"As soon as I bring you inside."

"No," she said swiftly, her eyes opening wide. "No. I want to stay right here. I'll be perfectly all right. It won't take you long. I promise to sleep afterwards. I'm not being stupid, Martial. I'm not being capricious, really I'm not."

"I know how important he is to you."

"Oh, more than he has ever been, more then he ever was to me simply for himself! He's the children's grandfather, their only grandfather—their only grandparent. That's more than important. So that's why I have to stay right here, that's why. I have to see him with the children. I have to."

He stood up.

"You saw him last week. Right here."

Her nostrils flared, her breath was labored. It was not good for her to engage in heated discussions.

"Oh, it's not the same thing, it's not the same thing at all. That was last week, not now. I haven't that many weeks left. Every single one is precious to me."

"You'll have more than that. Much more."

"It doesn't matter. Whatever I have will be good. Go and bring him, Martial. Please."

He bent and kissed her. There was nothing more to be said, it was time to give her some rest.

But for how long? He would ride to Poughkeepsie, and Doctor Bingham would turn him away, he knew he would, and then he would have to come back, and Anne-Marie would have to be told. Somehow. She would have to be told something, at any rate. Was there an invention, a fairy tale of some sort that would explain things, that would paper matters over? He had thought there might be, but now he doubted it. Nothing but the sight of her father would satisfy her, and that was, he knew, the one thing he would not be able to give her. All the tales in the world would not equal that. And all the tales in the world could not long forestall her knowledge of the truth. And would the truth kill her?

He mounted his horse and rode, more slowly than usual, toward Poughkeepsie, unaware of sun or countryside or even of time. He felt himself wishing his own ride could end in a ditch, his neck snapped, the whole thing ended. This was stupid and it was impermissible, he did not really wish it. What would happen to the children? It would be their grandfather who would raise them, and what tender hands *he* would have, what energy and life-sustaining warmth he would produce. Martial felt himself sneer, and tried to stop. There was no point to that, either.

There was not much point to anything. This much at least was clear. But he would go, as he was going, and he would come back, alone, and what happened would happen. He would lie if lying could help, but he knew it would be of no use. How much better if Doctor Bingham had had the seizure and died, rather than his wife! How much more appropriate if he should have the hemorrhage and die, choking on his own blood—him, rather than Anne-Marie. He felt merciless; anger tightened his throat and his grip on the horse's reins. He could kill Frederick Bingham, he could. But that would not help. Nothing would help. The next death was meant to be Anne-Marie's, and the Fates could not be held off. There was no way.

He was aware that he was riding as if to a funeral, and tried to nudge himself into a different and better frame of mind. Perhaps the old man would relent. If he would not see his only daughter's husband, his dying daughter's husband, the father of his only grandchildren, perhaps he would look at a note, if Martial had a servant bring him one. He began to rehearse phrases, he began to consider possible strategies. It was better than this hopeless, grim pounding along. Anything would be better.

But he never quite forgot that it was hopeless; there would be nothing to move Frederick Bingham. He could not forget that, because he knew it was as immutable as the sun rising in the morning and setting at night. He knew this was as fixed and determined as the fact that, one day soon, the sun would rise and the sun would set and Anne-Marie would not be there to see. He knew. But he rode on.

THIRTEEN

"Calamities are sometimes the lot of life. We can do nothing but submit, and hope that the dark ways of Providence will one day be explained. It is for the best, or it would not have been so."

—Daniel Webster, to Daniel Wright
27 February 1846

"And do you know what I told him?"

"No, Mr. Greeley."

"Well, he started out by saying he came from Mr. Brooks—James Brooks, you know; he edits *The Express*—who was running with me. 'And we'd like to do what needs doing,' he said, 'to make sure you and Mr. Brooks are elected.' Well, I replied, I'm only running for a ninety-day seat, and Mr. Brooks is running to take what Mr. Bingham has left him. 'Yes,' he pressed me, 'but it's important for the Party that you both win, and that Whig continuity be maintained.' Whig continuity: I like that. I already knew the Whigs would win and that by winning they would have utterly lost. We would not have to say, with Pyrrhus, 'Another such victory, and I am ruined!' No sir, we would not have to say any such thing, because this victory itself would more than suffice. The Whig Party guaranteed its disintegration and destruction, the very moment it nominated General Taylor—no matter how wise and good a President he may turn out to be. Well, in any event, my answer was pretty clear. 'Tell Mr. Brooks,' I said, 'that all we have to do, he and I, is keep still and let no attention be paid to us. General Taylor will carry us both in. Indeed,' I added, 'I cannot believe there are enough voters in the district who care enough about ether of us, one way or the other, to swamp the majority which General Taylor cannot fail to receive.' And though I have not been right about everything, not quite everything, you understand, I almost understated the case for our inactivity. The General had over eleven thousand votes in the district, and Mr. Brooks and I each received just under ten thousand. (Bye the bye, I did out-poll Mr. Brooks by almost two hundred votes.) Our Cass and our Van Buren competitors did not get much above eight thousand, added together, and the Cass candidate on his own did not reach so high as seven thousand. So, young man, your brother is out of Congress, and I am in it, fully entitled to the federal munificence. My salary, you know, will be eight dollars a day, while this retiring Congress still exists. Is that not munificence?"

"My congratulations to you, Mr. Greeley—and yes, I think it does seem pretty good pay, from where I stand."

"You will do very well for yourself, in time."

"I expect my brother will, too, when the state legislature meets next month."

"I doubt he would have left Congress, if he did not fully expect to do well in the legislature. Well, I wish him good luck. I shall be in Washington when the legislature meets, debating matters which may well reach him, in the Senate, when he arrives there. That would be droll, would it not?"

A copy boy arrived, there was work to be done, and Mr. Greeley fell to it. Jonathan was dismissed—and he, too, had more than enough on his hands, especially now that Bayard Taylor had left, sailing off to more romantic adventures. The *Tribune*'s readers virtually followed Taylor down the dock and onto his boat; they had a full description of the sailing, and of Taylor's cabin, and of some of his plans and hopes. They would soon be biting their nails as they read, over their morning coffee and bacon, the piece-by-piece narration of Taylor's high adventures: his columns would begin appearing almost before the boat docked. Taylor knew how to keep the adventure flowing and the reader turning pages, hands sticky with excitement.

But all the same, his absence created heightened activity for Jonathan. He was not expected to fill Bayard Taylor's shoes, but he was definitely expected to take up any slack created by other people filling in for Taylor. And he was expected to roam easily from books to domestic tragedy, from the President-elect's suspenders to the cable under the Atlantic. No one stood still at the *Tribune*—as Mr. Greeley had stood still for the election: there were no literary elephants who could charge the opposition as General Taylor had done for the Whigs. They were a herd of donkeys (the phrase was Mr. Dana's, not Mr. Greeley's, though as usual Mr. Greeley got credit for it), braying in chorus when they could, but all yoked together to pull the thing through. There was a lot of donkey work, and they all did their share.

It was November, 1848. General Taylor was elected, and James Brooks was elected, and Horace Greeley was elected, and it was expected that Theodore Bingham would shortly be elected, too, to take his place in a younger, invigorated Senate. Mr. Fillmore, the new Vice President, would preside over that body. And if the election had not solved much, or made the nation's problems disappear overnight, it had at least shuffled matters—and men—around, so that new blame and new praise would be necessary; it would in general be some little while before it was clear that truly new brooms were needed. Mr. Greeley's calm fooled no one: he was vastly delighted to be the Honorable Horace Greeley, and no one who knew him at all well could believe he would remain calm for more than five or six minutes, once he hit the floor of the House.

"He'll tear them apart—or try to."

"If they tear *him* apart, he won't admit it."

"Damnation, he'll never know they're doing it!"

It had been a protracted autumn, warm and bright until past the middle of November. Walking New York's crowded streets, feeling the unexpected heat, sensing the trees' unwillingness to go bare and bleak for winter, and with the scent of something more like spring than autumn in his nostrils, Jonathan returned over and over again in his mind to his dying sister. He did not know there had been a bad hemorrhage, two months earlier, and that she was headed rapidly toward her grave: Martial did not write to him about his sister's health, and his father did not write to him at all. Nor had he made visits, since the summer. He was, in fact, busy—but neither could he face the sight of her, and his father's pinched wrath, and Martial's weary sadness. He did not admit these things to himself: the pace of events at the *Tribune* was his salvation. Just the same, echoes of her kept pushing through at him. He would see faces that reminded him of her—or of Grace, his little niece, whose bright features were very like what Anne-Marie's must have been, almost thirty years earlier. He sometimes heard his sister's steps, in the clattering patterns of people clamoring past him. Every time he heard a scrap of music, from a piano or even from a barrel organ, he thought of her. He tried to avoid music entirely: it was too painful to be borne.

His Aunt Sophia, who knew even less about the situation in Poughkeepsie than he did, had somehow become aware of his disturbance. Jonathan did not know how she nosed him out—he was, of course, unaware of how many hints and clues he shook down from his unsmiling face, and his long silences, and the distant staring look so frequently in his eyes—but it was plain that she had. She was a tactful woman, and a subtle one, but the effort to nudge him into social things, into walks and conversations and tea-table gatherings, was unmistakable.

"You are almost nineteen, Jonathan."

"I am almost thirty, or forty, or even fifty, Aunt. Whatever you will. Close your eyes, blink, open them again—and presto! I shall be as old as my father. Or older."

"Do you think such literary shenanigans will divert me, Nephew?"

"Do you need diverting, Aunt?"

"Say what you will, young poet: you are going to carry cups and distribute sandwiches for me, this afternoon."

It was Sunday, the only day (this week) on which he did not have to be at the *Tribune*. She had come to his room at mid-morning. He had been reading. There had been too much time for books alone to fill, while he was still at Columbia, but now there was scarcely time enough to open a book, and sometimes there was not energy enough even when there was time.

"Aunt, do tell me why other people are congratulated for literary expression, and I am chided for it?" She made a quick face and he smiled. "And do tell me, also, why it was good for me to be locked away with a book, when I was a student duly enrolled, and it is bad for me now?"

"There are bad books, to be sure, Nephew, but I trust this is not one of them."

She was pretending to dust and clean. The room was actually in excellent order and there was nothing that required doing. Jonathan was an immensely tidy young man.

"It is poetry, Aunt."

"There is bad poetry, too."

"Oh, a great deal of bad poetry. I contribute to the total myself, from time to time."

"You require airing, Jonathan." She flung the window wide. "As your room does. It is indeed a good thing you do not smoke. It would smell like—well, it would not smell as it should in here, if you did."

"I am an exemplary young man, Aunt, bursting with virtue and good deeds."

"Are you, now?"

"Unquestionably. Don't you think, accordingly, that I have earned the right to relax with a book, on this the Lord's Day? Even the Good Lord rested on Sunday, after all."

"Are you trying to tell me, young man, that you have worked equivalently hard, the previous six days?"

He smiled and put down his book.

"You are determined to drag me out of my lair, I see. Well, I suppose there is no point to kicking and screaming about it. I will have to submit."

"Fiddlesticks! You make me out to be a busybody ogre, Jonathan. Is that my reward?"

"Surely, Aunt, you already know that your true reward can come only in heaven, and there is little point to expecting any portion of it here below."

"I will expect you down below in the parlor, young sir, in under an hour, dressed appropriately for your duties."

"I shall report as assigned, General."

Which he did, dutifully and not unsmilingly. He carried cups, and also saucers. He plied several trays of sandwiches—there were perhaps fifty guests, in all, most of them unknown to him, all of them singularly well-dressed, and virtually all of them marvelously hungry—and he refilled tea cups and water glasses. He made a snatch or two of small talk, on occasion, and when the afternoon's lecturer stood, for silence and elucidation to follow, he sat with the others and listened. And since his aunt and uncle were firm Abolitionists, as was their friend Mr. Greeley, he was not surprised at the speaker's topic—"Was Union With Slaveholders Possible?" The followers of William Lloyd Garrison did not believe it was, but as a follower of the merchant brothers, Arthur and Lewis Tappan, who supported abolition and abolitionists all across the country, but most particularly in New York City, the speaker most definitely believed continuation of the Union possible and also desirable. His arguments were modest, his speech not overlong—and then Jonathan was pressed back into service, as the audience needed to moisten their throats and refresh their spirits.

"Pray release me."

Jonathan took a moment to realize that the injunction was addressed to him. The voice was female and unfamiliar; when he turned, he saw that the face was young, pretty, and quite unknown to him.

"I beg your pardon?"

He had a small tray in one hand; it was empty and he carried it hanging down. She pointed, apparently in the direction of the tray, and he looked and saw nothing out of the way.

"Please," she repeated with some urgency, but not with ill humor.

He stood motionless, somewhat confused.

"Were you speaking to me?" he finally asked.

She smiled.

"Patently. Would you release me?" His confusion multiplied. "You're standing on the hem of my dress," she went on. He stepped back hurriedly.

"I'm terribly sorry. I hadn't noticed."

"So I saw." She leaned over, inspecting. "I don't think you've damaged it."

"I certainly hope not!"

"The fault is really mine, you see. I made it distinctly too long, and then there was not time to take it up. To shorten it," she added, suspecting—rightly—that he might not understand the term. "So, you see, if you choose to wear a dress with an excessive hem, well, you take whatever risk may be involved."

His confusion had not much abated; the whole subject was both alien and embarrassing. He drew a long breath and assumed the mantle of age and experience.

"The thought had not occurred to me. It has been some years since I wore a garment even vaguely answering to the description."

"Not *that* many years."

He swung the tray from side to side and smiled.

"All the same, I'm older than you are."

"So is our scullery maid."

"I might not, however, be old enough to be your father."

"Or our scullery maid? Besides, I already have a perfectly serviceable father. He answers to most of my needs."

Jonathan thought of replying that this serviceable father would not be answering nearly so well, before long, but decided that would be an impropriety. And risky: men got themselves into trouble for lesser offenses.

"Do you belong to the house?" she asked.

"After a fashion."

"French or English?"

This girl had a quip for every occasion, and several to spare. What manner of creature might she be?

"Only American. I'm sorry, that's the best available hereabouts." He was about to move on, to attend to his responsibilities, when his Aunt Sophia joined them.

"Did you like our speaker?" she asked the two of them.

"He was preaching to the converted, Aunt."

"He was speaking honestly," said the young lady, "and such things require to be repeated, over and over. We are an obdurate people, and our hearts do not melt readily."

"Mine lay unaffected," Jonathan put in. "And not overwarm, either."

"Ah," said his aunt, "I see you two have formed a debating society of your own. Very well," she said, reaching down and taking the tray from Jonathan's hand, "I shall leave you to your argumentation. But remember, Jonathan," she cautioned, as she whirled off, "how many true words have been spoken in jest."

"I am now discharged of all responsibilities!"

Her hair was brown, her skin fair, her eyes apparently brown, as well. She was rather tall, for a woman, and slender. Her nose was a bit thick, her lips on the whole rather thin.

"Only death can do that," she assured him.

"I spoke in a very limited sense. Do you always address yourself to eternity?"

"When I can. It speaks to me constantly."

"In French or in English? I do not mean to be rude, believe me."

She dropped him a mock curtsey.

"I do honor to your left hand, since your right does not know what its mate is engaged in."

"I should not like to debate with you in public. You are as quick to parry and thrust as an Italian swordsman."

"The race is of course not always to the swift."

"I was not even aware we were running."

She glanced to the side and saw someone or something that required her attention.

"Don't think me rude, but I am called away. Excuse me."

Her smile was swift and on the whole pleasant. He bent in a brief bow, and when he straightened she was gone. He rubbed his palms together. There was more to think about, in their fleeting interview, than he could conveniently digest.

The gathering was beginning to break up. Perhaps her father had summoned her. Or her husband? It struck him, abruptly, that he did not know her name. He shook his head. Where had his so-called brain been, these past few minutes? He would not forget to ask who she was, the next time they met. He had not met anyone like her, male or female.

But it was some years before he saw her again, and on that next occasion he did not need to ask her name.

It did not often snow, in Washington. Cold rain, and a bit of sleet, was as much as he had seen in his six years in the nation's capitol. But in December of 1848, as he waited for Morris Brady's telegram—they had arranged for a one-word transmission, "yes" or "nay": what did the details matter?—the snow came down as he had often seen it fall in Poughkeepsie. She had never seen it at all.

"Will it all melt, Theodore?"

He was trying not to look at his watch, or at the gold clock on the mantle.

"In due time."

She turned and smiled at him. He was standing near the window, in her best sitting room, his back to the snow. She was seated on a small sofa, in a bright gown that did wonders for her. He did not seem to notice.

"Is that a lawyer-like answer, or a politician-like one?"

"Arabella, I scarcely know if I live or die, let alone from whence I derive my expressions." He pulled out his watch, with a jerk, and consulted it for a quarter of a minute. "Confound it, where is that telegram?"

"Perhaps the snow has delayed it."

"I doubt that it is snowing in Albany."

"In December? I thought it snowed and hailed continuously, once winter set in."

"Soft, fat flakes," he murmured. He paced a bit, then caught himself up. "It will all melt, soon, very soon." His hands behind his back, he struggled to maintain even a vaguely statesmanlike pose. "And then it will be terribly sloppy. The horses will slip, the wheels will spin. Bad weather to be about in." But his heart was not in meteorological disquisition. He eyes scarcely took her in, his mind was far distant.

How like little boys they all are, she thought to herself. Thirty years ago it would have been a sugar stick on which he had set his heart, and toward which his whole being was directed. Now it was a seat in the Senate. And a seat in the Senate was indeed a grand thing, and worth struggling to obtain. She had encouraged him, mostly at a distance, as he wound up and down and around his home state of New York. She had sent him small presents, and carefully crafted letters, and done all she could. But the world would hardly come to an end for him, if he lost. He was a successful lawyer, he was a public figure and would clearly remain one, in the Senate or out of it. He was about to be a husband: he had her, or soon would have. Wasn't it possible to preserve just a bit of perspective?

She knew the answer: no, it wasn't. Her first husband had been virtually the same. He would set his heart on some transaction, some business coup, and stamp and fret until it carried through. "But once you've got it," she said to him more than once, "it will hardly matter to you. You'll set your heart on something else." She had seen it happen. "That's not the point," he would reply. "You don't understand." She was not sure she knew what the point was, in fact, and she was reasonably sure she did not care. Male perspective was perpetually awry; it was women's duty to at least help set it right, to do what was possible in the way of alleviating male tension and monomania.

"We needn't go about in it, then," she said cheerfully. She patted the sofa. "Do come and sit next to me, Theodore. I have the feeling you're almost avoiding me, this morning."

"Nonsense."

But he did not join her.

"Shall I send for some tea?"

"No, thank you." He turned and stood staring at the snow for a moment. "It won't last," he explained, turning back again. "There'll be sunshine this afternoon."

"I wish you were as sure of the legislature in New York as you are of the weather in Washington!"

He seemed impossibly young, as he sighed from the depths of his being.

"I can't control either one, Arabella, but the weather is at least predictable. What it has done fifty times, it is extremely likely to do fifty-one and then fifty-two times."

"Are you truly worried?" She held up her hand, as he started to respond too quickly. "No, I understand you are nervous. It is, to say the least, understandable. But do you think you might not be elected, after all that has happened?"

He sniffed, turned half to the side, and began to pace as he spoke. She could see the English in him, at moments like these. She wondered if his medical father had preserved any of that sturdy British woodenness? There seemed to be some diplomatic problems about the wedding and Doctor Bingham's attendance thereat. It would all be worked through: she knew herself too well to expect even a stodgy country doctor to stand up to her, even a doctor with an earl for a distant relation. She had not even met Theodore's brother. Or his reclusive sister.

It was a stranger family then she had quite realized. Never mind: Theodore was hers, and she knew him, and he was the only Bingham that truly mattered.

"I think I will be elected. I think there will be no problem. But a legislature—and a state legislature even more than the national one—is something like a large herd of sheep. If one of the senior rams bolts at the wrong moment, or some fat old ewe bleats danger when there really is none, the whole herd may stampede—and once they're stampeded, there's no telling what they'll do. In short, my dear, until I have that blasted telegram, and it says I'm all right, I can't possibly be sure. There simply is no certainty, in politics." He nodded dramatically. "As my wife, indeed, you'll learn that soon enough."

"I'm not sure I'll permit you to stay political, in that case."

His smile was weary. He had started to pull out his watch, when a servant entered, bearing a missive. Theodore paled.

"For Mr. Bingham," the man announced. Theodore wanted to step toward him, but could not make his legs move. The telegram, if in fact it was a telegram, had to make its deliberate way to him. It was a telegram. He held it, his hands shaking faintly. The servant left the room.

"You might open it," Arabella suggested.

He nodded, wetting his lips. But he did not open it.

"Would you like me to open it for you?"

"No, it's all right. Thank you, my dear." He pulled at the envelope. "Nothing ventured, nothing gained."

He got it open, at last, and tugged out the message. He read it, swayed, turned very pale, and half-staggered to a chair.

"God, God!"

"Theodore, is it 'nay'? Are you all right?"

He had his head against the side of the chair. She bent over him, tried to embrace him. He was like some living stone.

"Let me see it, Theodore."

He held out the message; she read it.

ANNE-MARIE DYING. PLEASE COME.
MARTIAL.

"Your sister? I thought she was strong as a horse."

"Here I was, thinking only of the election! My God, oh my God!"

"You'll have to go."

"Of course! At once. The election's not a matter of life and death."
Then he clapped his hand to his forehead. "Those poor little children.
And Martial. What can have happened?"

"I'll send James with you, if you like."

He put his hands on her shoulders. She stood very straight, he was
proud that she was to be his wife.

"That's very kind of you. But I'd rather take someone else."

She met his glance, understood it, and hesitated.

"Me?"

"You. Would you?"

She took a deep breath.

"How can I? We're not yet married."

"We can take Anna, instead of James."

"That doesn't make it right."

"It would help." He squeezed her shoulders. "Please, Arabella. I'll
need you."

Her hesitation was genuine. This was an insane notion. She did not
know the family, she was not a part of the family. It was not her place
to be there at such a time. Her presence might well be resented. Old
Doctor Bingham would not be pleased. But Theodore wanted desperately for her to come. And if she went, and if she conducted herself
as well as she knew she was capable of doing, he would be bound to
her forever. It would not be the easiest way to ensure her dominance,
to put down even the possibility of an uprising, but it would probably
be the fastest.

"How can I?" But her hesitation was no longer genuine, her mind
was made up.

"Oh please! I'll do everything I can to make it as easy as possible. And Anne-Marie would want you to come, I know she would. Do
please say you'll come, Arabella! I'll be eternally grateful to you."

Indeed you will, she assured herself. Indeed you will.

"It's hard," she said in a small voice, turning her face down. "But
if you want me to—"

His embrace was convulsively tight. They left the room hurriedly,
half a minute later, and began to pack. Even the journey would be hard,
in such weather. It would all be hard. But it would be worth every bit
of the effort.

They left an hour later, the horses slipping in the wet snow exactly
as Theodore, wise in the ways of snow, had predicted.

Which was why there was no one there to receive Morris Brady's telegram, when it finally arrived, in mid-afternoon, and why Senator-elect Theodore Bingham did not know for several days that the election had gone off without a hitch. He had won on the first ballot: it had been a triumphant victory.

But Anne-Marie had not, in fact, died. Martial Johnson, husband, may have misread what Martial Johnson, physician, ought not to have mis-read. Cut off from her family by waspish spite and distance—Washington was a long journey, nor was New York a quick jaunt—and even more by her unwillingness to allow anyone to know of her illness, he may have blown a loud, piercing whistle out of desperation and loneliness and overwhelming strain. Jonathan was the first to arrive, and then came his father, stiff and uncommunicative, stalking in, Bible in hand, as if to anoint the corpse. Theodore and Arabella were inevitably the last to come. No one came from Martial's side because, simply, there was no one left: his parents had both died when he was very young, he had been an only child, and what family he did have was more than a thousand miles distant, in the wilderness of Minnesota. He had been raised by a New England cousin, now dead. Only Binghams could help him, finally. Only Binghams would care.

Jonathan's telegram had come to him at the *Tribune*, where Martial guessed—rightly—he was likely to be most accessible. Jonathan had written a short note to his Aunt Sophia, explaining his abrupt departure, and told Mr. Dana, in the absence of Mr. Greeley, that he would get back when he could. He had then caught the first Hudson River boat leaving the city docks, rented a horse in town, and galloped most of the way to the Johnson house.

"Is she still alive?"

Martial embraced him, even held him.

"Yes. I did not think she could survive such a hemorrhage as she had last night—" and then he broke into tears, covering his face for a moment.

"How long will it be?"

Martial only shook his head.

"Where is my father?"

Even Jonathan was startled. Martial's face tensed, his eyes sparkled.

"He has not been here in almost three months."

"What are you saying?"

"The truth."

"Is he ill?"

"Not that I know of."

Jonathan held out both hands, as if imploring a fuller answer.

"Are you serious?"

"Perfectly."

"Would you explain? Can you explain?"

"He did not think I should have admitted to Anne-Marie, when she had already guessed it, the gravity of her situation. We had agreed, as medical men, that it was better for her not to know. But she *knew*!" he burst out, his burst out, his lips quivering. There was a longish silence, as he controlled himself. "He ordered me out of his house—"

"You can't be serious."

"Oh, but I am. And *he* was. He said he wished I had never met his daughter, he accused me of causing her illness by excessive child-bearing—oh, he said a fair number of things, and though I do not wish to repeat them, I have told you more than enough already, you will understand that I will never forget them. Nor forgive them."

They were standing just outside the front door. Martial's groom had led away Jonathan's rented horse. There was no snow on the ground, but it was snapping cold. The sun shone low in the west. A slight wind blew in the trees, shaking branches long since leafless. The ground was brown and hard.

"I knew he was angry with me," Jonathan said slowly, "for leaving Columbia and going to Mr. Greeley's *Tribune*. He would not write to me any longer. So I have not been in touch with him. I assumed it was pique, the foolish rage of an old man, and that he would get over it. I never thought he would—" He broke off. "It never would have occurred to me."

"You did not write to us, either."

"I know. I'm sorry. I guessed what was wrong, the last time I was here, and I knew you did not want me to know, and I knew my sister did not want me to know, and—I'm sorry. I could not do anything. I did not tell my aunt and uncle. No one knows."

"I sent a telegram to your brother, in Washington. He should be here."

"And my father?"

"I sent him a note this morning. He has not replied."

Jonathan kicked the door post.

"Damnation! Does my sister know how he has behaved?"

"How could she not? Even the children know, Grace especially. She is almost seven, now, and she has learned to understand more than perhaps she should. But they all miss their grandfather. They miss his visits here, and they miss their visits to the Grandvoort house. They love the old place, and they love him."

"I think my father cannot be well, Martial. My mother's death, and advancing age, have taken their toll."

"That may be."

"You don't believe it."

"He is your father, Jonathan. Why should I criticize him to you? What use would that be?" He glanced at the sky. "Perhaps he will ride over, yet. Perhaps he will care enough. I hope so." He took Jonathan's arm. "But I have completely forgotten my own obligations. Forgive me: do come in. Did you bring anything?"

They entered the house.

"Not a thing. I quite literally dropped everything." The house was as still as a tomb. "She must be asleep."

"Yes. I'd not have left her, believe me, if there was any immediate danger. She fell asleep after the hemorrhage, and for some hours I did not think she would ever awaken. But then her breathing improved, and her color, and she began to sleep quite peacefully. Nature's ways are strange, even to a physician. It was almost as if the letting of blood was necessary, as if it cleared away something and made her stronger rather than weaker. Of course, it may only be a false improvement, a false hope. But I actually think she is better, today, than she has been in some while."

They sat at a bare wooden table, near the fire. Jonathan realized that his hands were half numb and rubbed them in the waves of heat.

"Is there any hope?"

"How little we know! I have never wished more strenuously for greater knowledge than I or my profession possess. But no, I think there is no hope. None. She may die at any moment. There will be some advance notice, however. That at least is known; it is the nature of the illness."

"Who is with her?"

"You do not know her. She lives nearby and is a good woman. I would not have endured, I think, without her attendance. My practice has of course suffered."

"And the children?"

"They have also suffered. Immensely. Alice has some sense of what is happening. Grace unfortunately knows everything there is for a child her age to know. She knows her mother will soon be dead. She has begun to assume maternal functions—at her age! She has the younger ones in the nursery even now, leading them in some game or other. She has several times put the youngest to bed. Such a child, and so much responsibility!"

"It will be hard for them. And for you."

"It has *been* hard. I don't think I have ever known a time like this, not ever in my life. Perhaps I suffered when my own parents died, but I was younger even than little Mark, and he is barely three. If I suffered, it was as a little child suffers—and mercifully forgets. Whatever scars it may have left, they are invisible to me now. If it were not for descriptions I have been given, I would have no idea what either of my parents looked like. No idea at all. Isn't that strange?"

"I wish I had come sooner!"

"What could you have done?"

"Helped—both you and my sister. I'm not much of a nursemaid, to be sure, and probably even Grace is a better housekeeper. But I could have helped. I should have."

"I wish you had. But you also had a career to make."

"Nonsense! That is precisely what I am avoiding, with all of this newspaper trifling—as I dare say my father would be the first to agree. A career in journalism? I have scarcely learned how to write my name!"

"And we did not ask you to come, Anne-Marie and I. She did not want anyone to know, and I thought it was possible. It is not. I cannot blame her, it is perfectly understandable for her not to want her condition known. But I blame myself for not foreseeing how absurd that would become. It is not possible, Jonathan. I can say that quite without fear of contradiction: I have tested the possibility and found myself wanting!"

There was a noise upstairs; they both turned. It was a toy being dropped, or a door closing, and meant nothing.

"Well, it does no good for you to criticize yourself, Martial. Nor does it help for me to become a flagellant. We have proven ourselves imperfect—but I suspect we knew that before."

Martial was staring into the fire:

"It will be Christmas, soon."

"Very soon."

"I don't see how we can celebrate it."

"Of course you can! You must—and now that I'm here, by God, you shall! You owe it to the children. And to Anne-Marie. She's not likely to see another tree all decorated, or another goose roasted."

Martial stored silently at the flickering flames.

"You can't give into it like that," Jonathan urged. He was not sure what he meant, or if he was speaking the truth. But he knew it was important to buck up his brother-in-law. The truth or falsity of the statement was less important than its possible effect.

"I've been telling myself that for months," Martial answered slowly, still not looking away from the fire. "I suppose it's true. But I feel so tired, so worn, that I doubt there's enough life left in *me* to make anything possible. Celebrate Christmas, in that spirit? Christmas? It's almost like an exceedingly bad joke. However these things are arranged, and by whom, I'm afraid I have lost something of my sense of their appropriateness. This may be blasphemy, but if it is I can't help it. Can there really be any sense to what has been happening to my wife, and to what will happen to her children afterwards? Can that possibly be an act of anything which I would recognize as Providence?"

"You are not perhaps in the best position."

"Whose position might be better, let me ask you? Anne-Marie's? I wouldn't dare ask her."

"Does my sister protest against Providence?"

Martial stared into the floor, now.

"Ask her yourself. We have had better things to talk about, while she was still able to converse at all. I don't mean to be rude, Jonathan. I don't mean to be blasphemous. I can only say what I feel, and that is what I feel. I do *not* feel grateful to the Lord for this visitation. I am *not* willing to give up my wife—I would fight the Devil himself, with teeth and nails, if it would help preserve her. I would do anything. Anything!"

There were steps behind them. A moderately elderly lady came into the room and Martial jumped up.

"Mrs. Wilkins!"

The lady lifted a cautionary hand.

"She's only wakened, doctor. She'd like to see you. And she says, poor thing, she'd like a bit of soup. It can do her no harm, that it can't."

"I'll go right up."

"I'm Mrs. Johnson's brother," Jonathan explained, rising.

"The poor thing. Poor, poor thing. It's a miracle she's still with us."

"I came as soon as I could."

"Doctor Johnson, he was half out of his mind, he was that afraid. I'll fetch her some soup, if you'll excuse me, Mr. Bingham."

Jonathan put more wood on the fire, and he, too, sat staring at it. He'd come to sit at the deathbed, but that was possibly some little distance in the future. Never mind: he would not leave until it was all over. And perhaps not then: how could he leave Martial alone, distraught as he so plainly was? Would Anne-Marie want that? And what of their children? What if Anne-Marie asked him to remain, to come to live with Martial? What then?

But what if Martial eventually re-married, as of course he must—clearly, clearly. The brother of a deceased wife would be a difficulty. It would only make matters harder, not easier.

And the children, the poor little things. He would try to spend as much time with them as he could. Indeed, if Martial did not object he would ask to have his bed made up in the nursery. If they woke in the night, he would be able to tend them. And to keep the house as quiet as it should be kept, for his sister's sake.

And how could he think of Anne-Marie, lying in the bed she would now never leave—his lovely older sister, all her sweetness, all her charm, snuffed out forever, all her wizardry with music, all her love and grace—gone. How could he contemplate a world without her? She had been almost as much of a mother to him as his birth mother had been. He would mourn both longer and more painfully for Anne-Marie; he knew it already. He had known that, without knowing it, ever since he'd realized her illness. Oh, Martial was absolutely right! It was hard, terribly hard, and it was not going to get any easier.

"I see you, too, have been summoned."

His father had entered, unnoticed. Jonathan rose; his father accepted his greeting stiffly.

"I hope you are well, Father."

Doctor Bingham stood with his back to the fire. His appearance had not changed; the cold unfriendliness of his manner was predictable.

"It is not my health, I take it, which brings us here. Have you seen your sister?"

"Not yet. Martial is with her now."

"And who is ministering to her soul?"

It was impossible to sit, when his father remained standing. Jonathan retreated slightly, so that the table he had been sitting at was between them.

"I'm afraid I don't know that, Father."

"Naturally. It would not have occurred to you to ask."

"I think she is in good hands, with Martial caring for her."

"Martial is trained in the medical and not the spiritual arts." Doctor Bingham produced a black-bound book from behind his back. "I will read to her, if she is still capable of comprehending."

"She is not quite so low as she had been, I am told." Jonathan was not hopeful that his father could be dissuaded. To sit by Anne-Marie's bed, as she was dying, and read to her from the Bible did not seem to him terribly useful. If her soul had been traveling in the wrong pathways, surely this last-minute instruction would not help it. His father would not be headed off, but Jonathan would have preferred that they sing by her bed, or read poetry to her. "Martial indicates that the last hemorrhage has actually improved her."

"Purely temporary. The diagnosis was made a long time ago and is accurate. The disease is inexorable." He hefted his book. "I should like to see her as soon as possible. It is important that she receive what guidance she is capable of receiving, even now. I trust her husband will return shortly, and that I may be admitted at once?"

"I do not know, Father. I have not been here for very long myself. I had to come from the city, as you know."

His father did not respond. After a moment, Doctor Bingham left the fire and seated himself in the chair Martial had occupied. He opened his Bible and began to read. Jonathan realized there was to be no further conversation, no questions about his own existence. After a moment he, too, sat down, crossing his legs and trying to see only the fire and the walls and the windows. The only sounds were the occasional rustling as a page was turned. The fire had gone down, but he did not feel like renewing it. There were coals enough to keep them from freezing. He did not feel like moving at all. The silence was numb, empty, protracted.

"Doctor Bingham."

Martial had returned.

"Doctor Johnson." He father did not rise; neither man offered to greet the other. "May I see my daughter?"

"You may. You know the way." Before his father-in-law could respond, he moved toward and then spoke to Jonathan. "Why don't I show you to you room? Nurse will be back later, and I don't think we'd better put you in the nursery without consulting her. You'll see enough of the children, don't worry. And I suspect you can wear some of my clothing—enough to keep you for a bit, at any rate. It won't be very fashionable, we're not city people, here. But it will do, I fancy."

Doctor Bingham walked silently from the room, and Martial, who had been talking compulsively, as if to fill in the empty spaces, stopped. His face sagged, and he dropped into a chair.

"How is she?"

"As well as one can expect. Will he see the children, or is Anne-Marie's soul all that concerns him?"

"I don't know. He didn't say."

"He probably didn't say much."

"No."

"Did he even ask how you were?"

"No." Jonathan interlaced his fingers and stared down at them. "I didn't think he would, you know. My father is not an easy man. It will take him time to—to adjust, perhaps, to change."

"I wonder, Jonathan, if there is enough time in the world—but enough of that." He consulted his pocket watch. "I shall give him no more than ten minutes with her. And if he has disturbed her mind, I will bar him from the room. I will, by God!" There was sweat visible on his face. "I would much rather you had gone in first."

"His claim is not one I can deny."

"Nor I, damn it!"

"He will not harm her."

"He'd do well not to! I should be tempted to shoot him, if he did."

"I must apologize for him, Martial, since he finds himself unable to do it for himself. I'm terribly sorry. Try to forgive us."

"And what have *you* done, pray tell, which requires an apology? 'Us,' indeed!" Then he clapped his hands on his knees and rose. "That will be enough of that, my dear fellow. It will get us nowhere." He consulted his watch once more. "Come: there'll be just enough time for you to —" He stopped himself, then laughed briefly. "That's right, you have nothing to unpack."

"Not a blessed thing."

"Well, let me bring you up to the room. It will give me something to do, other than reflect on what he may be saying to her, in there." He shook his head. "That was a Bible he was carrying, was it not?"

"Yes."

"If I turn into a medical preacher, in my old age—if, that is, I have an old age—be a good chap and put a bullet through my head, will you? Come."

And he led Jonathan from the room.

She knew him at once; he could see that. It was a good sign. Her mind was very clear. Nor was there any mark of final dissolution in her eyes. He had practiced medicine for too long not to automatically inspect for the vital signs.

"Father. I'm glad you came."

Her voice was weak but plainly audible.

"Anne-Marie."

He stood by the bed, then reached for a chair and seated himself. "I am vastly relieved to be here."

She smiled weakly.

"I am very glad. It makes me happy to see you once more."

He opened his book, raised it.

"Let me read to you, Anne-Marie."

"Wait. Have you seen the children?"

He lowered the book. His face was pinched.

"No."

"Do please see them. They have missed you terribly." He did not reply. "I will let you read to me in a moment, Father. Please say you will see them."

"Very well."

Her smile was peaceful. She closed her eyes.

"Do read, then, Father, and I will listen as carefully as I can."

He read, his voice monotonous but, to her ears, cheerful. It was like the pattering of a familiar rain. She tried, several times, to make out the individual words, but they were not important and faded at once into the smooth flow, the comforting run of that well-known sound.

Jonathan was sitting near the window when Martial returned to the room.

"She's tired, but not too tired to see you. For just a minute."

"He did her no harm, I take it?"

"None." Martial's voice was crisp and professional. "He is with the children, now. I do not know if he intends to stay for dinner."

"Shall I ask him?"

"It's my house, young fellow. I shall ask him. If he does not choose to answer, that will be answer enough. If he chooses to stay, he will be welcome—though *I* am not welcome in *his* house!" He held up a restraining hand. "Enough. The subject is proscribed."

"I'll stay only a minute."

"Mrs. Wilkins is there. She is instructed to evict you."

"She won't need to."

Martial walked slowly down the hall toward the nursery, Jonathan quickly to Anne-Marie's room. He hesitated only a second, at the door, then knocked lightly and went in.

Her eyes did not open until he kissed her cheek. Then they opened and went wet, and her arms reached for him. They held one another, and did not speak at all, not a word, until Jonathan sensed Mrs. Wilkins behind him and, gently freeing himself, put his hand over her eyes so she would know she was to sleep, and quietly left her.

Doctor Bingham stayed only ten minutes with the children. Nor would he stay to dinner. Grace started to cry, but her father hushed her, whispering in her ear. Both Martial and Jonathan saw the older man to the door, where he had to stand for a full five minutes, waiting for his horse to be brought. There was not a word spoken, nor were there any farewells. Doctor Bingham nodded peremptorily, strode out, mounted, and rode directly off.

"Will he be back?" Jonathan wondered.

"I dare say."

"I hope so. For Anne-Marie's sake."

They went in to dinner, dining alone and rather miserably. The food was poorly prepared, but they did not much notice. There was remarkably little conversation. When the cloth had been cleared, Martial consulted his watch.

"Your brother isn't likely to travel at night, is he?"

"Under the circumstances, I don't know."

"I shall leave word, in case he does turn up. There is a bed, in any case. Why don't we turn in, eh? We can just peek in on Anne-Marie, thought I dare say she's asleep. She ought to be, with that draught I gave her! I wish I could take one, do you know?"

"Perhaps you should. You're dreadfully tired."

"Oh, I am, and I know it. But what if I'm needed during the night?"

"Is that likely?"

"As likely as anything else. I don't know, frankly. Even your authoritative father would not be able to tell you precisely—but you must forgive me, Jonathan. I keep telling you not to raise that subject, and then I constantly raise it myself. I am perverse."

"You are troubled, as how could you not be?"

"I am troubled. And I am tired. Let us sneak a look at your sister and my wife, and then to bed, eh?"

Theodore did not arrive until late the next morning. There were no taxis in Poughkeepsie, but he had located an old and rather dilapidated barouche at a livery stable, and he and Arabella rode up in state, pulled by a team of dingy horses and driven by an apprentice in working clothes and without shoes. It had taken the owner of the barouche—who had bought it, many years before, from the boarded-up stables of a Tory sympathizer, long since fled the country—nearly an hour to clean it. But for all that, it was just barely usable; not all the grime of years could be so readily removed. Theodore felt strange, creaking up the familiar streets in this heavy, pompous machine. Arabella felt still stranger.

"It hardly seems an auspicious start," she murmured, but either he did not hear her, over the rumble and squeak of the barouche, or did not choose to reply. And it was done, there had been no choice. This was the price she had known she would have to pay—but pay quite so freely, no, *that* she had not known. She would have come in any event, more than likely, but it would have been pleasant to have known. She had never before been north of the Potomac, except for a few brief summer sallies; there should have been a great deal to fascinate her eyes and enrich her senses. But she was nervous, and the clumsy old barouche seemed like a final ridiculous touch. She kept still and endured.

"We're here, my dear," she heard him say; then the barouche lumbered to a halt, and he heaved open the door and descended. He gave her his arm, and, gingerly, she stepped down beside him. The apprentice tossed down their luggage, which was not extensive; Theodore tipped him, and the barouche circled and creaked off.

"Good riddance," she said to herself.

The front door opened, and she saw a startlingly young man emerge. Could Martial Johnson possibly be so very young?

"Theodore!" Her fiancé was warmly embraced.

"Jonathan," he said quickly, "I have brought Arabella with me. This is, or very shortly will be, your new sister."

His bow was polished; she curtsied and tried to smile warmly.

"I hope I do not intrude," she said.

"Nonsense!" Theodore declared. "I very much wanted her to come, and in the end I persuaded her, rather against her better judgment. Anne-Marie will want to know her, I know she will. And I simply could not do without her."

"A womanly touch will be welcome. I would have liked to meet you under more cheerful auspices, but it could not be helped. I know my sister will be glad you came. So, do come in," he urged, turning toward Theodore. "Martial is with our sister, being medical, so I will for the moment assume his place."

"How is she?"

"She is still alive, thank God, and that is all we can expect. Father was here."

The door closed; he led them to the fire and seated them.

"Is that in some way startling?" Theodore wondered.

"Father quarreled with Martial. He hadn't visited in three months. He is angry with me, too, you know."

"No, I hadn't known. I have been immensely preoccupied."

"Obviously." Jonathan turned to Arabella. "Forgive us this introductory conversation. I do not mean to be impolite, I assure you. But there are some things it seems to me important that Theodore know at once."

"Of course."

It was a cheerful room, despite the occasion. Anne-Marie's new sister was obviously a good-natured woman, and a woman of taste, as well. She had heard of Anne-Marie's musical accomplishments, but not of her housewifely ones.

"Is our father ill?" Theodore asked directly.

Jonathan sighed.

"He is strange—stranger than before. His whole concern is religion. He was here, indeed, only to read the Bible to Anne-Marie."

"Impossible."

"But true."

"And why is he angry with you, Jonathan?"

"Because I have left Columbia and spend most of my time at the *Tribune*."

Theodore opened his waistcoat, to admit the fire's heat. The barouche had been something like an icehouse on wheels.

"Is that an irrevocable decision?"

"I don't know. But Father disapproves—strongly."

Theodore wanted to ask about Doctor Bingham's quarrel with Martial, but realized that he would need to quiz Martial himself. Was it about some religious question? It hardly seemed likely: Martial was as close to an agnostic as he had ever met, a man of intensely rational and scientific bent. Was it about the children, and their governance, their education? Well, he would have to find out, and to find out he would have to wait.

"We will have much to discuss," he said to his younger brother.

"Including your own affairs."

"I did not bring my affairs with me, I assure you, brother. My only concern now is Anne-Marie."

"So you have not heard . . . ?"

"Not as yet." Theodore felt a twinge of anxiety and tried to smother it. "All in good time. Do you think we will be able to see our sister?"

"I am sure you will."

Theodore turned to Arabella. "I wish you could have seen her—before."

"We will be friends," Arabella said.

"She is as sweet as ever," Jonathan said. "But she cannot talk for very long." He read the unspoken question in their eyes. "It is impossible to say how long it will be. Tomorrow, next week—Martial does not know. No one knows."

Arabella leaned forward.

"Perhaps I should make myself known to the housekeeper—is there one?"

"There is a Mrs. Wilkins, who helps my brother nurse her. There is a cook, I believe, and a maid, and the children have a nurse. But why don't we await Martial's descent? He will be the best person to speak to, don't you think?"

"Of course."

"And how was your trip?" Jonathan asked her. "Not all of it as elaborately awful as that barouche you came up in?"

He laughed and, discretely, she joined him.

"That *was* the low point," she assented, "and fortunately it came at the very end. I think it had not been used since before George Washington was in his grave!"

"Very likely," Theodore said. "You would not believe, Jonathan, how dirty the thing was. I did not let Arabella see it, at the start, or she would never have agreed to drive in it. They are considerably more fastidious, in Virginia."

"Not the thing for a Senator-elect, I would say."

"I do indeed have no final word," Theodore said. "So, at the moment, your immensely dignified older brother stands before you as a man without office."

"Ah yes: my employer, Mr. Greeley, now sits in your old chair in the House of Representatives."

"So he does—and an infernal nuisance he is making of himself, too!"

"Really? He does not convey that impression to us at the *Tribune*."

"He could hardly be expected to, could he? But let me tell you just what your precious Mr. Greeley has been up to."

So, with an occasional smile and an even more occasional word from Arabella, the two brothers talked politics. Not Theodore's own politics, and with no sense of urgency on either side. And they awaited their dying sister's husband. And finally he did appear, was introduced to Arabella, gave a report on Anne-Marie's condition, promised to admit them to her presence after lunch, and showed them to their room.

"I am extremely glad you came, Mrs. Davis. My wife will immensely appreciate your making the trip. And I am grateful, believe me, to have someone such as yourself to call on, at a time like this."

"I hope you *will* call on me, Mr. Johnson."

"I sha'n't have much choice, shall I? But I am indeed grateful to you. If I do not adequately convey that gratitude, I know you will understand."

"Of course."

He showed them their rooms and apologized, once more, for the rudeness of his hospitality.

"I dare say you can do a great deal better, in Virginia."

"You will have to put that to the test," Theodore vowed, and Arabella seconded him at once.

"I can hardly think so far ahead as tomorrow. "But I thank you."

Theodore started to press him, saw Arabella's faint sign indicating restraint, and was, as he increasingly permitted himself to be, guided by her.

"I will speak to the cook," Martial said. "It will be very plain fare, do understand that."

There were a few more politenesses, and then he was gone. Theodore turned to her.

"Aren't you glad you came?"

"It was the right thing to do, yes," she said firmly. "Shall we unpack?"

Anne-Marie did fairly well for four days. She was able to sit up in bed, propped on a mass of pillows, for half an hour at a time, and she was able to both listen and speak with normal concentration and acuity. Martial, as husband and doctor combined, steered them in and out of her presence as her feelings and condition dictated. The children were frequently in attendance, Grace of course for the longest periods, but only during others' visits. The children were always present, after their grandfather's visit, during his Bible-reading sessions. The words meant about as little to them as they did to their mother; they played quietly, as their mother dreamed and half-dozed and Doctor Bingham droned on. He never tried to instruct on his own, only reading to her out of the Book. He came every afternoon, at much the same time, stayed long enough to read to his daughter and to spend a few minutes with his grandchildren, then excused himself and rode off. Nor did Arabella's presence change his pattern. He was not overtly rude to her, but neither did he wax enthusiastic.

"He does not like me," she said to Theodore, after the first meeting.

"No. It's a strange time for him. My mother died so very recently, and now Anne-Marie. And they lost three others, you know. He's old, and he's bitter."

"Yes."

"And this religious fever has utterly swept him away. It's not that he doesn't like you."

"He *does* understand that we're to be married?"

"Of course. He's not quite so far gone as all that."

"May I say something rather negative?"

"Surely."

"Well, I have not known your father in any previous state, and I may well be wrong, but I would suspect he does not, in fact, like anyone. Perhaps that even includes himself."

Theodore was too startled to reply—and too impressed: she made leaping good sense, even to him, and yet no one had ever thought of this before. He kissed her on the cheek, very tenderly, and she smiled. They did not again discuss his father.

Jonathan made some conversation with his sister, telling her pleasantries about Bayard Taylor and Horace Greeley and Charles Dana (no relative of the sea-going Richard Henry Dana). He gave her some idea of how newspaper stories were conceived, hunted down, written, edited, slapped into print. It was all done with a very light hand and with many, many smiles: what was there to be serious about, in the face of her Imminent death? She smiled freely, telling him, over and over, how good her life had been, how much she had been loved, how deeply she loved oh so many things and people—her children, her husband, her family, her music.

"You can't measure things with an invariable ruler," she assured him.

He would not argue about anything.

"At my age, it's hard enough to measure anything against anything else."

She touched his hand. Her fingers were very warm, dry and feathery.

"I'm not afraid, Jonathan. Really I'm not."

"I can see that."

"It was harder, in the beginning. But once I grew to understand, once I accepted it, it hasn't been hard at all. It hasn't even been terribly painful, thanks to Martial. If it ever does grow painful, he puts the pain to rest." She framed a singularly large smile, and held it for some seconds. "Do you believe me, Brother, when I say that I die happy?"

"I'm deeply grateful. But I can't help feeling sad, too."

"Don't." She pressed his hand: hers was so weak he could barely feel the pressure of her fingers. "There's nothing to be sad about. That will only spoil things, Jonathan, for you and for me, too. I want you to be as happy as I am."

He managed some sort of smile.

"That isn't easy."

"No, but do, do, for my sake."

He made the smile disguise the most blatant lie he had ever told her.

"For your sake, yes." He bent and kissed her cheek, more to keep his feelings hidden than to express them. He held his face against hers for a long moment, struggling with tears, then straightened and went on smiling.

In the quiet moments of the day, when he was not with one relative or another, words began to take shape in his mind. Sometimes, before he went to sleep, he set down a few of the phrases beginning to haunt him. In the end, he saw that a funereal poem was composing itself—he felt as if that was what was happening, almost as if he had very little to say about it—and he determined to see it through, if only as a tribute to his sister. That process would take many months. And when it was finished, he would see it into print; what reputation he had as a poet ultimately would rest on that one poem.

Arabella did not want to obtrude herself: it was out of the question for her to seek an interview with the dying woman. But when Theodore was admitted, she went with him, at his strong urging. And Anne-Marie welcomed her with painful pleasure, holding out her thin arms and smiling so broadly that Arabella was for a moment afraid the intensity of emotion would harm her. Anne-Marie insisted on holding Arabella's hand; when Theodore rose to go, she did not want her new sister to leave.

"I think we could have been good friends," she whispered, when persuaded that Arabella did indeed have to leave, that it was time to rest, to prepare for the next visitor.

"I think we already are."

"Oh yes."

On the fourth day after Theodore and Arabella's arrival, Martial was late for lunch. He had instructed them to begin without him; reluctantly, they did as he requested. But when he did appear, it was obvious that dining was over.

"How long?" asked Theodore.

"An hour, perhaps. Two. Not much more."

They were all standing, pressing quietly around him.

"Shall I send for my father?" Jonathan asked.

"What use would that be?" Martial said wearily. "He'll come when he pleases, and he'll not come when anyone else pleases, Anne-Marie included." He took a heavy breath, then cried out, "He'll want to read to her corpse!" He choked, began to weep, and was half led to a chair. Jonathan wound his arms around him, Theodore stood with his hands on Martial's shoulders, and Arabella dipped a napkin in water and gently held it to Martial's forehead. This lasted only a minute or two.

"I'm sorry," Martial said, straightening, the tears stopping. "I sha'n't give in like that again."

"You've nothing to apologize for," Jonathan said at once.

"Nothing whatever," Arabella affirmed.

Anne-Marie wanted the children to be with her; they fetched all four of them, the two youngest sleeping in their father's and uncle's arms as Martial and Jonathan carried them into their mother's room. Alice walked, holding Arabella's hand, clutching it sweatily. She had begun to have some sense of what was taking place. Grace walked alone, just behind her father.

Anne-Marie was stretched out, her eyes closed, her face terribly pale. They sat and stood as near her as possible. The children made a noise, and she opened her eyes.

Her lips worked, then she spoke, hoarsely.

"Oh, yes," she said audibly. "Oh, yes." And then she said something no one could hear. Martial bent toward her.

"Just, my dear, what?"

But her eyes had closed again, and she was dead.

PART THREE

Daniel Webster (1782–1852)
"I was born an American; I will live an American;
I shall die an American."

"I am as unmarried, Judge Clayton, as a man can be.
As far as I can tell, my bachelor state is likely to continue
more or less indefinitely."

"The great majority of travelers only wish to 'get on.' Their first inquiry is how soon they can get to a place; the next how soon they can get away from it; they incur the expense of the journey, I believe, more for the power of saying afterwards that they have seen sights, than from any other motive."

—Daniel Webster, to Mrs. Lindley
6 September 1839

"You are probably aware, Mr. Bingham, that the secretaries to our ministers are, as a rule, somewhat more advanced in years."

Outside it was snowing. The fire in the Secretary of State's chamber was brisk and bright. Jonathan sat across the wide, polished desk and let Mr. Clayton go whither he would. It was Theodore who had gotten him this far, and it would clearly have to be Theodore who could get him any farther. A twenty-year-old newspaperman (soon to be twenty-one) would do well not to dispute with a distinguished jurist, a former Senator, and a man so in the confidence of President Taylor that even the staunchest Whig had not opposed Jonathan Bingham for a post once held by an even more distinguished Whig, Daniel Webster.

"Yes, Judge Clayton."

"On the other hand, it is also true that you are experienced beyond your years—and experienced, too, in precisely those areas where a diplomatic secretary most needs to be professional. Drafting memoranda and reports, and handling a good deal of correspondence, would be a principal part of your duties, were you to be assigned the post."

"To be sure."

Mr. Clayton looked down at his desk, then out the window. Plainly, he was not quite clear in his own mind what he wanted to do. Jonathan's background was in his favor; his comparative youth was against him— and Paris could be a temptation indeed for so very young a man. The most troublesome factor, and one neither man could discuss openly, was Senator Theodore Bingham of New York. The Whigs had come close to keeping control of the House, but had by a narrow margin lost to the Democrats—and in the Senate the situation was worse, with the Democrats having a ten-vote edge. Senator Bingham was even more important to his party, in their minority position, than he would have been had they controlled Congress. He was particularly important to the Secretary of State, who was, if anything, more closely supervised by the Upper House than by the Lower.

"I should perhaps mention," Mr. Clayton said carefully, "that the secretaryship is in no sense a sinecure." He held up his hand, to postpone response. "Did you know, Mr. Bingham, that across the globe we have twenty-six regular and two special missions—and but twenty-eight secretaries? I expect Congress every day to reduce that total; they complain incessantly of how terribly much money we spend on such useless matters as diplomacy! And yet, it has many times been brought to my attention that the secretaries in our principal missions—by which I mean precisely those in London and in Paris—are overworked to the point of exhaustion. Colonel Lawrence, who, as you know, occupies the mission in London, has himself said that he toils like a galley slave, being confined to his desk sometimes for ten or eleven months continuously. And he notes that his one secretary cannot possibly keep up with the volume of work." He shook his head. "There will be no relief; it can only get worse."

"Mr. Greeley is said to work thirteen or fourteen months to a year."

Mr. Clayton, who had no great affection for the radical notions of Horace Greeley, did not argue the point.

"And does he expect the same of his subordinates?"

"Indeed, no. He expects distinctly more of us."

Mr. Clayton smiled faintly.

"There is also the matter of expense. It is more costly, by a substantial factor, to live in Paris than it is in New York—and New York is by no means the least expensive city in our country, as to be sure you must already know. The minister, Mr. Rives, who has the advantage of prior experience in Paris, tells me that although his stipend, and that of Colonel Lawrence, are the largest offered to any of our ministers, he expends more than his salary on four significant items. Four!" Mr. Clayton ticked them off on an upraised hand. "House rent, carriage hire, fuel, and subsistence. Just those and no more." He shook his head. "Dreadful."

"It is perhaps appropriate to mention that I have a small annuity from one of my uncles, five hundred a year, with which to supplement my income."

Mr. Clayton rubbed his chin.

"And your French?"

"Moderately fluent."

"You are of course unmarried. The expense of a wife, in Paris, would be prodigious."

"I am as unmarried, Judge Clayton, as a man can be. As far as I can tell, my bachelor state is likely to continue more or less indefinitely."

"You'll be pining for no charming face, if you indeed go to Paris for us?"

"For one or two very charming faces."

"Ah."

"But none to which I am not related by blood. I am particularly attached to Miss Grace Johnson, daughter of my late sister. She is all of eight, I believe."

"Have you been to Virginia?"

"No, I'm sorry to say that I have not."

Mr. Clayton leaned back in his chair.

"A pity. Mr. Rives is deeply attached to his native state. He was educated at Thomas Jefferson's knee—did you know that?"

"I suspect that even Mr. Greeley did not know it."

Mr. Clayton nodded; his manner seemed to have distinctly mellowed.

"I dare say there are limits even to Mr. Greeley's knowledge. But it would become you, I think, to sniff out Mr. Rives' background and his connections. As a reporter, you should not find that difficult." He picked up a pen, held it a moment, then signed something lying on his desk. "There: I have just authorized your appointment—which does not need the advice and consent of the Senate, you know!"

"Thank you, Mr. Secretary," said Jonathan warmly. "I am grateful for your confidence in me."

"Let us be sure it is not misplaced. You're a very young man—but then, so is your brother, and there is no doubt whatever of his competence. I take it you are somewhat like him?"

Jonathan only smiled.

"You will find Mr. Rives exceedingly indulgent, I think, within the limits of what is possible. I think he will approve of my choice." Mr. Clayton consulted his watch. "Would you prefer to arrange passage for yourself, Mr. Bingham, or would you like to cross the Atlantic on a naval vessel?"

"Not as hard as I would have thought—and yet harder, too."

"Does that seem strange to you?"

Martial did not answer for a moment.

"Do you know, nothing has seemed either strange or not strange to me, since . . . . Well, it isn't that the whole world is upside down. I don't mean that. I have my practice, and the children. Things march along, whether you want them to or not. I don't mean that life hasn't just gone along. The children have been surprisingly adaptive—far more than I could have hoped. Your sister left them with something strong and clear, and it stays with them. They're very fortunate." He took a slow breath. "I feel *temporary*. It's a damnable odd feeling." He touched his chair. "Everything is as solid as ever, everything proceeds just about as it should, and I do, too—and yet I don't feel as though I'm truly here, as though I honestly ought to be doing, each moment, each day, whatever it is I am doing. Does that make any sense?"

"Did you think it would?"

"No, I'm not so far gone as that. I don't expect anyone to understand. I don't understand it, myself."

Jonathan crunched at an apple from the Johnson cold-cellar.

"Your fruit keeps as well as ever."

"And it's February, too."

Jonathan pointed with the half-eaten apple.

"*You* keep well too, brother Johnson!"

"You hint most delicately—most delicately. I've had hints that were substantially less gracious. I've even been told that I owe it to the children."

"Do you?"

"Perhaps I do. But there are limits, and I cannot exceed them, even wishing to exceed them. Could I stand at the edge of the Hudson, down there, wave my arms, and, wishing to fly across, *in fact* fly—flapping my arms like a bird?"

"I've not heard such talk since I left Columbia, Martial."

"I'm out of practice."

"I don't mean to put you off. I have, of course, considered the question, many times. There have been approaches, too, quite specific ones: the day of the arranged marriage is far from ended, Jonathan."

"I take it that not all widows are as forthright as Arabella?"

"Not in this part of the world, no. I might have had to flee, had they been so direct—not that Theodore was as backward as I have been, I dare say!"

"He has done well, my ancient and honorable brother."

"As has she."

"Indeed. I have just come from there: they are wonderfully well suited to one another. I begin to wonder, just a little, which of them rules the roost—but that does not matter, does it?"

"I wish I could be less backward, really I do. It might well benefit the children. But on the other hand, you know, it might also hurt them. Suppose I made a mistake? Can you see Grace as Cinderella, sitting in the ashes?"

"I don't think the story applies, not to either of you, father or daughter! But is it necessarily Scylla or Charybdis? Aren't there—surely there must be—women of sweet-tempered dispositions, willing and able to take on a decrepit widower and his four ill-mannered offspring?"

"I don't know. I simply don't know."

"And you're determined not to find out!"

"Not determined, no. Just cautious. Afraid, really. And not motivated to overcome these restraints. Could anyone really replace Anne-Marie?"

Jonathan walked out of the room beside him.

"But is that what another mother for the children, and another wife for you, should be expected to do? Could anyone replace *you*, Martial, should something take you from them? But wouldn't they still be entitled to guidance and care and affection?"

They stood at the door of the nursery, where Grace, now eight, and her younger sister and brothers, were so busily organizing whatever it was they were organizing that they did not see their adult visitors. Grace was forever the leader, and also the arbitrator. She was vastly taller than Alice, though the younger girl had a tough, tenacious way of getting what she wanted. The two little boys were still rather more like monkeys than men.

Jonathan led their father away.

"You are due in your surgery, Doctor Johnson."

"I love to watch them."

"Should you? Quite so much as you do?"

"Have I anything else?"

Jonathan clapped him on the back.

"Yes, damn it all! You need a wife, Martial, if only to knock some sense into you."

"Anne-Marie was very good at that, I admit it."

They stopped near a window. Martial stood looking out at the bare trees and the snow stretching deep and white all around his home. Jonathan stood facing him.

"I think even I could be good at it. You're remarkably in need of some sensible instruction, Martial. I'm almost sorry I'm going to Paris."

"You couldn't live here, in my event. Much too quiet for the likes of you, Jonathan."

"Touché."

"I'll think harder about it, really I will."

"I'll send you reminders by every ship. Grace sent me a charming little letter, this winter, by the way. I shall write to her, too."

"And Alice."

"And Alice. There will be no favoritism. I will be the most even-handed uncle in existence. Lord: when the boys are of an age, I will have to hire a copyist, just to keep up with your family's epistolary needs!"

"And what about you? Are you planning to bring us back a French bride?"

"Good Lord, no! Whatever gave you such an idea?"

"You're rather of an age yourself, you know."

"Do you know what Mr. Greeley's final advice was? 'Perfect your knowledge of their language, Jonathan. Learn their economy inside out. Study their literature, and their ancient monuments. But avoid their women like the plague.' Well, I propose to listen to him, brother Johnson."

"A pity. I am rather fond of this vicarious acquisition of sisters. I like Arabella very much, you know. Are you sure you couldn't be tempted by a countess?"

"Have you one for sale?"

"This is a splendid opportunity for you!"

"Don't I know it!"

"And even if you don't deserve it, you might as well make the most of it."

Martial ducked away, chuckling, from an imaginary fist from his brother-in-law—and Jonathan thought he had not seen that side of his brother-in-law in a very long time. He remembered Martial as rather a merry sort, before Anne-Marie's illness.

"All right, doctor. I'll settle with you in due course." He looked at his watch. "And now I shall ride over and bid my loving father farewell. There must be something in the training of a medical man, making you people refractory and eternally difficult."

"You'll be back for dinner?"

"Most assuredly. And I shall stay under your roof this night. The children offer a splendid excuse, you know. My father much prefers his own company, these days. He doesn't like noise in the old house. And I'm much too noisy for him. I think he sees me as the epitome of the horrible new generation that is taking over the country. And ruining it, of course."

"And his other son?"

"He never talks to me of Theodore. Or of anyone else, come to think of it. His conversation, such as it is, runs on religious themes. It's almost enough to turn me into some sort of idol worshipper. Just think how it would be if I returned home a follower of the pope!"

"That would do it, even more effectively than a French bride."

"But I sha'n't resort to either. You may depend on it. I will return as true-blue American, and as devoted a bachelor, as I leave." He struck a heroic pose. "Yankeedom forever! The red-white-and-blue! The Constitution! General Washington—and General Taylor, too!"

"You will be immensely popular in France."

"Well," Jonathan laughed, patting his chest with satisfaction, "there's really no telling where a man is destined to find his pot of gold, is there?"

"Just be sure you do return."

"Of that, Doctor Johnson, there is not the slightest doubt. Not the slightest. Unless Neptune personally sinks my ship under me, my return is as inevitable as death and taxes." He consulted his watch once more. "Now you go off to your surgery, and be sure you come back from there as punctually as I shall ride back from our old Grandvoort house."

"I was speaking, my dear fellow, of your return from France."

"One return at a time, Martial. I haven't even left yet!" They clasped hands, suddenly, and held the embrace a long time. "I'll miss you, as well as your children. I hope you will—take good care of yourself."

"I'll miss you too, Jonathan. There's a lot of Anne-Marie in you. The house is different, when you're in it. I know: don't bother saying it. We've said all there is to say, haven't we?"

"Never. There's always more to be said: that may well be the motto of my life." He touched Martial's shoulder. "And we'll say more of it at dinner. I propose not to be late."

"Nor I."

"Perhaps I can even wangle a brace of good bottles out of my father. He doesn't crack one a month, I suspect. We'll be merry, well enough. It can't do you any harm."

"Until the morning after the night before."

"There *is* no morning after! Carpe diem! Scatter the rosebuds—and all that."

"I shall try, Jonathan. I shall do my best. Honestly."

"Whitetowers is lovely, Mrs. Bingham—but this!"

They were standing on the front lawn, which stretched half a mile down a slowly descending slope, ending at a winding, tree-lined creek. There were stands of trees to right and left, but at some distance; discrete clumps of shade-trees, however, grew alongside the house.

"Blue Bell was my late husband's pride and joy. It had been a plantation, at one time, but he had all that ploughed under. And sold: he kept just enough land to also keep his privacy."

He shaded his eyes—it was February, but the sun was bright—and peered from side to side. The grass seemed astonishingly green. It was cut to an almost English evenness and regularity.

"I don't think I've seen anything quite like it, on this side of the Atlantic."

"Mr. Davis had never been to England, but he had seen a great many pictures."

"So," he smiled, allowing her to take his arm so they could continue their stroll, "this is where we will have to come looking for your husband, when we need him in the Senate and find that he has fled."

"I don't think you'll find Mr. Bingham fleeing very often."

"I suspect you're right. It is, of course, easier not to flee, at his age."

"Have you thought of escaping from the Senate, Mr. Webster?"

"Frequently. And as you may know, on at least one occasion successfully. But one must have somewhere to run to." He shook his head. "And not only do I have nothing like Blue Bell, I have nothing very much in general. I am a laboring man, Mrs. Bingham. If I do not labor, I do not eat. And my children's children will be deprived of that pittance they expect to have from me, after my death. If I do not labor in the Senate, therefore, I must labor in the law courts—and at my age, you see, that would be difficult. I am thoroughly out of the habits of the law; it would be hard indeed to resume them. All in all, accordingly, since I have to labor, I am satisfied to labor where I now am." He smiled. "As I know your husband will have told you, life as a Senator is scarcely one of deprivation."

"One cannot really aim much higher, don't you think?"

"Oh, it is easy to aim, and easy to fire. The trick comes with trying to hit anything. I have aimed and fired—and hit nothing—for quite some years."

"That can hardly be true."

"It is all too true, I assure you. But I have now done with both aiming and firing; that season is quite over with, for me. I shall live my years out, doing whatever a Senator is capable of doing—which is not, do believe me, always a very great deal. We are credited with more authority than we possess. I could wish, sometimes, that I had had more aptitude for the cultivation of the land. I regard myself as at least one part farmer, you know. But in truth I could never have survived, by my own efforts, had my father put me behind a plough. It was for many years a standing joke in the Webster family, that Daniel was sent to be educated because he could never get the hang of a scythe!"

"Have you kept the family farm?"

"I have, yes. But it is run for me by an agent—who is a genuine farmer, unlike his employer. We correspond, when I am forced to be in Washington, and I amuse myself with telling him how to plant potatoes and how to spread ash, and with instructing him in the mystical properties of guano. His letters are immensely cheering: all full of cows calving, and fields being readied, and buildings being repaired. I often say to my wife that every one of his homely letters is worth twenty subtle communications from anyone in politics. I sometimes think I do not belong in politics at all, and never have. Strange, is it not? Here I am, having spent most of the best years of my life in my State and my country's service, and at almost the end of it all I could wish I had done something very different."

"I would surmise, Mr. Webster, that you had something quite specific in mind."

"Oh I do, you're quite right."

"May I venture to ask . . . ?"

They turned in a large arc and started slowly back toward the house.

"It can do no harm, I suppose, to gratify you, Mrs. Bingham. It was an open secret, when I was a boy, that literature was where I was headed. I wrote reams of verses. On any and every subject." He laughed. "I still write verses, now and then, though I know, by now, there isn't much point to it. The good Lord doesn't gratify us as easily as I can thus gratify you, my dear lady. We may hunger and thirst for our soul's desire, and have to live our lives without it. His way may not be our way, and we must bow to Him." There was a small silence. "And do you know, your house has entertained someone with rather more talent for verse-making than I ever had?"

"During my tenure here, Mr. Webster?"

"Within the past month, I should suppose." He glanced around and saw her confusion. "Ah: I fear I may have betrayed a secret which was less than open. Shall we pretend, for my peace of mind, that I said nothing of all this?"

"But you must be speaking of my husband's brother!"

"I cannot tell of whom I speak—and shall we forbear to speak of it? A gentleman who versifies and does not talk of it would clearly prefer that others not do what he has not chosen to do."

"I hadn't known—and pray tell, Mr. Webster, how did you know?" He did not reply, but she immediately understood. "He left something in your room! Of course: he paid us a farewell visit just the other week. And he did seem to spend an unusual amount of time alone. I thought he was reading, preparing himself."

"Is the gentleman about to depart for China?"

"Not quite so far. France—and he goes as secretary to Mr. Rives, in Paris."

"I see," he said politely.

"Were you not consulted?"

"I'm afraid not. This was your husband's doing?"

"To be sure. But you should have been consulted! Is there another Senator who knows so much as you do of foreign affairs, Mr. Webster!"

"That I have been Secretary of State, Mrs. Bingham, does not necessarily indicate my fitness to be Secretary of State. Mr. Clayton is very well-placed in that post. He has managed for almost a year now, without troubling himself about my opinions. I have little doubt he will be able to continue doing without them. It is surely no great loss to the country. My opinions, just now, are not overly popular. Mr. Clayton and President Taylor are well-advised to leave me in the comparative obscurity into which events have placed me—deservedly, I have no fear of saying." He stopped for a moment, peering down at the creek. The sun glinted off it; the water shimmered with heat and light. "If I have sinned very desperately, as I assume I necessarily have, think how merciful the Lord is, to punish me with a seat in the Senate!"

"At the risk of embarrassing you, Mr. Webster—and I shall cheerfully take that risk—a country that does not consult its great men can expect serious trouble. And that you are one of this country's great men—well, that is not open to discussion, and what you choose to call your unpopularity has I think nothing to do with it."

"You are very gracious, Mrs. Bingham. To be told to one's face that one is a great man, and to be told that by so lovely a woman, in so lovely a setting . . . . Can you really expect me to return to the Senate, after this?"

They were almost back at the house. The other guests were inside; as they approached the long white steps, a liveried servant stood rigidly to attention.

"Is not General Taylor a Whig President, Mr. Webster?"

"I think it would be fair to say, with all due respect for the President—and I have a great deal of respect for him, as both a military leader and as a political figure: he has outperformed my expectations for him, in his current office—I think it would nevertheless be fair to say that General Taylor is not such a Whig as the likes of Mr. Clay or I may be considered to be. It was not clear, when he was nominated, that he was indeed a Whig at all. I supported him, you know, but not with the sort of enthusiasm displayed by Mr. Weed—or, in point of fact, by your husband."

They started up the steps.

"And so you are left out of things?"

"Can a Senator be said, with any degree of accuracy, to be left out of things? I would rather say that the President feels more comfortable with other advisors, which is his right, and so consults with those others rather than with me. A different President would choose still different advisors. That is the way of it. If I am indeed an outsider, Mrs. Bingham, it is a privileged status for all that." They stood for a moment just outside the large doors, which were flung back. "And so extensive are my privileges, as an outsider, than here in Blue-Bell-land I am a veritable insider. How much more blessed can a man be?"

They rejoined the others.

Dear Arabella and almost-as-dear Theodore,

Having decided to send me into exile—did you think I did not know from whence the fatal impetus came?—you will now have to endure regular reports on my exilic state. No, not even the sumptuous hospitality I was offered, at Blue Bell, will save you from this verbal flood: those who launch a craft such as myself into foreign waters must learn to accept the voyageuristic consequences thereof.

Besides, I am newly in Paris—less than twenty-four hours, in truth—and feel an absolute need to communicate my impressions. (Perhaps I shall write a book, yes. They say that travel books, especially those published out of New York by Messrs. Harper, are selling better than griddle cakes. My old cohort, Bayard Taylor, must have furnished a house and planted a garden, at least, with such ill-gotten gains.)

There is remarkably little to say about my lightning trip on the high seas. These days, New York to Calais is in truth something like stepping onto a long-distance train. The wind serves only to cool a passenger's heated cheeks, after an evening of wine and music. Coal burns away, in the bowels of the ship, and a crossing of as much as two weeks would be regarded as abominably slow. (How different, Theodore, when you accompanied Father to London!) Accommodations are luxurious; food is on the whole excellent; the wine is superb (very French); and if the companionship is a bit restricted, and likely to be dull, it is at least in good taste, with even a sprinkling (I believe) of junior lords and their ladies. I read most of the day and went to bed at night: like a Greek in training for the ancient Olympic festival, I did not think I had the right to frivolity. I traveled, after all, courtesy of the United States Treasury, and my mission was wholly official and impersonal. But the majority of the passengers seemed, I will admit, to treat the entire voyage as one extended ball. The ships' musicians did not complain of fatigue, but they might well have. The sounds of distant music were, however, never anything but pleasant.

Calais proved considerably less fearsome than I had been led to expect. As a sort of diplomat, perhaps, I was extended courtesies not generally available to my countrymen, but if so it was all very offhand. I was landed, inspected, stamped, and approved in less than two hours. It would be nice to think that my impeccable French accent had something to do with it—except that when I addressed the <u>inspecteur</u> in my best French, he answered me in still better English! Oh well. In Paris, I consoled myself, they will have less linguistic expertise, and will perforce have to deal with my French, though it be after the school of Poughkeepsie on the Hudson.

My luggage being modest, I hired a carriage and was wheeled off.

French inns have amazing food, immense insect colonies, and sanitary facilities the like of which even an Iroquois would be ashamed. I shall say nothing else on the subject.

I was four days on the road—and French roads, too, are best left undescribed. I should not wonder if the shaking they produce is not basically responsible for the shortened stature of Frenchmen, as compared to Americans. The human frame cannot but pay for such treatment, and in the only coin available to it. And we complain of the paving in New York City! Never again: I should have been blessed to experience roads only twice as pock-marked and pitted as those of New York. Ah, <u>mon dieu</u>. (I am trying to learn how to sigh in French. It does not yet seem entirely natural to me.)

But I am *arrivé*, <u>*mes cheres*</u>, and the shaking is done (*my arms still quiver from it!*). I have met our Minister here, Senator Rives. He is a handsome, full-fleshed man of not much over fifty. His grip is taut and his mind seems equally so. From a stray remark or two, Theodore, I gather that he does not think another French Revolution at all imminent—though I imagine he would not be distressed to have President Louis Napoleon metamorphose into Emperor Louis Napoleon. He is a Virginian, like your own sweet self, Arabella. I have been given the day to settle myself, with my official duties not to commence until tomorrow—or even later, if need be. I was ready, need I say, as soon as my carriage wheels ceased to roll. But Mr. Rives excused me, and a dismissal from such a source is not lightly to be disregarded. I do not think a secretary, even one trained at so lordly an institution as the <u>*Tribune*</u>, ought to attempt to countermand an American Minister in full flight.

Mrs. Rives is distinctly more puzzling. She is very much younger than her husband—though I shall not venture to be precise, since residence in Paris has plainly given her an opportunity, eagerly seized, to make use of devices and apparatuses designed for the disguise of such matters. She is also a Virginian, though so petite and so very blonde that she could walk on Broadway and be thought either a native or, better still, a <u>*Parisienne*</u>. (You know how well we love the French, in New York City: they are the North Star and the Flag Pole of our existence.) she offered me the hospitality of their <u>*hôtel*</u>—which is in truth an immense affair, more a mansion than I would have expected. There were, she assured me, rooms and rooms and rooms, any of which were mine for the asking. But—<u>*comment dit-on ces choses?*</u>—a little bird kept whispering in my ear, advising me to locate in lodgings of my own, and that is what, with some help from the porter at the <u>*hôtel*</u>, I have done.

I will not trouble you with details and measurements, except to say that I have a good-sized nest and pay only one hundred and seventy-five francs a month for it—plus, <u>*bien entendu*</u>, twenty-five francs to the concierge, and nine francs for washing. Oh, yes, plus twenty-five francs more for a large pile of wood, refreshed once a month in any quantity necessary. One heats by wood, here in Paris. It is cheery, though I expect by December it will not be be anything like so warm as I am accustomed to. Never mind: by December I will be more Parisian than the French, and able to bear their winter with the best of them.

Domestic chores call me away, my dear brother and even dearer sister, so I will seal and tomorrow I will post this garrulous missive. Do write. I should like to see the cherries blossoming at Whitetowers—but that too will come. First things first, and second things second—and am I not a philosopher, indeed, now that I am become a European?

Believe me your ever devoted and still faintly dazed brother,
Jonathan Bingham

Paris: Rue de Luxembourg 29: April Fools' Day, 1850

My dear Martial, by which I mean in these first paragraphs to encompass also the following:
Grace, Alice, Mark, and Michael:

I wish you were all here. Yes, even the rambunctious two last-named. Treat your little brothers well, Grace and Alice: when they are far from you, as in the fullness of time they inevitably will be, you will miss them even as much as I miss you, and all of you. I am in Paris, not in Heaven: and so I shall return to you, in due course.

I know I ought to tell you about the ocean, and its mighty waves, and about the soil of France, and what grows upon that soil, and about the taste of French butter and the walk of French women (not to mention their clothing, which is said to constitute, always, the very latest in fashion). Well, that may be, that may be—but I should prefer to save all such stuff for the travel book I will inevitably pen, sooner or later. Nor would you want, all of you, the same exact kind of information. Alice might be more interested in shawls and Grace in shoes. Michael might want military impressions, while Mark would hunt for agricultural data. And how could I tell you, oh Johnson pater familias, anything whatever that you did not know about French medicine?

The waves were—in a word—very wet.

You may ask how I know, since I stayed on the ship and did not venture into what the ship necessarily was immersed in.

You may well ask, but I do not propose to trouble myself with an answer. (Do not imitate me, children: it is a practice meant for adults and for adults only. Children should always speak when they are spoken to. They should also stand very straight and eat all their vegetables. And so to bed, little ones: the rest of this curious document is for your father's eyes alone. I kiss your soft cheeks.)

It does me good, as I think you will believe, Martial, to unbend with you and your family. The trip across was stolid, unending (though relatively short), and very productive: I was in truth writing very hard, harder, I dare say, than ever before in my life, and I think something may come of it. I will let you know if anything does. This is a project very dear to my heart, but it will take some while, still, to complete. It will have its interest for you, too—and that is all I will say on the subject. (It is an old axiom among authors, you know, that those who talk too much about what they are writing end by only talking.)

I have in truth very little to say about Paris. Or about France. I know very little about either, having spent less than a day in the one and less than a week in the other. Our Minister here, Mr. Rives (who was for some years Senator Rives: like our sister Arabella, he is a native Virginian), seems a sensible and pleasant man, not above fifty, a bit too large, but firm of both mind and hand. He has given me as much time to settle in as I may need, but I have promised to be ready on the morrow. And so I shall be. With the aid of his official porter, I have discovered this spacious and comfortable apartment; it is furnished, and very nicely furnished, so I have unpacked myself and moved in. Let us hope that Rue de Luxembourg 29 is an address destined to go down in American literary annals. (I do not think it is notable in those of France—but perhaps I am wrong. I shall endeavor to test my premise against the facts, when opportunity presents itself.) I am resolved that, at the least, it will not be preserved in any record as the locale for anything but serious and devoted labor. So there you have it.

Oh, yes: the aforesaid Mr. Rives is accompanied through life by a Mrs. Rives, younger by far, prettier by all odds, and to me rather strange. I had suspected that all Virginia belles were like our Arabella—but this belle, though belle enough, is—I do not know what. If I did not know better, I would have taken her (let me whisper the word) for a flirt. I must mistake both the manners of this country and those of her native place: she is the wife of the ambassador, after all, and I am a lowly secretary-clerk-transcriber-poet—and can one be lower, in this world, than that? Mrs. Rives offered me accommodation at their ministerial hôtel. I could not accept: do not ask me why.

It grows rapidly darker, I am alone, and I am hungry. My domestic arrange- ments do not as yet admit of dining here at home—but hold, I have just been pre- sented with a very presentable tray, displaying wine (to be sure), cheese, bread. Well: I am at home, make no mistake of it. I shall now dine, my dear Martial, and wish that you and yours could dine with me. Or I with you. I am already half-seas over with homesickness. It hope I shall recover in time: I have no terminus ad quem for my employment here. It will not be forever: you may count on that. Brace yourself, then, for I shall return, and that before too very long.

I hope you have been giving some thought to the very piquant discussions we had, the last time I saw you. I hope you are giving the subject more than thought, indeed. Do write, when you are able. Encourage the children to write also: I hereby pledge myself to give as good as I get.

Believe me, now and forever, yours faithfully,
Jonathan Bingham

FIFTEEN

Clarissa Rives seemed to be everywhere in the multi-storeyed, many-chambered *hôtel*—not a hotel at all, but more like some vast residential quarry, an almost endless series of plaster-and-wood caves in a tunneled-out warren. It was impossible for an American to understand what a *hôtel* was, or why the Parisians should want to live in them. Jonathan came to understand, in time, that there were rich *hôtels* and poor ones, too, and that social and fiscal differences made for domestic differences, as well. But all of them teemed; all them were noisy and full of so many people that it was impossible so many diverse individuals should reside where they were found. They did not: Jonathan also learned that Parisians scurried back and forth from *hôtel* to *hôtel* and—still more astonishing—that the proprietors of a suite were always at home when in fact at home. No visitor was ever turned away, despite inconvenience, despite other and possibly domestic arrangements. "They'd show you right into their bedroom!" he scoffed to himself—and then discovered that indeed they would. Was there no place sacred in Paris? Not, visibly, to Mrs. Rives, who flowed in and out of doors and windows equally, who passed through walls and ceilings alike, who was everywhere he went.

"Good morning, Mr. Bingham," she greeted him the first time. He had just managed to find his way from the Rue de Luxembourg, a ten-minute walk he had managed to prolong to something over twice that length. It was early April, and chilly in the early hours, but he was perspiring.

"*Bonjour, madame,*" he replied, trying to seem more cosmopolitan than he felt. Mrs. Rives was not only up and about, this early, but she was dressed in what, at home, would have seemed more like evening attire. Her dress seemed remarkably close-fitting, and the bodice had a scallop in it that, even perspiring and distracted as he was, he found upsetting. "*Comment allez-vous ce matin?*"

Her laugh, high and full, was about equally upsetting.

"Oh, no, Mr. Bingham. That is school French. You will have to speak only English to me, if you are to use such French. You will corrupt my accent, and I have been two years at its cultivation. Pray be more cooperative."

"And what ought I to say, Madame?"

She quite flustered him by curtseying.

"A lady does not instruct a gentleman, Mr. Bingham, in matters of address." She started to sweep off, then swung partly back toward him. "Perhaps *comment ça va* will be better?"

He bowed, fancied he saw an odd smile flicker for a moment on her face, then went in search of his employer as his employer's pretty wife disappeared through a side door.

Mr. Rives seemed a bit surprised that he had, in fact, found his way to the *hôtel.* Jonathan came upon him, seated at a kind of small writing table, enjoying a *croissant* and a small blue and white pot of *chocolat.* There were no writing materials in evidence.

"Ah, *monsieur le sécretaire!*" He smiled up at Jonathan, who of course remained standing. "You can see, my dear sir, how readily one habituates to Paris and to Parisian ways. One sinks into France as into a deep feather cushion." Jonathan bowed faintly. "Are you thoroughly settled, then?"

Jonathan briefly described his apartment.

"You *have* done well. Pierre helped, I dare say?"

"Immensely."

Mr. Rives brushed his hands lightly together; the *croissant* was gone, and the blue and white pot looked empty.

"I doubt that I could have done as well as that, my first day in New York. I doubt, indeed, that I would have tried. Well, then, young man, are you indicating a desire for work?"

"Such work as I may be capable of, sir. I am used to the ways of a newspaper, but not to those of the Department of State."

"You'll never accustom yourself to the Department, let me assure you. It is a strange hybrid monster, part griffon and part sphinx, with perhaps a dash of coyote. Does Judge Clayton bear up well?"

"He was in vigorous good health, when we talked."

"Good: he is an old Senatorial colleague, you know. He left us, to become chief justice, in Delaware." He held up one finger. "No, actually, that was not how it was. I had left the Senate some little while earlier. The people back home and I did not see eye to eye on the matter of the Jacksonian bank question. That was before your time, to be sure."

"I'm afraid virtually everything has been before my time, sir. But it was 1834, was it not, when you resigned from the Senate, and 1836 when Judge Clayton took the chief judgeship?"

"You are indeed a newspaperman, I see! And is your brother as well-schooled in the intricacies of diplomatic biography?"

"My brother, sir, is a Senator, and I believe it is a prerogative of the office to ask questions rather than respond to them."

"Quite true, usually. I hear good things of your brother—as indeed I hear good things of you. If old Horace Greeley was unable to corrupt you, I doubt that the diplomatic service can do you much harm!"

"I will be more concerned about what harm I am, myself, able to do."

Mr. Rives leaned back in his chair.

"Oh, I don't know that we'll give you much chance for that. I don't think even I could do a great deal of harm, if I set out to. If I badly offended Madame Eugénie—the President's wife, you know, and very Spanish she is, and very haughty she can be when she wants to—well, I dare say the worst that would happen is my recall. But do you happen to remember how much rope we gave Citizen Genet, back in the beginning of things, before we sent him packing?"

"We were as young then, sir, as I am now."

"Well said, young fellow. I'm told you have literary ambitions."

Jonathan nodded quietly.

"Well, you show talent, you do, indeed. Have you read this poet of theirs, Victor Hugo?"

"Oh, yes!"

"You like him?"

"He is quite marvelous, I think."

Mr. Rives scratched his chin.

"My French is none of the best, and in the way of poetry I frankly find it hard to appreciate much since Wordsworth. Perhaps you can be of some help to me. I should be pleased to find myself understanding this man they talk of, sometimes, as 'the French Shakespeare.'"

Jonathan had a sudden illumination as to the range of duties a secretary might be called upon to perform.

"It would be my pleasure, sir."

"I will be much in your debt, believe me. And how nice it would be, at dinner parties, to be able to roll a bit of Hugo off my tongue. The French are a good deal fond of quoting poets, you know. Have you a volume or two of his on your shelves?"

"I'm afraid I have no shelves as yet, sir. But bringing Victor Hugo to Paris would have been rather like bringing coals to Newcastle."

"Quite so." Mr. Rives sat thoughtfully for a moment. "Why don't you ask Pierre where you may find the nearest book shop, and you just lay in whatever stores you think we may need."

"Now, sir?"

"Why not? This would seem as good a time as any. What was it the Duke of Wellington used to say? 'In time of peace, prepare for war.' I don't say that Monsieur Hugo and I are engaged in outright hostilities, but a simple Virginia gentleman like myself surely has to struggle, to keep up with his flights of fancy. Why don't you go and seek Pierre's advice—he knows everything, as you've probably begun to realize. If they recalled me, I think I'd suggest him as my successor, if that could be arranged. You go and find us some suitable ammunition for the poetic battlefield. Keep the blessed things on your desk, here, so we'll have them by us when they're wanted."

And where would this desk of his be located, Jonathan wondered to himself, as he went in search of Pierre. All in good time: Rome was not built in a day; render unto Casear the things that are Caesar's. Comfort me with maxims, he assured himself. *Ecco il libro*! But all the same he felt odd, hunting down the Minister's factotum. Suppose he found, instead, the Minister's wife?

He found the factotum, and then the book shop, and then the necessary volumes. And then he found his way back to the *hôtel*. And there, finding that by this point the Minister was "in conference"—he did not ask with whom or about what, nor was that information volunteered—he asked for the location of his desk and, after some verbal uncertainties, was shown to it. And just then placing a small flowered vase on that desk, a vase empty of flowers at the moment, was in fact the Minister's wife.

"This is my part of diplomacy," she said. "I try to keep flowers in the gentlemen's working quarters." She stepped back, considering. "I think that will do very well."

"Very well. Thank you. But I trust your husband's desk boasts a multiplicity of such containers?" She did she not seem to understand.

"That is, his precedence, in this case, is clearly a double one, first as your husband, second as our country's minister."

She made no response. He considered the desk, which was a French style, unfamiliar to him. Rather than commanding a room, it seemed to command the entrance to a room—and judging by the double doors, carved and embossed, and by the portrait of General Taylor that hung across from the doors, he guessed that the anteroom in which he was located guarded the Minister's official chambers.

"Mr. Rives has a visitor. Have you been buying books?"

"These? Yes, but not for myself. Victor Hugo. Mr. Rives would like me to read some of that with him."

"Oh, Mr. Rives is a vastly ambitious man! I wish he could carry out all the projects he conceives of." Her eyes went to the books, and then swung toward him. "Are you a poet, Mr. Bingham?"

"In some fashion. But I think your husband will not often draw upon me in that capacity."

"If he will not, then I shall have to!"

He picked up the vase and pretended to examine it. What on earth was the woman up to?

"Do you know the origin of the word *secretary*, Mrs. Rives?"

"How should I, Mr. Bingham? I am neither poet nor scholar."

"Keeper of secrets, essentially. Confidant. If the secrets I am expected to keep are no more dangerous than the verses of Victor Hugo, I shall have an easy time of it in Paris."

"I can tell you very little of your official duties, Mr. Bingham. My responsibilities extend to flowers, and to social calls and dinners. I am obliged to have a new dress at every formal ball—isn't that a terrible thing to do to a woman?"

"It does sound arduous, yes. How do you manage to keep up with so urgent a task?"

"It takes several dressmakers, I can assure you. Nor does the Congress recognize its share of the burden. Mr. Rives' purse must pay for everything."

"I'm sure he does not mind, considering the excellence of the cause."

"He has not *said* he minds, but I rather fear he does. If anything of the sort is confided to you, Mr. Secretary, I would be much obliged if you would tell me."

"Your servant, Mrs. Rives."

She laughed and vanished. He had a few moments to explore the intricacies of his new desk, the beautifully crafted drawers, the handsome carving. And then Mr. Rives' great double doors were opened. Jonathan swung to attention. But the visitor who emerged did not require diplomatic services: this was the Minister's barber, bearing the obvious tools of his trade on a tray before him. The doors closed again, the barber whisked himself out of sight. Mr. Rives did not emerge, nor did any secretarial responsibilities. Jonathan wondered for a moment if he ought to knock, then realized he ought not to do anything until his employer summoned him. Did Mr. Rives realize that he was back from his book-buying errand? No matter: it would not be a difficult point to establish, when the Minister chose to seek him. Reportorial initiatives would not do, here.

Half an hour went by. Jonathan sat at his desk, stared into the polished wood, occasionally fingered the delicate drawer-pulls, and once or twice started to pick up a volume of Victor Hugo. But it would not do to be found reading poetry, even French poetry—even French poetry brought to his desk at the direction of his employer. It was one thing for Mr. Rives to indicate such an interest; it was something quite different for his secretary to sit and pursue matters on his own.

Was it always like this, at the Ministry? Jonathan had no experience of diplomacy, American or other. There had been virtually no briefing—none at all, if Secretary of State's Clayton's rather casual remarks could be ignored. Jonathan could not afford to ignore them: he had nothing else to go by. Where was all the immense labor of which other secretaries had complained? Did Mr. Rives himself ever *do* anything? If all that concerned him, indeed, were barbers and bookshops and ballgowns for his wife, then Congress' parsimony was not difficult to understand. What good did it do the United States of America to fund the Paris vagaries of the Rives family—and then add to them the vacuities of Mr. Jonathan Bingham, ex-reporter for the New York *Tribune*? 'Mr. Bingham reports that life in Paris is all very well,' he found himself writing in his head, 'but somewhat on the inactive side. His morning coffee was a bit strong, but on the whole highly potable. Paris streets were distinctly filthy'—but his readers already knew that. One did not come to France for the glories experienced by one's nose: it would be like riding behind a steam locomotive in search of pure, clean air.

"Would you step in for a moment, Mr. Bingham?"

It was Mr. Rives, standing in the doorway. Jonathan was more than startled: he had begun to voyage in internal waters, and the summons came like a message from outer space.

Mr. Rives motioned him to a chair, then went behind his own desk—which was, of course, a great deal larger, and heavier, though no more polished, than his secretary's. There was a large pile of paper in front of him. He plucked something off the top of the pile.

"Our mail bags arrive only once or twice a week, Mr. Bingham, so the pace of correspondence will necessarily vary—sometimes heavy, sometimes light. If you don't mind, when official letters are wanting, I will now and then ask you to be of assistance with private ones.

"I would propose some arrangement of the following sort," Mr. Rives went on, his eyes straying to the paper in front of him. "After I have finished looking through what our bag brings us, I will ask you to come in and discuss each item with me. You can make whatever notation you think helpful directly on the document, I would suggest—to avoid confusion, you see—and then you can dispose of the replies at your leisure." He glanced up for a moment. "Oh, yes, you must be wondering where all the official visitors are. In London, I understand, the Minister receives in the morning. That would, of course, be an utter waste of time, here. There are Americans in Paris who rise at a normal hour—a normal hour for Americans, that is—but most conform pretty readily to the customs of the country. And the French would not dream of doing serious business before noon. Or even later. So, we will have our visitors—and a fair stream of them, I assure you. But we will discuss that after a bit. For the most part, you will not need to be present, when I am being bored out of my mind by pests of one sort or another. I will from time to time ask you to serve as a translator—not that my own French is quite so bad as all that, but for diplomatic reasons, you understand. It is better if, sometimes, I do not seem to understand too easily what is being said to me in an official capacity. I wish, at times, I understood much less than I do. And there will be times when I will want you as a witness, or to take notes—you understand, I'm sure."

Jonathan again assented. The Minister's calm, organized, business-like stance made him uncomfortable. He had suspected this man of being a well-paid loafer! *Mon dieu!*

"Have you some well-sharpened pencils, and a good group of pens?"

"I'm afraid not, sir."

Mr. Rives opened a drawer and handed over a very good supply.

"If you are ready, then, Mr. Bingham, we shall begin." He thwacked the first document. "This is a note from Judge Clayton—his communications naturally receive our primary attention, he being my direct employer. As I am yours. Well. It seems that recently, in the harbor of Belize . . . ."

The pile was not unusually large, according to Mr. Rives, but the discussion—which was exclusively Ministerial: there were no Secretarial comments solicited and there were none volunteered—occupied something over an hour. Then each man was left alone at his desk, the Minister to compose such documents as required his personal drafting, the Secretary to accomplish the lesser items. It was immediately apparent to Jonathan that some training, at least, would have been immensely useful. He could write a clear hand, all right, even a fair approximation of the copper plate favored in official letters. But there were thorny questions of procedure. How was one to address a French general, who sought information on military structures and supply organizations? What title did the Minister of another country merit? Was the Secretary to write in his own name, in the Minister's, and, if the latter, was he to sign the Minister's name or present the document for signature? Ought he to send certain letters in French, rather than in English, or was the Ministry bound to the use of English? (He rather hoped it was: correspondence in French would require more than a little extra effort. It would be good for his soul, but he was not at the moment worrying about spiritual benefits.)

He began to sort the pile into separate categories. Those he could dispose of without further query he would do at once. For the others, additional guidance would be needed. He would feel singularly foolish, returning to the Minister, hat in hand, but it could not be helped. Who else could he consult for such precise information? He let himself realize, for just a moment, that even the Minister might not have the answers: he did not, after all, ever see this side of their joint labors. His predecessor as Secretary would know, of course—but who might that be and where on earth might he be found? Why was one Secretary permitted to leave before another was settled in? Why was there no neatly-bound compendium of rules and regulations? He pushed aside panic and did what he could.

Shortly before noon, warm and dazzled, he wondered if his health would prove adequate to such ferocious paper-shuffling. He felt the edge of a headache—and he was not usually subject to such pains. Well, it would either improve or it would not. He would either survive or he would not. He smiled grimly: how on earth had the sovereign state of which he was so insignificant a representative ventured to send such a pipsqueak as himself—such a puppy of ignorance and incompetence—on an errand of such weightiness?

"Will poppies do?"

He stared at her a moment. She stood just to the side of his desk, a small bouquet of red and white flowers in her hand.

"Do you mind poppies?"

He shook his head, and tried at the same time to clear it.

"Not a bit, thank you, Mrs. Rives. It is the flower of forgetfulness—and I was so absorbed in my work that for a second or two I scarcely knew where I was and what you were saying to me. My apologies. I trust I shall grow more alert."

She placed the flowers in the vase, adding a small quantity of water from a metal pot standing just behind the desk.

"Mr. Sanford had a good deal of trouble, at first, distinguishing this sort of letter from that sort. He was here before you came, you know."

He leaned back and wiped his forehead.

"I wish I could have him here, right now, for just an hour!"

"I believe he is in Cincinnati."

"I may soon be in purgatory!"

"I recall his saying, once, that all government people were whatever their titles said they were, and everyone else was honorable."

Was it that simple? Had she just dissolved half his troubles, with a laugh and a word? This *flirt*? He groaned to himself. A newspaper was supposed to train a man, help him see through pretense to reality! All he seemed to have learned was how to misjudge everything.

"And then the signatures," she went on, peering thoughtfully at the vase. She stopped.

"Yes?"

She bent and moved the vase more toward the center of the desk.

"That does look better, don't you think?"

"Much." He waited. "And the signatures?"

"Signatures? Oh, yes, on those letters. Mr. Sanford was not a poet, but he made a little rhyme that solved most of his difficulties. How did it go? 'When in doubt, leave it out.' I think that was it. A signature could always be added afterwards, he explained, so when he was not sure he put no signature at all—and left it for my husband to decide. Mr. Rives does not mind, you know. He is a very reasonable man, you will see that he is."

She was like a living training manual. It was as if a *danseuse* had stopped, in mid-whirl, and delivered herself of a compact, forceful lecture on constitutional law. It was as if Pierre had turned out to be Victor Hugo in disguise. It was, *tout court*, as if Jonathan Bingham was a first-class ass. How could he indicate both his gratitude and his regret?

"You have made the crooked straight, Mrs. Rives."

"Just tell me one more thing," he added. She cocked her head dutifully. "Did Mr. Sanford ever compose letters in French?"

Her smile seemed to say, for a moment, that it was impossible to tell what Mr. Sanford had done: such a man of parts! Then she replied, simply enough:

"I believe he did. Yes, I'm quite sure he did. It was very difficult, especially at first."

"Does a pin drop, here, without your knowing it?"

She turned to go, whirling with apparent pleasure.

"Lunch will be at two, Mr. Bingham. You are to dine with us. The cook has been forewarned."

His head spun, as he sat looking at his documents. The rest would be like child's play, thanks to her casual comments: like a master theologian, she had held up a grain of sand and from it explicated the entire universe. Was he in Paris or lost in some dream? His eyes focused on the poppies: they were indisputably real. He gripped the edge of the desk. Yes, that was real too, as solid as flesh. He was in Paris all right, and he was awake; it was April of 1850, and he had come across the ocean for just the work he was now doing. But was this Mrs. Rives what she seemed to be? Was she, perhaps, not so much a master theologian as a master spy—all her disarming simplicities and absurdities simply a cloak for deceptive activities vast and complex beyond his comprehension? He shook his head. It was, in truth, beyond his comprehension, and so there was not much point in trying to comprehend it. He picked up a document, sharpened a pen, and set to work.

The hours before lunch had been even more of a whirl. Visitors approached him: he would rise and bow, and there would be minor discussion—in the end, he would seek admission to the Minister's chambers and, if authorized, would escort in the visitor; if not authorized, he would fabricate an appropriate dismissal, something not so much denying access as postponing it. He was not requested to stay for any conferences, this first day—and that was just as well. His own desk was crowded with work. It was hard to keep leaping from letter to visitor and back; it would have been still harder had the interruptions been longer, had he been obliged to take notes on what was said, had his services been required as an active translator. His mind seeking a precise phrase he wanted for a letter, he wondered if this was merely a postponement of his translating activities, and a deliberate easing of the new Secretary's burden? He found the phrase he needed and began to set it down on paper, leaving the speculation unresolved. He also knew his speculative powers were vastly less powerful than he had ever suspected. Would he improve?

Would it rain?

Would lunch be *à la française* or *américaine?*

Would he please mind his business, and his *p*s and his *q*s?

Lunch was plainly *à la française*. Mr. Rives emerged to escort him to table, and the lay of the cloth alone told him that the customs of the country would be observed.

"I do sometimes bring our visitors to table," Mr. Rives had explained, as they went up the carpeted stairs. "But lunch is more our own than is the evening meal." He showed Jonathan through the door. "Almost a family affair, you know. I'm sorry you won't be lodged here, as Sanford was. I grew rather accustomed to having him about. Perhaps you chose wisely, you know. I can't very well summon you, at three in the morning, from the Rue de Luxembourg. Well, not unless it's a true state emergency, at any rate." He consulted his watch. They were in a comfortably furnished room of medium size; there was no table in evidence. "I think we can go in."

The table was set *à la française*, but, in variance from the customs of the country, they were joined by the Rives children, two girls of about eleven or twelve, shy and invariably quiet. Their mother—Mrs. Rives was their mother, wasn't she?—sat at the foot of the table, the Minister at the head, and Jonathan on his right. The two children sat together on their father's left. Each course was produced from the hands of a servant—French, to be sure—and afterwards was cleared by the same servant. The cook remained totally unseen, as did the kitchen.

"We hope you will lunch with us as a matter of course," said Mr. Rives as soup was being served.

"My daughters have been anxious to meet you," added Mrs. Rives.

"You're definitely a celebrity," said the Minister.

"For now, perhaps. But I shall try, hereafter, to be as inconspicuous as the woodwork."

"That may not be permitted."

"Or tolerated," Mrs. Rives added.

"The point being," Mr. Rives summed up, "that we do most warmly welcome you, and we hope that you will be happy here—as well as
busy."

They addressed themselves to their soup, continuing in an easy
conversation.

"Paris is an immense city," Mrs. Rives said. "We have been here
for more than two years, and my daughters and I are fond of rambling
about. But we have not begun to know the city, and I suspect we never
can, given a diplomat's limited tenure."

"New York is perhaps easier to know," Jonathan said, "though it,
too, is growing rapidly."

"You are not a native of the city?"

"Not yet, Mrs. Rives."

"The young man is a diplomat, my dear. In addition to knowing
what words to use, he knows what words not to use."

"I was born in Poughkeepsie, Mrs. Rives. My early years were spent
there. But I have family in New York, so we visited regularly. And I attended Columbia College, in New York, before I joined the *Tribune*."

"Do tell us about Poughkeepsie. Is that how you pronounce it,
Mr. Bingham?" She signaled for the soup bowls to be removed. "Is it
located in the United States?"

"So I am told, Mrs. Rives!"

They discussed Poughkeepsie, and then New York, and dined quietly and well. Diplomacy was not either broached or breached. Mention
was made, in passing, of a succession of official evenings out, at many
of which the new Secretary of the Mission would be expected to attend, but that was as close to the bone as things came.

But while he was walking in the small garden, behind the *hôtel*, waiting for Mr. Rives to rise from what was apparently a usual post-prandial
rest, Jonathan found himself again confronted with the Minister's wife.
She was wearing a bonnet and there was a straw basket on her arm. She
seemed to be heading toward the gate, but she stopped, seeing him.

"To market, to market!" he greeted her.

"Not really—but there are so many little stalls, and they offer so
many delightful surprises that I am always tempted." She lifted her basket. "And with this on my arm, you see, I am always prepared."

"I would offer my services, but I fear I shall be on duty in a very
few moments."

"I fear you are right. It is kind of you to offer." Jonathan bowed, thinking the encounter ended, but she made no move to leave. "I would not venture out alone, in the United States. But it is very different, here. There is no impropriety in my taking a stroll unaccompanied. I am told, you know, that Madame Eugénie, the President's wife, would like to be able to do this. She expects, however, to be Empress Eugénie, before too long, and it would not do for royalty to behave as we commoners are permitted to do."

She smiled cheerfully. He decided to seek higher ground.

"Your daughters must be at their lessons."

"Oh, yes. Their tutor, at the moment, is French. We alternate the French variety and the American, so they learn both worlds—and both languages. I do not want them to be in a French school. I have a horror of that sort of formality—and I do not want them exposed to the Roman religion."

"To be sure."

"It is hard for Europeans to understand: you will find that out for yourself, I have no doubt. They do not fear Rome. So many of them are, in name at least, themselves Catholic! They do not seem to take it seriously. But I fear it, nevertheless."

"The man my brother defeated, in the first instance, when he went to Congress, was an Irish immigrant. And a Catholic. It was something of an issue in their debates."

"It will be more of an issue, don't you think? The immigration is enormous, I believe. And growing."

"Indeed."

"Do you expect to write about Europe, Mr. Bingham?"

"For the *Tribune?* No, I think I ought not to, while I am in the government service."

"Not for the newspapers, no, but for more thoughtful readers perhaps?"

"If I become sufficiently expert, Mrs. Rives, I may find myself producing a treatise of some sort. But I should be surprised if I did."

"Are you already thinking of leaving us?"

"Oh, no, not at all. But if your husband's tenure is limited, what must mine be?" He tried to keep his smile crisp; her eye seemed to pierce his armor without the slightest effort.

"Are your quarters comfortable, Mr. Bingham?"

"Astonishingly so. That is the principal difference between New York and Paris, in my limited experience. Though even that may be a nonexistent difference, created out of inexperience."

"I think you will be happy, here," she affirmed—and still did not go on her way.

"I should be most inattentive, as well as ungrateful, if I were not, Mrs. Rives. It is a splendid opportunity. I propose to take full advantage of it."

"Of course. And you will permit us, will you not, to be helpful whenever we can? Though I dare say that, before long, you will be better equipped to guide us about Paris than we would be to guide you. You are, after all, a poet—and this is a poet's city. But I need not tell *you* that."

"Every city is a poet's city, I think," he replied quietly, feeling suddenly more secure with her. She was a woman, and he was a man: what could she do to him? She plainly sought him out; the number of occasions, in this less than one day, when he had found himself alone with her could not be a thing of accident. If he was so worthy in her eyes, having done nothing to establish any claim on her, then his was the ascendancy, not hers, and he was perfectly safe. Why had he felt threatened? "Even such a poet as I am."

"You will read me some of your work?"

"In time."

"You are very diplomatic, exactly as my husband says you are."

"I am a Yankee, Mrs. Rives, and the blood on my mother's side is pure tradesman, as far back as one can see. I spent some months in my uncles' counting-house, in New York. A handshake can be worth fifty thousand dollars there, and a nod of the head a hundred thousand. One learns to guard one's words. And even Mr. Greeley, my late employer, though he may have the reputation of being loose with words, is, in fact, a veritable miser. He says only what he means to, not a jot too much or too little."

Her smile did not seem in the least out of countenance.

"But you will read me something of what you have written?"

He bowed, silently, and this time she left him.

A moment later he was summoned to Mr. Rives' office, and the afternoon's labors had begun.

*"I assure you, it is not often that good wine is under any roof where
I am without my knowing it."*

—Daniel Webster, to his friend Stephen White
August/September 1832

Whitetowers, 15 April 1850

Dear Brother Jonathan,

*Exile would be more peaceful, right now, than the internecine warfare being
conducted in the Senate. As a Virginian by marriage, and with a wife who is indisputably a slaveholder, your brother finds himself in the unique position of being
mistrusted by both sides. The Northerners are suspicious that, in marrying to the
South, he has irretrievably sold himself to the plantation owners and growers of cotton. The Southerners are, of course, aware that he has done no such thing and is and
will remain a Senator from New York rather than from Dixie. Mr. Webster—who,
by the way, followed you to Blue Bell: did you know that in his youth he, too, aspired
to Olympus?—several months ago came down hard on the side of—neither side.
He advocated compromise, for the sake of the Union, as also has Mr. Clay, newly
returned to the Senate and a great force for good. But how it will all end, Theodore
tells me, he cannot yet see. President Taylor is, to be sure, an obstacle: he does not
believe in compromise any more than he did in military retreat, when he was no more
than a general.*

*So much for politics, which are no more interesting when seen from close up than
from three thousand miles distant. You are quite right: there should be no politics in
our representation abroad (or at least as little as possible). Your two letters would
seem to indicate much more interest in Mrs. Rives than in President Louis Napoleon. To be sure, you see a good deal more of the lady than of the President—but do
be discreet. Or, if you find yourself unable to be discreet, at least be careful.*

*We have been to Poughkeepsie, and environs, recently, though the trip was not
of long duration. Theodore has had some mysterious dealings with your father, the
purport of which he does not propose to confide in me, so that, alas, I can confide
nothing in you. I do love to pass along secrets; it is a pity your brother is so close-fisted
about them. We visited your brother Johnson, too, and though I tried mightily to*

persuade him of the superior virtues of medical practice in Virginia, I quite failed. Arguments about the educational advantages for his children, and fairly soon the social advantages for his daughters, similarly failed to move him. He has, however, permitted his oldest daughter, Grace—I cannot say little Grace, she being quite a young lady—to make us a visit, and she is here now, having come south with us. Theodore will return her to her father in good season, but no sooner than necessary. I enjoy her company immensely. I do not know that she would have been an ideal daughter, had I been privileged to have one: she is too formed, too serious, perhaps. But she has a quick eye, and a quick tongue, and she has a marvelous gracefulness. Just to see her enter a room is a pleasure to me. I doubt that I have myself ever moved with such catlike smoothness. She is a remarkable child, and will be, without fail I think, an even more remarkable woman. Your sister would be proud of her. I can assure you that I am—and never more so than when it is assumed, here where she is not much known, that I am in fact her mother. It would have been nice, from time to time, to be taken for her older sister, but I seem to be too far gone for that, I am sorry to report. What charms I have had, indeed, might never have been adequate to such a pretension: Grace Johnson is already a singularly beautiful young person.

She tells me, candidly, that although she admires her uncle in the Senate, her uncle in Paris is her favorite. You do seem to attract feminine attention, Jonathan! If it were possible, she would dearly love to visit you as she has the Washington Binghams. She knows it is not possible, but Grace does not strike me as easily reconcilable to the impossible. I think were I her mother and responsible for her to that degree, I might feel some concern. It is not stubbornness, nor is it disobedience. But it is a striking and vigorous independence, certainly, in one so young—and female. I questioned almost nothing, at her age, and would have been rather severely reprimanded, I suspect, if I had. My father was a seventeenth-century Englishman, when it came to the behavior of his female children.

Your brother has had some interesting law cases, of late. They have not made much law, as he puts it, but they have made a great deal of money—for him. It is just as well that we do not try to farm Blue Bell, and Whiteoaks, but only rest on their undisturbed surfaces. An uncle of mine, also a lawyer, used to say with a peculiarly wry smile that he knew without a doubt that there was money in farming—he had put so much of it there! Theodore and I would rather put our money by, for those old ages which seem to creep up so slyly on each and every one of us.

Not on you, to be sure: it is not until a man is old enough to vote, I think, that age begins to seem a burden rather than an accomplishment. Were you at home, you would vote this next year, would you not? Being in Paris will therefore doubly preserve you young and safe.

Perhaps it is our privilege of not voting which keeps us women as free as we are of the problems of age! Government—as you must be learning—is a dreadful burden on those who must do the governing. I could almost wish that Theodore restricted himself to the law, and not to the making of laws. But he insists that the Senate is a very great place. It is filled, to be sure, with very great men—though some of the greatest are growing too old to remain much longer with us. And we have lost one great man, Mr. Calhoun. His passing will not make much of a stir abroad, I believe; he never achieved really great office, though he deserved it. But he is gone and we of the South, in particular, mourn him deeply. It is always a dark time, I feel, when the great ones begin to leave us. There will be others, there always are, but the great that one knows are unlike the great that one has to grow accustomed to. We of the South knew Mr. Calhoun, and knew we could trust him. As to his successors—well, we shall see.

What, you must be saying to yourself! My sister Arabella so philosophical? I had not thought it possible. But do you begin to see, dear Jonathan, how easy it is for a clever woman—and I am one of that breed, you know—to fool a man, any man? It is not a secret I reveal to you casually, but in the express hope that, circumstanced where and how you are, it may be of some use to you. If Arabella could be so cleverly feigning, just think what ———— or even ———— might be capable of. Do think of it: it will be of use to you, believe me!

And since I hear your niece approaching, across the lawn, from a game she has been at, let me assure you, Brother, of my pure affection as, now and forever, your sister,

Arabella Bingham

Washington [Whitetowers], 20 April 1850

Dear Uncle Jonathan,

I am visiting my Uncle Theodore and Aunt Arabella at Whiteoaks. They keep me too occupied to miss my sister and my brothers, though I do miss my father. I think my brothers must keep my father too busy to miss me!

No one in New York State pays much attention to a child, but here in Virginia—I think Whiteoaks is in Virginia: is it?—I am spoken to like a real person. Ladies and gentlemen talk to me, and even listen to me. It is very pleasant. It may not be right—I do not know if my father would agree with it—but it is very nice. I am asked what I think of things. And then my answers are regarded. Perhaps they go off and laugh, where I cannot see them, but perhaps they do not.

I miss you very much, Uncle Jonathan. It is very nice to have letters from you. I try always to answer them very quickly, so you can write more. It is also very good practice for me. And I try very hard to make my penmanship clear and easy to understand. Is it?

What are you doing right now? When you write to me, tell me just what you are doing. All right? Do you speak French a great deal? I have begun to learn some French. It is very beautiful, as you have always told me it was. But it is so very different. I had not expected it to be so different from English. How can people use so many different ways for saying the very same thing? That seems very strange to me. Perhaps I will think differently when I am grown up.

I think my Aunt Arabella is a very grand lady. She has so many Negroes to do things for her. I do not know if they are happy, belonging to her. But she is nice to them. I have heard of slaves being beaten, but she does not do that. I am not allowed to play with the Negro children.

My Uncle Theodore spends most of his time at the Senate. It is very important. He is often very tired when he comes home. But Aunt Arabella is very nice to him.

I have been to a Ballet. It is too splendid for me to tell you about. Do they have Ballets in Paris, where you are? Do you go? If you go, you will know what I mean.

This is a very long letter. It has taken me two hours to write. I am very tired, but I hope you are not tired reading what I have written. I wish I could kiss you.

> *Your loving niece,*
> *Grace Johnson*

"I am grateful to you, Mr. Bingham. My husband can ill spare you, but he knows how much I wanted to attend this exhibition."

"The École des Beaux Arts is hardly the place for an unattended lady."

They sat quietly in the Minister's carriage, letting the streets unroll. The Parisian spring was translucent: it seemed, sometimes, as if there was no difference between the daylight and nighttime skies. Neither contained anything but faint streaks of cloud, and the bluest of all the blues Jonathan had ever seen. The Hudson was a beautiful river; the Seine, along which they rode and along which the École des Beaux Art was located, was still more beautiful. The sun was at mid-summer brightness, if not yet at mid-summer heat. And everyone in Paris seemed to be in the streets, walking, shopping, riding, seated at small café tables. The trees were full, having been blossoming for over a month, but not yet dark with summer green. There was still a laciness to the foliage, and a wonder to the grass, which made the entire city almost ethereal.

"Is it really as beautiful as it looks?" Jonathan murmured, half involuntarily.

"Close your eyes. The test will be if it is more beautiful when you see it than when you do not."

"It's the same sun; it should not be more beautiful here."

"And pray tell, why not, Mr. Bingham? Everything else is."

"That makes no sense."

"But does it have to? By whose proscription is sense required of," and she waved her arm widely, "this great beautiful city?"

He did in fact close his eyes for a moment. It made no difference: he could still see the crowded streets, and all the filigree of men and foliage. He opened his eyes, stared, and shook his head.

"I would have thought there were rules, that there was a logic. Are we subject to such things, in America, and here in Paris they are immune? It would hardly seem fair."

"There is nothing quite so amusing as a disappointed romantic."

He turned and met her glance.

"Is that what I am?"

"Of course! Didn't you know?"

He looked out the windows once again. He felt like something between participant and spectator, watching a living canvas unfold and at the same time moving through it.

"I feel utterly alien."

"Ah, *au contraire!* You must feel how intensely you, too, are a part of Paris, at least for now. It is true: you *are* as much a part of it as any of those good people out there. Half of them are probably from England or Germany, in any event. But they are as much a part of the scene as—as you are!"

He leaned back on the cushions.

"They say that Goethe, when he first saw the Alps, pulled down the curtains of his carriage and muttered, 'mountains, ugh!' I feel a little like that."

"How spiteful."

"No—though I suppose it is jealousy. If I can't have it, if I can't be really a part of it, then I don't want—"

"The solution," she interrupted cheerfully, "is that you must be a part of it. Or it must be a part of you."

"I doubt that it's possible."

"I know that it *is*."

"Then you know more, Mrs. Rives, than I do."

Her laugh was high and bright.

"Did you ever doubt that, Mr. Bingham? How could you!"

Jonathan's first diplomatic dinner—to which he was invited, at the last minute, because of an unexpected shortage of one gentleman—was given by his employer, Mr. Rives, in honor of the English ambassador, Sir Alexander Stephens. This was one of those evening affairs at which a person of his lowly standing would not ordinarily be present (though the Minister was far too polite to phrase it in such terms). It would be a fine opportunity to see how the inter-governmental aristocracy conducted itself; he would have many opportunities, later on, to view the diplomatic *hoi polloi*. He felt, as he smoothed down his black tie and squinted at himself in the moderate-sized mirror that was all his apartment offered, a little like an explorer in darkest Africa—except that he was to be exposed to brightest Europe. The English guest of honor was a knight, and his wife was, in her own right, Lady Molly Stephens. He could not suppress a faint smile: Lady Arabella Bingham? Lady Grace Johnson? We manage these things better at home, he assured himself, for all his nervous anticipation. A lady either is or she isn't; giving her a title doesn't make her any different. And yet, somehow, at least if the lady was English and not American, it did. He did not know why.

He closed his door behind him and strolled toward the Rives' *hôtel*. The guest list included the Russian *chargé d'affaires*, who had the unlikely name of Marano d'Acquitano; and a Belgian diplomat whose status escaped him but whose name was Ferdinand Saint-Jacques; and the Papal Nuncio, Monsignor Vitalli—who was, he recalled, also an archbishop; and Lady Molly's niece, Miss Engle; and Sir Alexander's nephew, Michael Bestwood, and perhaps Mr. Bestwood's wife (who was either ill, or pregnant, or both, and either would or would not be in attendance).

There was someone he was forgetting: it was not to be a large dinner table, and he ought to have all the guests clearly in mind. How else did one decide matters of precedence, which were so vitally important to these people? Suppose a nobleman were put behind a mere commoner: empires would shake, and diplomatic bags would bulge. *Mon dieu!* The French something-or-other, yes, Monsieur Delgado, from the Quai d'Orsay: of course. They were, after all, in France. What would a diplomatic dinner in France be, *sans* Frenchmen? He had heard that Madame Delgado, in her palmier days, had been the reasonably famous Lucille d'Estaing, late of the *Comédie Française*. That would be plainly impossible, in Washington, and he imagined highly unlikely in London. But whether this was a matter of better ordering, well, he did not know. He hoped he would have some better idea, after having met Madame Delgado. *If* he met her: it might not seem worth anyone's while to present a featherweight newcomer to the wife of a French something-or-other: what *was* Delgado's office? An important one; that, at least, was clear.

Children smiled and nudged each other, seeing his formal attire. He smiled: in New York they might have flung catcalls at him. Or even stones, if he seemed a bit infirm—or slow of foot. But then, in New York he would not have walked to an occasion of such weight. Odd: it did not seem out of place, in Paris, where things were so much more formal, to appear on foot. Very odd indeed. Different strokes for different folks: that was certainly the name of the game.

Oh, yes: there was an American grouping, too. How could he have forgotten his own countrymen? A Mr. Winslow, of Boston, with Mrs. Winslow, and *les demoiselles* Winslow, two in number as he recalled, as well as a Mr. Parker and a Mrs. Dennis, the latter apparently Mr. Winslow's aunt. Or was she Mrs. Winslow's aunt?"

What a nuisance, confronting so many tender questions, and so many unknown faces.

What a pleasure, what an opportunity, meeting so many strange and, to him, interesting personages.

And they would be eighteen at table, or even more if Mrs. Bestwood put in an appearance. Ah, the ferrying of the ladies to table would be an experience, not to speak of the jealous guarding of precedence. And what language or languages would they converse in? One could speak English to an Englishman—but to a Papal Nuncio? To a Russian *chargé* with an Italian name? Would M. Delgado prefer his native French?

Would Mr. Bingham step right in? He would, and did.

"Are you long in Paris, Mr. Bingham?"

It was one of the Miss Winslows, probably the older of the two. She was a cheerfully plump girl, sufficiently pretty; her eyes had a modest intelligence.

"Less than a week."

"Oh. I had hoped to prevail upon you to guide us about the city. We are just arrived."

"It would be a case of being led about by the blind, I'm afraid."

Her smile had an American bluntness. Jonathan was already aware that one did not see smiles of that sort on the faces of European women.

"You must be extremely busy, in any case, being so newly arrived."

"Oh, yes. I have to guide my Minister through the intricacies of Monsieur Hugo's verse, and the other day I escorted Mrs. Rives to an exhibition of paintings. But I do write a very great many letters, and I am required to read even more of them than I write. I think Mr. Rives is being kind to me, perhaps so I don't panic and flee when I learn what the post truly involves."

"You're not from Boston."

"No. Is that an insuperable handicap?"

The butler announced Monsieur and Madame Delgado. (He was, Jonathan shortly learned, *directeur* of the *bureau de l'extérieur*, Quai d'Orsay. A most formidable man, too.) M. Delgado was short and roly-poly, with small eyes, a bald head, and very active hands. His wife, the former *comédienne*, was a full four inches taller, not much above fighting weight still; her dark hair was piled extravagantly high, as was also her very white bosom.

Sir Alexander Stephens, who finally arrived with his *entourage*, was a modestly portly man, with large eyes not unkindly of aspect. His wife was even more extravagantly protuberant than Madame Delgado, but unlike the French lady she seemed more a tightly laced ice cone than a restrained volcano: her hair was a tired blonde, her mouth had a sour downturn in the corners. Miss Engle was painfully thin, as if her parents—whoever *they* were—had not bothered to feed her in some years. She was also painfully shy, with her eyes perpetually on the floor. Mr. Bestwood, on the other hand, shook hands almost fiercely, but there was an opacity in his eyes, a dullness in his entire face. He had the energy of a man of parts, but he seemed to have none of the other attributes.

There were no preliminary refreshments, as there would have been had the evening's entertainment been a ball rather than a dinner. And not much more than five minutes after the British had landed, dinner was announced. Jonathan had expected that there might be some milling about, as this one and that one jockeyed for position, but it went so fast, and so effortlessly, that he barely had time to note who went in to dinner on whose arm. It went, in tabular form, the first first and the last last, like this:

Sir Alexander Stephens took in Mrs. Rives;

Mr. Rives took in Lady Molly Stephens;

Baron Marano d'Acquitano took in Miss Madeleine Engle;

M. Delgado took in Mrs. Winslow;

Mr. Winslow took in Madame Delgado;

M. Saint-Jacques took in Mrs. Dennis;

Michael Bestwood took in Marcia Winslow;

And Mr. Jonathan Bingham, *secrétaire du Ministre des Etats-Unis,* gave his arm to his countryman, Miss Sylvia Winslow, age sixteen.

Following them, though not arm in arm, came Mr. Parker and Monsignor Vitalli, the Nuncio.

And it looked, when the unrehearsed but impeccably executed maneuvers had been completed, like this:

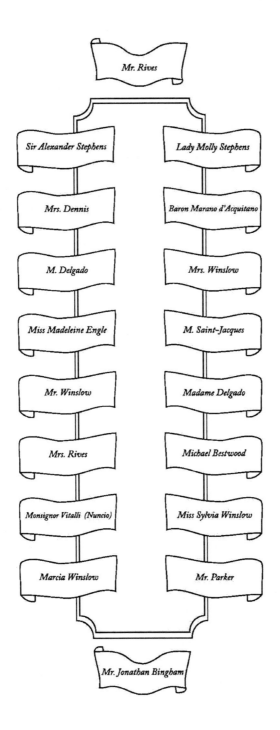

Jonathan's conversation, which he had resolved would be diplomatic and dutiful, began with Mr. Parker, of whom he asked, civilly and dispassionately, the nature of his business.

"Here in Paris, do you mean?"

"I imagine *that* is not business so much as pleasure."

Mr. Parker contemplated the notion, which seemed foreign to him, then shrugged it away.

"Cotton mills. Not the gins, mind you, but the mills. From warp to woof, you might say."

The Nuncio, who was seated directly across from Mr. Parker and apparently deep in conversation with the older Miss Winslow, to his right, and Mrs. Rives herself, to his left, flicked a glance at them.

"*Qu'est-ce qui c'est un* mill?" he murmured quickly.

"*Moulin*," responded Jonathan, and the priest smiled fleetingly and, without missing a verbal beat, went on with his socializing.

"We build them," Parker continued. "We design them. Sometimes we run them."

"In Boston?"

"Anywhere. Mostly in New England, but we don't aim to be particular. We've been talking to a man about setting up in California. Probably do it, too."

"That would be profitable."

Mr. Parker tilted his head thoughtfully.

"Maybe. Maybe not."

"But the gold . . . ."

"It's transportation costs I'm thinking of. And keeping the machines in service. What good's a mill that don't run? It might be six months out of service, waiting for some ding-dangled part to come sailing around the Horn. No, all in all I'd just as soon leave it up to the sending in of goods already manufactured-up. But Mr. Winslow, he's got the itch to try it, and he's the boss, in the end. What he says goes."

"What is it they say of us in England?" laughed Mrs. Rives, leaning slightly toward the two Americans. "That we itch for their wool and scratch for their gold?"

"Do the good gentlemen of Virginia," murmured the Nuncio, "have many compliments for *their* former slaves?"

"Touché," smiled Jonathan.

"I wouldn't listen, ma'am," explained Mr. Parker earnestly, "if they talked like that. An Englishman is like to be a bull in our china shop, when he gets half the chance."

Mrs. Rives smiled:

"A John Bull, indeed." Jonathan laughed, and she turned directly to him. "Have you lived in England, Mr. Bingham?"

"I've scarcely had time to live in the United States."

"A strange country, really and truly it is. It might not worry *you*. To be an English gentleman could, I fancy, be distinctly pleasant at times. But an English woman, ah, that would be a hard lot. So circumscribed. So pinched. I should not like to be so held in, not for all the glories of British civilization."

"And the rain, ma'am," put in Mr. Parker. "Why, it rains half the day there."

"How right you are, Mr. Parker. Very accurately observed."

Jonathan winced, but Mr. Parker smiled happily and proceeded to discourse on British weather, with many accompanying meteorological details and some lengthy measurements of rainfall.

It seemed hours later when, just after the ladies had left the room, Sir Alexander rose to his feet, glass in hand:

"To the Queen, gentlemen, and to friendship among nations!"

Mr. Rives stood for "President Taylor, and prosperity across the globe."

Baron d'Acquitano proposed to "His gracious majesty the Tsar, and the spread of Christianity and civilization."

M. Delgado offered to "President Louis Napoleon and the hospitality of my country to all the gentlemen and their ladies."

There were other toasts; it all took considerably less time than, to Jonathan's experience, it would have done back home—where toasting was something akin to dueling. The brandy and cigars seemed of much greater interest, here. And then, glass in hand, the gentlemen began to wander. M. Saint-Jacques, who was after all a commercial consul, was soon deep in conversation with Mr. Parker. Mr. Winslow and the Russian *chargé* paired off, with Mr. Bestwood more or less listening at the edge of things. M. Delgado and Sir Alexander were clustered around Mr. Rives, deep in what was, Jonathan thought, most likely the true diplomatic purport of the evening, if there were one at all. And he was himself immediately engaged by the Nuncio, who spoke fluent French with only a trace of Italian accent.

"You are very young, my son."

"Not quite twenty-one, *Père*."

The Nuncio nodded and sat down in the seat vacated by the younger Miss Winslow. Jonathan was pleased to see that he drank brandy just like anyone else, though he did not smoke. The black habit he wore was, in fact, very like a kind of formal dinner dress—a uniform, as it were.

"And this is all very new to you," the Nuncio gestured briefly around the room. "All of this."

"Some of it, but not all. I spent the last two years working as a newspaper reporter, in New York."

"*Pour le Tribune?*"

"*Oui,*" Jonathan acknowledged, pleased that the Nuncio knew the paper, and had somehow guessed his affiliation correctly.

"Tell me, my son, if you would, something of this Mr. Horace Greeley."

"Something turned into ten minutes' talk of this Mr. Horace Greeley.

"Do you think you will like Europe?" the Nuncio suddenly asked.

"After less than a week in Paris, what do I know of Europe? I do know that I am American, not French—not that I can be sure, as yet, what it means to be French. We are your children, in a sense, we Americans, but we have begun to go our own way, and it is not the same."

"Of course. You speak French well."

"*Merci.*"

"Do you also know Latin?"

"More or less. I spent a year at a university, in New York."

"Do you happen to recall the line, *Nescio quid meditans nugarum, totus in illis?*"

"That's Horace, is it not?"

The Nuncio patted him on the knee.

"Excellent. Do you know what it means?"

"Pretty much. 'Dreaming about some unimportant matter, his mind is all absorbed by just those trivial things he focuses on.'"

"Oh very good, very good. You have been well taught." He raised his finger again. "That would be my warning to you. Or as Our Lord put it, 'Where your heart is, there will your treasure be also.' He knew— as did Horace, though a pagan—and a poet."

"We Americans are a religious people, Father, even though mostly not of exactly the same dispensation you observe. We are a moral people, I think. I'm not here in Paris for any sort of debauchery, believe me."

"Good, good."

"Except perhaps poetic debauchery."

"Ah, I suspected as much. You are yourself a poet?"

"Possibly. I propose to find out."

"And," put in M. Delgado, appearing to his right, "you are already pledged to set Mr. Rives to rights, on the subject of Victor Hugo. That will not be easy. Mr. Rives is, as you must surely have learned, an obstinate man."

"This young American gentleman," M. Delgado said at once, as they rejoined the ladies—he conducted Jonathan directly to his wife—"has favored us with a superb recitation of the poetry of M. Hugo. And he is himself a poet."

Madame Delgado's graciousness was awesomely polished. She might have been Dona Sol, in Hugo's *Hernani*. Jonathan wished he could ask her if she knew, and if she had ever taken, the part.

"Strange things are occurring, on the other side of the Atlantic," she smiled, with a nod including Mrs. Rives in her observation. "Once upon a time you would send us only wild Indians and the furs of even wilder beasts. Then you sent us tobacco. And now, *grace au bon dieu*, you send us gracious ladies and accomplished gentlemen—even poets."

Mrs. Rives laughed.

"Wait. In fifty or a hundred years . . . ."

"Shall we say," Jonathan ventured, "that there is now no shortage of beauty, or of merit, on either side of the ocean?"

"Ah," exclaimed Madame Delgado. "You will come to my next *salon, mon poète americain?*"

"Infallibly," he bowed.

"We shall have a celebrity among us," whispered Mrs. Rives, a few moments later.

"Should I not go to the lady's *salon?*"

"By all means, go. It will be, I suspect, educational. Madame Delgado is not such a *bohémienne* as she is sometimes thought."

"She strikes me as a very grande dame. Is that more my own ignorance than her true nature?"

"Who can tell a woman's true nature, eh? And a French woman's, at that? No, on the official level, dear Mr. Bingham, you are quite right to accept the invitation. I know my husband would want you to expose yourself to as much of French culture as conveniently you can."

But her eyes seemed to be saying something quite different.

"You, my dear lady, are pulling my leg."

"Not at all."

"Indeed. You are taking advantage of my inexperience. And of my youth."

She gathered up her skirt, preparatory to moving on.

"It has been *my* experience, Mr. Bingham, that gentlemen who talk quite so insistently of their vast inexperience, and of their hopelessly naïve and youthful state, are not in need of any further experience, and are never so young as they make out. Do you know, Mr. Bingham? I begin to think that a stone, dropped inside you, would echo for hours and hours." Then she laughed. "You're not accustomed to being found out, are you? Or, at least, not so quickly?"

She was gone before he could formulate a proper response. If he had been found out, he wished the discovery could be shared: he found it impossible to follow Mrs. Rives, and was relieved when a flicker of Mr. Rives' eyes brought him to his employer's side and, a moment later, to the aid of Mr. Bestwood, who might otherwise have sunk to the floor. He was not so much inebriated as sodden; Jonathan quietly conducted him to a side room and arranged him on a sofa. Mr. Bestwood did not so much as change his expression—indeed, drunk or sober he remained the same. How did one know when an Englishman had passed out? Perhaps, he smiled, when you refilled his glass and it remained filled. Mr. Bestwood did not require further services, and his employer and his employer's guests might: he returned to the main room.

"You should be careful of him," M. Delgado said softly. Jonathan followed his glance, which was aimed at the Nuncio, some yards distant.

"I think he is surely well-intentioned."

"Ah, that is exactly what you are supposed to think. One traps fish with minnows, you know, not with beating on the surface of the water. It is one thing to be raised under the Church, Monsieur Bingham. One can then escape it with ease, when discretion strikes. But to come under that fearsome umbrella, when one is too old to have developed a sufficient defense, that, I assure you, is dangerous. I have, indeed, seen it happen. Often."

"But you are yourself Catholic, are you not?"

"As any educated Frenchman must be, *oui*. The Italians say of us, as I believe the Moslems of Arabia say of their less observant brethren, that we are no Catholics at all. But tell me, how do you find *la belle France*, eh?"

"Would you be able to see Mr. Bestwood home?" Mr. Rives smiled. "I have only now been advised of his indisposition."

"Shall I return here?"

"But where else?" Mr. Rives said. "Ah, yes, I see: will we still be making merry? I expect we will. Sir Alexander is a gentleman of some endurance, and so is M. Delgado." He glanced around the large room. "I expect the ladies will keep pace with us. They always do, you know."

"It will be my pleasure to return."

"It should not be a long trip. The gentleman's wife will be there to receive him, so your obligations will end when he is safely delivered at his door." Mr. Rives chuckled. "I can recall being delivered in just that way, as a very young man. Except that it happened to be my mother, rather than a wife, who received me—and do you know, I sobered myself up pretty quickly. Mothers are not so indulgent as are wives, I'm afraid."

"Should they be?"

"Oh no, to be sure. Wives have a great deal more to forgive us for. You will see, Mr. Bingham. Matrimony is a luxury, for our sex, and a necessity for theirs. That makes a difference."

But when Jonathan returned, well after midnight, the lights were lit and blazing, but the party was visibly over. The room was empty, except for Mrs. Rives, seated on a chaise near the fireplace.

"It seemed proper for someone to greet you, Mr. Bingham, after you returned from your errand of mercy."

He stood a bit to the side, wondering why she was the bearer of greetings and not her husband.

"If the evening has ended . . . ."

"It hasn't, not quite. You needn't run off. Would you like a glass of claret?" He shook his head. "You seem immensely at home in European society, Mr. Bingham. One would think you a battle-scarred veteran."

"Do you know what the younger Miss Winslow said to me? That there really was no difference; it was all pretty much the same thing, no matter where on the globe you went."

"Did you agree with her?"

"I changed the subject."

"I find you baffling at times, Mr. Bingham."

"Ah. That was exactly what I said of you, when we first met."

"To whom?"

"To my brother and to my sister," he explained, a little regretting his indiscretion.

"And have you remained baffled?"

"Did you intend that I should?"

"Is that an answer to my query, Mr. Bingham?"

"You are perhaps too logical, Mrs. Rives."

"I do not know," she said briskly, "whether you are to be congratulated—or spanked."

The familiarity even more than the annoyance registered strongly on him.

"Have I offended you, Mrs. Rives?"

"I don't know," she said at last. "Do you think that might be possible?"

He tried to retrace his actions and his words.

"I cannot think of anything, to be perfectly honest."

"Of course not."

"Then I have offended?"

She rose and stood a moment.

"Perhaps. I propose to leave you in the dark, Mr. Bingham."

"Is that not excessively cruel?"

Her laugh rolled a bit more easily.

"That will depend, Mr. Bingham. That will depend."

Even had her husband not rejoined them, Jonathan would not have asked on just what it depended. He was not at all sure he wanted to know. Mrs. Rives was more than baffling; she was quite possibly dangerous. And she was his employer's wife.

SEVENTEEN

> "I see little female company, but that is an item with which I can
> conveniently enough dispense."
>
> —Daniel Webster, to his friend James Hervey Bingham
> 25 February 1802

Poughkeepsie, 22 April 1850

My dear Jonathan,

*There having been, of late, some transactions as between your brother Theo-
dore and myself, and your portion of what might be termed your patrimony being
involved, I take pen in hand to advise you of what has been done. It would, to be
sure, not be easy to undo what has been done, but it would perhaps be possible if it
seemed to you of sufficient urgency. I regret that I did not consult you beforehand;
your decision to reside temporarily abroad made that, as you will understand, a bit
difficult. But I do not think you will object.*

*I believe you were somehow aware, on your last visits here, that the Grandvoort
house, as you are pleased to call it, was no longer a source of gratification to me,
nor even, now, a comfortable residence. It is too large, it is too empty, and it contains
far too many memories, some of which I would prefer to extinguish. I am not, like
your Uncles Peter and Karl, a man of property. I cannot uproot myself lightly, nor
re-settle myself casually. Nor have I the right to high-handedly dispose of property
which though legally mine is morally my children's. This has presented severe restrictions to another intention of mine, one increasingly dear to my heart. I will speak
of that in a moment. Indeed, I have not yet advised your brother Theodore of this
latter aspect of matters. I will do so, I assure you, in the same post as I dispatch this
message to you; he will have heard what I have to tell him, accordingly, well before
you are able to read this letter. Theodore is of course already possessed of the other
information I began by alluding to.*

*In a word, accordingly, I am no longer the owner of this house. The purchase
price, which I am assured by competent persons is a fair one, has been paid by your
brother Theodore, who is also in possession of a deed to these premises. Only one-*

half of that sum has, however, been paid to me. The other half has been irrevocably deposited in trust for you: the income will automatically be paid to you, and after you have reached your majority the principal, too, will be at your disposal at any time you wish to have it. The sum is not a large one, but I do not imagine you could have expected any substantial sums from me, now or ever.

    Nor shall I be long in residence here. I have explained my departure, but as I have indicated, not my destination, to your brother. It seemed to me better to postpone this latter revelation: your brother is no closer to my way of thinking, I believe, than you are, and misunderstandings would be likely to occur if we discussed these things in person.

    It is not Theodore's intention, at this point, as I understand it, to reside in this house himself. He intends to rent it out, for some specified period. I have not concerned myself with what in truth no longer concerns me in any way whatever, so I can tell you nothing about the future tenancy. A good part of my allotted three score years and ten has been spent under this roof, but it will not shelter me much longer.

    I believe there is some political reason for Theodore's wanting to own a house in New York State, and in particular this familial house. You will have to refer to him directly for information on this subject, however. Political matters have never been close to my heart, and they are even more distant now.

    Whatever time remains to me, and to be sure it cannot and should not be long, I intend to spend in the place where Our Lord suffered and died. My passage is already booked, and what few things I intend taking with me are already packed. If all goes well, indeed, I shall in fact be gone from here by the time you read this letter, and with God's mercy I shall be in the Holy Land before the first of June.

    I will write to you from Jerusalem, as God wills.

Your father,
Frederick Bingham

"I trust, as one diplomat to another, I will have the opportunity to pay my respects to your husband."

"What would a *salon* be, eh, if one's husband were regularly in attendance?" She looked around the room, which was full, though not crowded. There were distinctly more men than women, though to Jonathan's mind the ladies present were more than sufficiently striking to redress the balance. "A *salon*, Mr. Bingham, is something professional, do you know, not something domestic. One entertains for one's husband, and one entertains for oneself. A dinner party is a diplomatic affair. I then become Madame Directeur; I shed what sense of humor

I may have that day, and I allow at least half my mind to go peacefully to sleep. It is not bad—do not mistake me. I do it cheerfully, and it is expected that I will do it well, and indeed that is how I do it. But here, tonight, *my* night, my guests would not dream of calling me Madame Directeur, and I hope that some at least among them would not know to whom you spoke if you so addressed me. These are the people I knew and lived with and worked with when, not really so many years ago, I was Lucille Lalonde." She laughed modestly. "I think perhaps Lucille Lalonde is still a better-known name than Henri Delgado." She took Jonathan's arm and steered him to a long table with a white cloth and many delicacies spread across it. "Come: you will take a small glass with me, and perhaps eat a small morsel, and then I will turn you loose, and you will be able to graze in my pastures."

"And be grazed upon."

"But of course! A *salon* is necessarily a reciprocal affair, M. Bingham. One takes and one gives. Is it not like that in your country?"

He accepted a small glass and a small bite.

"We have nothing quite like this, to my knowledge."

"Indeed! How is that possible?"

He thought for a minute that she was joking, but then he remembered that she was French, after all, and could not know his homeland's habits.

"We have educational evenings," he said a little hesitantly, remembering suddenly his Aunt Sophia's crowded room, and the pro-abolition, pro-unionist speaker that night, and, most vividly of all, the girl with whom he had exchanged some piquant remarks. He had not seen her again. But he knew her name, now, and he brought her to mind, occasionally, at odd moments, wondering when he would see her. There was no urgency; he simply wondered.

"You are wool-gathering," Madame Delgado chided him.

"Quite true. The mind of man is a strange thing."

"Not nearly so strange as the mind of woman, which is well able to read the mind of man! Are you fortified and prepared to venture forth, *cher poète americaine?*"

With a smile she delivered him into the company of a large and portly man in a plaid waistcoat and a long, lacy-sleeved jacket.

"Jacques, I present you a young American poet—and diplomat. M. Bingham, M. Silvestre."

She left them.

"Our hostess has already spoken to me about you," the Frenchman explained in a voice so suave, so controlled, that it was immediately plain his living was made on the stage.

Jonathan bowed.

"You have the advantage of me, sir—but not entirely. You are surely with the Comédie Francaise."

M. Silvestre looked rapidly down at himself.

"What have I done to give myself away so readily!"

"Only that you have spoken half a dozen words, I assure you. No one who had not been on the boards could possibly speak them so elegantly."

"Ah, you are a poet, indeed. Tell me, what is the state of the opera in your country?"

M. Silvestre was shocked to learn that opera was essentially a non-existent phenomenon, in America. They strolled a few feet, then stood chatting about music and drama. M. Silvestre seemed to accept Jonathan as a fellow professional, one whose opinions were well worth being listened to. It was both startling and embarrassing.

"And you are not yourself a musician?"

"Totally non-musical, I'm afraid."

"But that cannot be. You know too much—unless you have been playing a part with me. And, after all, as an actor I should recognize such things."

"My sister was an excellent musician. I suppose I learned from her. It could not have been from any other source; it certainly could not be from the slightest degree of talent."

"She has left music for motherhood, I dare say?"

"She has left this world for the next."

"Ah. I am sorry."

"I have heard no one play like her, not to this day."

"You will have to hear M. Liszt. I wish you had been in time to hear M. Chopin—ehh, *that* was an experience."

"Tell me something of him," Jonathan asked. M. Silvestre, was also an acquaintance of George Sand, and of Lamartine, and of De Musset. A series of anecdotes unfolded, until they were interrupted by a very tall, very slender woman in a black gown of so unornamental a nature that its very bareness was an ornament.

"Do not believe a word he says," she told Jonathan.

"Marguerite!"

The lady bent slightly toward Jonathan.

"He is really a pig farmer, from Brittany. He comes to Paris twice a year and pretends to a career on the stage, and to an acquaintance with men—and yes, with women—who have never set eyes on him. It is really frightful how Lucille allows him to impose."

M. Silvestre bowed and presented her, laughing.

"M. Bingham, Mademoiselle Sherif."

"Now if *I* told you a story of Madame Sand, *eh bien*, you could count on its being both first-hand and true."

"To the very last drop," M. Silvestre affirmed, "even though, *ma chère*, you are too young to have ever met the lady, and too discreet to repeat any stories of her, and too beautiful to need to prevaricate."

"You speak like a hopeful lover, Jacques."

"What is it you say in English?" he asked Jonathan. "Hope springs eternal in the human breast?"

The lady winced.

"Jacques, Jacques," she murmured in protest. "Confine yourself to the butchery of one language, please."

With a flourish and a mock bow, M. Silvestre left them.

"You must be very good friends," Jonathan observed, "to insult one another so freely."

"I have been Desdemona to his Othello, and Juliet to his Romeo."

"Ah."

She seemed to stare at him for a moment. Her eyes were even deeper than her laugh.

"Have you wondered about my name?"

"I've not had time. Is it French? It does not sound so."

"It is Arabic."

"Surely, you are not . . . ."

She stared for another moment, then, with a little laugh, winked.

"I'm from London," she said softly, and in English. "My name is Sybil Smith. You can't admit to that, here, not if you want to be heard from. So I turned myself into Charisse Sherif." She smiled. "It worked, too."

"Your French is impeccable."

"And yours."

"I did wonder, though, if you had married an Arab."

"*Horreurs!*"

"And why did M. Silvestre call you Marguerite?""

"I told you not to believe a word he said."

Not all the guests at Madame Delgado's *salon* were so unusual. All however were of interest. Jonathan preferred not to seek out the literary folk; it would be time for that when he had proven his claim to the title so freely bestowed on him, in Paris, and by so many. It did not seem to him that an aspiring poet was quite the same thing as a poet in deed. He was pleased that the writers present—and he knew the names and in some cases something of the work of those who were pointed out to him—did not regard him as exclusively their concern. It was, he quickly realized, a singularly cosmopolitan world. If anyone had asked him, and he was glad no one did, he would have had to admit that there was nothing like this in the United States, either—nothing. But perhaps there would be, before too long, when the country and its writers had been mellowed and seasoned.

When he went to make his farewells, Madame Delgado seemed taken aback. "Why do you leave us so soon?" she wondered. "It is only a very little after midnight."

"Ah, the curtain at the Comédie may not go up until eight-thirty, but the day of an official Secretary begins a great deal earlier than that!"

"Do you have no days to yourself?"

"I have time to myself. The United States of America may be a slaveholding country, but at least in its official capacity it does not treat its employees as if they, too, were slaves."

She held onto his hand, keeping him.

"And do you spend long hours at your writing desk, on those days which belong only to yourself?"

"As a matter of fact, Madame, I do."

"You are working hard?"

"Yes."

"At a poem?"

"Yes."

"Ah. About what?"

She released his hand. He stood thoughtfully in front of her.

"That is harder to say."

"Is it a secret thing?"

"No. Nothing I do is important enough to deserve secrecy, believe me—aside that is, from my official activities at the Ministry."

"Tell me, then, if it is going well."

"I think it is. It's—" He raised one had, then slowly lowered it, trying to find the exact words."It's not a poem of the sort one writes in French, you see."

"Ah?"

"I'm afraid so. It's funereal, for one thing."

"Not a sermon, I trust?"

"Not a sermon, no. It will be a memorial to my sister, who died very young. She was a splendid musician, and a very great loss. And it will be something of a philosophical poem."

"It does not sound excessively lively."

"Perhaps not."

"*Eh bien*, M. Bingham. When your solemnities begin to bore you, please let me know."

Her smile was subdued but gracious. His leave-taking was cordial. He felt buoyed and at the same time disciplined, he did not know on what grounds. But plainly he would also have to discipline himself, if his memorial were to continue toward some effective realization. How easy it was to waste one's substance. How tempting were the ways of the world.

"But that way, too, lies madness," he murmured to himself. "I shall end in Jerusalem, too, at that rate."

It was a fine, bright summer night. The streets were almost deserted, but he did not mind having them to himself as he strolled briskly back to the Rue de Luxembourg, some two and a half miles distant. The exercise would subdue the evening's excitement; he would sleep soundly, and with luck he could put in half an hour or a bit more at his desk. He had, in fact, written nothing since his arrival in Paris—nothing, that is, except a stack of letters half his height tall. "I'm the one who ought not to be believed!" he scoffed. "Why did I tell her so flaming a falsehood?"

He did not even attempt an answer: the stars were too clear and lovely, and he watched them instead.

The porter had summoned him; there were, he was told, *deux femmes américaines*, who had been to the Ministry before. Their French was so utterly wretched that he, Pierre, could not understand what they wanted. And he had, to be sure, more important things that required doing. What were two insignificant ladies to the polishing of furniture, eh? Or to the correct piling of the next season's firewood? Would le Ministre understand if he, Pierre, did not attend properly to his proper functions? Would he listen to any explanations about two wretched ladies, eh?

Jonathan agreed to come at once, and Pierre went off with a grateful sigh that was also an indignant sigh. Americans!

"Ah, Miss Winslow, Mrs. Dennis."

"It hardly seems appropriate, young man," said the older lady, "for the offices of the government of the United States of America to be staffed by people who speak no English."

"To be sure. Pierre is the porter, and he has quite enough trouble speaking French. But I am reasonably fluent in our common language, ladies, and I am very much at your service. Can I be of any help?"

Marcia Winslow, who clearly found it difficult to keep silent, even in the imperious presence of her aunt, hastily produced a page torn from a newspaper.

"We were hunting this exhibit, Mr. Bingham. But no one seems to have heard of it."

"I do not think the cab drivers in this city are familiar with the written word," Mrs. Dennis sniffed.

Jonathan consulted the page, then handed it back.

"I'm terribly sorry, ladies. But you seem to have found one of the most interesting happenings of last summer. The exhibit you wanted, I'm afraid, has been closed for almost a year."

Miss Winslow made a very sour face.

"How stupid!"

"Do be a good girl and keep such things to yourself," Mrs. Dennis sighed. "I should never have agreed to chaperon you and your sister. I experienced nothing like this in Boston!" She took something from her reticule, sniffed at it, then stepped rather feebly back, while Jonathan hastily brought her a chair. He helped her into it. "Thank you," she said distantly.

"Shall I fetch some assistance?"

"I shall be fine in just a moment." She closed her eyes.

"She will be fine in just a moment," Miss Winslow repeated, standing out of her aunt's sight and making an even sourer face. "Do not go to any trouble, Mr. Bingham."

"It is so disappointing," Mrs. Dennis sighed. "To come all this great distance, and live through such troublesome things, and all in search of a reward that seems so very unlikely." Her eyes were open, now; she sat very straight in her chair and looked straight at Jonathan. "If we had wanted to be Europeans, why, we should have arranged for it back in seventy-six. It would have been possible, then. I dare say France would have been delighted to have us—and I would now understand your Pierre with no difficulty whatever. But it is too late." She glanced at her niece. "I have been telling you this, and your sister, and yes, your blessed father, too, I have been telling you this for months. But you Winslows have a way of not listening. I told your mother that very same thing, Marcia, and she did not listen, either."

"Aunt. Pray rest yourself."

Jonathan offered a glass of stimulant, but Mrs. Dennis refused with great firmness.

"Not even in France will I descend to the consumption of alcoholic beverages."

"Shall I fetch you a cab?"

Miss Winslow's face darkened, and she muttered something inaudible.

"I will thank you to do that, if you please," said Mrs. Dennis. "And now, my dear girl, will you go back to your father in peace?"

The ladies' departure was rapid, and orderly, but not peaceful. Had she dared, Jonathan thought, Miss Marcia Winslow would have refused to accompany her aunt. But she did not have quite the gumption required. The best she could manage was a singularly long face and a surreptitious kick at the carriage door.

Jonathan turned to resume his copying work, interrupted by Pierre's summons. Mrs. Rives, standing in the doorway, interrupted him further:

"I do not find all our countrymen equally amiable."

"Indeed."

"Do you know what that old lady said, the other night?"

"I can almost guess."

"She announced, in her skinny voice, that if this were in truth a *mission*, we would drink the plain cold water provided by the Lord. She apparently confuses my husband with her neighborhood preacher. But she got her water, and she drank it. Much good may it do her! It's not exactly what the Lord provided, here in Paris."

"So I've been told."

Mrs. Rives stepped back inside, and he joined her, closing the small side door through which he had conducted their visitors.

"You have been very busy, Mr. Bingham."

"I have been trying to lead two lives, Mrs. Rives."

"Has Paris so changed you, and so easily as that?"

"Not at all! I meant that I've finally managed to shake off the weariness of my voyage, and at least some of the shock of my arrival. I meant, that is, you see, that I was working very hard at a poem, one I'd started some months ago."

"I see."

"My first obligation is to Mr. Rives, of course. So I cannot sit at my desk quite every night. But I do try."

"Of course."

"Though what will come of it I can't say." He felt he'd successfully diverted her. "I can't so readily reveal my literary interests, in the United States. People would ask to see what I'd put in print—and the truth of it is that, in the way of poetry at least, I've so far put nothing into print."

"You will, I dare say, put quite a lot into print."

"I hope so! But not without great labor, I can tell you that. Perhaps it comes easily to some great minds—like Victor Hugo's, for example—but it comes painfully hard to me."

"And so it should."

"Indeed."

"Where would we all be, if things came easily to us? I ask you, Mr. Bingham: where would we all be?"

And without waiting for an answer, she left him. He was not at all sure he could have given her an answer—in fact, he was not at all sure he understood what she meant. She had seemed very contained, very sure of herself, and she had gone off with an impressive floating grace. Mrs. Rives, he reminded himself, was a very pretty woman. Mr. Rives was a very lucky man.

And he, Jonathan Bingham, had better become a very busy man, *tout de suite.* He laughed at nothing in particular and climbed the stairs to his desk.

Paris: Rue de Luxembourg 28: May something-or-other, 1850

My dear Martial,

I don't know how one becomes a reformed character, without truly having sinned, but I think I have managed it. I may or may not deserve congratulations; I cannot yet be sure. At any rate, I do know that I consider myself reformed—and here in Paris, far from the true reformed of this church and that one, I am, I am, afraid the sole judge of my standing in such religious questions. And I feel reformed! Surprisingly, it does not make me feel any better (nor, for that matter, any worse). No, I feel much as I have always felt, aside from the consciousness of a change—and indeed, reform seems to me to be a matter of what one does more than what one is. Who knows what unpleasant thoughts may lurk in the heart of the most benevolently smiling man? But what he does, how he acts, what he says: these are things one can measure.

That final word, "measure," brought me up short, and I sat here for some minutes, reading and re-reading what I had written. Am I turning into some sort of quasi-scientist, I asked myself? Worse yet, am I leaning toward that unamiable and hard-faced whore, Philosophy? Or worst of all, is there some venomous virus of Theology deep in my bosom, slowly working its poison into my veins, and destined in the end to utterly dominate my being? These were, you will agree, fearsome notions, and I worried no end. For perhaps five minutes. And then I came to the realization, or perhaps more accurately to the remembrance, of the fact that I was a callow mind in an equally callow body, whirled by the multitudinous impressions of a new residence abroad, speaking and to a large extent thinking in a foreign tongue. How in all sanity could I not display some alarming symptoms? False intellectuality is to my mind probably the single worst symptom one can display—and seeing this in myself I applied the sovereign remedy for all such diseases: laughter. I pushed back from my writing desk and bellowed at my own fatuity, howled at my pompous stupidity—and then felt (it all comes back to feeling, does it not?) a great deal better.

I have had quite a correspondence with Grace: that may well be what is motivating me to turn so philosophical.

And—to turn from the ridiculous to the veritably sublime—in what state do I find your heart? No, never mind your heart (again, it is action rather than internal resolve with which I am concerned—and with which the world should be concerned). In what state do I find you? Still unmarried? I trust some measures are in train to end that most deplorable of all deplorable states—for a man with a motherless family, that is. I am, as you know, barely a man, and I have come nowhere near the parlous state of paternity. (It is, I am told, somewhere west-n'or-west of the equally parlous land of matrimony.)

Well, you must surely have realized, from all of this verbal fuss and bother, that I have been poeticizing again. Deeply. Lengthily. Ponderously, more than likely. There may be men who can so indulge themselves, one moment, and return the next to civilized deportment, undamaged, even unaltered. I seem, on the contrary, to be of a different (and very much inferior) breed. Poetry may bring out the metaphors and similes in me; it may musicalize my tongue, but it also seems to bring out the fool. After balancing a pentameter beam, I find myself unable to walk straight lines on a simple floor. After twisting up my tongue, I find that it does not easily or readily untwist, certainly not of itself. I can only ask for your forgiveness; I cannot even pledge that I will refrain and desist. It is in sober truth a kind of madness—a kind of disease, good doctor. I suffer, I endure, and in the end (why do I insist on prating of the end of everything?) I recover. But am I cured? Surely I am—until the next fit. Like a true and proper madman, am I not?

I am become, for all my madnesses, a most proficient copyist. That, too, was sink or swim—for in <u>very</u> sober truth I would have drowned in papers, had I not polished my penmanship and swung my elbows manfully. The language of diplomacy, which I dutifully employ in the composition of such original epistles as I am asked to turn out, is distinctly easier to acquire than the language of France. Diplomacy is distinctly unlovelier, too. I would quote you an example, if it were not that I am at home and all the examples are piled across my other desk, at what I sometimes now call the <u>hôtel des Rives</u>. (Did you know—the poetic fit reasserting itself—that in French "rives" can mean both the shore or bank of a river and also the edge or rim of a wood or forest? I do not mean to turn dictionary-maker: the concealed pun seems to me appropriate, I'm afraid. As one can drown in a stream or river, or in a sea of papers, yes, so, too, one can lose one's way in a wood. To end this parentheses in a simple word: I am become somewhat fearful of Mrs. Rives. What is that British schoolboy rhyme? 'I do not love thee, Doctor Fell. The reason why I cannot tell. But this one thing I know full well: I do not love thee, Doctor Fell.')

There! Had I not extricated myself from that parenthetical bog you would have begun to fear most seriously for my sanity.

Tell me—for you have become a sluggish correspondent: I hope that means you have been occupying your energies on the amatory front—something of your shining children. Has Alice lengthened these past months? Has Michael learned to sit his pony? Has Mark learned to distinguish all our English vocables, one from the other? These are slight matters, I admit, but they interest me mightily, especially at these distances, deprived as I am of the opportunity to watch trivial matters turning slowly, like ripening apples, into serious ones.

Do not tell me of my father. I know everything, of course: he did me the favor, if favor it was, of writing me. I thoroughly approve of his leaving the Grandvoort house, and I am naturally delighted that it will stay in the family even if Theodore will not at once occupy it. My father needed to remove himself from all of his history: his instinct was so far accurate. But to remove himself from all of civilization? To travel half around the world, and to end of all places in so miserable a hole as Jerusalem? <u>Jerusalem</u>? Good Lord—and I do not jest—what is that abject Turkish colony to him or he to it? If there was a notable Passion there, once, well, in two thousand years it has baked clean out of those dirty sands. I have no personal knowledge of the place, but I have personal knowledge of some who have that personal knowledge, and believe me I do not speak lightly. I do not know whether to *hope for letters from there, which I am promised (or threatened with), or to hope, with what may be a still greater sense of filial propriety, that he is somehow diverted along the way, even by illness. By anything, very nearly, which might conceivably divert him. Jerusalem? Had you any notion, Martial, when you married into this strange family of mine, that we were that strange? But then, you had the best of us: of that there is no doubt whatever.*

I have just looked back at the date penned near the start of this letter, and I find there perhaps the most fitting metaphor of all: I do not know what day it is! Could anything better express—all that there is to express? Well, if ashes and dust could yield up a man it may well be that a life—temporary, I do hope—of incoherency can ultimately yield me up a sense of coherence. Would you write me on that subject, please, if you address yourself to no others? A word of assurance from so sane a mind as yours will be of deep comfort to

> *Your poetically afflicted brother in exile—which is like his poetry a self-affliction of yours, believe me, etc.,*

> *Jonathan Bingham*

The concierge had said, with plain disapproval—for it was after nine in the evening, and the streets were totally dark, and Jonathan was irrefutably a bachelor—that there was a lady to see him. Jonathan had blinked. Did the man have the right door? The right name?

"*Bien entendu.* She asked for M. Jonathan Bingham." He peered loweringly at his tenant. "That is truly your name, is it not, Monsieur?"

"Oh, yes. Have no fear of that."

The concierge scowled and shook his head.

"Monsieur. This is a respectable house. We wish to keep it a respectable house."

Was the lady so visibly unrespectable? *What* lady?

"Well, whoever she may be, please tell her I am at home?"

The scowl persisted.

"Monsieur, this is a respectable house."

"You can accompany her, you know. I will speak to her with you in the room, if you like. I was not expecting a visitor. I do not know who this mysterious lady might be."

The concierge's scowl turned faintly leering.

"Monsieur." He managed to find just the right tone to sound insulted and scandalized.

Jonathan frowned.

"*Eh bien.* If you will not show her up, I will go down."

He started through the door, but the concierge took his arm.

"Monsieur. That would be worse." The shock in his voice had taken it to a whisper.

Jonathan did not know whether to upbraid or laugh at him.

"Do I go down, or does she come up? Alone or with you *en train?* It doesn't matter to me, you see." He gestured to his writing desk. "I have work to do, and I will thank you to allow me to get back to it, before my night is entirely flown away."

The spread-out papers, the pen so obviously in active use, seemed to settle things in the concierge's mind. The Word—with which he had only the slightest of acquaintance—was almost as holy, almost as sacred, as the Church. Seeing that Jonathan was actually engaged in *writing* was apparently, for him, like receiving a blessing from some sacred font. The air cleared at once.

"I will send her up at once, Monsieur." His voice was strong and respectful. "I am deeply sorry that you have had to be disturbed. Excuse me, Monsieur." He bowed himself out, closing the door with the softest of clicks.

Jonathan glanced at his desk. It might appear scattered and disheveled, to one who did not know, but he had a beginning sense of the shape and the weight of his poem. Only a beginning sense—but once dawn began, how could the light hold back? He could see, in his mind at least, how intractable a body of material he had been wrestling with. Much of his months of effort had been wasted, as he thrashed and struggled with his material and with himself, fighting to get his bearings. It was coming; he was finding some irreducible truths. Interruption would be a further waste. But only a temporary one: there was no longer any possibility—except death itself!—to keep him from finishing. For better or worse, he would soon be a poet who had in fact written a poem. A real poem. Whether he managed to write another or he did not, this much would be done. Soon.

The knock was almost inaudible.

"*Entrez.*"

He stood well back from the door, whether from caution or some other emotion he did not know. There was no particular quickening of the pulse, as, say, a lower might have felt, waiting and watching for his beloved. He was neither waiting nor watching for anyone; he had no beloved, and he could not, had his life depended on it, have said who the lady about to enter his room might be. He did not speculate, either. He stood and watched.

She was well-wrapped in a black street cloak, wound around her shoulders and most of her face. The concierge had seen no more of her face than Jonathan could see: the fellow would never know who the visitor had been. But Jonathan knew at once.

"I had to come," she said simply.

He was too startled to offer her a chair, or to take her cloak, or to extend any of the usual courtesies due from a gentleman to a lady.

"Nor could I count on an invitation." She tugged the cloak partially off her shoulders; her face was calm but unsmiling. "You seem, in truth, something less than overjoyed to see me, Mr. Bingham." And then a faint smile crossed her lips. "I should dearly like to call you Jonathan. I never have, you know, though I have much wanted to." She stood surveying him. "You may, if you like, call me Clarissa—here, at least. I would like that."

"Forgive me," he murmured, trying to understand what his role was supposed to be. Principally, he wondered how he could get out of this with the least damage. Was there a way? "Your husband?" he finally said, biting his lip at his own inability to preserve any kind of outward calm.

She took a step toward him, then stopped, looking around the room.

"I am free, and white, and more than twenty-one. He has as much of me as he requires, and quite as much as he is entitled to by contract. The rest is mine." She had finished her survey. She smiled at him, her face softening. "Well, Mr. Bingham? Are you so frightened of me that you forget all the obligations of a gentleman?"

She swirled the cloak entirely off her shoulders and held it out; he automatically took it. She was wearing a simple house dress, but all her dresses, simple and elaborate, were close-fitting, and virtually every one had a deep and deeply disturbing neckline. Was she blushing, now, as she stood watching him watch her?

"Well? Do I pass inspection?"

He hurriedly disposed of her cloak. She did not move, visibly extending him the initiative. He did not want it; he did not know what to do with it.

"Oh, *mon cher*, you are terribly frightened!" She raised her arms, almost as if inviting him into them. "What can I do to put you at your ease?" He could not answer. "I will tell you what you can do, to put me at mine."

"What?" he stammered.

"Pour me a small glass of wine. Have you such a thing?"

"Oh. Yes."

He moved stiffly to a sideboard.

"Jonathan." He voice was soft, but not gentle. "There: I've said it. I hope I am fated to say it again, many times. Do pour us each a glass. Thy need is as great as mine!"

He poured two small glasses, trying not to spill the wine. His hand shook, he could not control it. It was shaking as he held out a glass for her to take. Mercifully, she said nothing.

"Will you also offer me a chair?"

There were only two in the room, one of the two rooms in his apartment. He quickly brought her the best chair, which had been placed at his writing desk, and brought the other for himself. He set it, however, very nearly ten feet from hers. She seated herself and smiled winningly.

"Are you afraid I am likely to eat you?"

He shook his head, dumbly.

"Are you aware of the risks I have taken, Jonathan, to come here tonight?" She held up her glass and took a small sip. He sat, clutching his in both hands, and nodded intently. "You are?"

"How could I not be?" he said suddenly, his voice freed. He took a long, slow breath, and then a substantial drink of wine. "It is a very perilous thing."

"And you do not know why I have done it. Isn't that so?"

She was staring at him; there was no possibility of evasion.

"I am young, Mrs. Rives, and I am inexperienced in very many things. But I do not think I am a fool, and I do not think you think I am one."

"Could you call me Clarissa? Please? It will make it somehow better that I now call you Jonathan. That is a lovely, strong name. I have wanted to say it to your face, as I have so often said it to myself. I have, you know. Many times. I have stared into the mirror and wondered what you saw, when you looked at me. Whether indeed you even noticed me."

"Oh, yes."

"And what have you thought of me?" She smoothed her skirt with one hand. "Can you tell me? I would terribly like to know." Her eyes were wide. She seemed, abruptly, vulnerable: the cloak of assurance seemed to have slipped away from her.

"Mrs. Rives—"

"Clarissa. Please."

He experienced a moment of vertigo. He fought it off, taking another long draught of wine. His glass stood largely empty, hers still quite full.

"Clarissa." There was perspiration on his forehead.

"Thank you."

Her voice had become deeper. He rose, quickly refilling his glass. His hand shook just as much, but he had no fear of spilling anything, this time. He strode back to his chair, planting himself a little defiantly.

"A gentleman ought not to speak of such things to a lady," he said.

Her laugh rolled over to him, like far-off thunder on a hot summer night, trailing down from a mountain peak.

"Not even if the lady invites him so to speak?"

He shook his head, found himself starting to lean perilously far on the back legs of the chair, and quickly righted himself.

"And especially not when the lady is married."

With a sweep of her free hand she rose, then plucked up her chair and shifted it right up against his.

"There! I think that will be better."

He sat very still, and very silent. She raised her glass in a toast.

"To a resolution of all difficulties." He did not respond. "Won't you drink to that, Jonathan? Mr. Bingham?" she added in a sly whisper. He drank to it, as did she. "Now. How, then, shall we resolve matters?" He did not reply. "You say that my being married is the ultimate difficulty. But *you* are not married, Jonathan. The responsibility of marriage is then mine—and only mine. Are you required to assume it for me?"

"I did not mean that," he noted, somewhat confused by her argument. He was trying to avoid her eyes, at so close a range. It was not easy. "I frankly do not know what to say," he admitted, taking more wine.

"That is a beginning," she said quickly, her voice rising. "We can perhaps proceed from there, I think. You could go on, you know, and answer the question I asked you earlier."

"What question?" He felt unbearably stupid. "Forgive me. I am somewhat addled, this evening."

"I quite forgive you, now and in the future. That's a blanket dispensation, please note. It will serve you in all sorts of circumstances, and it is freely given. But what I asked—and it is the sort of question a woman needs to ask, and needs to have answered—was how you saw me." The room was oddly silent. "I assume you have noticed, at moments, that I am a woman?"

"You know I have."

"Do I? How would I know?"

His breath caught, but his courage mounted.

"You cannot be as lovely as you are—Clarissa, and not know it. Even though you are married—and to my employer, at that—I could not possibly fail to notice."

"So. You think I am lovely?"

"You are toying with me."

She threw back her head and laughed vigorously.

"Oh, Lord! That is exactly the sort of thing a *woman* is supposed to say to a *man*. Do you recall that?"

"Yes."

She put her hand on his arm, for just a moment.

"If this is a game, Jonathan, it is—as we said at the start, when I first came tonight—a singularly dangerous one. But it is not a game. I am not toying with you, believe me." She peered down at her glass. It was empty. "Please, sir," she smiled at him, extending the glass in his direction. "May I have more?"

He laughed, to his own surprise, and went and refilled both their glasses. She had risen, he saw, as he started back, and she was drifting around his room.

"What were you doing, when I was announced?"

She looked up at him, as she took the glass, and he had the fleeting thought that she intended to—he did not know what. But she only smiled and sipped.

"I was working."

She moved toward his writing desk.

"At diplomacy? All alone, in this snug little apartment?"

She bent over the desk, scanning the papers sprawled there. He wished he knew how to command her away, but knew he could not.

"No. I was writing."

"Poetry, I see."

"Yes."

"And very sad poetry."

"Yes."

She went to the single window. The curtains were drawn, and she did not open them. She stood with her back to him, then turned.

"And do you ever write other kinds of poetry?"

"Sometimes."

"Do you ever write—love poetry? Have you written any?"

How in God's name was he to deal with her?

"Clarissa," he began firmly, then faltered. She stood waiting, truly waiting. Whatever he would say, and he did not even now know what he would say, was a thing of moment to her. It mattered. He mattered. He could not understand very much else, but that was unmistakable. There was something almost meek in her stance, suddenly, something vaguely pleading. Her eyes were deep and very round. "Clarissa," he began again, but there was nothing else to say.

She took a step toward him and somehow, he could never recall having moved, he was standing directly in front of her; she was still waiting, still looking up at him, and there were neither resolutions to be effected nor obstacles to be surmounted: it was all perfectly clear. Holding his glass carefully in one hand, he bent and touched his lips to hers. She began to tremble, and his one free arm went around her. She dipped toward him, and it was all as the day that follows dawn, as bright as it was inevitable.

EIGHTEEN

"The true science of life is to mingle amusement and business, so as to make the most of time."

—Daniel Webster, to his friend James Hervey Bingham
23 December 1803

Boston, 4 June 1850

My dear Jonathan,

You are become so literary, indeed, that I can already see, even in your letters, the writer I expect you will shortly become. The public writer, that is: I have no doubt, now, of the private portrait. It is just as well that you left university, I can quite understand all that, as I could not entirely understand it earlier. Not that I was critical: you are more than old enough to decide things for yourself. All things, I should say. And by leaving Columbia, plainly, you guaranteed yourself two essentials: first, the diversity of experience which I imagine a writer absolutely requires, so that he may have the wherewithal for his writing, and second, no less important, the competency in life to ensure that he can survive and write. As newspaperman, as diplomat, as whatever you turn to next (I suspect you will do a lot of turning), you will undoubtedly earn a larger competence than at whatever profession the university might have fitted you for. (Though you could then have turned to the law. You still could, you know. But I do not think you will.)

Well, the long and short of all this is, my blessings on your career—and when will I be permitted to see this first product of your workshop? Will you have it printed there, or will you send it here? As an American, I would hope you would want to see it into print here. Never mind Europe, and England especially: if they want to read what you (or any other of our countrymen) have written, let them. Or let them refrain. What is an Englishman, or a European, to us, any more than a heathen Chinee?

You can perhaps see from this letter that I am in Boston, as I have openly admitted. I do not think that even New York, for all its brimming ambition and its undoubted success, is as American as this old town. We do not have many old towns, in America, and none, I think, quite like this one. Well, there is Philadelphia, but I suspect it is more embalmed than truly growing. Boston is as alive as New York, believe me, and in its literary activity it is even perhaps a bit more alive. It is grow-ing, too: there will be cannon shots from this city heard across the country, before long. Perhaps across the world. And I cannot but agree with Mr. Emerson, who said almost a quarter of a century ago, speaking at Harvard (of course)—and I wish I had been there to hear him say: "Our day of dependence, our long apprenticeship to the learning of other lands, draws to a close." I could not be in his audience, that day, but I have heard him this past week, and his friend Mr. Thoreau, and also Mr. Alcott, and Mr. Channing—this town fairly bulges with literary energy, I tell you. I am immensely happy to be here.

And what, you ask, am I doing here in the first place? That is a legitimate question, considering that I am the sole support and guardian of four children, who happen also to be your nieces and nephews. They are in good hands, by the way: Grace is still luxuriating in Virginia, and Alice is luxuriating, for the moment, in having suddenly become the oldest child on the premises, and I have left Mrs. Wilkins comfortably in charge of all their well-being.

To the point: I fear I sound as addled as an adolescent.—And in so saying, Jonathan, do I not already tell you why I am here? Not quite, actually, because I did not come here with matrimony in mind. I needed to consult with several medical people, on a ticklish case, and I needed a rest, and it seemed sensible to combine busi-ness with pleasure. On my arrival, I found that some of my friends here had been thinking along precisely the same lines as you, and for quite as long. The difference, however, was that they did not confine themselves to persuasion. If I chose to be scientific (or gross), I could indeed say that they spread out a trap, and baited it— baited it most prettily. It seems just as well to me, now, that I did not listen to you as fully as I might and even should have done—for if I had acted earlier I could not act now. And, believe me, I want to act now. I have already spoken my piece, as you can imagine, and I have been listened to, and I have been rewarded with a positive response. And though I cannot quite manage to bring a bride back with me, on this trip, I will do so the next time I come to Boston, and soon. It will be better to have at least Grace at the wedding, don't you think? And Alice, of course. The boys are too young to attend, or to remember that they had attended if they were permitted to.

Do you know what my first question to her was, once I had conceived the notion of the thing? No, you are wrong, believe me you are wrong. I asked if she played the piano. She assured me that she had never so much as approached a piano. Had she said she played like an angel, I think I would have had to flee the house. If Grace should want to play, some day, I suppose I would have to relent. But no one else. I am, I dare say, slightly insane on this subject, but a man who has loved and who has been loved, as I have been, is, I maintain, entitled to his insanities thereafter.

Well. Your sister was twenty-one when we were married, and I was six years older. I am now ten years older than that. Miss Lydia Holt, soon to be yet another

Mrs. Martial Johnson, is a full fifteen years my junior. She is, however, strong-minded beyond her years. For some years she has been, in fact, about as politically active as Theodore, although with substantially less chance of immediate result. Her activity has been focused, you see, on the matter of slave-holding, which like the rest of us she opposes—but unlike the rest of us she has striven mightily to abolish. In a word, she has been active, quite singularly active, in abolitionist politics, which is a strange sort of politics, less concerned with power than with principle, and although ultimately desirous of electing government officers of the same persuasion, first and basically concerned with the convolutions in all our hearts. I admire her work; I expect I will have to admire it, since she is not likely to abandon it, even for such splendid matters as a husband and home and, all in a bundle, four new children. She is a warm soul; I would not entrust my children, and especially my daughters, to a woman who was not full-blooded and sympathetic. But she has an energy most untypical in the women of our day, at least. And she has a wit, and a tongue, to match anyone. Lord: how she cut me up, the first time we met! There was nothing malicious in it, she did not speak out of rancor or ill-will. But it was no contest, in the fencing sense. I was touched, slashed, and bleeding before I knew I needed a weapon. This should have upset me. I am perhaps perverse, but it only encouraged me. It was some time before I realized why. I think my Boston friends were aware at once—or, as I have suggested, even earlier than that! It does not matter. No man can be, in truth, entrapped who does not entrap himself. I suppose I was ready to be entrapped. No, I suppose I was ready to be entranced: these are not at all the same things, as you will in season learn. (Or have already learned, in wicked Paris?)

Her person requires that you observe it in person. But I can say, in the flatness of words (my words, at least: yours are pearl-shaped and round), that she is rather dark than light, with brown eyes and hair. Her skin is—well, I had better omit that, as between gentlemen. She is very nearly my height, in shoes at lest, and on the slender side. If her face has a flaw, it would have to be her nose, which is a bit over-substantial, even thick. Her lips are of a delicate thinness. A commendable addition to our ranks, all in all. We are to be married, in the Unitarian church (of which she is already a young pillar), on July the ninth, at about ten in the morning. If some Turkish carpet can fly you here for the occasion, you are promised a slice of cake, a glass of champagne, and a peck at the bride's cheek. Failing that, you are promised as warm a welcome as ever, when you do appear again on these shores.

It is, I think, hard for me to be as serious as I feel, Jonathan. Perhaps I cannot fully credit what I have done—though indeed I have only promised as yet to do it. But I will not back out, believe me! Perhaps I wonder how my children, and Anne-Marie's, will take to their new mother. I do not fear disapprobation, though some of that there is sure to be. I have never discussed slave-holding with our sister Arabella, but she is a Virginian born and bred, and she does, in point of fact, as you know, hold slaves. That may prove sticky. What do you think? And Theodore, though a Northerner, and not in any sense a representative of the slave-holding population, is required not to offend where he can refrain from offending. I may become an embarrassment to them both. I hope not, for I have no choice. You are unlikely to see me on a public platform, nor do I have any talent for public debate—or private, as Lydia has proven! But I am not the man who could marry a woman like Lydia without thoroughly sharing her views. Anne-Marie did. My wife, when she becomes my wife, will have my full and complete support. It will likely be sticky, as I say.

But whatever it is, my dear brother, it will be good—good for me, good for the children, and I trust good for Lydia. We are apt to be as much of a challenge to her, and conceivably more, than what she is apt to be to us. It does not strike me as anything but pleasurable—and that is a quantity and a quality, I now see, that has been sadly lacking in my life these last two years. That was, I dare say, what you and all my other friends were trying to tell me. I was, alas, unable to really listen. But I can appreciate your words, now, and I am even more grateful to them, having at last managed to understand them.

So, it will be done, His will be done, and my happiness, and my children's, infinitely bettered. I am very happy; I fondly hope you are in some way as enamored by my news as I am of my situation! There: have I succeeded in manufacturing a proper literary phrase, with which to end this monstrously overgrown epistle? Success or failure, I am done.

Yours, etc.,
Martial Johnson, M.D.

(me doctarum . . . Horace, is it not—though you, not I, should append it to your name, because as I recall it is about the glory of being a poet—well, I am in any event again a lover, though unpoetical . . .)

Jerusalem, 4 June 1850

My dear son,

Did you, as did your relatives, expect that I should not reach this holy place, diverted by old age, or by sickness, or by something considerably more final than either of those? It must have passed through your mind, as it did Theodore's, and his wife's, and that of your brother-in-law, Doctor Johnson. I stopped briefly in New York, before taking ship, to say farewell to your Uncles Peter and Karl (who both think alarmingly well of you), and they expressly warned me I would never arrive. Their wives must have thought the same, but they had the grace to stay silent.

Well, despite all invocations to the contrary, prayers have brought me safely here. I cannot say that Jerusalem is a golden city, as it was in the time of King David, or as it still was, I am informed, in the years on earth of Our Lord Jesus Christ. It is a very hot and dirty city, decayed, and poor—quite remarkably poor. I have seen such leprous sores, and a variety of ulcers, in a week of walking these ancient streets, that no doctor in America, I suspect, will ever glimpse. I am not here to medically treat the citizens of this Turkish principality, of course. I am here, solemnly and humbly, to retrace, day after day, the steps on earth of Our Lord: may it renew my flagging soul, and purify my worm-ridden heart.

The purpose of this letter being to inform you that I am here, and to put on record an address where any communications, should you have occasion for any such, can reasonably be expected to reach me, I will not unduly prolong this epistle. Your earthly father is still walking this earth; he is well and as healthy as a man of his age has any right to be; and he is doing what he knows he has to do. There is no more to be said.

Your father,
Frederick Bingham

Whitetowers, 4 June 1850

Dear Brother,

Were I a wagering man—and how could any man involved in political af-fairs dare to wager on anything, being already committed to so splendid a form of gambling!—I would speculate that father did not tell you for what exact price he sold me the old Grandvoort mansion. I am reasonably sure he did tell you of the sale that had been effectuated, and of the temporary disposition we agreed to make of your share (one-half) of said price. I do not think he has become unworldly so much as other-worldly. All the same, you have a right to know the sums involved. The price was set, I should say, not by me, nor even by our father, but by the general agreement of some half a dozen knowledgeable persons in Poughkeepsie, people whose names you would know but with which I will not bother you now. (Though if you write and ask, tell me their names, that I may execrate them, publicly and privately! Then of necessity I will furnish you with full particulars.) They are all long-term residents, as also their fathers and grandfathers before them, so they seemed to be the right and proper parties for making this determination. In a word, then, *the price was established at no lower than ten thousand and no higher than fifteen thousand dollars—never mind what our father paid for it, lo these many years ago. Indeed, I do not even know that figure—and I have resolved that fairness required me to select the larger of those two sums. Accordingly, father was given a cheque for $7,500.00 and an equal sum was put in trust for you, at a reasonably good rate of interest. The interest will be paid to you, yearly; after you are twenty-one (when does that interesting event take place, bye the bye?), you may draw down all or any part of the principal, at your pleasure.*

There: even as a lawyer I take no delight in these hum-drum details. They are, however, a necessary part of our existences, and I think you will appreciate knowing with at least this much precision where you yourself stand in the sale of the old manse. Would you let me know if there remains anything still to be done, from your side? I will be glad to act as your attorney, gratis, provided that you do not overburden one who is, after all, busy in the governance of our country.

Even after two years, you know, I do not always feel like a Senator—a true Senator. Webster, Calhoun, Clay, Cass—and <u>*Bingham*</u>*????*

Well, I do, as I have done, my best. We will see, in another four years, if our home State is pleased with my performance. They may send me back to this place, or they may send me—elsewhere. Since my marriage, as you can imagine, I feel distinctly less anxiety on such subjects. To be the squire of Whitetowers, of Blue Bell and now of the Grandvoort mansion, well, that does not seem to me too terribly worrisome. How many men have three such roofs over their hands, in point of fact? To worry overmuch about having the marble arch of the Senate extended over my noble brows strikes me as fatuous.

I have heard no complaints, officially or privately, about your performance in Paris, and that strikes me as a very good sign, and an indication that Mr. Rives and Mr. Clayton are at the least not unsatisfied with their new employee. They have done, in my opinion, at least as well for themselves as you have done for yourself, and more than likely they have the better of it. I have formed the impression that Secretaries are not the most carefree and unburdened of creatures. Am I correct? Is Mr. Rives as distinctly a slave-driver as he is a slave-holder? You must of course be aware that I cannot reduce his impact on your quotidien self. Mr. Clayton is Secretary of State, and Mr. Rives is our Minister to—I almost said, to the court of Versailles, though I believe France has not yet replaced her President with an Emperor or a King? Well, you will write and tell me these details, as I have written to tell you those I had in my possession.

Your letters, such as they are, tell us that you are well, and turning more Poetical by the day. Will all of this result, before long, in a slim volume, bound in (say) green silk, and seen for a season on erudite and fashionable coffee tables? Our Uncle Peter, who had never struck me as a literary soul, tells me that you are indeed a man of talent. I respect both his opinion and your endowments, brother. But I also exchanged words with our Uncle Karl, and he made it very plain that you would have done well had you stayed in his charge. I fancy, though he did not say anything directly to the point, that he would welcome you back to his house and also to his counting-house. You are, in any event, very well loved in New York. I heard such cheerful news of you that even my own ears began to burn; yours must have fairly flamed, despite the ocean of separation.

If you are struck by the paucity of political news, as I dare say no writer for the Tribune *could fail to be, I can only say that politics has for the moment gone rather sour and confused, here in Washington. We had much less difficulty subduing all of Mexico, and they in arms against us, than we seem now to have in subduing our own tempers. California, that golden land, has become a part of the United States, and so is what we are calling New Mexico—but what are we to do with them? We are a nation, for the moment, of thirty States, of which fifteen are happily free and fifteen are, unhappily but tidily, of the slave-holding persuasion. To disturb that neat but precarious balance is not something one wants lightly to do. And some do not want it done at all, under any circumstances. Mr. Clay, as he has so often before, is leading us toward the course of compromise—I can nearly predict that historians of this nation, a century or two from now, will write of him as the very Father of Compromise, and not in any pejorative sense, to be sure.*

There is substantial sentiment on every aspect of all the various questions involved. Some would have us admit all the new lands sans restriction. Mr. Calhoun's last speech—he was so ill that it had to be read for him by Mr. Mason of Virginia, who is incidentally a distant relative of Arabella's—was of this view. Mr. Jefferson Davis, of Mississippi, quite agrees, not really to anyone's surprise. Mr. Salmon Chase, of Ohio, is determined that slavery will be forbidden wherever the hand of the Federal Government can now forbid it. General Cass, returned to the Senate, will follow Mr. Clay's lead; just as important, so too will both Mr. Webster and Mr. Stephen Douglas, of Illinois. But, again, what will we do? Will we recognize a separate Utah territory, and make it indeed a new State? What will we do about the claims of Texas, once a sovereign republic, and now determined not to let "New Mexico" escape it a second time? I assume we will have to make California a State on terms inimical to slavery, since it grows gold and Mexicans rather than cotton. But where do we proceed from there?

There are those among us, too, who would place the slave trade of this District at issue in the entire matter. And there are certainly those on both sides of the question, North and South, who are exercised about the disposition of what we in the North call free slaves and they to the South call escaped slaves. Are we to return this species of "property," when it has delivered itself into our hands, believing and hoping itself free? Believe me, this is not the end of it, and though it may be the end of us, we are fated to dispose of at least the majority of these issues, one way or another, sink or swim. I sometimes fear we may sink. Can a Union persist, this torn? There are those who ask that question, too, and many Southern voices do not seem to think the Union can persist. I confess I do not know what will happen, not only here in the Senate, but throughout the land.

The President, further, compounds our difficulties by being firmly and articulately opposed to the admission of <u>any</u> new territories at this time. It is whispered that, having conquered those places once, he does not want to be forced to conquer them a second time, and this time from the political rather than from the military stance.

But we are a troubled nation, brother, with these boulders crammed into our craw, and with the likes at our helm of your equally troubled brother,

Theodore Bingham

P.S. How could I forget? Have you as yet heard from Jerusalem? I do not know what to expect, or whether it is better to expect nothing. We have heard nothing. Arabella, who fondly asks after you—as also (Lord! I am, I see, more of a political reporter than a fraternal correspondent) does your charming little niece, Grace Johnson— thinks that we shall be months without word. I dread a formal letter from some obscure consul in some dirty, obscure place, enclosing father's cravat and apologizing for the crocodile that has eaten him while he knelt at prayer. I do not know what to think—there was nothing I am afraid that I could do, short of locking him up, and that I neither could nor would do—and I do not even know what to hope for. If by chance you have any news, and suspect we may not have any, do please communicate as rapidly as possible. We are as anxious as we are helpless.

"I doubt very much if my government will take any position whatever." Mr. Rives was able to speak to his visitor in English and to expect reasonable comprehension, but in order to be sure he had invited Jonathan to be present. "Did you expect some difficulty, perhaps?"

M. Delgado smiled. He too spoke in English—fluent, though somewhat accented, a basal French overlarded with British vowels and some occasionally quite startlingly accurate reproductions of British clipped consonants. Jonathan found it hard not to listen to his accent, rather than to the meaning of his words.

"May I be indiscreet?"

"Please," Mr. Rives answered.

"Article forty-five will be much debated. Much debated, and for, I would think, a very long time." This was, Jonathan knew, the constitutional prohibition against long-term presidencies in the Second Republic. The French President was actively pressing for its amendment. "We are, as a nation, expert in debate."

"I much prefer your debates, myself, to those of our English cousins. There is a certain—how shall I put it?—a certain snap, a flair, to your debates."

"Ah, yes. I would have to admit that we do it beautifully. But then, *hélas*, we pay no attention whatever to anything that has been said. All the lovely words, all the logical arguments, all the passionate rhetoric, run down the gutter. And we roll up our sleeves and knock each other on the head until we are all tired, and the least exhausted is declared the winner, more perhaps by default than by virtue of true success. And then this very process of exhaustion leads, inexorably, to further combat, since the defeated party is aware that it is never truly defeated and can always rise again, if only it can recover its energy. We have done this time after time, for almost a century now. I cannot see any hope that we will change."

"Do you expect violence?"

"Who knows?"

"Should *we* expect violence? I would need to lay in some stores, here at the Ministry, in case I had, shall we say, an influx of unexpected boarders, for some unpredictable time."

"Most unofficially," M. Delgado answered calmly, "I would think that might be an excellent idea. It could of course be a precaution taken in vain. But I do not know. Much will depend on the next several months. And on the army. And, to be sure, on the President's patience."

Mr. Rives nodded, thoughtfully silent.

"The British," M. Delgado went on, "will recognize any new government with eagerness, if it is of a monarchical nature."

"To be sure."

"As will the Russian government, and the various German states, and Austria."

"You have nothing to fear from us. Even were the Marquis de Lafayette still alive, and in personal danger, I doubt my government would interfere, beyond perhaps some form of protest. But with Lafayette dead . . . ." He smiled. "You do not take us for a military power, do you, Mr. Delgado?"

"Not yet." The Frenchman paused significantly. "We are keenly aware of the growing power of your country, in all respects. Your time on the world's stage is fast approaching; you will inevitably be a military power, once your population has grown, and your economic power has swelled. You will have, then, what we in Europe like to call 'interests.' And you will choose to protect them, when they are threatened. One thing leads to another."

"Well, I should like to have been present, if you had ever had the opportunity to say those things to General Andrew Jackson! I think he might have had an apoplectic attack!"

"The good *général* is in his grave, and the world has rolled onward. And I, who speak more as a friend than as a government official, also speak not to M. Jackson"—he pronounced it more like "zzhaxSOHN"—"but to my good friend, M. Rives." He spread out his hands. "It is better for things to be understood than misunderstood. That is why I have come."

"I am very grateful to you, M. Delgado. I, too, would like to avoid misunderstandings whenever possible. And I am deeply concerned that there be no injury to persons—or to property."

"Persons, of course, are a great deal easier to protect from injury. They are—*comment dit-on?*—mobile?"

"*Merci bien,*" Mr. Rives repeated, his accent heavy.

M. Delgado bowed, and as Jonathan rose the Minister waved him back to his chair, indicating that he would take the Frenchman to the door himself. Southern courtesy, Jonathan murmured to himself. Mr. Rives was every inch a Southerner. They probably should constitute the American diplomatic service, solely and exclusively. No other American could touch them for suavity and grace. He certainly could not.

He sighed. He did not, rather to his surprise, feel guilty. Mr. Rives' relations with his wife were his, and their, affair. He had wondered, after Clarissa left, whether he would readily be able to face her husband, this next day. It had proved remarkably easy; everything was just as it had been. So long as the injured husband did not know he was, in fact, injured—or if he knew, then so long as he did not know who had injured him—official existence would continue unchanged.

And private existence. Mrs. Rives was a forceful woman, as well as a lovely and a desirable one. He did not need to focus on her probable history to realize, without consciously bothering to reflect on it, that he was not apt to have been the first. Nor would he be the last. She would be expert—as expert as those French debaters—at covering her, and their, tracks. She, too, was a Southerner, after all. She knew, without a doubt, what would follow if Mr. Rives found them out. So, too, did Jonathan, and he again surprised himself by not being afraid. It was not much of a risk, he judged, and Clarissa was certainly worth it.

He forced his mind away from remembrance of her, the night before. That was not useful. He would unfairly tax his work; he could conceivably reveal himself, somehow. It was inappropriate—though it was glowingly pleasant—to remember what had been. Patience. His time having come, it would without fail come again. Clarissa would not lightly abandon him, having taken such extraordinary measures to capture him, nor would he abandon her. All the same—and again and again—he tried, without notable success, to divert his backward-looking thoughts. It had been a glorious evening!

"And are you the new Minister, Mr. Bingham?"

Clarissa smiled at him from the door. He rose at once, untangling himself from his chair and his daydreaming. He had not felt awkward, seeing her husband, but he felt swiftly uncertain, almost childish, seeing her.

"I am, dear Mrs. Rives, your most obedient servant."

She shook her head, as he started toward her, and he halted, confused.

"Later," she said simply, then smiled, turned away, and was gone. He stood where he was a moment, then dropped back into his chair, limp and drained. He touched his forehead with the back of one hand: it was damp, he had begun to perspire. Was that how a man reacted, indeed? She was his mistress, now, was she not? He slumped into the chair, holding onto the arms for support. Was she? In a technical sense, yes, surely. But in reality? Was he the architect of their coming together, the engineer, the general? Hardly.

He straightened, stiffened his spine, and made himself look more like a proper Secretary. Did it matter, after all, who had been the prime mover, or whose hand lay firmly on the tiller? She was a fine woman, devilishly fine, and he was as lucky as he could be. He smiled with satisfaction. He was very lucky. He laughed softly. There might be somewhat less poetry, for a while, but in the end there would be more. Oh, much more!

Her long dress did not seem to hold her back. At worst, she tucked it up with one hand, and climbed, or leaped, or tip-toed, over any obstacle that presented itself. Nor did she catch her sleeve—or her hem. There simply were no obstacles, where Clarissa was concerned.

"How glorious!" he exulted, stopping near the swell of the hill. She turned with him, holding lightly to his arm, and he covered her hand tightly with his own. "*La belle France*," he affirmed, then bent and brushed her cheek with his lips. "*Et la belle française—ma belle française.*"

There were almost no fences; the pastures and tilled fields spread one upon another, as if this whole vast landscape belonged to a single fabulous landlord, rather than to a horde of hungry peasants. And it was all flung open for whoever chose to clamber across it, to ascend its hills and sit beside its small, clear-flowing streams. One did not walk like this, where he came from. And where would one find a bear, here, except perhaps in a zoo?

"It makes me very happy," he told her. "All of it." He squeezed her hand. "And you. You make me very happy, Clarissa."

She smiled up at him, her eyes bright and somehow deeper than, still, he was able to fathom.

"And if it were to rain?" she wondered, and laughed.

"I would pull down some trees," he replied extravagantly, "and build you a log cabin. We are very good at such things, we Americans."

"Do you all live in log cabins, still?"

"With our Indians, to be sure. And also our cows, horses, pigs, and chickens."

"It must be very warm, in the winter."

"Oh yes," he assured her, turning once again toward the summit, where they were to picnic. "It gets fearfully cold, in the winter. Sheep are particularly useful, you know."

"But the odor!"

"We are accustomed to it. Besides, is it not said, in France, that an American smells even worse than his animals?"

"That, *mon cher*, is a bit *de trop*. Even for a poet, and a fabulist, you exceed yourself."

"I am an American. It is impossible that I could ever exceed myself."

"And it is said that Germans have over-large egos!"

He only laughed and swung the picnic basket.

"Careful," she warned.

"I could not be more careful."

"But the wine . . . ." And he stopped the swinging. When residents of France mentioned wine, you knew they were no longer jesting. The only subject more serious was food. And money, to be sure. Possibly love.

The hill was well-wooded, which was fortunate, the day being very warm and the sun totally unobscured. Still, they were both perspiring when they reached the top. He spread out his coat, which had long since come off his back and been draped over his arm.

"*Assis toi*," he invited. She held out her hand and he helped her, then placed the basket alongside her and himself just the other side of the basket.

"It is only a little past eleven, but I find myself thinking of what may be inside this basket."

"Americans! You are primitives, you eat like cows and horses."

He threw back his head, laughing, then let the sun glint through the trees, straight into his eyes. The sky shimmered; the blue broke into rainbow colors. The world seemed suddenly to have disappeared. He could see no earth, no dwellings, no sign of humankind. Except that he knew she was seated just beside him.

"Enough. You perhaps think you can talk to the sun, if you pay attention only to its rays?"

He swung back to earth. She had opened the basket, but all she removed was two delicate glasses and a flagon of wine. He watched how deftly she poured. As she handed him the glass, he tried to bend and kiss her wrist. She pulled back, in mock alarm.

"You will spill the wine!"

"*Horreurs.*"

They cooled themselves in comparative silence, sipping, watching the leaves shake, listening to birds. He did not recognize all the calls but did not ask her to identify them. She sat with her legs demurely tucked under, her ankles and even her feet invisible. Her dress was considerably more modest, out of doors. The high collar of her dress covered half her neck and uncovered nothing else. Her sleeves, delicately puffed, were long and though not quite prim—he could not imagine her wearing anything prim—were nevertheless clearly proper. When she raised her glass he could see her wrist, as the sleeve slid back. It was a marvelously pretty wrist, but, though he wanted to, he did not attempt to kiss it. She had a firm procedure for educating him, in these things, and he usually required only one lesson.

"Your visit to the dressmaker's," he said with a sudden smile, "will not be terribly productive."

"On the contrary." Her voice was as firm and sure as Arabella's—more, even, since Clarissa had taken on that peculiarly French—or was it European—authority? A woman on her own ground was *maître chez soi*, just as the *charbonier* of the school proverb was also master in his own house. Though they were both Virginians, even so masterly a woman as Arabella was not, in the United States, quite so securely the dominant force in her own domain. "I will have a most productive fitting. You will see."

He stared, for the moment bewildered. She was not making what struck him, wildly, as a bawdy jest. No, she was serious.

"What are you saying?"

Her laugh was flute-like, but gay.

"I will have had an excellent fitting. You don't understand?"

"How could I?"

"Of course. How could you?" She leaned forward a little, treasuring her joke. "Do you know where my dressmaker lives?"

"Most assuredly not."

She rocked slightly back and forth.

"It is a very good address. Some most reputable people reside there." She turned and grinned at him; he was unable to follow her. Her eyes brightened inordinately. "Oh, you are a most miserable conspirator, *mon petit amércain*."

"Concededly. I haven't the faintest idea what you're talking about, Clarissa." Her name in French, Clarisse, reminded him of the French for Michael Angelo: Michel Ange. He would say that softly to himself, sometimes, as he was drifting into sleep. If angels spoke, that was how they would sound. He loved all things French, even more now than ever before.

"I don't know that I ought to reward your ignorance."

But he knew she would tell him, in her own good time. She was not good at keeping such secrets. What good was a secret, when the whole point of it was to exhibit, to demonstrate, your own greater cleverness?

"But I will be kind to you."

"You mean, you will prove my ignorance, and your own—"

She reached out and closed his lips. It was a decisive gesture. All the same, he managed to kiss the palm of her restraining hand. And she did not at once remove it.

"*Comme tu es bête*," she murmured, but he did not take that seriously. She could play the make-believe French woman game as hard as she liked.

"*Eh bien, madame?*"

"She lives in a very small apartment, to be sure," she said as slowly as possible. "It is in the fourth *étage*; one has to climb some very long and very narrow stairs to reach it. But she is a very good dressmaker, and of course I do not mind."

"The more you climb, the less she charges?"

She pretended not to hear him.

"And her address, *cher* M. Bingham, her address," and she paused lingeringly, "is thirty-one, rue de Luxembourg."

He gasped and clapped his hand to his forehead.

"Ah!"

"Precisely. I was first at thirty-one, and then I was at twenty-nine."

"How clever. And how convenient."

Her smile seemed to say, had that not been available, I should most readily have found an equally clever device. And he knew it was true.

"In time, you will realize just how fortunate you have been."

"I realize it now! Believe me, I realize it fully." She only smiled and shook her head. "And besides, how can you talk in the past—already!"

"Because I am realistic."

"I am much too happy to be realistic."

"And you are much too young."

He swung himself around, and put his arm around her.

"I should like to do more than enjoy you. I should like to keep you."

"Could you?"

"Why not?"

"I am a very expensive toy, *mon cher*."

"I will earn vast sums."

"With your copying? Or with your poetry?"

"My uncles are in business, in New York. They are very wealthy men, Clarissa. I have worked with them, a little. I could work with them again."

"Would they have you?"

"Most certainly!"

"Would you have them?"

He bent and scuffed out a tuft of grass.

"Do you have to be quite so realistic? And so perpetually?" He tried to rub the grass on her cheek, but she leaned away. "Isn't it pleasant to dream?"

She raised her glass.

"To dreams," she proposed, and they sipped. "But all the same, even dreams should be realistic."

"Oh, that word."

"Consult your chronometer, Mr. Romantic Poet. It may well be time for our lunch."

He stroked his stomach instead.

"It is time. I do not propose to live by the clock."

She began to open the basket.

"All the same, when it is time for us to take the train back to Paris, we will be there."

"Must we?"

She did not bother to answer, but busied herself with their meal.

NINETEEN

New York, 19 March 1851

My dear Jonathan,

   I have seldom begun a correspondence, or heard via the mails from someone once a part of my daily existence and now removed by much distance, with feelings of such pleasure. It is evident that you have attained your majority in more ways than one. I am moved, as it is yet too early for you to fully understand, both by the visible signs of your maturation—as a man and as a figure on your American literary scene—and by the fact that you chose to honor me with that extraordinary production, your poem Memento Mori. *I have just about enough learning to understand your title: "remember, you too shall die!" But I think my long years of reading poetry in our own tongue, and my practical experience as a writer and editor, allow me to declare this one of the finest productions of any American pen to date. You ask me to look through the poem, criticizing where necessary. I have looked; I cannot criticize, it seems to me too fine for anything but praise. Let posterity, which will surely read it, also have the license to analyze and comment upon it—for I do not think that even posterity, for as long as this English of ours is spoken or read, will have much to animadvert on.*

   You have suggested, with far too much modesty, that if I happen to find any passages, or even any single passage, of sufficient merit, I am to feel free to dispose of any such item as I may choose. I take it, Jonathan, that you are here offering me the privilege to first print your poem, and though the Tribune *is by no means such a literary organ as I sometimes wish it could be, I am, I assure you, proud and happy to tell you that I propose to print the whole of the poem, in sections consecutively for as many days as it takes. Mr. Dana enthusiastically agrees: he thinks, as I do, that you will have a brilliant career ahead of you, if you but continue as, here, you have begun.*

I must say, since you have generously and I hope not foolishly given me the disposal of your poem, in terms, that is, of print, that I have used the good offices of Mr. Dana to conduct the manuscript also to the offices of Messrs. Harper. One of the Brothers will, I suspect, be in contact with you shortly, and with an offer of publication. You deserve to be enriched by this work; I doubt, knowing our country-men, that this will be the result, but a book—and such a book as this will plainly be—will very likely lead to other things.

I can only congratulate you. You say (at age barely twenty-one!) that this is a work long meditated, but however long you have meditated, you have more impor-tantly meditated well. And you have not shirked: the issues are dealt with openly, but with a rare passionate calm. How you have done it, I cannot know: it is not to the likes of me that poetry comes, descending from Heaven. But it has come to you, and I am doubly honored, both to print the poem and to arrange for its more permanent publication, and also to know that I have in some sense helped, however minimally, to nurture what is destined to be a major talent on our American stage.

Politics? (to descend, lamentably, from the sublime to the very nearly ridiculous) You deign to ask my impressions of the latest developments. I am very much an ex-politician, as you know, my ninety days of elected leadership having long since van-ished into memory. But we are not the nation we were, even when you sailed abroad. President Taylor's election was, I thought at the time and even after, very much the lesser of two evils; I remain warmed by the thought that that oaf Cass was denied the office. But President Taylor's death has brought us, in his stead, President Fill-more, and President Fillmore is in his way as much a mutton-brain as is General Cass. We have more States in the Union, and less unity. We have more arguments with our Southern brethren, and we have more slaves escaping to our shelter, and we have more slaves being heartlessly and brutally returned to their "Owners." The South has thrown us a sop: there are to be no slave battalions marching through the streets of the nation's capitol, chained together for the market-place to dispose of them. But in those areas where slavery flourishes—for who grows cotton in front of the Supreme Court? or behind the White House?—we have spinelessly permitted them to throw an iron vise of oppression over their illicit fields.

I do not mean to insult you by a mildly negative reference to your brother, in this context. But he does not seem to me precisely the man we want, in the Senate. He did not, frankly, seem to me the man we wanted, when he campaigned for the office. I dare say he will be re-elected, and as often as he likes; he has tried not to offend. And if that is not the road to immortality, it has been proven to be at least the road to stability in office. But we shall see about that. A great many old saws may tumble

*to the ground, before too long. A great many proven ways may prove to be in vain.
You may apply to your other brother, Dr. Johnson, for further information. He is
slowly becoming less of a medical man and more of a force in what the dunderheads
are pleased to call "abolition." (I am told he is a sterling example of a man much
improved by marriage.) As if the so-called rights of one man to dispose of the body
and the labor of another, solely in his own interest, was something we as a free people
could consider anything that needed "abolitioning!" What is there to abolish, when
it could not conceivably be legitimate, in God's eyes or in our mortal but supposedly
democratic ones, that such a thing as slavery should continue to exist, much less
flourish, on our native soil? We—and I am enlisted under the banner, indeed—do
not wish to abolish anything. We wish to restore freedom. We wish to re-establish
decency. We wish to see bondage replaced by liberty. It is in truth exactly that simple,
though no one is better aware than I am that it will not in reality be anything like
that simple. Before the great day comes, as in the end it must, there will have to be
shibboleths smashed, and parties dissolved, and men wounded. There may have to
be men dead: I do not know, I hope not, but I fear it. I am not a prophet, but I will
venture to predict that no Whig will ever again sit in the highest seat of power in this
country. Mr. Sumner, a so-called "abolitionist" from the State of Massachusetts,
will very likely take a seat in the Senate, come this fall. He will be joined by others.
There will be forward movement, let me tell you—or there will be dis-union. It will
come to that. I do not see any other course.*

*I do not know if your Aunt Sophia Andrée quite agrees with me. But more
and more of our countrymen are seeing the inevitable truth. No one wants to see it;
for many years I did not want to, I thought that Mr. Van Buren might lead us out
of the wilderness, I hoped that Mr. Clay might, I prayed that Mr. Webster might
have the opportunity. But false gods are not worth praying to, and we as a people will
come to know this, as I at last know it. It will be a different country, we are slowly
but surely learning, or it will be no country at all. The mantle of freedom is not to
be worn by a slut. I think the Andrées will come to understand, as indeed such colleagues of theirs as the Tappans already have. Money is not such a bar to wisdom
as some would think!*

*I wax philosophical; let me return to business, and then let me have done.
How much poetry, worth twenty times twenty of this scribbling of mine, could you
have penned in the time it has taken you to plough through all this turgid—but
still true—plumping and preening! And perhaps, nay more than likely, you have
yourself come to know these things unaided by my self-serving wisdom, if wisdom it
be. Never mind: truth is not worn out by repetition.*

*I began to say: the poem will appear in our unworthy pages, beginning on Mon-
day next. I will send you copies as they emerge from our presses. And Mr. Dana
has pledged himself (gladly, I may say) to furnish you with such evidences of critical*

and popular reaction to the work as come to our hands. It will be a success; there is no doubt of it. You have every right to be proud—though on the evidence of your poem it would seem clear that you will permit yourself, at most, a variety of gratification considerably lessened than pride. Do you know, when you first came to us, at the <u>Tribune</u>, *and Bayard Taylor showed me that deft and vastly amusing review you wrote, very much to his order, I was sure that you would grow into a humorist, or even a satirist. I never contemplated—so much for my wisdom!—the kinds of depths you display, in* <u>Memento Mori</u>. *It should make us all, and it does make me, humble, indeed, to contemplate how little we know of one another, and of how inept our powers of prediction about one another continue, eternally, to be. You are very young, and it would be easy to excuse myself on that score. But I neither excuse nor do I blame myself: I only repeat, and wish I had the immense pleasure of repeating more often, not only to you but to others, my deepest, my most profound congratulations, my admiration for your gifts, and my gratitude for what you have already given us, along with my anticipation of what you will in the future bring to us from who knows what heights. And as you know, there is remarkably little rhetoric that ever flows out of the dogged, quotidien pen of*

Yours, etc.,
Horace Greeley

"I would have stayed at Columbia, had I been you."

She had brought a cup of tea to his desk and lingered. They did not have much chance for conversation, during the day, nor could they frequent public places when they were together of an evening.

"*You* probably would have. I think you would have made a superb Secretary of State. Perhaps a good President, if you cared to have the post. No: there is no doubt, you would have made a good President, a very good one."

He hoped she would push aside the papers on his desk and perch there a moment. He wanted more time with her, as much time as he could find. He could not find a great deal. But she only bent and flicked away a spot of dust, then straightened and stood over him, arms crossed, unsmiling.

"Columbia would not have admitted me, nor would any other university in our benighted world. Nor do I think I am quite so ignorant of the political world as the gentleman who now occupies the White House."

"General Taylor is a man of some power."

"General Taylor is a fool."

"And you are bitter."

"Shouldn't I be?"

"I would say not. You are very beautiful——." She made a sour face and he stopped, uncertain. "You are, you know."

"Do you praise General Taylor for his person?"

"I wish I had the right to praise yours as it deserves to be praised." She bent toward him, and he wondered if she meant to kiss him.

"You are indeed a fool," she whispered, and then she swept out of the room.

Boston, 19 March 1851

Dear Jonathan,

Why did you not tell me—but indeed, how could you have told me?—that you and Lydia had met, some years ago? You do not, perhaps, recall the incident, in which you had the ill luck to begin by very nearly tearing the bottom off her dress, and to close by being baffled by that strange and stalwart wit she still practices. Nor, in truth, did she at first recall it—but when I described to her who this Paris-dwelling brother of mine was, she did recall, and we both of us laughed mightily, as much at her conduct, I assure you, as at your discomfiture.

I have not abandoned our home, no. I have not moved to Boston: we are here so that Lydia may speak at a meeting. Did you know that Charles Sumner, the lawyer and teacher of law at Harvard, is very likely to be elected Senator from this State? It is not certain; the Massachusetts Legislature has its weak men. But if it is to be, it will be a very great thing, indeed, for Sumner is implacable, especially on the issue of the spread and even the continuance of slavery on these shores. He is said to be a noble man; I can in part confirm this, for I have recently had the pleasure of meeting him. It is almost enough to drive one into the political arena, to see that a man of such depth, such learning, and such immovable high principle, can conceivably ascend to one of the highest offices in the realm. But then, you already know about such high officers, since we continue to have one of our very own, in the family as it were.

There is not, so far as I can tell, a literary bone in my body, but since my wife is afflicted with the gift of tongues I seem to hob-nob with writing people, when we come to Boston. (We come surprisingly often. I could not live here, but is it assuredly a remarkable place to visit.) There is one aspect of this which puzzles me. I would have thought, as an outsider, naïve and unknowing, that the fate of our country's literature would pretty much equally concern the writers of all regions and centers, and that each would look to the other for support and help, praising and sustaining with *energetic good cheer. This appears to be the very farthest thing from the truth. One has only to read the New York papers to see how jealous those writers are of Boston: the <u>Knickerbocker</u>, now, though its editor himself is, I understand, a transplanted New Englander (perhaps they are the worst kind, however), perpetually sneers at all things coming out of Boston. And I have heard no less a man than James Lowell condescend, politely but damningly, at the aspirations of New Yorkers—<u>his</u> theme, visibly, was that there is in truth only one literature worth remarking, in America, and Boston infallibly has it all. And will keep it. This is surely wrong, as well as dangerous. Tell me, my poet brother, does this strike you as a fair portrayal? Am I in error? Are my impressions only superficial ones?*

Your nieces and nephews are well. Grace, indeed, is more than well; she is positively blooming. Her long stay in Virginia and Washington, last year, seems to have struck a deep spark. She dances, now, all the time. Do you recall how she seemed, even as a small child, to flow about, leaping and almost flying? She has begun to organize herself, to transform accidental grace into (forgive me the pun) deliberate, even artistic Grace. She has her mother's infallible sense of rhythm, and she has that strangely liquid motion so totally her own. (How does the old poet put it? "When as in silks my Julia goes, then, then, methinks, how sweetly flows that liquefaction of her clothes." You'd think he'd seen my Grace, by God!) Anne-Marie's music gave so much to the rest of us, and so terribly little to herself. May Grace's gift, for that is what seems to be emerging, somehow do more for her and no less for the remainder of the world. Perhaps this second half of our century will be a better, more sustaining time to grow into adulthood, for a woman of talent, than was the first half.

Lord: you are only a dozen years Grace's senior, I had forgotten how monstrously young a man of parts you are, Jonathan. You have no right to be so young, especially as I see the accursed number "FORTY" writ large in the clouds and sliding toward me, inexorably, terribly. (Plainly, there has been some literary influence on me: I am sorry for it, and will try to amend myself in what follows.) You are of my generation, though—are you not? Or are you of Grace's generation? Or neither? Do I seem like an middle-aged gentleman whose bearings are become unsure? I am that, lad.

Do you think of ever returning to these shores?

What have you been a-writing, eh? You have been damnably silent, on that subject, you know. There were some hints, as I recall, of something stewing, even before you sailed for the Old World, but since you have landed, smack as I would guess into the waiting arms of Temptation, you have fallen into non-productive paths, from all that I can see. Do correct that, as I would beg you to chastise and righten any other of my numerous misapprehensions. When I see your first volume of poems, Jonathan, then I will know to which generation you truly belong. You can disguise yourself from others, but you can not disguise the self of your poems. Nor can poems smile and wink and charm, as their author may, when secrets are close to being pried into the open. Be forewarned, therefore: I am on the watch for one Jonathan Bingham, and expect to catch him unawares in his book, if I cannot catch him in his person.

Your father does not, of course, write to me, not even from his Holy Land. I do wish he would deign to notice his grandchildren with an occasional line. I cannot, to be sure, suggest this or anything else to him, but perhaps you or your brother Theodore might? I would be grateful—and the children ecstatic. They are obliged to suffer from a void of grandparents on their father's side, and now to be forced to add to that indignity the deprivation of, first, their maternal grandmother and now their maternal grandfather—well, it is not truly fair, it cannot be fair. We are agreed, naturally, that children should ideally be seen and not heard, but cannot their father, at least, and it may be some one of their uncles, be heard on their behalf?

Like an underwound clock, I wind down. This town fatigues me: it is not as bustling as New York, and I would guess it is not so prosperous. But there is a kind of continuous current running through all the streets, and thereby through all the inhabitants, linking them together in a virtually common—what? Neurasthenia would be too strong, but something nervous it is, for all that. Medical science knows it not, but the visitor to Boston, be he political, literary, or medical, feels it on the soles of his shoes—and, after a bit, in his brain, located (perchance) some centimeters to the right of the medulla. Persiflage? Only partly, let me assure you. Those who survive, or even better, those who <u>overcome</u> this strange psychic tension, like Mr. Emerson, or Mr. Lowell, or even Mr. Alcott and Mr. Channing (whom I like less, the both of them), they give off a kind of reverse electricity, a very special and wonderful sort of tension indeed. But those of us who cannot overcome, who can barely survive, well, we grow tired. And in my case, dear Jonathan, I require, as I now will take, a frequent nap, to ensure my making it through. Have you seen a surer sign of approaching age? But my hair has not yet whitened, believe me it has not!

I am charged by my wife to tell you that she wishes to see you again, as our guest, and that if you had not been in France the while, thus guaranteeing cavalier status, she would thoughtfully shorten her skirts for your visit. There: I have said it. We all wish you were with us; we would seek to tie you in some more palpable style, if we could. (But Lydia has no sister, alas, to tie you with. I shall endeavor to think of something, never fear.) Grace, who has always found you a veritable fund of warmth, grows misty-eyed when she talks of you. I do not jest! Were she a few years older than she is, she might be our bait, might she not? Cousins make remarkable couples, I have noted.

Enough of this: I grow more than tired; I suffer from brain weariness and all the concomitant symptoms. I prescribe rest, and as my own patient I faithfully obey. May you experience a delightful Parisian spring, and never fall.

Yours, etc.,
Martial Johnson

Cliff Street, New York
26 March 1851

Dear Mr. Bingham:

We are pleased to offer you publication of your poem, <u>Memento Mori</u>, upon the terms set out in the enclosed brief agreement, the which, if it meets with your approval, you will kindly sign and return to us at the above address. Without speaking to my brothers and partners, I cannot be precise as to time of publication nor as to size of the first printing, but I would venture, in a preliminary sort of way, that books of this sort (though I speak here only in the rough, and do not at all speak of the unique quality of your work) do best in the season immediately before the Christmas holidays. I am informed that Mr. Greeley intends serial publication, in the <u>Tribune</u>, which will I expect help rather than hinder sales of the volume proper. If it proves possible, we shall gauge public reaction from that newspaper appearance, and estimate the likely sales therefrom.

We are most impressed with your work and trust to see, in time, more than one sequel.

Yours, etc.,
J. Wesley Harper

The garden was lovely with late summer colors. The carriage was being brought around and he was attending to her, while she waited. It seemed to him a singularly unarduous duty.

"I trust you will return with mountains of lace."

"I propose to purchase a pair of gloves."

"With lace."

"Without lace. Jonathan, you are sometimes insufferable."

"Frequently."

"Frequently. If you were not so—"

"Please do not say poetic."

"Good Lord, no. That is the very last thing I would have said!"

He heard the carriage wheels.

"You still baffle me, Clarissa."

"And you, my dear Mr. Bingham, have no secrets from me. None whatever. If you were a book, indeed, I could put my hand on your first page and divine all the rest."

The coachman opened the gate.

"It is a book dedicated to you."

"Do you know, I used to read a great deal, when I was younger. I seem to have gotten out of the habit, recently. It's a pity, I suppose, but what can one do?"

The coachman closed the gate behind her, after tipping his hat to Jonathan.

Jerusalem, 4 July 1851

My son,

This is a lazy, dirty city: therein is a lesson, to be learned at pain and of necessity. Do not trust the earthly appearances of anything whatever. The only clean objects in all of Jerusalem, other than the insignificant persons of European and American visitors, are walls and roofs, which are painted with whitewash, more I think to deflect the sun than to ape holiness—or cleanliness. There is nothing sacred, here, and yet everything sacred. Beggars abound, seeking only the gilt and tinsel of this world, while under their scabby feet lies the very ground where the most sacred of feet have walked, leaving stamped on all our souls the most imperishable of prints.

And all about this crumbling town, this laughable fortress which any two companies of New York militia could lay waste in any hour they chose, lie the most holy of hills, purple in the twilight, white in the sun, yellow under the great oily moon. The stars above, oh my son, are the same stars which shone on Him, as He strode those hills, teaching, exhorting, His lovely voice lifted in wisdom and song. Men do not hear Him, now, even though His words are recorded. He left us, from one of those hills, but beggars teem across it, today, whining at the stubborn Christians, or supposed Christians, who pay dutiful rather than feeling tribute both to beggar and to Christ.

If He cured the lepers, ought I to salve the sick and the lame? I do not: I am not here on any earthly mission. Clergymen, so-called, flock here from civilized lands, to convert the faithless, the Arabs and the Hebrews. It does no good, I can tell you. Few are converted, and in the process many are subverted: one look at the fat, lazy "monks" of Jerusalem tells all.

I have acquired some words of the languages spoken in these streets. I can, when I will, converse with those who crowd them. I do speak with them, at times, perhaps to break the occasional monotony which settles on me, willy-nilly, as I tramp my rounds, following endlessly in His steps. There is, I suspect, some feeling that I too am sanctified, except in my case by madness rather than by any true sanctity. Never mind: it keeps the highwaymen off, though not the highway insects, nor am I troubled by the painted sluts who also, though more discreetly, pass up and down these filth-encrusted streets. The garbage of the world: how it ennobles the mind! To walk in refuse and to lift one's eyes to Heaven: there is the ultimate, and I sometimes feel that I have approached close to it, and that I will come closer and closer as the days go endlessly by.

There seems no end of time, but there is an end, my son, and it comes upon us, upon all of us, before we know it is drawing nigh. Live, since you do live, with that end ever in your heart, and you will come to glory when it is upon you. Such is the prayer, and such is the life, of your dutiful, Christ-loving Father, here in Jerusalem, this fourth day of July, in the year of Our Lord eighteen hundred and fifty-one.

Amen.

Whitetowers, 9 August 1851

Dearest Uncle Jonathan,

I am again in Virginia. My Aunt Arabella has been good enough to invite me once more, and my father has sent me here, and I am very glad of it. Not that I am glad to be away from my new Mother, and my sister and my brothers. I do miss them—as I miss you all the time, Uncle Jonathan. I love you dearly. But do you know what? One of the ladies who dances in the Ballet that I saw here last year, and which I will see again in a week or so, has agreed to give me lessons in dancing. Is that not splendid? Of all the things in the world—I mean, apart from all the people—I like dancing the best. So it is wonderful good news.

Having a new Mother is very good too. It is perhaps less wonderful for me than for Alice, and less wonderful for Alice than for Michael and Mark, who are too little to really remember Mother. I mean, our real Mother, who is in Heaven now. I remember her perfectly: do you? Of course you must! She was your own sister. If anything were to take Alice from us, I would never forget her, and she would not forget me. It is something like that, only more special too, with Mother. Every time I hear a piano I think of her, and I hear her playing. No one plays her piano, now. Our new Mother does not play. She is also too busy, when she is not with us, in trying to help the slaves, and also the Negroes who are no longer slaves.

Aunt Arabella only smiles when I tell her of my new Mother. I think this must be because there are ever so many slaves here at Whiteoaks, and Aunt Ara-

bella would not like it if they were to go away. It would be very strange for her, and hard. I wonder what my new Mother would say, if she could see Aunt Arabella with her slaves? I wish I knew. It is hard to understand, some times. What do you think?

If I came to Paris—I know I cannot yet, I am too little still, but perhaps when I am older?—would I be able to dance there? Do ladies dance, in Paris? Mostly they do not, here, Aunt Arabella says. I have called the lady who is to give me lessons a lady, but I think my Aunt does not so consider her. She is very beautiful, and she dances beautifully. You ought to see her. You would love her, I think.

My father thinks there are no slaves in Paris. Is that true?

I do wish I could see you. I would give you such a nice kiss, if I could see you. It is not fair, and I know I ought not say it, but you are my very special Uncle. Did you know that? I wish you would come home. Or I would come there. I wish—but you will think me a very strange girl, and so I will not say anything more.

But do come home soon. Please?

Your loving niece,
Grace Johnson

"Are you growing tired of me?"

"Oh, I have been tired of you from the start." She laughed and touch his cheek gently. It was early evening; they were in his apartment. She had come in the middle of the afternoon, and they had made love, and they had taken tea together, and now they were sitting on his bed. It was growing dark rapidly; she would shortly have to leave for the *hôtel*, and her formal dinner, to which this night he was not invited. "I was tired of you before I met you."

"That's a fascinating thought."

"As I am tired of all men. Because they are not women."

He half turned and glanced at her. Her face seemed cheerful, even radiant.

"You are growing into a *philosophe*."

She pried the chronometer out of his pocket and consulted it.

"I am growing late, *mon cher.*"

He tugged her back.

"No. Not yet."

She laid her head on his shoulder.

"Only a little longer, Jonathan."

He could almost hear her slow breathing. Seasons flew one on the other's heels, in Paris. At home he had scarcely noticed time's flight, but here he could mark it as on a sailor's chart, each day, sometimes each hour. It was too dark, suddenly, to make out the yellowing leaves he had seen, just a few minutes before, on the tree outside his window. It never snowed much, in Paris, but there might be snow any day now. It seemed to come early, just before the leaves were all gone, and then would come the wet, cold winter. And the spring. An election year, in the United States. Mr. Rives might return home, willingly or unwillingly. And his Secretary?

"My poem will shortly be a book."

"And you will be famous."

"Will I?"

"But of course! What an idea! Is there any point to publishing a book, if one is not to be famous for it?"

"Will fame make me more attractive—or less?"

"Neither."

"You can't be serious."

"But I am. Totally."

"I can't believe that. You're being deliberately perverse, for reasons I cannot decipher. How could it not make a difference? I don't understand."

She sat up.

"How little you know of me. How little, indeed, you know of women. Do you think I, or any woman, loves a man for what he is?"

"Could there be another reason?"

"*Comme tu es bête!* How stupid you are, Jonathan. A woman who loved a man for what he is, right now, this moment, would have to have some vital part of herself disconnected." She put her hand under his chin and slightly raised it. "I look at you, this minute, and what do you think I see?"

"Me."

"Idiot. No, I see what you can be, what you may perhaps be. And I see what you are to me—which is not, be assured, at all the same thing as what you may seem to be to the rest of the world."

"Feminine logic."

"Not a bit of it. Simple truth."

"How can you be so all-seeing? How can women as a group—no, it makes no sense."

"Not to you. Or to other men. That is our strength: you cannot see what lies directly under your noses. As long as that remains true, Jonathan, you may keep the trappings of authority. True strength, and true direction, will continue to emanate from us."

"That is an argument I can recall hearing before."

"But you did not listen."

"I listened. I simply could not credit it."

"Good." She slipped off the bed, stood smiling down at him. "Remain obtuse."

"But loveable?"

"Sometimes."

"Will you be here Thursday?"

"There are limits to even my husband's flexibility."

He made a face: "New limits?"

"The same ones. You do not want him to be suspicious, do you?"

"Is he?"

"I think not. Can I ever be sure?"

"You were, just a moment ago."

She took his arm, as they walked into the sitting room. Her shawl lay across a soft chair (which she had given him: it could seat two, relatively comfortably, and one superlatively comfortably). She put out her hand but did not pick it up. Her rings glittered against the plain wool.

"There are no limits to my flexibility," she said quietly.

"Indeed!"

She faced him.

"Is that amusing?"

"Shouldn't it be?"

"No. A woman would be quickly broken, in this world, if she were not a creature capable of adjustment."

"And a man, too."

"Not so much."

"You're right. Not so much. A woman has to make more adjustments."

She laughed, and spun around, whipping her shawl into the air and over her shoulders.

"You are more educable than most, Jonathan." She stood on tip toes and kissed him. "That *does* make you more loveable."

They started toward the door, he just behind her. She was not holding his arm, now.

"And more durable?"

"Definitely!"

He put his arms around her; she wiggled free.

"Should I be late . . . ." she warned, holding up a scolding finger.

"What then?"

He watched her quick eyes scanning his. He was tired, suddenly, of all the deception, all the concealment.

"End of the matter," she informed him quietly. "I am, after all, a married woman."

"How well I know it!"

She pretended to cuff him, chidingly.

"*That* again. You would not marry me, Jonathan, if you could."

"How do you know?"

"I know. And so, too, do you. You may pretend that you do not, but even if you can succeed in fooling yourself, you cannot fool me." She turned to open the door, then swung back. "And what a fool you would be, indeed, if you seriously thought of marriage to me."

"I do happen to love you, Clarissa."

He could almost see her making herself smile.

"As best you can, *petit.*"

"You have a nasty tongue, at times."

"*Bien entendu.* If Little Red Riding Hood had had a nasty tongue, do you suppose the wicked wolf would have gotten her—or her poor innocent grandmother?"

He rested his hands on her shoulders, staring into her face, trying to read it. He had never seen eyes so bright and yet so impenetrable.

"You're playing with me."

She lifted her hands and wound them into his.

"Isn't that what I do best? Truthfully?"

"I don't think so."

"As I suspected. You *are* a fool." She kissed him once more, a definitive leave-taking peck. "I must go." She dropped her hands from his shoulders; in a moment he let his fall from hers. "I will see what I can do about Thursday."

"Please."

When she had gone, he stood for a moment in front of the closed door, not looking at it, not seeing it. Then he walked to his bedroom, but did not remain there. He turned around, and walked rapidly to his writing desk, straightened it, sharpened a pen, uncovered the ink well, smoothed down a sheet of paper—and sat staring at it. It was very white. His pen was not heavy. The evening was very dark. He could just barely make out, if he strained his ears, the faint sounds of feet on the stairs. Was it Clarissa returning? Hardly. She had a dinner to be readied: that was no pretense; he knew it was sober fact. What could possibly bring her back? But he wished there could be something, he did not know what.

And where would he eat *his* dinner, this night?

He sighed, leaned back, and dropped his pen to the desktop. After a moment he screwed the top onto the ink well. There was nothing to write, nothing to say. Was there some hidden poetry in her going, in the downward curve of his relationship with her? He could not have drawn a graph of that curve; he could not have documented it, but he felt it, and he knew he was right. She had had many lovers: that was and always had been clear. There had been many other Jonathans, and there would be still others to come. His predecessor, now, about whose work she had mysteriously seemed so informed: that did not seem so mysterious, any longer.

Should he withdraw, before he was withdrawn from?

But to what? To whom?

Or should he return to America? His book would be appearing; his reputation would be created. Greeley would welcome him. But he did not want to be back at the *Tribune*. It had been a fresh adventure; it would now be drudgery, no matter how highly he was regarded, no matter how well he was paid. He did not, in truth, need much money, not with the regular payments of his uncle's annuity. All time beyond that remained blank, unreal, not something he could in any way anticipate. He did not want to anticipate it.

Should he find himself another *maîtresse*? The French word was so much more elegant, as well as pleasanter. "Mistress" had an ugly sound to it. In America, to have a "mistress" was to behave immorally. In Paris, a *maîtresse* was, if not quite *de rigeur*, at least socially sanctioned. Some of the leading ladies of France, under any and all sorts of regimes, had been somebody's *maîtresse*. No one's mistress was worth a box of salt, in the United States.

But who could he turn to, in this delicate business? Young Americans—and even more, young Englishmen, the higher the class the more true it was—seemed to flock into the arms of Parisian *grisettes*; the *grisette* would come after you, if you were male and if you wore sufficiently expensive clothing and in general seemed to have sufficient wherewithal to make it worth her while. Jonathan had, of course, been approached. Was it American prudery that had made him shake his head, invariably, and walk straight on, not looking back? Perhaps it was. No matter: he would not turn to *grisettes*, even after Clarissa found her way out of their relationship.

He rose and stood at the window but did not look out. The blinds were not yet drawn; he could have seen the street below, the carriages, the passersby. He had often stood and watched them, counted them, categorized them, even imagined from whence they were coming and to where they were going. This dark evening he simply stood and saw nothing.

She would find her way out, nor would he resist. What good would it do to try holding her? She was stronger than he was, certainly, in such matters, and how could he pretend to hold her? With what? She had come to him of her own accord, and she would leave when she was ready. That leave-taking was somewhere not too far off. How would he remain in her husband's employ, when she was no longer—his *maîtresse?* He had managed both with her and without her. He could probably manage whatever he had to manage. But he did not relish the idea. She would be very correct; he would be very correct; it would all be immensely civilized. He was tired of civilization. He was tired of—of Paris? Or of himself?

He walked past his writing desk but left it untouched. There was nothing to say: he had learned that already. Was he truly a poet, when he felt so deeply and yet could find no words to express himself? Did he feel so deeply? What did he feel? Did he feel anything?"

He threw himself into the soft chair she had given him, but immediately bounced up again. It was time to go out. There was nowhere he had ever been, in America or here, where walking was so satisfactory. He had thought it was best in New York, but that had been before. He took his hat, slipped into a coat, and went down the stairs very quickly, suddenly anxious.

He stopped on the pavement, glancing up at his own window. It was dark. What was he in a hurry about? He smiled and shook his head. Was he in search of adventure? Hardly. His stomach grumbled, reminding him that he would shortly have to be in search of dinner. Very well, that was what he would search for: dinner. He would treat himself to an excellent meal, excellent even for this city of gastronomes. He would dine well.

Perhaps he would pay a visit to the Follies. Or to the Comédie. Perhaps one of Madame Delgado's old friends would be performing— he had been neglecting her and her salon, as indeed he had neglected most things, in favor of work, Clarissa, and his poem. If he knew the performer, perhaps he could stop by in the dressing rooms, afterwards, and chat. Perhaps he could take some jolly dancer out to a late supper.

A dancer?

He straightened his hat and laughed almost too loudly. It was time to set himself in motion, and he walked quickly off, trying to observe closely, to store up impressions for future use. And this time the only person he did not fool was himself.

"We are predestinated not to be great in the field of battle. . . . Our battles are forensic; we draw no blood, but the blood of our clients."

—Daniel Webster, to his son Fletcher,
15 January 1836

South Street, New York, 20 December 1851

My dear nephew,

It is not my custom to pen letters, other than a very few pertaining to our affairs here. I do not write letters when I am at home, and as you know well I do not linger long enough indoors, when I am here at the counting-house, to have the opportunity, even had I the necessity, of penning letters except in cases of stringent necessity.

I think, however, that Andrée Bros. can afford me a few moments of leisure, under the extraordinary circumstances of your appearance in print, and the even more extraordinary nature of that appearance. I do not myself read Mr. Greeley's newspaper, no more does your Uncle Karl. But thanks to my sister Sophia I was well aware that the Harpers were putting your <u>Memento Mori</u> in print, this season, and I made sure to have one of the first copies delivered to me, thanks to the kindness of young Fletcher Harper, with whom I have had some occasional dealings in a business way.

I am told that the appearance of the poem, in the pages of the <u>Tribune</u>, was distinctly an Event. Well, if we do not, in this country, have a great deal of Literary Achievement to be in an uproar over, nevertheless we do still have men of taste and discernment, and it is better to be talked about, as an Author—provided the talk is not inimical talk—than to be ignored. So I am pleased that your first major production, in a literary way, has been Noticed. I am told, too, that there will be a good deal more notice, once the magazines, which of course appear less regularly and so take a good deal more time to get around to things even of such importance as your poem, have had the chance to swing into action. Some large guns will be trained, or at least fired: I hear that Mr. Evert Duyckinck will notice the book, and even Mr. Clark of the <u>Knickerbocker</u> is said to be impressed. One does not often find those two gentlemen on the same side of things, but I understand they are agreed, and you are to be declared Poet of the Hour.

Well, that is as may be, and though I know you must be pleased to hear of it, I know you too well, Nephew, to think that such fussing in a literary teacup will mean a great deal to you, or linger long in your mind. It is in truth less important than either the poem itself, or than the large and truly meaningful matters you have yourself already discussed, in the poem. <u>Memento Mori</u>: it is not the title I would have imagined you appearing under, certainly not at your young age, Jonathan. But then, not many of your readers can know better than myself, or indeed any member of the family, how rightly you have chosen, and why. Your sister would be proud, it seems to me, to know how deeply her death has moved you, and how beautifully she—and all who die young—have been mourned, in your lines. How true it is, and I can do no better than to quote you, that

> *All that tread*
> *The globe are but a handful to the tribes*
> *That slumber in its bosom.*

It is not startling, you have not sought to startle us. But what you have said is too well-framed to be ignored hereafter. Many have thought as you have thought, at least in fragmentary part, but it has been for you to wrap that thought in imperishable language. And I have read, over and over, your parting injunction, in the final lines, to

> *Like one who wraps the drapery of his couch*
> *About him, and lies down to pleasant dreams.*

However many years I may have, Jonathan, I would dearly love to be able to depart in just that way! That is the nub of your achievement, indeed: to have enabled so many of us less gifted mortals to find, in your words, the aspirations, the prayers, the tears we could not so well utter for ourselves. A poet who can do so much, and at so early an age, is more than worthy: he is to be treasured.

I do not overpraise you, Nephew. I tell you the simple truth, as I am myself, to your own knowledge, a simple man. I would not deceive you if I had the power. May you go on as you have begun. May the world soon know what manner of man walks among us, quietly recording us in steel and bronze, for all eternity. May the Lord shine His face on you, and keep you, and preserve you, is the heartfelt prayer of

> *your loving uncle,*
> *Peter Andrée*

Jerusalem, 1 January 1852

To Mr. Jonathan Bingham
American Ministry
Paris

My dear Mr. Bingham:

    I have just finished advising your brother, The Honorable Theodore Bingham, United States Senator from New York, of the melancholy circumstances which it is now my solemn duty to communicate to you.

    On the twenty-eighth of December, last, your father, Doctor Fredrick Bingham, was found lying in front of what is here called a mosk—that is, a place of Islamic worship—and brought fairly promptly to my quarters, situated not very far distant. I was not at home, being obliged to make certain calls to the Turkish authorities here, but my wife ordered Doctor Bingham brought directly into our living room and placed, there, on a sofa. He was barely alive, and raving. Seeing his condition, my wife endeavored to soothe his fever and calm his mind, though not with any great success, the fatal illness which had seized him working rapidly to its destined and ineluctable end. His steaming forehead was bathed in such cooling substances as were available, in this torrid zone, and several attempts were made to secure the ingestion of various liquid potions, none of which, however, could be prevailed into his mouth, he thrusting all such succor away.

    Meanwhile, a messenger was sent to me, and another to the German doctor who, failing one trained in our American procedures, ministers to the sick and to the dying among the comparatively few civilized members of this community. As it happens, Doctor Haufstadt being committed elsewhere, I was the first to arrive. I found your father conscious, and somewhat less inflamed with fever, my wife's ministrations having mercifully obtained that much effect. He was sufficiently coherent to dictate to me your brother's address, and yours, and to express the wish that his belongings be collected and sent to your brother. This wish cannot, alas, be honored, as I shall explain in due course, the manner and the nature of your father's death having been as they were. I assured him that I would do all in my power and he seemed somewhat relieved. He insisted on engaging me in a discussion of eternity, and of the nature of sin, in which discussion I of course obliged him as best I could, but in which inevitably I found myself somewhat handicapped in my inability, at all points, to completely comprehend the argumentation he was pursuing. I am afraid this agitated him; it seemed to assume a very large importance to him that I must totally understand, for my own future welfare, and I did my best to dissemble an

understanding which was regrettably denied me, thought I do not believe I truly suc-
ceeded in disguising my confusion.

This discussion endured, I believe, something over an hour, during which time
we momently expected the assistance of the medical man we had sent for, but for the
time being in vain. Your father angrily and I believe contemptuously rejected even
the possibility of medical aid, informing us that he was himself of that professional
persuasion and quite aware that he was dying, and no one and nothing would be able
to save his life. He did not appear to wish that it be preserved, saying a number of
times that he was (you will forgive me the words, but they were transcribed shortly af-
ter his actual demise and are, I trust, accurate, though not precisely cheerful: in these
sorts of situations I do, however, believe it to be my duty to pass on the deceased's
final remarks, whatever their nature: it is not as I see it my role to act as a censor of
the departed), and I quote him, "rotten with sin, death, error, and pestilence of the
soul." As I say, he declared this of himself repeatedly, I do not know exactly how
regularly or how often, but many times indeed, and most forcefully. He also declared
that his life had "less merit than a worm's," and deserved to be put out "like a gut-
tering candle." He was, in his final moments, a most elegant and eloquent man, and
spoke with the obvious accents of an educated and well-read mind. It would have
been a delight to hear him, under other circumstances and saying things of a lighter
and less desperate nature. From time to time he would fall back, quite exhausted
by his efforts, but he would not permit himself that little leisure, and immediately
returned to his—I very nearly wrote sermon, but it was more like a preachment, if
you happen to be familiar with that colloquial but useful term, applied in that part
of the United States where I had my maternal nurturing.

When the medical man arrived, your father was displeased to see him and
made his displeasure immediately apparent. He was terribly articulate, even at the
end. "Take that infernal monster, and his infernal tools of the devil, back to hell
where he belongs!" That indeed was exactly what he said: I have checked with my
wife, who was as struck as I was by this singular utterance, and who confirms to me
that I have it accurately transcribed, to the very syllable. Doctor Haufstadt only ap-
proached some ten feet or so distant, but your father's exhortations appeared to drive
him back. I say appeared, but the Doctor informed me, shortly, that there was noth-
ing to administer, your father being in the final stages of a disease called the kolera,
fortunately unknown among us in the United States, but a dreaded predator in this
part of the earth's surface. Alas, those who succumb to this fever cannot, by Turkish
law, strictly and harshly enforced, be preserved to their families in corpselike form,
but must as soon as certifiably dead be burned, and all their domestic and personal
affairs along with them. This is in order, if so it may be, to keep others from the pes-
tilence. You need not worry yourself about myself and my family: we are somehow
immune to this disease, as my five years in the Holy Land will of themselves testify.

There was accordingly no danger to us in your late father's final illness, nor in his demise, which took place, as I recall (my notes do not speak to this point), at roughly four in the afternoon. He had become quiet and apparently more composed. He shot up from his bed—I do assure you, the word is not misplaced: your father bolted erect, as if propelled by some mysterious force—and screamed, most terrifyingly, "You be damned!"—and then fell back. I was the first to reach him, having been seated no more than a few yards away—I was indeed so startled by your father's fervent declamation, and so unprepared both for its force and for the words he uttered, that I spilled quite widely across my wife's carpet a cup of tea I had been endeavoring to consume. I am told that the stains will largely be removed, after some applications of the servants' devising: I say this only so that you will not be troubled on my or on my wife's account. We were only too glad, more as fellow Americans, I assure you, than as official representatives of our United States Federal Government, to do what little we were able to do, in the way of relieving or possibly soothing your late father's final moments. He was dead when I reached him, and you will, I know, be pleased to hear that there was a smile on his lips, as though Our Lord had heard his final prayers and granted him eternal peace. I know that he has gone to a deserved reward. And though inevitably you will mourn his passing, it is perhaps fitting if I observe that the death of a man so full of years and wisdom and goodness ought not to be mourned as, say, the death of a child or of a young mother would be mourned. I know you are as aware of such things as am I, but I say them, even briefly, in the hope of performing, my dear Mr. Bingham, one more small service to a member of a family prominent in the affairs of our nation, and as some small sign of my appreciation for, in particular, your brother's notable and enduring labors on behalf of us all, whether from your natal State or from some other of our sovereign entities, mine or indeed any other.

This is my melancholy task; I trust I have performed it to your satisfaction. I should be glad to try to inform you of any particulars I may unintentionally have omitted in this account, though I have, believe me, endeavored to be as complete as my recollections, aided as I say by my wife's and by the notes I took immediately after the late Doctor Bingham's departure, can possibly be. You will understand from all that I have here written that there is no necessity to make funeral arrangements, the Turkish authorities having confiscated the body of your father, and also that there will be, I regret to say, no final belongings which I might have the honor to transmit to you, they along with the corpse of your late parent having been consumed in the cleansing fires lit, as per the law, by Turkish hands. Were it otherwise, you may, believe me, be assured that all my best efforts would have been strongly exerted to ensure the safe transmittal of anything entrusted to my care, to the ancestral home, or to any other destination specified. It would have been the very least I could do.

Nor, let me finally assure you, are there any consular fees to be remitted, under the double circumstance of your own employment in the diplomatic service of our mutual Government, and of your Senatorial brother's distinguished standing in our country's capitol. I have recorded a memorandum, for the eyes of Mr. Webster, once again the Secretary of State, advising him of the acts here outlined and the measures taken, as herein described. Believe me, sir, your most faithful and obedient servant,

Marcus Barnard
United States Consul, Jerusalem

Rue de Luxembourg, Paris
18 January 1852

Dear Martial,

We are a rum lot, we Binghams, are we not? Who would expect to go halfway around the world to make a reputation in New York City? Or to go all the way around the world, indeed, to find death in Jerusalem? Or to cross the Atlantic to discover the existence of the female sex? Or—and your oldest daughter, mind you, is half Bingham, a fact which neither she nor you would be well advised to forget!—to travel to Virginia to unearth what Saint Petersburg and Paris have long since perfected, and von Weber written about, namely the art of the dance? I need say nothing about us Binghams and the national ferment, because we seem there at least to have a minimal effect, despite the presence of a Bingham in the Senate. I would give more credit to a fiction, even, lately published in the National Era, *an abolitionist journal put out in Washington, which fiction is soon I believe to appear in book form. (Do you take the journal in question, you who have been so thoroughly recruited to that cause? Do not wonder that we here in Paris are so well-informed: we are, after all, in touch with the capitol on occasion. The name of the novel, by the way, is* Uncle Tom's Cabin, *and it is written by a woman, the sister of Henry Ward Beecher, I believe.)*

As for what ferment may be thought to exist here in Paris, well, I assure you I have no hand whatever in it. Mr. President Louis Napoleon did not think to consult me, some weeks ago, when he launched the so-called coup d'éat by which the Second Republic is being transformed into the Second Empire, and Monsieur le Président into Sa Majesté l'Empereur. There was some fuss then, you know: early in December, last year, when the plebescite was first announced, and everyone knew the monarchy was to return, there were barricades thrown up, in the Faubourg St. Antoine, and the troops of General Saint-Arnaud opened fire, and there were bod-

ies all over the streets. The unfriendly members of the Fourth Estate, who expect by the way soon to be muzzled by this no-nonsense new government, have taken to referring to that unequal clash as the Massacre of the Boulevards. The new constitution—pasted up on the walls just four days ago, so you may not have heard of it as yet—continues the process begun last December. The plebescite, not surprisingly, gave Louis Napoleon seven and a half million votes, as against less than a million on the other side; the constitution gives him "free and unfettered" authority to do as he pleases, to be sure in the name of the people as a whole. It is such a democratic emperor-in-nascence, then, who has sent ten thousand Frenchmen to Algeria—a fate probably worse than death.

But I do not choose to discuss ferments and fusses and politics with you. Do you know, my medical brother, how badly I use you? I do use you, at any rate: I write to you instead of confiding in a journal or a diary. Did you know that? There are people, I know, who can confide only in themselves; they lock their secrets into a diary and suppose that they have made confidences to the whole world—of the future. I do not live in the future, I live here and now, and only here and now. As do you—so I confide in you. Failing, that is, a proper wife in whom to confide. Enjoy my correspondence, therefore, while you have it, for matrimony is fated, I dare say, to put an end to it. Not to me: I am brave in its contemplation—especially since there is no cloud of marriage in my bachelor sky.

Do not reproach me. I know I have urged matrimony upon you, and so successfully that you are happily wallowing in it once more. I also know that I have committed indiscretions of which, I am sure, you were not guilty, in your state of marital inter-regnum, and of which I would not have been guilty, had I remained in the pristine state of innocence in which I came here, wrapped and enshrouded. But— eh bien—I am here, and I have been here almost a brace of years, and how could I not be somewhat different from what I would have been, had I not come here at all?

Do you see? I use you in lieu of Columbia College and Professor McVickar and all the high-minded discussions I could have had, had I stayed enthralled in his and its tutelage. There are, of course, no high-minded discussions of that sort, here in Paris. You would be laughed out of the room, I can affirm, if you attempted any such nonsense—as the French look at it. One can be serious about money, or wine, or even love: morality is for clerics, and clerics are for old women, and old women are not present at salons. And there you have it, in a nut-shell.

I wish my father had thought fit to die at home, in his bed. It seems hard that he spent his entire life, and spent it on the whole well, tending the sick and the dying in New York State, then whisked himself around the world to a dirty province of Turkey and died there, in the streets. Nothing of him will now be left to molder peacefully, productively in his native soil. I think of that often, you know. I do not quite know why death is so real to me, and the dissolution that follows death, but so it is. This does not seem to me morbid—but does it so strike you? I would wish, on my own death, that I could lie in American soil and lend my otherwise useless corpse to the growth of some tree, some flowering shrub. That does not seem to me unfit. Indeed, it seems terribly fine. One is not reborn as a rose or an azalea; it is only the rotting flesh, but that, too, has been part of us, in our earthly life. I do not wish to disregard the flesh. I do not wish to pretend that it is not—but there I am again, drifting into jejune philosophizing. Would I inflict the same balderdash on myself, if I were communing with my belly button, in a diary? I hope not, but I fear I might. I seem to have a fearful tendency to second-rate mush.

Well. Let me, as they say in Poughkeepsie, straighten my socks. I am told, perhaps I ought to be embarrassed to repeat it, but I am too much of an egotist to consider embarrassment—I am told, bluntly, that my little book has been very well received and is much talked of, if not much read. It is too early, still, for the heavy gunners to have located me in their sights, but the early popguns have the charming euphony of champagne corks. I am labeled Poet in Truth; some, for reasons of their own, seek to enlist me, permission unrequested, under assorted banners, most of which flutter largely in their own front yards, some of which do not flutter at all. I wonder, if I publish another book—and I suppose that, having begun, I will in the nature of things continue, if not progress—how different this will become? I have noticed, you see, that in literature it is with us much as it is in politics. We welcome a bright new recruit; we hail his ability to march and to flash his shiny new weaponry—until he is no longer a recruit, at which precise moment we absolutely abandon enthusiasm and appreciation and all other good feelings, and demand to know why, with all his firepower and expertise, he has not long since conquered the North Pole for us, or at least the plains of Canada? We adore the New, we condemn the already known. We are a singularly restless people—too restless, perhaps, for the development of that distinctively American literature of which we hear so much, in the journals. Am I "Young America"? A chilling speculation, that!

How is Grace, the dancing girl? Do you mean to have her continue, now that she has begun? Will it be up to you, indeed? (She is half Bingham, remember.) She has entered upon the double numerology: I can well recall my own magnificent entry into my tenth year. I fell into a mud pool, and I tore my coat, and my father lashed me with sarcasm, and my mother wept. I believe it was dear Anne-Marie who cleaned my dirty face. Your Grace will have done things differently. She is already a creature of much loftier talents than her declining uncle—I am, mind, of an age to vote, and our dear sister Arabella assures me that voting and senility are intimately connected. (How has Theodore managed, all these years?) I may choose, on that basis, to remain the rest of my life in France, where neither I nor anyone else needs to vote—Louis Napoleon devotedly shoulders all our burdens—and I can stay green forever. In the eternal spring of Paris, yes. And I wish it would come soon. I am dreadfully bored with Parisian winter, and with these bright-blazing wood fires that shed so much light and so little heat. I grow colder, I believe, each winter I spend here. British coal may be as black as sin, as black as their political careers and their deep diplomatic maneuverings, but oh, how warmly it burns.

Do you see the advantage of being, now, proclaimed a writer, a __true__ writer? One can dither across endless pages of perfectly good white paper, scratching words of no meaning, and one is considered __un vrai poète__. __Ah oui, je suis un poète__—and do you know what that means, in my poor case? It means, dear Martial, that delicacy will not permit me to speak openly, certainly not in a letter, of the one thing which most nearly concerns me. It means that I have to cascade you with literary fluff, when what I would most love to do is sit down across the table from you and open my heart indeed, and seek your good advice. I will be able to speak to you, and how well I know it, only when it is done with, when the whole subject is a forgotten and a buried one—and what would be the point to speaking then? I think you must have some notion of what I mean; I cannot say more, or say anything more openly for reasons you will have guessed with no difficulty whatever. Our mails are indiscretion itself, as too many have over the years learned to their sorrow. I must therefore be totally discreet, foreign as it is to both my nature and to my need. And you must accept my chaff in place of wheat, and make what you can of it.

I am well, in body, and whole in mind, if not entirely secure in heart or satisfied in spirit. I hope that this finds you and all of yours, including the rapier-like Lydia—how could I possibly forget her, when she left me bleeding on my aunt's neatly polished floors?—in good health and happy. Exchange a snowball or two with Michael and Mark, on my behalf, and plant kisses on the Misses Grace and Alice (plant them, mind, somewhere inconspicuous, so they can grow until my return), and buss your Lydia (on your own behalf, but with my greetings in mind: I do not wish ever to be indelicate!), and believe me, Martial,

Your affectionate, etc.,
Jonathan Bingham

Washington, 16 April 1852

Dear Mr. Bingham:

I am writing, under a separate seal, to Mr. Rives, to request his compliance in a proposal which necessarily requires, as well, that you concur in what will be of some inconvenience to both of you. We have suffered a grievous loss, at the Department of State, in the death of Mr. Lewis Simpson, for many years as much an architect of foreign policy as any of the more transient Secretaries who have occupied the chair where I now sit for the second and surely the last time. Mr. Simpson has been our architect, our draughtsman, our interpreter of official documents from the French, and always an indispensable companion of his purely nominal superiors. The business of the Department urgently requires someone who can approximate Mr. Simpson's manifold abilities, and such persons are as ever in short supply. But without someone to hand, believe me, the Department will founder, and I will go down with the rest. It is a matter of such prime importance that I have sought the advice and consent of the President, rather than that of the Senate, and he concurs in my urgent desire that the hiatus be cured at the earliest possible date. He concurs, too, in my recommendation as to the filling-in thereof.

I suggest, in a word, that for so long as you may be willing to exercise the functions, you immediately be transferred from Paris to Washington, and be forthwith labeled and denominated Acting Chief Clerk of the Department of State of the United States of America. I have transcribed it as glamorously as possible; I am of course well aware that the glamour is all in the writing, and not in the <u>ding an sich</u>, or the thing itself, as the Germans put it. But can you find it in your heart to help us, to help me, in this our hour of desperate need? To ask so young a man to give up Paris, in exchange for the barrens of Washington, is to ask that bread be baked out of sawdust. No one, believe me, is more keenly aware that I am, how little you can be offered, and how much is being asked of you. On the other hand, I do not dissemble, and the need here is exactly as great as I have outlined it—greater, as each day goes by, and Mr. Simpson's chair remains empty. I have myself given up much, for the service of my country. It is my way, you may reply, for I am a politician. But though I would not wish to do you the disservice of turning you, too, into a politician—you are already something more meritorious, as a poet—is it possible that I can beg of you at least some little while of sacrificial labor in your country's behalf? Not many are so called; you are in sober truth both called and required.

With your consent, then., as well as Mr. Rives', I hope that we will as quickly as possible be in a position to end this lacuna, and restore the Department of State, and the foreign policy of the United States, to a proper level of efficiency. If I may be so presumptuous, I would urge you to terminate your affairs in Paris as rapidly as may be possible (I do not speak of what may be convenient, please note), and make your way on the most seaworthy and speedy vessel available, directly to these shores and to this address. You will be most anxiously awaited. I have promised Mr. Rives, in what I trust is the likely event that you will both agree to my suggestions, that I will scour the countryside for some acceptable successor to your duties there, and post him across the Atlantic in the opposite direction, as expeditiously as may be arranged.

May I add, on a more personal note, that I have felt an interest in your literary career, far beyond what might be expected of even so devoted a reader of American poetry as myself. This had its commencement when, by the purest of accidents, I chanced on some fragments of what has now turned into your superb <u>Memento Mori</u>, lying forgotten on a desk in Virginia. I do not I think need to specify the noble house or the owners thereof. At any rate, I quizzed my hostess on the authorship of what, as a failed poet myself, I knew to be sterling work, and as I say from that moment I conceived a singularly lively interest in what was then only a nascent, but is now a full-blown poetic career. Your book is an honor to American and to all letters; your presence in the Department of State would, believe me, do honor to that institution and give great personal pleasure to,

Yours, etc.,
Daniel Webster

Cliff Street, New York
18 April 1852

My dear Mr. Bingham,
    This will serve as a brief notice of our intention to reprint, I suspect in an edition somewhat larger than the first, your book <u>Memento Mori</u>. It has attracted a good bit of attention, virtually all of it favorable, and though the sales, as might be expected from a volume of verse, are not quite so brisk as author and also publisher would desire, or as the merit of the poetry deserves, still they have been quite good, and we are close to sold out on the first edition.

    I trust you will not take the brevity of this note as any indication of lack of concern on our part, either for this volume or for those which we hope will in due course follow it. My brothers and I are deeply pleased with <u>Memento Mori</u>, and gratified to have begun what we hope will be a long and mutually satisfactory association.

    I shall post a copy of this second printing to you—we are considering, I should add, some small changes in the binding as well, to make the book both more handsome and, we trust, more durable—as soon as it is in hand.

    Believe me, my dear sir,

Yours, etc.,
Fletcher Harper

"I'd have liked to take you dancing."

"A ball gown would have presented problems."

"Everything presents problems."

"Indeed."

The waiter had brought their aperitifs; he returned, now, for their orders, and Jonathan waved him off. It was too soon.

"Don't you feel, really, that we're entitled to something more than a working-class *bistro*?" He sipped his wine. "Or is that foolish?"

"I don't feel entitled to anything." She leaned back, setting her glass on the table, and peered around at the other patrons. "Except, perhaps, to surviving our evening here." She nodded at a crowded table across the room. "Those *gaillards*, now: if they knew you had more than a hundred francs in your purse, I dare say they'd be happy to cut your throat—and mine—to relieve you of the burden."

"Nonsense. But all the same, I hope no one here speaks English."

"I dare say half of them don't speak French." Her cloak had slipped onto the back of her chair; she gathered it up. "I know it was important to you, Jonathan, that we have this evening. You're leaving, it's the only kind of farewell we *can* have." She glanced quickly around, then shuddered. "But I don't mind telling you how nervous this—place," she paused, stopped, then resumed: "*eh bien, à votre santé.*" She lifted her glass. "Never mind my fears. Women are afraid of everything, aren't they?"

He noted, but did not remark on, her return to the formal *vous*. He *was* leaving, after all. It was as good as over.

"Would you be so distressed, in Virginia?"

"In Virginia, my dear Jonathan, I would never be in a situation of this sort. Have you forgotten? We do these things differently, in the United States."

"Not in New York."

"Do you patronize such establishments as this, in New York?"

"Have *you* forgotten, Clarissa? I was a reporter. Mr. Greeley's employees are obliged, on occasion, to go where even angels might fear to tread."

"You couldn't have persuaded me to accompany you."

"I'd not have tried. We have no female reporters, you know."

"And a good thing you don't." She pulled her chair as close to the table as it would go, and touched, for just a moment, the faintly grubby cloth. "We are a democratic country, I know, but sometimes I do regret that democrats—oh, never mind me. I'm a spoilsport tonight, am I not?"

"Yes."

She reached out and stroked his hand.

"I'll try to be jollier."

"A farewell needn't be a funeral."

"I know that. Believe me, I'd rather it were a celebration. You have a lot to celebrate."

"I do?"

"It's a distinct advance, your new appointment."

"If I were intending a diplomatic career, perhaps."

"You'd be extremely good at it."

He stared at her.

"*Ah, vraiment*"? He was suspicious, suddenly, of her motives. Was she trying to turn his thoughts from their primary focus, namely his loss of her? Did she not feel it to be a loss? He had suspected that before: did this confirm his suspicions, or was she in fact only attempting to cheer him, and herself, with what comfort was available? "Because I have so successfully deceived *Monsieur le Ministre américain?*"

"Don't inflate your importance. The task of deception was essentially mine."

"Perhaps *you* ought to go to Washington, to aid Mr. Webster."

She reached out and squeezed his hand, held it for a moment.

"Have I offended you?"

"That would be most unlikely."

"I'm glad."

"All the same, do you recall our conversation, lo these many months, when I intimated that you were, I feared, growing tired of me?"

"Many months ago? Ah, if I had been tired of you so long ago as that, Jonathan, I should have found a way of—how shall I say it? Of disentangling myself."

"How diplomatic. And true, I dare say."

"I am not a patient woman. You know that."

"Except when you want something."

"That, of course, is another matter entirely." She burst into laughter that was just a shade too bright. "Don't tell me about feminine logic, pray don't!"

"I sha'n't." He emptied his glass, then stood it like a miniature obelisk on the cloth in front of him. Only the faintest trace of wine remained. The rest was as colorless and empty as if there had never been anything to savor. "I don't feel remarkably logical, myself."

"Or cheerful."

"No. Nor celebratory. Shall we order, finally?" She did not object; he signaled to the waiter, and they ordered.

It was a singularly quiet meal, eaten slowly, meditatively perhaps, but above all silently. She seemed to respect his melancholic mood—or to humor it? He never quite knew, with Clarissa.

"*Avez-vous un Jupiter, Monsieur?*"

A large man in a dirty sweater stood next to their table. Jonathan handed the man a match.

"*Ici, Monsieur.*"

"*Merci, merci,*" the *gaillard* muttered, lighting his hand-rolled cigarette as he swaggered back to his own table.

"How did you know what he wanted?"

"A man is often in need of a match. Did you think we were in danger?"

She shivered.

"I was frankly not thinking of you at all. Did you see how he looked at me?"

"No."

"I doubt he came for a match, that was simply an excuse." She reached out and this time held tightly to his wrist. "Can we leave, Jonathan? I don't want to stay here."

"Why?"

"Because I'm afraid. Can't you see?"

Jonathan called for the *addition*, paid it, and they left arm in arm. He would ordinarily have asked that a cab be called, but it was not a service one could summon, at a place like this. Workingmen did not patronize cabs, in Paris. Nor could he leave her alone, while he secured one himself. She was not dissembling—her fright was apparent. She clutched his arm fearfully, holding her skirt to her. Nor did she speak while he waited for a cab to appear, and then signaled to it. They were lucky; it was a wait of no more than ten minutes.

"Oh, I'm so glad," she sighed, as the cab started off. "I was frightened half out of my wits."

"So I saw."

"Are you mocking me, Jonathan?"

"Not a bit of it. But neither do I understand. I've given up trying, in any event. It's no use, I'll never comprehend."

"Had you seen the beastly glances he gave me . . . ."

"It's an immensely respectable establishment, however."

"Respectable!"

"Yes."

She was angry, her voice rose slightly.

"How can you say that?"

"It's not the first time I've been there. I'm not a fool in *all* things, Clarissa."

She pushed back against the seat.

"Very well," she said crisply. "Very well." Nor did she speak again until the cab drew up in the Rue de Luxembourg. "I sha'n't come in," she announced flatly.

He had started to open the door, but closed it.

"Are you serious?"

"Perfectly."

He leaned back, crossed his arms, and considered.

"Isn't this a bit ridiculous?"

"I shall leave that for you to decide, since it seems to matter to you. Will you be so good as to tell the coachman where to take me?"

"It is our last night, you know." He kept his voice carefully mild. "I don't mean to pressure you . . . ."

"How good of you." Her voice was not at all mild. "Will you oblige me to address the coachman for myself?"

"Just a moment, Clarissa. Please. Have I sinned so grievously?"

She refused to reply.

"I should be glad to apologize," he continued gently. "Except that I need to know toward what my apology is directed."

She directed him to open the door on her side, to speak to the coachman. He quietly performed the task for her, climbed down, and stood watching as the cab rolled off, quickly lost in the darkness. She had not said goodbye; she had not even looked at him. Their final evening together. He was to leave in two days. It was likely he would never see her again—leave it to Clarissa to make sure of *that*! And they had been lovers for the better part of two years. Not a sound, not a glance.

He climbed slowly to his apartment, which was virtually denuded. Only bare necessities remained, and the furniture that had come with the rental. His books were packed, his papers, the pictures he had bought, the gifts for his relatives and friends. It was just barely still his dwelling place.

She had been his *maîtresse*. She had just barely been his *maîtresse*, and she was that no longer.

He was nothing to her, any longer.

It had all happened so rapidly.

He sat in his soft chair, which he was not taking home with him, and reflected. He was surprised, after a fashion, but not depressed. How could that be? Had he known something of this sort would happen? Had he secretly wanted something of this sort to happen? He had looked forward to quite a different ending. Or, in his heart of hearts, hadn't he? Had he been as anxious as she to wind matters up, to close the books, to draw a thin red line under all the accounts and write in a large, plain hand, *FINIS*?

She had been very anxious: that was plain. She must have been waiting and watching for a pretext; it did not matter how good a one. A pretext was a pretext—it either served or it did not. She had made sure it did.

He sighed quietly. Very well, it was over. He could bow to her most formally, at the *hôtel*, tomorrow. He could shake Mr. Rives' hand with renewed confidence and good cheer. He could return to the United States with his slate as vacant as it had been when he came. That was a good thing; it was without a doubt a good thing. And on the whole what he felt, softly breathing in his mind, was a quiet glow of relief. A stray thought flickered, briefly: had Clarissa plotted his recall to Washington? What a droll notion, that. And suppose she had? What of it? He shrugged. Was there, still, a bottle of wine on the premises? He rose to look. He wanted only a small glass, before dropping into bed, a kind of nightcap. He proposed to sleep soundly, to wake refreshed, and then to go about his business. It was over. He was leaving.

As they said in Poughkeepsie, "Another day, Another dollar."

PART FOUR

"How long has it been, Jonathan, since we
gathered at this house?"

TWENTY-ONE

"I see enough to convince me that our affairs at home are in a very bad and difficult state, and I do not profess to know who was born to set them right."

—Daniel Webster, to his friend Hiram Ketchum,
29 August 1839

The servant appeared without being summoned; her tray bore two tall drinks. Arabella did not seem to recognize the human agency involved: she quietly took her glass and continued to listen to her niece.

"Thank you, Lisa," Grace interrupted herself. She sipped, knowing it would be inadvisable to continue, now, as if nothing had happened. In her aunt's eyes, indeed, something fairly serious had happened, though nothing could be said about it until the servant was out of hearing distance.

"You *are* incorrigible," Arabella finally said, sighing.

"I can't help it."

"That, of course, is what is always said when one is disobedient."

"But my father—"

"You are in Virginia now, not in New York. And you are my guest at Blue Bell."

Grace could see Lisa disappearing around the side of the great house. She and her aunt were seated in a blue and white gazebo. It was late May, and already warm. They had been talking about matters more interesting to Grace—but the thread was temporarily broken.

"How can I not say thank you, Aunt?"

"Was it acknowledged?" Reluctantly, Grace shook her head. "Nor will it ever be. Lisa knows her place."

Grace took a slow breath.

"Would you punish her, if she acknowledged what I said?"

Arabella smiled.

"I don't need to, my dear. She didn't, and she won't."

"Would you have her whipped?"

"Grace! What nonsense are you talking? Ah: you've been listening to Lydia again. Lydia thinks we in the South torture and abuse our servants."

"Slaves."

"Servants," Arabella emphasized. "I don't think of them as anything but servants."

Grace did not want to argue. She forced herself to keep silent. But she could not help asking, silently, if these servants could leave whenever they wanted to serve no longer? If these servants were paid for their labor? If these servants had any kind of control over their servitude? It did no good to ask, or to argue. Arabella was immune. She was also very kind, both to her servants and to her niece. And Grace spent three months of every year with her aunt: it had long since become a fixed pattern.

"Will you try, Grace?"

"I'll try. Really I will."

"But you're not sure you'll succeed."

Arabella laughed, and Grace managed a smile.

"I haven't done very well so far, have I?"

Arabella leaned forward and patted her shoulder.

"You've done very well, really, considering what foolish ideas are stuffed into your young head, up there in your frozen North. If *I* heard nothing, morning noon and night, except abolitionist rant, I'd probably think all the landowners in Virginia were monsters, too. Even seeing with my own eyes that they were not, I'd more than likely go on believing it for at least some while. You'll see for yourself, my dear. And then you'll be recovered—until you go back North again."

"How can you be so polite to my new mother, when she comes here?"

Arabella smiled hugely.

"The day she asks to conduct an abolitionist meeting at Blue Bell— or asks me to distribute some of those infernal pamphlets—well, she won't. She's a lady, your new mother, and she knows when to speak and when to hold her tongue. As do I, I think. As you will, when you're grown. You will: it only takes time. And practice." A flock of ducks flapped noisily overhead. They bent their heads back and watched the scattered formation disappear. "There are girls who take on much more responsibility that that, at not much more than your age. A married woman has to be a lady, and the mistress of a house—not to speak of children, and servants."

Grace giggled:

"And a husband."

"To be sure. Many of my friends, when I was your age, were married at fifteen." Arabella's smile softened. "It was not unusual."

"It does seem very young."

"They were good marriages, for all that. Happy, and productive: what more can one ask for?"

"If one proposes to be married."

Arabella pretended to open her eyes very wide.

"Has one much choice? Do you propose spinsterhood? It hardly seems a viable alternative. Besides, at fourteen you can propose a great many things that, in just a few years, will no longer occur to you. Believe me, I know. I remember."

"We are to be fruitful, and to multiply. I know, I've heard it so many times! And it's a woman's burden."

"It *would* be unusual for a man to have children."

"But can't a woman do other things?" Grace's smile slowly faded. "My mother would have liked to tour Europe. As a musician, I mean."

"And you'd like to tour it as a dancer. Is that what you were about to say, a moment ago?"

Grace made a face.

"It may be. Ought I not to?"

Arabella's smile had not faded.

"I won't attempt to answer that, my dear. One day, before too very long, you'll be able to answer for yourself—and it won't make any difference what I might say. You won't need my opinion."

"Because I'll have adopted everyone else's?"

Arabella laughed.

"Oh, I was going to be a rebel, too, at your age. But it doesn't last."

"Why should it not?"

Arabella again leaned forward and stroked her niece's arm.

"Would it do any good if I told you? You wouldn't believe me, not yet. Suppose I asked you, Grace, if you'd enjoy not being able to visit your friends, not being received by your relatives? I couldn't receive you here, you know." Grace was scowling tremendously. "I couldn't. It would be the social death of me, if you had turned from a lady into a traveling *artiste*. My friends and neighbors would consider you, well, a sort of fallen woman."

"That would of course be nonsense."

"Perhaps. But all the same that is how they would see it. And how would you live? In dingy hotels and boarding houses, eating loathsome food, in the company of loathsome people."

"Miss Kemble? Liszt? Chopin?"

"Lovely names to listen to—but to have at one's table? I think it's an experiment most people of quality would cheerfully dispense with. And you might not be able to live at all: had you considered that? Very few attain even to the station of Liszt or Chopin. Most starve. Or very nearly. And your Miss Kemble left it all just as soon as she was able to marry."

"Are they any the less happy?"

"For starving? I should think so, yes. Have you ever tried it? I don't recommend starvation, Grace. No, being a rebel has its price—and it's a fearful one for anyone, still more fearful for a woman." Arabella shook her head easily. "I for one could not contemplate paying it."

Grace rose, silent, and walked to the doorway. Small birds were chirping in the nearby trees. There were blossoms on some of the shrubs and in some of the flower beds. The air had the soft eagerness of spring, and none of the sharp attack of her own part of the country. She had been in Virginia only a week; it was still, especially at this season, something of a miracle. She turned back to her aunt.

"I might."

Arabella's smile was gentle.

"You might. But I hope—and I expect—you won't. Do you think your mother would have wanted you to?"

Grace stepped slowly outside. In a moment Arabella had joined her.

"Your Uncle Theodore will be at home, soon. Shall we walk in that direction?"

They went very slowly toward the house, stopping to peer into clumps of newly greened trees, occasionally bending over a blossoming branch.

"It isn't fair," Arabella said carefully. "True. But that isn't a very useful demand to make of existence."

Grace stayed silent. They strolled slowly on.

"You might as well ask to join your uncle in the Senate, or your other uncle at the Department of State." Grace stopped to fondle a silky cluster of leaves. "Or," Arabella continued quietly, "to run a shipping enterprise in New York, or a medical practice in New England."

"Or to lead any sort of normal life?" Grace said, not forcefully but with a distinct aura of truculence. "I might as well join a convent!"

"It isn't quite so terrible as all that," Arabella said softly, taking her niece by the arm. "There are things women can't do, but a great many things they can. An increasing number. And it is possible, you know, to be very happy. I think I have managed it."

Grace did not reply.

"Why, you could even be a kind of politician, like your new mother!" Arabella laughed. "I suspect my father would not have been able to be polite! He was a terrible reactionary, at least about women. But wonderfully protective."

"I don't need to be protected!"

They reached the winding path that led to the front entrance. It was well cropped, and paved with small stones.

"I wish that were true."

"I'll go to Japan!" Grace's voice cracked slightly. "Or somewhere."

Arabella squeezed her arm.

"Commodore Perry was known to my first husband, but I don't think even that would be enough to gain you passage. Nor do I think you would want it, if you knew how sailors are forced to live, especially on so far-ranging a voyage. Men do not always have it as easy as you might think, you know. They too have to give up this, in order to gain that. As we do. And if we operate in different spheres, why, is that really so bad a notion? We're not much alike, after all. Can you see me rising on the Senate floor, to engage in passionate debate?"

Grace's expression was immensely solemn.

"Yes! I think you'd do it wonderfully well, if you wanted to."

"But I don't want to. I would think myself an awful fool. I would feel desperately out of place."

Theodore was waiting for them, leaning on the balustrade around the front entranceway.

"Has it been a lovely day?" he inquired.

"Beautiful," said Arabella at once, going to him. "But something has happened. Your day was not so fine as ours."

"There is fighting in the Kansas territory. One set of ruffians against another, each proclaiming high and mighty principles, each trying to steal the other's land. It's almost a war!"

"How terrible."

"Well, it's even worse than that. I hadn't thought to speak of it, but I suppose I must. Preston Brooks—you know, old Butler's nephew, he's in the House—went out of his head. He felt that Sumner started it all, with his flaming speeches, and he felt Sumner had tried to blame it all on Butler instead." He hesitated. "They're both right, in a way. Well, Brooks came over to the Senate and attacked Sumner. With a heavy cane."

"Lord!"

"Almost killed him, in point of fact." He grimaced. "Terrible. It seems to have been known, at least to some, that Brooks would do this thing. And no one came to Sumner's aid—at least, not quickly enough. He is not a popular man, in Washington. I do not doubt that he deserves his unpopularity. He speaks most unrestrainedly. But he does not deserve this."

"What will happen now?"

"To Brooks? Nothing, I dare say. If he is expelled from the House, which I must doubt, he will be returned at once. He will be a hero, here in the South, Arabella. Mark my words. As Sumner will be in the North—if he lives. Mr. Greeley, too, was assaulted some while ago: did you know that? Well, it wasn't nearly so desperate an affair, just fists, I believe, but I dislike it—I dislike it very much. It portends a spirit of violence all across the land." He started to smile, but ended with a grimace. "I don't think I can have much to say about it. Mr. Pierce will do nothing much. I think Mr. Buchanan will be the next President, and he will certainly do nothing!"

Arabella took his arm and led him into the house. Grace followed.

"But Mr. Buchanan is from the North, is he not?" Arabella queried.

"Are we all to be Northerners and Southerners, then?" Theodore's voice rose slightly. "Are there no alternative stances any more? Am I to disown you, Arabella, put you aside, because I happen to have been born in the North and you in the South?"

"I certainly hope not!"

They came to the drawing room. At a sign from Arabella, Grace left them.

"There will be government troops in Kansas, Arabella, before this thing is done. There will be more fighting, perhaps a great deal more. I do not know what else there will be."

She rang for a servant.

"There will be a cool drink," she declared. "That much I can still accomplish for you, Theodore!"

"Perhaps we ought to turn it all over to you women, the whole lot of it. Can you imagine Mrs. Brooks assaulting Mrs. Sumner?"

"You will have to tell that to your niece, you know. She was advocating my entry into politics, not half an hour ago."

"Clever girl," he murmured, taking up his coat tails and dropping into a chair. "Lord, I'm tired. I should confine myself to the law, it may be—though who knows? We may be settling those arguments with swords and daggers too, before long!"

Arabella told the servant what to bring, then hurried to her husband's side. She stroked his forehead.

"Grace also suggested going to Japan. Would you like to try that?"

He threw back his head and laughed heartily.

"My sister would be proud of that girl!" He took Arabella's hand. "I sha'n't put you aside, my dear. Not even for being so morally delinquent as to have permitted yourself to be born elsewhere than in the chaste and pure North. I doubt that even Lydia would make such a suggestion."

She seated herself near him.

"Lydia is a woman of sense—on most subjects."

"You're much alike, you two. Did you know that? Strong, and capable—and lovely. Well, at least *you're* lovely. Unmistakably so, thank God."

"You're not a bit like Martial, I'm afraid. But I rather prefer you, in spite of that."

"I shall explain your decision to him, when he comes here, this next June."

He sipped his drink, closed his eyes for a moment, and then they discussed matters of no importance whatever.

"It was not an affair of great moment."

"Fortunately!"

Greeley smiled.

"I suppose, Mrs. Andrée, that I ought to deem myself fortunate. I have seldom been subjected to personal violence."

"You are fortunate, Mr. Greeley," said Karl Andrée, who had been sitting very quietly through most of the conversation, "that you are not on your death bed, as Mr. Sumner may well be!"

"I take it," said Sophia, "that the Mr. Rust who attacked you, Mr. Greeley, must be a large and powerful man?"

"Indeed."

"That is of course the sort who chooses to act in such a detestable way."

"But standing over a man who's trapped in his chair," Karl muttered, "smashing away at his head with a heavy cane! Lord!"

"Oh, I was on my feet right enough," Greeley explained. "The House was just out of session, and all in attendance were returning to their lodgings. It had been, you will recall, a singularly spirited contest, to determine who might be the next Speaker. A stout, athletic man approached me—I did not then know that this was Mr. Rust, of whose acquaintance I had not then had the pleasure—and abruptly asked, without any preliminaries, whether I would resent an insult? Those were his exact words, I recollect them vividly. I am not inclined to personal combat, and I am afraid I did not even then think in such terms. 'That depends on circumstances,' I replied, and I suppose it was far too lawyer-like a response, for the next moment I was struck by a powerful blow, which I neither saw nor anticipated, and I staggered, stunned and not quite sure of my bearings, ending up against the wooden railing of the walk that leads down through the public grounds, from the Capitol to the Avenue."

"Villain," Karl muttered.

"He has since said he did not intend to strike me, but felt himself too provoked by my response to contain himself."

"I'd contain *him*!"

"Oddly enough, there were dozens of people present, but no one interfered, or came to my assistance. Mr. Rust whirled on his heel and walked off. I waited until my head had cleared, then proceeded toward my hotel—where I found Mr. Rust awaiting me, together with some of his friends. This time he quite anticipated Mr. Brooks, trying to assault me with a cane instead of with his fist. I raised my arm and rushed at him. I meant to strike him back if I could. He broke the cane over my arm, which was badly swollen, and again spun around and headed off, this time for good."

"You are most fortunate, Mr. Greeley."

"I was badly shaken up, I can tell you. Indeed, once I had repaired to my room at the hotel, head and arm both swollen and aching, I was unable to leave it for some days. And though the Speaker was not at once elected—the House spent a full nine weeks on the matter!—in the end the man I and many others supported was, as you know, elected. And a good man he is, our Mr. Banks, and a good Speaker, too."

"I trust you instituted proceedings, Mr. Greeley."

"I did not."

"But you should have!" Sophia cried.

"Some weeks after Mr. Rust's assault, Mrs. Andrée, I was, in fact, waited upon by the Marshall of the District of Columbia. He requested that I appear before the Grand Jury of the District, as a witness against Mr. Rust. I declined."

"Oh, you should not have. He should not have been allowed to escape unpunished!"

Greeley took a deep breath.

"I do not think it appropriate that I should punish him, however. And when at least a score of persons witnessed each assault, none of whom were apparently prepared to come forward and testify, though any and all of them must have had better opportunities for observation than I could possibly have had—well, I did not then, and I do not now, see why I should be required to be either an informer or a complainant. If society does not mind Mr. Rust acting as he acted, of what use would it be to placate the wrath of the law by a fine of twenty-five or thirty dollars? No, I preferred to do nothing; indeed, I explained to the Marshall that I would refuse to speak unless forced so to do by process of law. He did not choose so to force me, and there it all ended."

"You are quite recovered, by now?"

Greeley's smile was a trifle sly.

"I trust so. I was warned, do you know, that other men favorable to the slave-holding interests were only awaiting their chance to assault me further. I was threatened with a pistol shot, and with horse-whipping, and oh, I do not know what else. I recollect that several of us contemplated the purchase of pistols; there may even have been something of the sort effected. But nothing came of it all, in the end."

"Thank the Lord!" Sophia sighed.

"It was not pleasant. But I fancy all our Southern cousins will need to learn that we are not quite such milktoasts as they may think us, though we do not, as they do, swagger about and utter loud boasts and fierce threats. I am not physically powerful, to be sure, but neither am I to be dissuaded from what I see as the right path by a show of force. If it were necessary that I perish, in defense of the truth, I would go to my grave before I gave in. It is in fact as simple as that, and they will have to learn."

"We will likely have to teach them," Karl said slowly.

"Indeed."

"And that is, in fact, why I asked you to come by today, Mr. Greeley."

"Do I seem to you to be doing too little, Mr. Andrée?"

"Not at all. I assure you, you are doing all that one human being can. No, you do not seem to me in any way lacking, Mr. Greeley. I admire and commend and support you, with my whole heart."

Greeley bowed, smiling.

"I am gratified."

"He speaks soberly, and accurately," asked Sophia.

"My brother and I are not rich men, though popular report vastly multiples our fortunes. We have families to maintain, and to provide for after we are gone. We have obligations to our church, and to other charities for which we have over the years given as generously as we have been able."

"You are well known for your philanthropy, Mr. Andrée."

"Be that as it may, Mr. Greeley, our consciences, and I must add our hearts too, are much stirred by the abominations lately perpetuated. We have come to realize that we have been too long quiescent: this country cannot continue as it has lately begun to proceed."

"You are aware of the recent outbreaks in Kansas?"

"Yes."

"They may be only the prelude to worse things. I am inclined to believe, Mr. Andrée, that there will be a great many worse things. I do not foresee the end of it."

"I feel, Mr. Greeley, that my investment in life in these United States is worth many percent less, so long as freemen are locked up and sent, in chains, back into bondage. I am a businessman; I do not like to see any investment depreciated. It has become plain to me, therefore, that I must do anything I am able to do to stabilize and protect what, foolishly, I have until now largely taken for granted. My brother, with whom you are of course acquainted, feels much as I do, and because his family obligations are somewhat less than mine, will be able to give somewhat more. We will hope to involve other men of conscience, and of means."

Greeley's eyes were bright.

"What project did you gentleman contemplate?"

Karl rubbed his chin thoughtfully, noting Greeley's enthusiasm; his words were very carefully chosen.

"We thought we might consult with you, before anything was actually begun. I have no doubt, Mr. Greeley, you would be able to think of ways for the disposal of such funds as we might be able to make available."

Greeley's smile was intense.

"Quite probably."

"But we do have the notion that the abolition of slavery is where we want to aim. The problem, therefore, is how to use our expenditure for the greatest possible good—for the largest and most forceful possible effect. We wondered, and thought we might ask you, what would be the result of gathering information in one central place, and publishing it. Information, and also the views of concerned and feeling citizens. Not by way of interfering with your noble work in the *Tribune*, to be sure." He nodded at Greeley, who was now squinting faintly. "Not another newspaper, and not a magazine. We are not literary people, nor do we have literary goals. The publication could not be called by any usual name, more than probably."

"I would see it printed in red, if I could!" Sophia said suddenly. She had been sitting to the side; her passion was evident, thought she did not speak again.

"Would that be a useful thing?" Karl inquired.

"It could be a marvelously useful thing," Greeley replied slowly. "There are publications with similar goals. They too are useful."

"Our purpose would not be to compete with anyone who is doing what needs to be done."

Greeley began to pace.

"Surely, surely," he said, his voice squeaking as it always did when excitement dominated him. He clasped his hands and rubbed them together. "My only concern, as you will appreciate, is to see that what needs doing is *best* done. If you and your good brother were overflowing with gold, Mr. Andrée, it would perhaps be possible to go directly to the southern masters and buy up their slaves, to set them directly and immediately at liberty. Such schemes have in the past been talked of. But they are not practical, no one has such funds at their disposal, and the amounts would be staggeringly huge, moneys to buy, moneys to transport, moneys to educate and outfit and support—no, it would not be practical, though I dearly wish it were." He was pacing quite rapidly, now, whirling just before he reached the wall, drumming hard till he reached the wall opposite, then wheeling and marching back once more. "No, we must be practical. As businessmen, you and your brother do not wish to fritter your hard-won resources. You wish to concentrate your funds and your efforts, as one focuses a beam of sunlight with a glass, so that it may gather unto itself and burn."

"Indeed."

Greeley's hands were behind him, his face was wet with perspiration, his voice squeezed as high as it would go.

"Where to set the fulcrum, where to exert the leverage, where to lift and heave so that the rotten edifice crumbles and falls!"

"Perhaps," Karl began, "you would like to –"

"Ah!" Greeley came to a dramatic stop, his hand raised perpendicularly over his head. "I have it!" His face glistened with delight. "Why not combine your notion, which is after all a sound one, with the resources already available to me? The publication must be free to deal with its one primary concern as it sees fit, from week to week, and it ought to be a weekly, so that it need have no truck with the idle matters of daily existence. It can thus be as long or as short as may be necessary, from one issue to the next. And we can distribute it, at one swoop gathering in all those who now read the *Tribune*, all the thousands from Maine to California, by attaching it to a particular weekly issue of the *Tribune* itself, say the Saturday issue, or the Sunday, it does not greatly matter." He lowered his arm and pounded his closed fist into his other hand. "By God, yes! It can be totally separate, printed and folded as the kind of independent entity it would be, and then tipped in—as one tips in illustrations, Mr. Andrée. For that, in truth, is what it would be! An illumination, an indictment, a forum, a call."

"Not I trust to arms?"

Greeley stayed silent. None of them were smiling: it was a sober moment.

"A decade ago, Mr. Andrée, I would have answered, ringingly, *never!* But who could say anything so positive, today? I cannot, nor will I. I do not wish for a resolution by force. But if it comes to that, I do not think I for one could shrink away and still say, as once I could, *never!*"

They were all silent.

"Would you see yourself, Mr. Greeley," Karl finally asked, "as the editor of this—whatever it may turn out to be?"

"I could perhaps contribute, from time to time. I do not see that I could take on the editorial responsibility. For it will be a high responsibility. It will be, in plain truth, more than a fulltime job, and it will require someone with very particular and even distinguished abilities."

"Have you someone in mind?"

"My mother would have said, God will provide. Whether He will take on the responsibility I cannot say. But we here below should, if we all put our heads together and ponder well, be able to do it reasonably—even perhaps seasonably." He smiled, then laughed. "Why perhaps your nephew might be persuaded into assuming the task."

"I have thought of him. But let us not hurry ourselves. Were I to assemble a few men of standing, and of some resources, Mr. Greeley, do you think you might find the time to join us?"

"I will do better still, Mr. Andrée. I will see to it that sample pages are struck, with something more or less like the sort of material that might be wanted. You gentlemen would this be enabled to see, concretely and specifically, what the possibilities would be, and you would very much more readily, I think, be able to make your decisions."

"Would a fortnight be sufficient for you, Mr. Greeley?"

"A fortnight," Greeley agreed, and strode over to Karl, who rose and shook the editor's hand.

"Your fertile brain may well have spawned yet another creation, Mr. Greeley!"

"It will be your creation, not mine, Mr. Andrée."

"You will be the midwife, then. Well, let us see. I may be in error, I am not the man to see so far as you are able to, but all of us, you and I and whatever others will join with us, we may have set another nail in the coffin of the most damnable institution this country has ever known." He nodded at his wife. "Forgive me, my dear. I do not often feel moved to such expressions. But the sight of that poor black man being dragged through the street, in chains . . ." He took a long breath. "Well, Mr. Greeley. Would you take a cup of tea with us, before we release you to your editorial desk once more?"

"It's not jealousy, you understand."

"I do. Of course!"

They were strolling across the wide lawns of Blue Bell, on a hot, lazy Saturday early in June. The season was not yet at its peak; warmth seemed to stroke across them with beneficent rather than murderous intent, and the grass was able to absorb it all. In a month or less, waves of reflected heat would flicker and blow, the grass would seem to be a sea, green and gray and shimmering. A lady would be in absolute need of a parasol, and no gentleman in his right mind would keep a lady out in the sun for more than five or six minutes. For the moment there was no need for parasols, no need even for a hat, and they walked fairly rapidly, and with no concern for overexposure to the elements.

"Nor is it that I lack belief in myself. At least, I do not think that is the problem."

"You have done a great deal, for someone your age."

He turned and laughed at her.

"Listen to you! You might be my grandmother, instead of my niece."

"It's still the truth," she repeated stubbornly, blushing and trying not to blush. "You oughtn't to make fun of me for my age. I'm not a child anymore. Aunt Arabella says lots of girls married at fifteen, when she was younger, and some still do. And I'm fourteen."

"Indeed you are. I keep forgetting. You are in fact a youngish lady, and not a child."

"Do I *look* like a child?"

He kept his eyes studiously in front of him.

"That, my dear Grace, is not entirely fair. You know as well as I do that you are a singularly lovely youngish lady."

"I wish you meant that, Uncle Jonathan."

"But I do mean it. I've always meant it."

She made a face at him, but he did not see it.

"Yes, and you're waiting to marry me when I grow up."

"Of course. Isn't that what I've always told you?" He took her arm and helped her over a low fence. They were leaving the main house behind. Fields, some cultivated, most not, lapped about them, quiet and deserted in the June sun. "Have I gone and married anyone else?"

"But I *am* grown up, don't you see? You can't just amuse me, and yourself, with talking about marriage."

"Have you ever known me to deceive you, Grace?"

She did not reply. They walked up a small hill, and he found an old and very dry tree stump, lying propped against two large boulders. It was simple to climb the rocks and sit on the stump, their feet dangling over.

"The view is singularly beautiful. Theodore knew what he was doing when he married!"

"Uncle Theodore did not marry for money."

"Of course not, and I didn't say he did." He glanced around. She was staring down the slope, her lips slightly compressed. "Either you are tired, or in a wretched mood suddenly, or I have somehow—God only knows how, for I am such a mild mannered fellow—managed to offend you." She stayed silent. "But this Whitman, now. He's absolutely a phenomenon. He breaks all the rules in the book, he uses forms and styles no one has ever heard of, he ignores rhyme, he even ignores meter, he writes about subjects no one in his right mind had ever considered suitable for poetry—and he succeeds, gloriously! I can't account for it." She did not speak, though he waited. "How indeed could one be jealous of such a phenomenon? I've never met the man, but he must be—well, odd, at the best. I don't think he's elderly, though he speaks of himself, often, as if he's as old as the hills. At any rate, now that I've stumbled onto his book, which I suspect he must have had something to do with producing himself—he's more or less a printer, you know: I had heard of him, when I worked with Mr. Greeley's *Tribune*—I can begin to understand why I've written so little, these past few years."

She turned and stared directly at him.

"Why?"

He swung his legs and looked down at the moss below them, and at the worn surfaces of the rocks. His feet moved like a pendulum, his legs swung like the moving parts of a clock. To what rhythm did his feet refer? Where were they meant to take him?

"Grace," he finally said, speaking both slowly and softly, "there's been a lot of fuss made about my book. I don't say it's a bad performance; it's certainly deeply felt. I loved your mother, I loved her very very much. I wanted to honor her, in death, as I tried always to honor her in life. She was a splendid woman; you are a fortunate girl to have known her even a long as you did."

"I hardly remember her," she confessed, her voice and her face softening. "I try to, but I hold unto less and less every year. She's fading. I don't want that to happen!"

He reached over and patted her hand.

"Well, the old saying seems still to be true. Man proposes, and God disposes. And I comfort myself with the thought that if I were meant to make a large career as a poet—as the Brothers Harper wish I would: they keep writing to me, inquiring about my next book!—I would be turning out verse as a carpenter turns out chairs. He wears a carpenter's shirt, by the way, in the picture at the front of his book."

"Mr. Whitman?"

"Yes. He's not of course a carpenter—but he does seem aptly dressed, I will admit it. *I* would not look quite right, attired as he is!"

"You are a gentleman."

Jonathan winced."

"And *he* is a poet?"

She raised her hand, as if to push him, then let it drop to her side.

"You know quite well I meant no such thing. You are perverse, Uncle Jonathan. You are, I begin to suspect, distinctly vain, too. And who knows? You may be other things that have been kept from me. The temptations of Paris, I understand, are not inconsiderable."

"And *you* are a ninny."

This time she did push him, her face growing red.

"And *you* are an old goat!"

"If it were not so warm, young lady, I would offer to race you down this hill. That would show you what an old goat I really was!"

She swung down from the stump and dropped off the rocks onto the grass, unaided, before he could move to stop her.

"Come on!" she challenged, her hands on her hips. "Or are you afraid I might beat you?"

"Do proper young ladies, a year or so away from marriage, still run races?"

"Catch me, if you can!" she called, and turned and ran. He leaped down, and raced after her, but she was swifter than he had realized. He was taller, and his legs were longer, but she was young and singularly agile and, though he gained a little, she reached the bottom before him.

"I told you, I told you!" she exulted, standing under the last tree on the slope. Her face was quite red, and very wet with perspiration. But her voice was strong; she was not puffing in the least.

"Well," he admitted, wiping his face with a kerchief, "you are quick. I will concede it. If you dance half as well as you run . . . But you do, don't you? You should perhaps have been a filly rather than *une fille charmante.*"

She tossed her head.

"I despise gallantry!"

He patted his lips dry.

"Oh, I do too. Probably because I'm not very good at it."

Her face sobered instantly; she put a hand on his arm.

"What *will* you do, Uncle Jonathan?"

"It will be revealed to me, I dare say."

"Will you stay at the Department of State?"

"Anything is possible. I've stayed there four years, and even a little over. Was I meant to be a diplomatic chief clerk? Perhaps. I might already have found my niche, Grace, without knowing it. These things happen."

They started back toward the house. She did not take his arm. She walked, he was increasingly aware, with a firm, sure step that was some-how still feminine. But it was unlike any female's step he had ever seen. Even Anne-Marie had not had so athletic a stride.

"We seem to be so happy a family," she said carefully. "So success-ful. Uncle Theodore has risen to the Senate. But I don't think it has made him happy to be there. You have written a successful book; you are well-known and well-respected, but you, too, are not happy with what you are doing. My father practices medicine less and less, and politics more and more. My own mother was meant to perform at the keyboard, but she never could. And I . . . I want to dance."

"Dance, then."

"Aunt Arabella says I'd be excluded from everyone's home, if I did. Even from hers."

He tried to keep silent but found it impossible.

"It would be her loss. And theirs."

"And perhaps I'd not be good enough."

"You'll not know if you don't try."

They crossed onto the smooth lawn that led directly to the house.

"Would I still be received in *your* home, Uncle Jonathan?"

"My dear lady. If you are to be the mistress of the house, how could you possibly be kept from entering it?"

She laughed, but this time did not blush. And then they marched back to the house, as if on parade, silent, rigidly in step. He stopped at the bottom of the steps, stood back and made her a sweeping bow. She did not curtsey in reply, but gathered her skirt and was up the steps and in through the door before he could follow.

TWENTY-TWO

"The country is very well, if extremists and ultraists would let it alone. There is a strong feeling of union, North, South, and at the centre; and I do not think folly and faction can easily extinguish it."

—Daniel Webster, to Dr. Perkins
18 February 1849

"Well, Theodore! I can hardly see you playing the part of a Simon Legree—even if, like him, you do come from New England."

He pretended to grimace.

"I am disowned everywhere I go. A plague on both your houses! First your friends tell me I am a blackguard, Arabella, and now my sister from the North not only mislocates me—for I am a New Yorker, Lydia, and that is not quite the same thing as a New Englander—but seems to suggest that I am become a tyrant with servants who, in truth, belong to you, my dear, and not to your poor misrepresented husband. Perhaps this is why we are in the disordered state in which we now find ourselves—everyone thinking the worst of everyone else, sectionalism rampant, no trust in people for the government, or in the government for the people."

Lydia's dark eyes, so brown as to be almost black, gleamed.

"Ah, there's a theme that would indeed interest me, brother—if you had broached it seriously."

"As I hope he did not," Arabella smiled. "Afternoon tea is one of the few graces we have left. It would be hard indeed were my husband to take it away from me, prattling of politics and the like." She helped herself to a small biscuit, then sat contemplating it for a moment. "We do not get the flour we used to, when I was a girl."

"Lydia would probably like to reply that, in faith, we receive the flour we deserve—precisely and exactly."

"Lydia will say nothing, especially since you, brother, have chosen to speak for her! But that is perhaps the chief difference between North and South, is it not?"

"That our biscuits are better than yours? or worse?" Arabella smiled gently. "We have never exchanged recipes, Lydia."

"Was it not Mr. Graham who argued, most vociferously, that Americans ate far too many biscuits—thought not of your cook's making, Arabella! No, I meant that we in the North, probably because we have had no choice, have permitted ourselves to be led into the future."

"Kicking and screaming the while," Theodore murmured.

"But since we *do* have a choice . . . ." Arabella paused to refill her husband's cup. "I have heard it argued, Lydia, by serious gentleman of this region, that all the primaeval American virtues have been under massive attack, these many years, and that most have succumbed. A few have, however, survived, and we in the South would seem to be their precariously hospitable hosts."

Lydia rose, tall and extremely slender. Unkind critics, masculine in gender, had been heard to maintain, with considerable heat, that Dr. Johnson's skinny wife would not have so much time for things that did not concern her, and much more for things that did, if her husband had seen fit to give her children to rear. They had also been heard to sigh for these same hypothetical children, exposed to so fierce a maternal parent.

"It was Monsieur Voltaire, I believe, who maintained with some cleverness that we each ought to stay in our own garden, and till it as best we could."

"One ought really to drink to that!" Theodore brightened. "If he were less indecent, Voltaire would be a man worth spending time with."

Lydia walked to the long French doors, standing open to the garden.

"I shall investigate, sister Arabella, and see if you have cultivated yours as you should."

Theodore leaned back in his chair, smiling.

"Or had it cultivated for her?"

"Well, perhaps it comes to the same thing, in the end," Lydia said quietly, as she stepped out.

Arabella stirred her tea:

"You ought not to tempt her, Theodore. She strives mightily to be inoffensive. It is most ladylike of her, all things considered."

"And ungentlemanly of me?"

"Must you tease her?"

"I must, yes—but I shall try not to. Is it distressing to you?"

"She is our guest."

"I'm sorry, then, my dear. I shall try to sin no more. You see? An unregenerate Northerner can change his location, but not his spots! We do not have your graces—and especially not in New England."

"I would say that Lydia displayed rather more grace than her senatorial brother-in-law."

He smiled and was about to say that Lydia, of course, was a woman. But her smile, soft as it was, made him think that it was perhaps better to say nothing. Which was what he said.

"To see *you*, my dear. And our dear brother and sister, who are so gracious as to receive you. You are almost your Uncle Theodore's daughter, by now, as well as mine!"

Grace had conducted her father to the blue and white gazebo where she and her Aunt Arabella often sat. The sun was brilliantly hot; they could feel its warmth even in the dim, airy little room.

"And my new mother does not talk with people from Washington?"

Martial grinned.

"You are very nearly a grown cat, my little puss."

"Why do men refuse to take my sex seriously?"

"I can no more speak for all men, my dear, than you can speak for all women—but if what you say were true, would it not be I who spoke to people from Washington, rather than your new mother?"

Grace frowned.

"You are perhaps an exception, Daddy—with your wife, at least."

"And you, my dear, are still a child."

Grace scowled.

"My aunt says that girls my age have been married."

"To be sure. Girls your age have worked in the fields, too, and done a great many things that you, my daughter, are not required to do."

"Did my mother ever wish that she had been born a man?"

"I think not. She sometimes wished that women were able to be more in public—"

"As my new mother is?"

"Am I to take that as an impertinent remark, young lady?"

"I hope not."

"How, then, was it meant, Grace?"

"As a query." She hesitated. "Perhaps, as a reflection of changes already taking place. I wonder if Mother had wanted to conduct meetings, and even speak at them on occasion . . . ."

Martial scratched his ear.

"She did not want to."

"But she did want to perform in public, as a male pianist surely would have done. You've told me that yourself."

"You want something of me, Grace."

"No."

"Yes. You are leading up to something."

"No, Daddy."

He leaned back, rubbing his chin.

"All the wisdom of the centuries leads inescapably to the one conclusion: you have something difficult on your mind, and you are having difficulty speaking about it. Let me cut the Gordian knot for you—is there anything, after all, that a daughter ought to have quite such difficulty saying to her father? I sha'n't disown you, no, not even if you say that you—well, I'll let you tell me what it is you want."

She could hear a bird, whose call she did not recognize, singing quietly outside the gazebo. She could hear the soft rustle of her father's coat, as he shifted in his chair. She could hear her own blood beating in her temple, and in her wrist, and tried to still it.

"I want a great many things, Daddy." Her voice was soft but steady. "Many, many."

"Quite right. And I trust you shall have a fair number of them, before you're done. But the something in particular?"

She felt like screaming, suddenly. Her legs had tensed; it was hard to stay where she was, unmoving. It would have made much better sense to jump up and run out—run anywhere; it did not matter. But she did not move.

"I don't know."

He waited; she did not continue.

"I take it, Grace, you're still afraid to tell me?" He spoke gently, and his face wore a kindly smile. "Well, then, I can—"

Her arms flailed at the wicker table, her body twisted forward, and her face fell between her arms, pushing against the table's wooden top. Sobs broke out of her, uncontrollable, deep and desperate. He knelt beside her, his arms around her, but it did not help. She cried blindly, miserably; his words, his caresses, did not affect her—she did not know he was there. While the episode lasted, she was as totally alone as a human being can be.

"It is kind of you, Mr. Bingham, to walk out this way."

"Not at all, Mrs. Johnson."

"But you have had a taxing day in Washington, and then a long ride."

Jonathan bent his head.

"I am also of an age, I trust, to do all those things in a single day—and more. And, may I say, the opportunity to converse with you once again, after so many years and so very brief an initial opportunity, spurred both me and my horse."

"You have indeed been in Paris, Mr. Bingham."

They strolled on much the same path he had taken, some months earlier, with her step-daughter. Lydia was taller and brisker than Grace. Nor did she look around her as much: her eyes seemed to see through rather than simply to look at the things she encountered. And, he added silently, the people, too.

"I have become, I think, about as much a fixture in the dusty offices of the Department of State as the great seal or the Secretary's favorite desk chair."

"Does the chair never change? Are there no new favorites?"

"No, I assure you! The Secretary changes, fairly regularly, but the favorite chair has been in the same position since, I believe, Mr. Madison occupied it."

"And it was not burnt by the British?"

"Our British cousins are too amiable for that. They might burn a building, or even shoot a man or two, but destroy an object of personal comfort? No, never!"

Lydia glanced up, briefly, at a passing bird.

"That, I take it, is what is meant these days by civilization?"

"I think, Mrs. Johnson, that is what always has been meant by civilization."

"I should prefer, all in all, to be a barbarian."

"I'm relieved that anyone's preference, in fact, has so little to do with it."

Her quick glance, this time, was directed at him. Her eyes seemed to hit out, like bright beams of weight and substance.

"Don't you believe in the precious freedoms for which we are supposed to have fought?"

"I sometimes wonder, these days, if I believe in anything, Mrs. Johnson."

"You require shaking out of *that*, Mr. Bingham."

"Quite probably. Your stepdaughter, little Grace, seems to feel much the same way."

"She adores you."

"Oh, that is a habit she will break, believe me, just as soon as she meets someone more to her liking."

"I doubt that."

"I will defer to your superior knowledge of all things female."

"Tommy rot," she snapped. "Is there a man alive who has not made the study of my sex the principal object of far too many of his hours? Why would a woman pay that sort of attention to other women?"

"Indeed," he laughed, "I have always assumed that you would pay it to other men."

"Mr. Bingham, some of us have better things to occupy our minds. Some of us do indeed *have* minds, and we are obliged by the Creator who gave them to us to use them."

"I have never doubted it. Do I strike you as a male disbeliever?"

"To be very frank Mr. Bingham, you suddenly strike me as a man who has stayed in Washington too long. You ought to have been out and doing long before this."

"But doing what?"

"Oh, Lord," she exclaimed brusquely. "If you need to ask the question, there is no way to answer it for you."

"Is not one politician in the family a sufficiency? No—two, or even three, if what Martial tells me of your activities, and of his, is at all accurate."

"It is accurate."

"Should I not then be a complement to your activities, and to my brother Theodore's, rather than a mere imitator of them?"

"I had not considered imitation, Mr. Bingham."

"But there is something you had considered?"

Her silences were never very protracted, but they were always significant. Lydia functioned at something like twice the pace of most people he knew. He braced himself.

"I had considered, Mr. Bingham, that you might be worthy of the editorship of a new publication, intended to assemble and make public the facts of our developing controversy over slaveholding. I came to Washington, indeed, with that consideration primarily in mind."

Jonathan could not mistake the intensity of her sudden disapproval.

"I see."

"Do you?"

"I think so, yes. Even some males have been endowed with the power of mental activity. I do not say we always use it properly; I certainly do not claim that I so use it."

"You are become quite professorial, Mr. Bingham."

"That is not, I believe, meant to be a compliment."

"I do not practice compliments, or insults for that matter. I tell the truth, to the best of my ability."

Jonathan did not immediately respond, nor did she pursue him. They walked silently for some hundred yards.

"Under whose sponsorship is this new publication to be born?"

"Would you be less interested if you knew?" She swung briefly toward him; there was no smile on her face. "*Are* you interested?"

"You would not have come to ask me the question, Mrs. Johnson, if you had not anticipated quite considerable interest on my part."

"I may have been wrong about you. I am frequently wrong, and I just as frequently admit my errors."

How had Martial found this woman? And wooed her?

"Shall we rest a moment, under this tree, and consider things a bit more coolly?" He indicated a large oak, ancient and productive of a dense shade. She remained alongside him, though she had yet to lean on his arm.

"Is that a reproof, Mr. Bingham?"

"I do not reprove ladies."

She actually stamped her foot.

"Then, I suggest to you, sir, it is time you began!"

Jonathan leaned against the thick trunk. It was warm, though the sun was low in the sky. He dried his forehead with a kerchief.

"We seem destined for a disputacious acquaintance, Mrs. Johnson."

"Do you assign the responsibility for that to me, Mr. Bingham?"

He closed his eyes for a moment, then let them re-open. Nothing had changed. He could see small distant signs of life, but everything was remarkably still. Blue Bell was no longer a plantation. It was an artificial garden, and of vast extent. It was an artificial island, a kind of created paradise; the life that twisted and swirled outside its boundaries did not cross and come in. Arabella and her first husband had planned it that way, and they had been outstandingly successful.

"I do not want to quarrel, Mrs. Johnson."

He heard her quick intake of breath.

"It might be the healthiest occupation you have engaged yourself in for a very long time, Mr. Bingham."

"Indeed."

"You have permitted yourself to grow into the wallpaper, here in Washington." Her voice was faintly less harsh, but still brusque. "Nothing of consequence, of true consequence, has occurred here in years. The real life of this country, the true pulsing heart and soul of it, are elsewhere. May it not always be so! But it is so, now, and has been so for years, perhaps since General Jackson departed. This has been a government of backing and filling, and a series of men have occupied its seats of power, men who were chosen, I believe, exactly for their capacity to continue that demonstration of moral paralysis and political cowardice."

He wondered, fleetingly, if Charles Sumner had inspired Lydia, or she him? They sounded very alike. Their rhetoric was equally abrasive. But were they perhaps correct?

"Washington is not an active capital any longer—that is true."

"It does not encourage activity, Mr. Bingham. How much poetry have you written, since your coming to Washington?"

"Is that truly a measure of activity, Mrs. Johnson?"

He thought for a moment that she would again stamp her foot.

"You surprise me, Mr. Bingham. Indeed you do. I had been led to think a great deal better of you. We may have been wrong, your uncle and I, to think of you as a possible editor."

"I hadn't known—"

"There was, I believe, no reason why you should have."

He felt, and tried not to show, a stab of acute irritation.

"My Aunt Sophia, of course, has had connections with the antislavery movement. We first met, as you may recall, on one such occasion. But neither her husband nor my Uncle Peter Andrée has been prominent in that movement, though both have been distinctly charitable men."

"The elimination of slavery, Mr. Bingham, is not a charity. It is quite simply an obligation."

"And my uncle—I assume you refer to Mr. Karl Andrée—has recognized his obligation?"

"Exactly."

There was no irony in her response.

"And he is supporting this new endeavor?"

"He is. As is your Uncle Peter. And many others of sense and means."

Jonathan reflected that her assertiveness, unusual and even charming when she was young, had become terribly tiresome now that she was more matronly. He found it difficult to deal with her as, ordinarily, he dealt with women.

"Your uncles are involved, and so is your former employer, Mr. Horace Greeley. Mr. Greeley's judgment, I must say, is that you would be exactly the right person for the post."

"I am flattered."

"I beg your pardon, Mr. Bingham. I do not believe that you feel flattered; you are merely polite. And Mr. Greeley's judgment is merely mortal."

"A limitation we all suffer from, I suppose."

She did not miss the irony, this time.

"You do not care for plain talk, do you, Mr. Bingham?"

She was facing him, her dark eyes fixed on his.

"On the contrary."

"Ah. You do not care for it, then, when the subject is yourself."

"You do disapprove of me, don't you, Mrs. Johnson?"

"I scarcely know you, Mr. Bingham."

"That is true, yes. But how, then, do you form such clear opinions as to my behavior—no, more than my behavior. My very soul, which you take, if I understand you correctly, to be that of a remarkably slothful, apathetic creature."

She shook her head vigorously and her hair swung out and back, almost as if puffing itself. He had not realized that her bonnet was in her hand; he had not seen her take it off.

"You do not understand me, Mr. Bingham."

"I have been trying, believe me."

"What credit should I put in that claim?"

Something faintly but recognizably like a smile flicked across her lips.

"None that a banker would recognize, I suppose," he answered quietly, stretching his arms over his head until they touched the bark. He felt very like a kind of dryad, without stopping to wonder at so odd a notion.

"Are you opposed to the institution of slavery, Mr. Bingham?"

He lowered his arms. The smile seemed to have disappeared; she was nothing if not grim in her inquiry.

"Totally."

"But the government for which you labor is in full support of it—even worse than that, indeed, since it does not admit its support."

"Very true."

"How then can you remain in its service?"

"Have you asked that same question of my brother Theodore?"

"Most certainly not. I do not trifle with triflers. You will pardon me the expression, but neither I nor anyone else concerned with the abolition of slavery can take your brother seriously. He is, in point of act, a disgrace."

"You are harsh, Mrs. Johnson."

"Am I any harsher than the whip with which slaves are daily beaten? Or the legal and the palpable, forged chains which bind them to their masters' service?"

Jonathan took a long breath.

"I wonder, Mrs. Johnson, if we will ever be able to agree on anything, you and I? There seem to be walls and moats between us, in every direction."

She did smile, though not with any great enthusiasm.

"You find me difficult, do you not?"

"No, not difficult. But different, yes. Shall we walk on?"

She nodded, and they left the shade and proceeded, more slowly this time, across a half wooded slope. She walked with her bonnet in her hand. Her hair was thick enough to repel the sun.

"Abolition is a cause, Mr. Bingham," she began after a moment. Her voice had lightened and softened, had become almost agreeable. "Those who labor for its realization can never afford to be merely pleasant. And when it comes to choosing one's fellow warriors, well, it behooves us even more to be on our guard, to pick and choose with great care."

"You have been testing me, I gather."

"Do you recall what Mr. Garrison, to whom we all owe so much, said at the start of his own great work? I have long since committed his remarks to memory." She half lifted her hand as she spoke, and emphasized the words with a series of small downward motions. "'I will be harsh as truth, and as uncompromising as justice. On this subject I do not wish to think, or speak, or write with moderation. I am in earnest—I will not equivocate—I will not excuse—I will not retreat a single inch—and I *will* be heard!'" Her voice had risen; she was almost chanting. "I have taken that as my creed, Mr. Bingham. I am, as you remind me, only mortal, and like most creeds this one requires more than a mere mortal can accomplish. But I try—I try mightily—to live up to it."

She had stopped walking, though he suspected she did not realize it. She had turned toward him, her eyes gleaming. It was suddenly as if the virago had been transformed into a kind of demi-goddess.

"It is a very great cause, Mr. Bingham. A very great cause. I have dedicated my life to it. More and more of our countrymen are joining with me and with those who think as I do, and we will prevail; we will topple the monster from its pedestal. Our opponents do not expect us to accomplish anything, much less to prevail over their established powers and their long-settled doctrines. They are confident; they are even arrogant. But we shall beat them, Mr. Bingham, we shall win. I have not the slightest doubt we will! In your lifetime and in mine: the cause of righteousness cannot be defeated; it cannot be delayed. We will win, Mr. Bingham, because there is no other way to be obedient to God's will."

Jonathan wished, suddenly, that she had never met Martial, or that he had somehow managed to be the first.

"May you be proven right, and speedily!"

She reached out her hands, abruptly.

"Will you join with us, Mr. Bingham? Will you leave your sterile diplomatic dust and consign yourself to something greater than yourself, greater than any one of us? Will you join us?"

He took her hands, and she laughed, for just a moment throwing back her head.

"I could dance with joy, Mr. Bingham! Oh, I feel that I have this day recruited a strong arm, a powerful pen!"

He swung their joined hands into the air.

"Dance, then!"

They swung around and around, leaping and then pounding down on the ground. She put her head back again, and he did the same; they seemed to hang at the end of each other's arms, which stretched between them like a railroad track. He laughed, and he heard her do the same. And then sobriety returned, and they slowed, stopped, dropped each other's hands, and stood, panting but still smiling broadly.

"I am glad, Mr. Bingham, I am very glad!"

"No gladder than I am."

She bent her head, stood quietly for a moment.

"Lord," she said softly, "bless this man who is about to enlist in Your holy work. Grant him Your favor and Your support." She glanced up at Jonathan, whose smile had become a bit uneasy. Would she drop to her knees, right here in the open, and pray still further? "I sha'n't ask if you are a religious man, Mr. Bingham. You are a good man, and your heart beats to the right tune. No one has any need to ask more than that."

"Would you permit me to say, Mrs. Johnson, that you are a most unusual woman?"

She laughed, energetically and with apparent pleasure.

"I suppose I am. Does it matter?"

He shook his head.

"I do not know what to make of you!"

She laughed again, almost as loudly.

"Well, Mr. Bingham, you are not the first to say that to me, or words to much the same effect. My husband said pretty much the same thing, when he first met me."

"Men are not accustomed to a woman of such—independence."

They had turned and started back toward the house.

"That is I think very true, very true. Your uncles, both of them, and your aunt, and Mr. Greeley, and a great many others, all spoke of you in glowing terms, Mr. Bingham, but do you know what perhaps most recommended you to me?"

"Not that I had nearly ripped the hem of your dress?"

"Assuredly not! No, what impressed me most was how Grace spoke of you. Are you shocked?"

"No, but I cannot help being surprised."

"She is, herself, a most independent creature. I do not know what she may do, in this world, but I feel she will surely do something, and perhaps something notable. There are not many women, even today, of whom one can expect such an accomplishment."

"Indeed."

"And it is not simply that she loves you, loves you with all her heart and soul, though plainly she does that, and has for years. No, she is a tough-minded observer, even at her age. She does not know or understand what she will someday know and understand, but she understands a great deal, and she sees, I think, even more. I will not, I think, tell you in so many words what she said of you, when I mentioned the possibility of your taking on the editorship. But she saw, with remarkable clarity, just what you might be capable of, and what she saw was what I wanted."

"Was yours the deciding voice, may I ask?"

"Oh, no. But I have been charged with this particular part of the process of selection. Whoever becomes editor of our proposed publication—and I ought, now, to take that out of the conditional, shouldn't I? Well then, you will have to work pretty closely with me, for much of my responsibility is to coordinate abolitionist work in most of the country, and to dispatch speakers, and to furnish materials, and the like."

Blue Bell suddenly appeared on the horizon, and Jonathan stopped walking for a moment.

"Mr. Marcy—the Secretary of State—will have to be told at once."

She touched his arm. It was a gesture not of intimacy, but of comprehension and of support. He caught a glimpse of what it would mean to work close to this strange woman.

"Will he be inconvenienced? Are you fond of him?"

"Inconvenienced? He is a lawyer, you know, and has been a judge and the governor of my home state. He is a very able man, very able. And very much a professional man. He has negotiated, and is in the process of negotiating, some excellent agreements with other nations. What can I say? I admire him. I have liked working with him, too."

"Are you regretful?"

"A little, yes. That would be inevitable, you know. This will be a large change."

Her smile was warm.

"I should think so."

"Am I secretly, have I been secretly, a political man all these years, and not known it of myself? Is that what Grace said of me?"

She took his arm, companionably, and they resumed their walk.

"Never mind what Grace said! And do you know what, Mr. Bingham? You ask too many questions of yourself."

"Impossible!"

"Oh, no. It leads to an excess of introspection, which in turn leads—to all sorts of undesirable places."

"Like the writing of poetry?"

"You are also excessively facetious."

Her tone was easy, but he was aware that she spoke seriously.

"Who now is being professorial, Mrs. Johnson?"

He felt how she almost bounced, as she walked along, lightly holding his arm.

"Of course! I was meant to be a professor; my father always assured me. It would have been the ideal solution, if I had not been born a woman."

"And are *you* regretful?"

She did not laugh, and she did not answer at once.

"A little, yes. That would be inevitable, wouldn't it?"

And then they both laughed.

TWENTY-THREE

"I have passed my time very agreeably . . . seen a good many people, and enjoyed much. But I now feel a strong wish to get home. I feel that my place is not here; and that I ought not to stay longer than to gratify a reasonable curiosity, and desire to see an interesting part of the world, but not my part."

—Daniel Webster to Edward Everett
16 October 1839

"Well, you can see what dispute has accomplished for us." Theodore's smile was thin. "Beecher's Bibles, rightly so-called or not, are not to my mind the way to hold this country together. You may feel differently; I rather suspect you do—or you would not have accepted this new assignment."

They were in Theodore's senatorial office, the younger brother seated in a stout oaken chair familiar to them both from their childhood. Senator Bingham, not quite two years into his second term, sat behind his heavy desk, one hand toying with a marble paperweight, carved in the shape of a Revolutionary War cannon. It had been an election present from his wife; he found himself reaching for it whenever talk proved difficult or uncomfortable.

"Neither of us runs the country," Jonathan said, "and of the two of us, you know, you have had and will continue to have the greater say in things. I will be only the editor of a new and unheard-of periodical. No one has ever elected me to anything whatever, Brother, and I doubt that anyone ever will." He pursed his lips. "I'm afraid—it is my largest fear, in taking on this post—that I will be a preacher to the converted, and only to them."

"That cannot be a very comfortable feeling; I understand, Jonathan, that you wish for more. But who has elected Mrs. Stowe to high office, or indeed to any office? She seems to me to have had as much to do with the governance of this country, of late, as President Pierce."

"That would be Mr. Pierce's decision, if it were the fact, would it not? Had he chosen to be the sort of chief executive Jefferson and Jackson were, well, the powers of the office have been for these four years at his disposal. Wouldn't you agree, brother, that it has been the man and not the office at fault?"

Theodore frowned.

"Damn it, I'm seriously concerned. Pierce is doing all he can, all anyone reasonably could, to keep the peace in Kansas. It's just not good enough. He'll call out the federal troops. Maybe that won't be good enough. Where is it all leading us? And isn't it time we called a halt, stopped bickering, and put things back together? It may be too late, before too long. Is that what you want, Jonathan?"

Jonathan put his hands in his lap and stared down at them.

"Mr. Pierce has made one slave-holding appointment after another, Theodore. The rest of the country will not see Kansas turned into a slave-holding territory, and then a slave-holding state. What answer does a free people have, to a slavery government, except Sharps rifles and an absolute determination?" His voice was just barely audible. "I am not disposed to break up the Union; it is not mine to dissolve. But I do wonder, brother, if temporizing is the way to true harmony. Peace between the regions of our country cannot be a mere word. I will support Colonel Fremont, if he is nominated."

Theodore's frown deepened.

"And," Jonathan went on, "I have no choice but to support John Brown. His methods are not my methods, but his goal is the one I also seek."

"Civil war, that's what you'll bring us to!"

"I hope not."

"But you'll not struggle to avoid it."

Theodore had leaned forward, his finger pointing at his younger brother.

"Are the opponents of slavery to be held solely responsible for everything of a negative sort, brother? Are we so very powerful, then? I wish it were true. We could settle matters out of hand, if the power you impute to us were in fact ours."

"You're strong enough to bring us all down, that's how powerful you are."

"And is anyone strong enough to hold us together?"

"Well, now. You *ought* to be working with Lydia, Jonathan. You've taken on her tone, and her arguments, and even her sanctimonious smile."

"It is our uncles who have provided me with the opportunity, not our sister Lydia."

"I love our Uncle Karl and our Uncle Peter, but I do not love what they are doing to this country, Jonathan. It does not belong to any of us, as you say yourself. No one has the right to destroy it." Theodore smiled. "Nor our family ties, brother. I promise not to denounce you on the floor of the Senate, no matter what you say. Or do."

"I will not hold you to that promise, Theodore."

"Of course not. You are a man of honor, Jonathan. I respect your honor. I respect our sister Lydia's. She is a lady. But I abhor your principles—hers and yours, if indeed there is any difference between them!"

"I could wish you shared them, brother."

"So I could argue your case?"

"You have a formidable legal reputation."

"Damn it, Jonathan! I'd sooner give the country back to England, than turn it over to a —." He stopped himself and forced a smile to return to his face. "Well, I've no desire to quarrel, not with you nor with any man, Jonathan. It is people like me, I'm afraid, who will be squeezed between a rock and a very hard place. I could wish you would stay in the Department, brother. You are well thought of. You could do much good."

"What is it our Shakespeare has said, brother? 'There is a tide in the affairs of men which, taken at the flood, leads on to fortune.' Well, if by fortune we understand that which is important, or useful, or even good, then I am bound to leave Washington. I have no choice."

Theodore rose.

"Suppose we take our chances, for now, at the eating house? My choice, I can tell you, will be a chop and a stein."

"Mr. Marcy can spare me for a while, I dare say. If I had ever conceived of myself as more than an insignificant speck, brother, these years in Washington have reformed me."

Theodore clapped him on the back.

"It's the confounded specks that do all the damage, Jonathan! Your Mrs. Stowe, now, she's expert at throwing dust—and it sticks, that's the damndest part of it. It's only dust, specks—but it sticks!"

They strolled out of the office, arm in arm, smiling as if enormously pleased with life and with each other.

"Do you think," he began, then had to plant his foot and brace against a sudden rolling of the deck. She came to the tips of her toes and leaned one hand on his shoulder. It was a brief yawing. "Do you think," he resumed, as the ship straightened, "we were right to leave her?"

"Of course."

They walked along the narrow deck passage, occasionally looking out to starboard, where the ocean stretched endlessly, and to port, where in the middle distance the coast slid gently by, one mile indistinguishable from the next. They had embarked at Baltimore; they were to be carried all the way to New York, a route Martial preferred to the slower, safer, steadier, duller path of railroad and coach and ferry. They had come south the slower way; he had vowed to return the quickest, shortest route possible.

"She's very young. And impressionable."

Lydia tucked her hand through his arm and leaned briefly against him.

"You worry far too much, Martial. I doubt that I have ever seen a stronger-minded young woman than our daughter."

"Oh, I dare say she could handle Theodore and several legions like him. But Arabella?"

"I would trust our Grace, Martial, with an Amazon on the one hand, and a Sybil on the other."

"I sha'n't tell her that." They reached the stern and the end of the passage allotted to promenades—no one else was taking advantage of it, most of the passengers having had one look at the grey sky and then fled indoors—and he paused, sniffing the heavy air. "Marvelous aroma. Aseptic. Bracing. Restorative."

They turned and headed toward the bow once more.

"How physicianly you are today."

"The purport of which, eh, is 'physician, heal thyself'?" She did not reply. "And are you also satisfied with the other piece of business you transacted, Lydia?"

"I am satisfied that Washington is become a useless city, full of self-satisfied, corrupt men and indifferent women."

"So much for Washington! No, I meant the recruiting side of our journey."

"We are none of us perfect."

"Did you mean yourself, for your judgment in recruiting him, or him for accepting?"

"All of us." He noted yet again how easily she kept stride with him, though he was taller and had neither skirts nor tall heels to impede him. Lydia always kept pace. "Our brother Jonathan is worthier than he knows himself to be. But not necessarily for the things he thinks he values."

"No, he is not, nor has he ever been, what might be called a run-of-the-mill sort. Even as a boy, you know, he was distinctive. Those intense eyes: he seemed always to be noting things that children ought not even to be aware of."

"He will do the work as it should be done."

"I dare say you're right. It takes his sort of mind, doesn't it, to see how a straight road needs to be bent?"

"To elaborate on the metaphor, he will perceive how to pull thread through the eye of an invisible needle. Less metaphorically, he will, I think, bring a strain of imaginative perception that is badly needed. The worst thing we could do, I fear, given the opportunity that has presented itself, is to deaden precisely that imaginative perspective, that vivid sense of the awfulness of enslavement. He will quicken the public pulse, Martial: that is what he will do best. Do you think that an accurate judgment?"

"I don't think I have disagreed with you, Lydia, in something like a year. Or even two."

"Am I so very close to perfection, then?"

"I sha'n't answer that, either! No," he added softly, "you're infernally mortal, my dear, but terribly remarkable."

"Do you often remark me?"

"All the time. I remark you even when, I suspect, you do not realize that I have eyes for no one else. You needn't be flattered, however. I have some indication that other males, less fortunately situated than myself, do exactly the same thing."

"Am I a prize trophy, then?"

He squeezed her arm.

"Of course! Did you think I sought your hand for any other reason?"

Her smiled narrowed.

"I'm afraid it must sometimes be difficult, having a wife like me."

"Good God! If I were a follower of Brigham Young, and it were possible to have a dozen like you, I'd snatch at the opportunity."

"Your first wife, for all her gifts, remained very much a model of domesticity."

"Anne-Marie had four children to tend."

"Do you wish we had children of our own, Martial?"

He stopped them, turned, and put his arm tightly around her waist.

"Four seems an admirable number to me."

She leaned her head against his chest.

"I wish for a child, sometimes."

"You are a young woman."

"It seems like a celestial exactment, sometimes—a kind of impost, a price to be paid for other things."

He hugged her, then set them back to walking.

"That, Lydia Johnson, is the sheerest nonsense you have ever spoken."

"Oh, I'm much more of a pagan than even you know."

"Are you now? Do you expect Triton to swim up to us, waving a parti-colored banner and shouting out prophetic messages?"

"I expect I'm tired, Martial."

"And no wonder."

"Perhaps I ought to lie down for a bit." He immediately steered them toward the glass door. "Will you join me?"

"I'll see you into the arms of Morpheus, the only other male in whose arms I am prepared to trust you. And then I will, if that does not offend you, continue to breathe in this beneficent air. Landlubbers like us do not have enough such chances. We have only another day, you know, or at most two." She put her hand to her forehead. "Have you a headache, my dear?"

She managed a small smile.

"I am suddenly too weary to know."

He hurried her to their cabin.

"Are you sure I will be welcome, Uncle Jonathan?"

"Without a doubt."

"Are girls often to be seen in the places of government?"

He held the door for her.

"You will not be welcomed as a girl, Grace, but as a charming young lady. And charming young ladies, as you will in time learn, are generally welcome everywhere, in government and out." The porter tipped his hat to Jonathan, who nodded. "I'm told the porters are instructed to forget your face, once you leave for good, but I don't believe it."

"Have you much business to conduct?"

They walked through a narrow corridor, their steps clattering—it seemed to Grace—terribly loudly.

"Very little. I'll only be a minute."

She pulled on his arm, and for a moment they stopped.

"What if Mr. Marcy appears?"

"He may do that."

"Oh, no."

"I shall simply introduce you, and even though he is no Southerner, Mr. Marcy is very much a gentleman. He is also from our home state, you know, so you are almost a constituent. Stop fretting, eh? There's not a more proper-looking lady in ten miles of here, and I dare say not a more attractive one in considerably more than that."

His desk was exactly as he had left it. His successor had not yet been appointed. There had been talk of his waiting before he left the post, so that the transition would be smoother, but that was no longer possible. He picked up his favorite gold pen, and several small morocco volumes in which he had kept track of appointments and obligations and meetings. The drawers were already empty, but he opened them, swiftly, just to be sure. There was a portrait of George Washington over the desk, but it had been there when he arrived, and he did not feel it right to disturb what must have been a long tenure. That same picture would probably still be hanging on this same wall, long after he was dead.

He sat down in his chair and stared at nothing.

"Have you writing to do?"

Grace was perched uneasily in a wicker chair, just to the side. It was a very small office: one more person would have crowded it.

"Tons."

Her face fell.

"But not here, dear Grace! I referred to the obligations of a life time, not to any obligations here." He straightened. "I could show you —"

She rose.

"No, please. I'd just as soon be gone."

"You'll never have so good an opportunity again, more than likely." She shook her head, her mouth pressed shut. "Just think what you'd be able to tell your grandchildren."

"I sha'n't have any grandchildren, if we don't leave here directly!" she burst out. "What if someone comes?"

He leaned back in his chair.

"And what if they do? We have more than a perfect right to be here."

"*I* don't."

"Nonsense. I am still by law the head clerk in the Department. You are my guest. And also my relative." He waved her back toward her chair. "Do sit a moment. We can chat and you can feel history slowly accumulating around your ears."

She remained standing.

"Uncle Jonathan," she declared firmly, "I will leave by myself, if you do not escort me."

"Lord. I shall have to send for a federal marshal, to detain you."

She started toward the door, and he rose and quickly intercepted her.

"I will not be found where I do not belong!"

He moved his hand, as if to rough her hair, but thought better of it and simply put it lightly on her shoulder.

"May I have just a moment more?" he asked softly. "I have spent a great deal of my life here, you know, and it isn't the easiest thing in the world to simply walk out, shut the door, and forget it all."

"Why didn't you say that, then?"

"I suppose I've learned to dissemble. It's one of the vices of diplomacy. And not one of the vices I'm proud to have acquired." He walked back toward the desk and slowly ran his hand along the edge. "I shall have to acquire a whole new set of vices, in my new post."

She came up behind him, and leaned her forehead on his arm for a moment.

"Or virtues."

"Oh, I already have all I'll ever have, of those." He turned and put his hands on her shoulders. "Thank you for letting me stay just a bit. I suppose I needed to soak up a little of the air, to carry away with me. I've breathed it long enough!"

"And they say that women are nesting creatures!"

"I'm at least one part female, surely. Aren't all poets?"

"Are you still a poet?"

He nodded carefully.

"A very fair question. I don't have the answer. Do you?"

Her deep eyes looked directly at him, but she did not reply. There was a trace of a smile on her face. Her mouth was soft, now, and just barely open.

"You *are* a most attractive lady, little Grace!"

She frowned swiftly.

"I'm not little Grace any more, Jonathan!" It was the first time she had ever called him by his given name, without adding an "Uncle" in front of it. It had not been intended, but neither was it retracted.

"I stand reproved," he apologized.

She bent forward, swiftly, and gave him a small kiss on the cheek.

"You stand saluted." Then she turned and walked to the door. She stood there, smiling back at him, and it was like a summons. He had no choice but to obey.

"Come," she invited quietly, but it was not necessary to say anything and she seemed very aware of that fact. She's quite right, he said to himself, she's not little Grace any more. Those days are over. He gave her his arm and felt a strange new sense of just who it was that was walking beside him. He would have to be a great deal more careful; this was a woman, not a child, and he did not want to do her any damage by avuncular tomfoolery. Even if he had been serious about marrying her, which he did not think he had been, not ever, it was unlikely that either the family would give its consent or that a respectable minister would perform the ceremony. An uncle and a niece, of blood relationship, were not exactly like a brother and sister, but it was sufficiently close to classical incest to be frowned upon. It might well be prohibited (though not, he knew, in France, or more than likely in other European countries). And no matter what the legal situation, this was his sister's child, and he loved her not as one who marries, but as one who nurtures. He loved her more, in that way, because her mother had died. He had felt a need to fill what part of Anne-Marie's place he could. But Grace, no longer a child, did not seem to understand, nor did she seem to want to understand. She was a headstrong girl; she would very shortly become a headstrong woman.

He would be remarkably careful, starting on the instant.

"Let me give you a bit of lunch, and then escort you back to your Aunt Arabella."

"Fie on Aunt Arabella!"

He turned, startled, in time to see her face crinkle into pleased amusement. She was pleased with herself, pleased with her rapidly growing powers. Her laugh was virtually pleasure incarnate. And she was, indeed, becoming a very lovely woman.

"Laughter in these hallowed halls," he said with as much hauteur as he could muster, "is singularly inappropriate."

But that only made her laugh still harder.

It would not be easy, this business of being careful. It was just as well that he was leaving, very soon, for New York, and his new editorial post. Then he remembered: she, too, lived in the North, and not very far from New York. And her stepmother, Martial's new wife, was to be his close, his terribly close associate. There would, of course, be visits back and forth; there would be a great deal of contact, whether he chose it or not. It was unavoidable. Did he in fact want to avoid it?

He brought her out into the sunlight.

"I don't know that just a bit of lunch will do, Jonathan. I'm dreadfully hungry."

"Diplomacy does do that to you, yes," he murmured dryly. What was he going to do with this blossoming creature? What was he going to do with himself? How was he going to manage? One thing at a time, he cautioned himself. There is absolutely no need for panic.

"*Eh bien?*" she inquired, tugging lightly at his arm.

"This way," he said decisively, and was not at all sure he had deceived her.

TWENTY-FOUR

> *"The worst verses cannot hobble so badly as our politics, and none of the muses gives such inspirations as that fury, party madness."*
>
> —Daniel Webster, to Mr. Plumer
> 7 March 1842

"You need more poetry," Greeley had said, early on, but *The Weekly*, as it was informally and later on formally called, had raised Greeley's subscription rolls, and would probably have been a self-supporting item within a year of its first issue, perhaps even without the huge network of *Tribune* readers who had helped it along. But it did not have to do without that network, and Greeley and the *Tribune* did not have to do without the steady subsidies provided by friendly merchant-philanthropists. It was an ideal arrangement for Greeley, who gained everything and could not lose: the policies of *The Weekly* were basically harmonious with his own, so he could not alienate supporters or further embitter enemies already totally opposed. He could not lose financially; he gained both in publicity and readership, as *The Weekly* attracted favorable attention. Nor was there editorial interference: the merchants knew both who and what they wanted, and that was what they had gotten. Jonathan was editor, but he worked hand-in-hand with Lydia Johnson and the organizations of which she was an active supporter and participant. Jonathan drew an adequate salary (Lydia was, of course, unpaid— as a woman, and a married woman, to boot) and did far more than an adequate job. His satiric side, for example, helped immensely: in pillorying the Dred Scott decision, in 1857, he had written, in part:

> So the Negro in bondage is not a citizen, eh? A citizen, after all, is a *man*, and what could be plainer than the plain fact that a descendant of Black Africans is not a man? Except when he is, of course. A free Negro is Constitutionally en-citizened—

by a mysterious sacrament even more profound and dazzling than any known to mere Christianity. But an enslaved Negro is, well, more like a horse. Or a cow. Or a talking parrot. Society encourages good morals among these beasts of burden, to be sure, since one never knows when the mystic transformation into a human being is likely to take place. It even establishes Christian churches which these non-men (and non-women, too) are led to make use of—for the cultivation of their non-souls, surely, since what mere beast possesses a soul?

But where lies the greater madness: in this absurd discussion, or in the minds of those to whom it is literal truth and even Holy Writ?

When in 1858 Senator Stephen Douglas accused his opponent, Abraham Lincoln, of being "jet black" in the north, a "decent mulatto" in the Midwest, but "almost white" in Egypt, Jonathan thumped a mocking drum at the Little Giant:

> Senator Douglas has our intense sympathy, if not exactly our support. It is hard to be in favor of six things at the same time, any three of which are wholly incompatible each with the other. And the Senator has done, we admit, as well as any man could, given the tangled web he was woven, and which he hopes to turn into a magic carpet, carrying him straight into the White House. We might, however, gently suggest that the time for web-spinners has passed, and the time for truth-tellers has arrived.

Lincoln lost the senatorial election, and Horace Greeley was pleased, for he hoped to recruit Douglas for the Republicans. But Jonathan knew that a bright star had arisen, in Illinois:

> "A house divided against itself cannot stand," says Mr. Abraham Lincoln, and we hope the tenant of a certain house in Washington is listening. Can you hear him, Mr. Buchanan, and if you can, what might you think of doing about it? Nothing, as usual? Well, come the next election, perhaps some of our wonderfully indifferent public tenants can be turned into the street.

That election was to be in 1860, only two years off; like most Northern-ers, Jonathan suspected that William Seward, his brother's New York colleague in the Senate, would have the Republican nomination—and the presidency. But much could happen, in two years, and *The Weekly* did its best to prepare the way for the best candidate possible.

It was not a season for poetry. Whittier and Lowell and even Long-fellow poured out jingles on the folly and sinfulness of all slavery, and everyone called it poetry, but Jonathan knew better. All the same, when in the autumn of 1859 John Brown captured the federal armory at Harpers Ferry, Virginia, and was two days later himself captured by Colonel Robert E. Lee and the U. S. marines, and when Brown was within two weeks tried, convicted, and sentenced to death for treason against the state of Virginia, and for conspiring to incite a slave rebel-lion, Jonathan published one of his rare pieces of verse. It was called "A Letter Not to be Delivered, Not to be Read, and Not to be Forgotten":

> Oh, there's no help for John Brown, none,
> And there's no help for his men,
> Like the wearer of humanity's crown, One
> Who came before, and went
>
> To His grave, and was lost to the earth, our home,
> But won us peace, and our souls.
> Oh, John Brown's holy bones, these bones,
> Will take their bloody toll
>
> Before there's peace in this land, our land.
> He did what had to be done,
> He lifted a nation's guilt in his hand, that hand,
> And his battle has just begun.

Jonathan did not think a great deal of it; it was topical and it seemed necessary. Greeley reprinted it in the *Tribune*; many praised it. But Jona-than knew better, nor did he mind: poetry was poetry, and polemic was something different. His job was to inform and stir, to move his countrymen's hearts and shake their spirits. John Brown's death was a tragic fact; it had to be converted into living energy, into mass energy. If his brief lines helped, and they seemed to, that was all they were intended to do. He offered his readers poetry of a distinctly different kind, early the next year, when Senator Jefferson Davis introduced a set of resolutions clearly intended to bring the North to its knees. No state could interfere with the rights of other states; an attack on a state institution, like (for example) slavery, was an attack on the Constitution; no one, and no state, could interfere with property rights, like the rights of those who owned fugitive slaves; and so on. Jonathan's poem neither had nor needed a title:

> Jeff Davis, here's my hand,
> Your plans are mighty grand.
> You suck on Federal eggs,
> And pull on free men's legs,
> And laugh behind our back.
> You give our heads a crack,
> And knock our brains on wood,
> And swear it's for our good.
> But Jeff, we know your kind,
> We've seen the yarns you winds:
> No matter the tales you tell,
> We know they're born in H—;
> Though black is hardly your color,
> We see you're a devilish feller.
> Three cheers for your brazen gall
> As you nail your flag to the wall
> And paste your words in the air:
> The South has spoken: there!—there!

Greeley laughed out loud; Jonathan hoped that a good many of their joint readers would first laugh and then weep—or even curse. For, by the twenty-fourth of May, 1860, the Senate had actually adopted Jefferson Davis' resolutions. And was a federal Senate which could support such notions worth saving? *The Weekly* of course dealt with that issue, too, and at some length.

"It's going to blow up," Greeley kept predicting. Sooner or later, indeed, it seemed likely to do exactly that. Was the South worth fighting to keep? "A false issue!" *The Weekly* explained. "We do not want to keep the South, or the West, or any other part of the Union that wants to go its way. Let the South conform to the law of nations, and the law of God, and release its bondservants, and we will wish them hail and farewell. For can they think us so dull, though perhaps from our representation in Congress they well might, that we could permit on our borders a state hostile to all that we and the rest of the civilized world stand for, a state that would inevitably engage in subversion and incitement to riot, that would seek to sell its slave-derived wealth through our ports, and draw from us our hard-won manufactures, to be paid for in slave-earned gold? No, we do not seek to retain them, but neither can we forbear to protect ourselves, and those enchained souls for which each one of us is responsible, here on earth and ultimately in Heaven."

Twenty days after Davis' resolutions were introduced, Abraham Lincoln stood in New York City's Cooper Union and said, carefully but bluntly, that "There is a judgment and a feeling against slavery in this nation, which cast at least a million and a half of votes. You cannot destroy that judgment and feeling by breaking up the political organization which rallies around it." *The Weekly*, and not only *The Weekly*, began a crescendo of drum-pounding for Abraham Lincoln as the next president of the United States.

> "Let us have faith that right makes might," said Mr. Lincoln, and we say, "Let us have faith that he will see the right and use the might, and let us, whether we have been Whigs or Democrats or Republicans or nothing at all, let us unite to give this man of sense and feeling the last chance this nation may have."

"I know we have been doing right. My only question remains, have we been doing good—any good at all?"

"If we have been doing right, how can you doubt?"

"I understand how you can ask that, but I'm afraid it doesn't answer my question."

She glanced up from the stack of papers in front of her.

"Is this one of your black days, Jonathan?"

He fanned out his fingers and held them up to the light. It was almost three in the afternoon; the June day was sunny and bright. He could see lines that were surely veins. He was staring at his own mortality, dim against the glare of the sun.

"Well, one-half the Democratic Party has nominated Senator Douglas, and I have just learned that the other half has nominated the Vice President, Mr. Breckenridge."

"Mr. Lincoln will defeat both of them, plainly."

"Plainly."

"Is that not satisfactory?"

"Lydia, I don't know any more if anything is satisfactory!"

She put down her pen.

"It *is* one of your black days. No, don't argue. I propose to take you out of the city, and drag you, kicking and screaming if necessary, to the peace and quiet of—"

"Not today, Lydia. Thank you, but not today."

"Grace tells me you're avoiding her."

"Oh, most certainly. She's quite right."

"I did not think you so cruel, Jonathan."

"It's not cruel at all, I assure you."

"She loves you most desperately."

"And I love her, yes. In my way, as she loves me in her way. I am her *uncle*, Lydia. My task is not to charm her, much less to marry her. She needs other company than mine."

"Even if yours is what she wants?"

"She is not old enough to be the judge of that."

"She is eighteen."

"To be sure. And Arabella was married—the first time, that is—at what was it? Seventeen? Sixteen?"

"And Grace's own mother."

"To be sure, Lydia. Your facts are, as ever, strictly accurate. You will be a formidable public speaker, if you survive into the next era, in which women will speak, and vote, and hold office."

"For a man of thirty, Jonathan, you are sometimes devastatingly juvenile."

"Oh, indeed, yes, I quite agree."

She half raised her hand.

"Were I a man . . . ." She lowered her hand. "But it wouldn't do any good, would it?"

"Not a bit. I am, as my late mother could have told you, and would have told you, had she been given the chance, incorrigible. I was apparently born incorrigible."

"It is worse than a black day, I perceive."

Jonathan leaned back in his chair, closed his eyes, and wished he were a small boy once more, fishing in the Hudson off Poughkeepsie. He wished his feet were bare and his mind were blank. He wished he had never been to France, never written a poem, never turned out a weekly anti-slavery magazine. He could not wish that he had never met Lydia, but he wished that he could wish so. How important she had become to him! And how helpless and hopeless this whole situation was, since she had met his brother-in-law, Martial, long before he had managed to meet her once more, and she was now Martial's most happily married wife.

"Would you have me marry your step-daughter, Lydia?"

His eyes remained closed; her sharp voice could cut through thicker things than voluntary darkness.

"I have expected that you would—the decision, however, being yours and hers, and not mine."

He wished he were lying in the mud, in a particular shallow where he had often covered himself, letting the sun bake him brittle and hard. He wished he had become a veterinarian doctor, so his life could have spent with animals, who were mute and sensitive—and totally apolitical.

"It is not, however, lawful, an uncle marrying a blood niece."

"Fiddle!"

He opened his eyes. She was not smiling.

"It is," he pronounced slowly, "what the law terms incest."

"And the law is an ass!"

"You mean, dear sister, that such things are, in fact, done. And by reputable people."

"As you yourself know, Jonathan."

"Indeed." He nodded and shut his eyes again. "This is a lawless time. We have been urging non-obedience to the law, for years now, in fact, and we no longer respect it in any particular. But it is the law, still, for all that."

"Do you want to marry Grace?"

She was doubly difficult to argue with, brighter and more aggressive than most of the men he knew, and at the same time a woman and so entitled to a wide variety of social exemptions.

"I think any man in his right mind would regard her—"

"I did not address the question so generally, brother, but most particularly, and to you."

He opened his eyes and tried to smile at her. It came out as a woeful affair, a mere stretching of the facial muscles.

"Would it be advisable to confide in you, do you suppose?" But she had no idea, no idea whatever, of how monstrously inadvisable it would be!

"I am, for better or worse, her mother!"

"To be sure. Oh, yes."

"You have managed to avoid my question, Jonathan."

"Inevitably."

She pushed the pile of papers away; her motion was sudden and expressed mounting irritation.

"I have been meaning to discuss this with you, Jonathan. It has become an urgent matter, of late. And since you appear willing to discuss some aspects of it, at least, we need to discuss the rest."

"Should not Martial—"

"I have had more than sufficient opportunity to learn my husband's feelings. He and I are one, in this."

"And in law, too, you know."

"Jonathan are you quite sober?"

"What a silly question, Lydia! What on earth made you ask it?"

"I do not know how else to account for your behavior, suddenly."

"I am desperately sober. I do not in fact think I have ever been truly un-sober. More's the pity, perhaps."

"You are an odd creature, Jonathan—a man of towering potential—do not, pray, interrupt me." She sat silently for a moment. "You do not think it of yourself, but all who know you are aware that you could be famous in a variety of ways. Nor do I mean, as I trust you know, the fame of mere show, but the reputation of solid and significant accomplishment." She held up her hand. "Let me go on, please. As I say, this is well-known, and not in dispute. You are also a man of wildly fluctuating mood, and sometimes of such moods that you appear to un-man yourself." She permitted herself a small smile. "Do you know what I term you, sometimes, in my own mind?"

"I would like to know," he said simply. He crossed his arms over his chest, almost as a protective gesture. "I care a great deal, you know, what you think of me."

"And you do not know?"

"No. I fancy, at times, that I have glimpses, but that is all I have. You are not an easy woman to comprehend, Lydia."

"Nor are you, Jonathan."

"I do not try to be difficult, in this or in anything else."

"Do I?"

"I do not know."

She surprised him by laughing, a vigorous peal of amusement.

"I do feel, every now and then, that the Good Lord made a fatal error, in creating two sexes instead of one!"

"And that one," Jonathan said at once, "female."

"But of course. Still, the mistake was made, alas, long before my opinion could have mattered. And we must live with it, as men and women alike have always had to. Do you see? I should, indeed, have been a professorial philosopher. Do you recall my telling you that?" He nodded silently. "Think—what pains you and our other co-workers might have been spared! But I was asking you if you had any inkling of the nickname I have for you, in the solitude of my own fancy. And you said you had no inkling. Well, after four years of hard labor at your side, perhaps you will forgive it to me. I hope so. I sometimes think of you —" she paused for only an instant—"as a kind of Don Quijote."

"A great creation, one with which I should be proud to have any association."

"On your honor?"

"Oh, I'm not sure I have any of that. But honestly, yes. Did you think I would be displeased?"

"I know you, in truth, about as imperfectly as you say you know me. I do not myself think I am impenetrable as you make me out."

"I fancy myself as clear as glass. Nor do I mean mirrored glass."

She glanced at the papers she had pushed away, earlier.

"I wonder if we have the right, while the work is as yet undone, to sit and prate of our insignificant selves?"

"Unlike Don Quijote, I do not always have the appetite for tilting at windmills."

"Is that how you see our work, and *The Weekly*, when the mood is on you?"

He hunched down in his chair, his hands in his pockets.

"You have a knack for asking leading questions, Lydia. I'm not sure if your father was, in truth, accurate, telling you how professorial you ought to be. I can see you, really I can, as a lawyer."

"Do you feel interrogated, cross-examined, pilloried at the bar?"

"Quite."

Her smile was distinctly gentle.

"Do you want to tell me your feelings about Grace?"

"I *have* told you."

"She has not gone to her Aunt Arabella's, this year—not yet, at any rate."

"On my account? I hardly think so."

"You do not at all understand."

"She is no longer a child—as you yourself insist, Lydia. She is free to decide her whereabouts. She is totally free."

"A woman in love, and especially a young woman, is not free."

"Am I to blame?"

"Possibly."

He had to say something, and he took a quickly calculated stance, hiding behind a weak fence of thin, scrappy boards that any wicked wolf, or witch, could have blown away with a solid puff.

"*I* am not free," he declared, aware that he might well back himself into a corner. Fine: he would still not give in. She was never to know who it was he had come to love. Never. On that he knew he could stand, never giving an inch.

"Are you to be married to someone else?" The rest, all the well-chosen words, were mere talk.

He shook his head, slowly, like a stubborn child.

"It's nothing like that."

She waited; he did not go on.

"Grace has been giving lessons to young ladies, you know." Her voice had become winning, almost coaxing. "She has been spending vast amounts of time developing dance techniques that are, I truly think, new on the face of the earth."

"She is vastly talented," Jonathan agreed. "There has never been much doubt of that. I saw it in her when she was a small child."

"And she has just come into a bit of money, a trust that her father created for her when her mother died."

Jonathan met her eyes, then looked away once more.

"Are you afraid she'll do something rash, then?"

"I do not know if Grace can do rash things; she is too realistic, too sensible. But she is capable, indeed, of the unexpected, even the bizarre."

"As, for example?"

"It would not be bizarre, would it, if I could predict its nature?"

"But you are wishing, and perhaps you are even asking, that I fore-stall it—whatever it may turn out to be—by marrying her?"

"They say that marriages are made in Heaven, not here on earth!"

Jonathan leaned over, extending his arms, and pushed the pile of papers back to her.

"Enough. Shall we return to what we are supposed to be doing?"

She did not move.

"I also wonder, sometimes, what directions you might have taken, had you not gone to France."

"We never blame the British for our faults, do we? But they are, in fact, much more responsible for them than are the French."

She waved the objection away, casually, with a flick of her wrist. He found himself staring at her tapered fingers—and wishing he could touch them.

"British, French—what does it matter?"

He was obliged to close his eyes.

"Let us not discuss foreign entanglements," he said softly, almost whispering. In the flicker of darkness he had created for himself, he could virtually see—like a kind of waking vision—her face smiling up at him. He quickly opened his eyes and saw the worn boards of the table at which they were sitting, and the papers, and the full glow of the June sun. "Or any other entanglements," he added, trying to laugh. His emotion suddenly ran away with him, ran very high, and burst out before he could check it. His throat caught, instead. But his luck held, and though he had risked an almost fatal revelation by even so much as mentioning matters of "entanglement"—a word with deadly connotations, with each and every one of which she was ordinarily fully familiar—so intent was she on his relationship with Grace that she did not notice its application to a very different pairing.

"Will you come, this weekend?"

"I can't."

"Are you afraid?"

It was not an ironic query, or a taunt.

"Probably, yes. It is, I find, my besetting sin. I realize it more and more vividly, the older I grow."

She pulled the papers to her, but did not resume work.

"Odd. Women are supposedly the fearful sex. But I do not think I can ever recall being afraid. Not of anything. Or anyone."

"You have been singularly blessed!" His voice had risen, suddenly, and after the hushed tones that had been their conversation, it seemed almost operatic.

She plucked the topmost paper off the pile.

"Have I now?" She laughed gently. "I do not think that is the view of me which is entertained by most people."

It took an effort not to reply. He did not see her as most people saw her; he had known that from the start and had learned more than she could possibly have known about her own immense qualifications for marriage most joyous. But there was nothing to be said.

"She asked me most particularly to invite you, this weekend," Lydia concluded, starting back to work.

"I shall think about it," he mumbled, catching at his lip with his teeth. To keep himself silent? In pain? He could not have told.

"Do," she murmured, already lost in the paper in front of her. Her powers of concentration were phenomenal. She was phenomenal. And she was his married sister; she was Martial Johnson's wife.

The girl stood with her long, white skirt raised just above her bare toes, her arms spread at the elbow. But she did not proceed, only stood rather squatly and squinted at Grace.

"But I'm not really a bird, Miss Johnson."

"Indeed you're not, Dorothy!" The child looked, in fact, much more like a penguin than the gull she had been instructed to imitate. Or perhaps more like an overfed pet rabbit. "But you must try all the same."

"My father says I'm to learn to dance."

"And would your father like to teach you, Dorothy?"

"Oh, no. He don't know how!"

Grace moved toward her, smiling.

"And I do. So, you will mind what I tell you and if you're a good girl, and try very hard, you may in the end learn how to dance and make your dear father terribly proud of you. You'd like that, wouldn't you, Dorothy?" Grace stood behind the girl and grasped her arms. "Now. I'll help you do it properly, in case you need helping."

"But my father says—"

"Bother your father, child! Will you do as you're told or won't you?"

Dorothy did as she was told, as nearly as she was able, and in the effort was stilled. The lesson continued, first Dorothy, and then her friend Susan, both of them twelve, neither of them notably graceful. Susan was somewhat more promising, but Grace would have been pleased to be free of them both. But what was she to do, as a dancer, if not give lessons, passing along the secrets she was beginning to discover? Earning respectable fees was somewhat more promising. She did not charge much, but she was paid, as a professional should be. It was very professional, *very* professional. It was all quid pro quo, as her Uncle Theodore had said, laughing. It had been a kindly, tolerant laugh, not ill-intentioned—but was that why she had not gone to Virginia, as for years and years she always had at this season? It was surely not out of loyalty to her few students, who could very well have done without their lessons. The girls liked her well enough, but for *dancing* lessons, not in order to be turned into seagulls. Their parents wanted them to move lightly on the dance floor, so that when the time came, there would be young men trailing along behind them, like bees after flowers. That was proper dancing—and if Miss Johnson's new-fangled methods led to the old established goal, well, they could be tolerated. But had there been any talk of waltzes in Miss Johnson's classes, they asked their children? Or polkas? Or any real dances, indeed? The answer was usually no, and the parents, very plainly, were concerned.

And Grace was concerned. She was concerned for her students: she had taken them in charge and she meant to do as well by them as she knew how. Her methods, though still slightly fumbling, were well-founded; she knew they would work, in time, if given the chance to run their course. But she was concerned, too, for herself. She had been instructing children for the better part of a year and a half. There was no reason, so far as she was aware, why she could not go on indefinitely. It might lead to an academy of sorts, though for that she might have to remove to Boston or to New York. But was that what she was meant to do? Her mother had never given lessons; she might have instructed her children, had she lived. But one's own children were different. And Grace had none, as yet. She did not have a husband, either.

The carriage came for Dorothy and Susan, by now properly shod young ladies, and Grace was left alone with her brothers and her sister. Alice was on the verge of turning seventeen and very much more resembled her father than her mother—darker, physically more compact, and a great deal quieter. She might have been a doctor, too, had such things been possible. As it was, she read rather too much and would frighten away a good many young men—that was easily foreseeable—before she found one with sufficient courage. She would be a very fine wife and mother, and she would not rebel, as her older sister did. The girls were friends; they were not particularly close. Mark was a boisterous fifteen, beginning to simmer into young manhood and lose at least some of his childish rowdiness. It was impossible to tell what he would do, except that he would do it noisily. He was destined for Harvard College, fairly soon. As was Michael, only fourteen but already better read and intellectually more agile than his brother. Michael would end as a professor: they joked about it, proudly rather than naughtily, and Michael only smiled. He had his father's face but his mother's eyes; he was slender and light-boned, and would not be of more than medium height. He walked with something like the smooth effortlessness Grace had always displayed: in their games, earlier on, he had usually been assigned to play a cat, or a silent burglar, or the young prince turned into a mute and beautiful swan.

Mark was off somewhere, in the crowd of boys he played and ran and fought with. Michael was reading. Alice was sewing. None of them would want to be interrupted, and she did not want to interrupt them. She would likely be the first to fly from the nest—wherever she flew to!—but it was already palpable, the growth, ripening, and imminent dissolution of the childhood family they had known for so long. The very youngest of them, Michael, was not what one could call a child, not any more. Alice was a young woman; there were no more nurses, and no more nursery. It was all very different, and likely to be a great deal more so. And soon: the pace had quickened, for her and for all of them. Years had barely crept by, once, but they did not creep any longer; they skipped and ran and leaped, and they were gone, and a new one was in place, almost before the coming could be properly appreciated or the going sensed.

She saddled her pony, swung lightly into the saddle—she could ride as beautifully, side saddle, as most men could with the horse between their knees: her father swore to it—and let the animal walk slowly toward the river. Her father did not like her riding in the open fields, alone, and she respected his injunction. But she was permitted the relatively short ride to the nearby stream, called a river but, in fact, more a creek, and she took advantage of the permission whenever she could. Her father was newly back from Boston, where he'd gone on some political business. He was very nearly as political as his new wife, and his medical practice was much diminished. It did not seem to trouble him, though former patients regretted his new preoccupations: Grace had a vague sense—these things were of course not openly talked of—that Lydia had brought quite a lot of money with her, and so the family income had not visibly suffered. Right now, her father was making medical calls. Her new mother was about to return from New York, where she, too, had traveled on business.

And would Lydia return alone?

Grace bent her head, to avoid a low-hanging bough. The stream was only a quarter of a mile farther. It was still at its fullest, the spring freshets not yet having dried away. By August it would be a trickle, and in some years it was bone dry by October. She had no favorite occupation, on its banks. She liked to hear the faint, almost bell-like rush of the flowing water. The sun made odd and lovely patterns on the shifting surface, bounding crazily off smooth rocks at the stream bottom.

As a child, she had skimmed flat stones by the hour, and she knew that Mark still did. She and Mark had built dams, too (the others were not interested in such activities), regularly swept away by the current until Grace persuaded her brother that damming off only a part of the stream, rather than trying to obstruct its entire swift movement, would be more practicable. Mark would then catch small fish, and stock their man-made pools; as he grew older he would even return for days in a row, to feed and to observe the fish making new homes for themselves. And he always cared enough to destroy the stone walls around them, when he grew tired of the whole enterprise. Grace had praised him, just as regularly, for that considerate care.

Would Jonathan come with her mother? It would be a telling sign, this time, if he did not. It would not be hard to understand, after all that had gone before.

The pony stopped, at the top of the final slope. Sometimes she liked to ride him down; sometimes she liked to dismount and walk slowly alongside him, the reins loose in her hands. She would pick flowers, now and then, and the slower she strolled, the more he got to eat. He waited for her to dismount, if she were going to. She did not, and with a small shake he continued toward the water.

Jonathan would not come: she had a growing sense of some such final token, a waxing conviction that he did not want her and would never come for her. She knew, as she seemed always to have known, that she wanted him, that she loved him more than sufficiently. She was sure she would always love him: he had always been there; he had always been her very reason for growing up, for becoming a woman. And in his way he did love her, that, too, was clear. But not sufficiently. Or he was afraid, though of what she did not know: the incest notion had no reality to her. Who would dare to disapprove? Or perhaps he loved someone else more, and more deeply, than he loved her? She did not think it was the lady in France, whoever she had been; she knew there had been someone. But that was history.

Jonathan's editorial work tied him pretty stringently to his desk. When would he have found time to fall in love quite so desperately? The only woman he saw with any degree of frequency, so far at least as she knew, was his sister Lydia. But Grace had not inquired, and Jonathan had not told her, whether there had been other opportunities. No one would tell her, to be sure; perhaps even her new mother would not tell her, if by some coincidence or special power of divination Lydia herself knew. Women did not often know what men did, when they

were not in plain sight. Women had no great means for learning anything that men did, behind female backs. It was, in truth, very hard to
be a woman: that, anyway, was starkly evident.

She tethered the horse, loosely enough so he could graze, then
walked down to the edge of the running stream. She did not feel like
sitting: that would have been much too inactive. There was too much
stirring inside her; she could not place herself in ladylike poses and
gently meditate. And what was there to meditate about? Either he came,
and all might yet be well, or he would not come, and it was finally ended.

The sun was behind her. She could see her shadow on the water. Slowly, she lifted her arms over her head, then spread them out,
watching the patterns of light and shade, how the sparkling stones were
snuffed out, turned into mere wet rock, as the shadows passed across
them. Mr. Hawthorne, most of whose writing she admired, had done
terrible, heavy-handed things with light and shadow, in scenes alongside just such a stream. *The Scarlet Letter* fairly dripped with obvious
moralisms of that sort. All the same, it felt a little like some strange, hidden source of power, to be able to alter nature by the mere raising and
lowering of one's arms. God had summoned light, and then darkness,
in that way. She smiled. Lydia would laugh at her, and her Aunt Arabella
would gasp, hearing such prattle. Her father would smile indulgently.
And Jonathan?

She let her arms drop. No one, she sometimes thought, knew him
as well as she did. But at other times she wondered if she knew him at
all, if he had not been playing a subtle, skilful, lifelong game of hide-
and-seek with her. Or something worse than a game, perhaps, something so woven into the fabric of his existence that he could not have
helped himself. Was Jonathan, in fact, that kind of incarnate magician,
a spinner of soft fantasies, a teller of gorgeous lies? And not exactly
lies, because—and she was quite firm about this—Jonathan had never
meant to deceive her. Or himself. There was no conscious deception,
no realization of deceit. But was there deception, was there a pattern of
subtle lying? Was it all fantastic? The very thought was devastating, but
reality seemed to be marching inexorably in that direction.

She whirled, suddenly, then crouched halfway down. Then she
threw herself into an abstract dance as wild and free as anything she
had ever experienced. Her long skirt flew; her arms twisted and inter-
twined, while her legs took her into the air in leaps that felt as soaring
and light as some mythical dance to Diana or to Apollo. She felt herself
to be floating, flying, half-animal and half-human. There was no audi-

ence; she did not need an audience. It was not a dance of display, but a dance of fundamental tension, an unwinding, inch by inch, of the taut forces unbearably twisted up inside her. She was not expressing herself but freeing herself. Her art became, as she swung from grassy slope to placid rock, from bent huddle to flashing flight, a kind of internal pathway, a road into deeper and calmer regions waiting to be discovered, places of certainty and knowledge located, both miraculously and un-surprisingly, far inside herself. She was not aware of discovery; she did not reflect on either surprise or the full sense of rightness, of certitude, that flowed into her. But she knew, her body knew, and she danced with an authority that was new even for her, that was grounded in realities she was able, now, to make use of even without understanding. Art and understanding were no longer the same. They would not be the same, when the dance was over. Nothing could be the same, though she did not yet know that, and the dance had not ended; the dance went on and on as though it neither would nor could ever end.

TWENTY-FIVE

"I feel a vacuum, an indifference, a want of motive, which I cannot well describe."

—Daniel Webster to his friend, Mrs. E.B. Lee
18 May 1828

Theodore met his brother at the door.

"How long has it been, Jonathan, since we gathered at this house? The Johnsons are already here; Arabella is with them. Come in, come, in. I was sure you'd make it, though Lydia expressed some doubts."

Jonathan entered. It was the same big, old house, little changed. Theodore owned it, but he had not much lived in it. Plainly, the tenants had done little except dwell for a bit, like campers on vacation.

"I wasn't sure there'd be a boat, on the fourth of July. But there was." He paused, looking slowly around. "The same old Grandvoort house, isn't it?"

"The family may come and go, but the house goes on forever. We are much reduced, aren't we, as a family? I've done nothing to add to the rolls—and come to mention it, brother, neither have you!"

"I at least have time, brother," he replied, and Theodore laughed again, then took his arm and led him into the drawing room.

"Jonathan!" Martial called out at once, rising. "You've become a stranger, blast it. I thought we had you well roped and tied, when you took on *The Weekly*, but you've used it as an excuse to stay away!"

"He has, however, worked," Lydia smiled. "I can testify to that."

"Bosh to his work! I consider family ties, and the ties of affection, distinctly more important." Martial was reluctant to stop shaking Jonathan's hand.

"Which is perhaps why you are, yourself, so rarely at home, Father?" said Grace, who had not risen.

Martial pretended to scowl at her, but he released Jonathan, who approached and took Grace's hand.

"*Enchanté, ma princesse,*" he murmured. Grace smiled quietly but did not reply. Alice, and Mark, and Michael, came to be greeted. There was a minor hub-bub; Theodore plainly enjoyed it.

"We have not seemed so much like a family," he declared firmly, "in a great many years."

"But we are divided," Arabella added, "only by geography."

"Indeed. Will you have a sherry, Jonathan?"

"Even Michael and I have one," Mark announced. There were smiles all around the room.

"You'd think it was Christmas," Jonathan laughed, "rather than the fourth of July!" He took a sherry and stood warming it in his hand. "Reluctant as I am to agree with my older brother, I must admit it is very comforting to see so many Binghams, and Johnsons too, assembled in one place. I had almost forgotten there were even this many of us."

"Some of us," Martial put in, "have been dutifully obedient to the Biblical injunctions."

"I have the feeling there may be a conspiracy afoot. Perhaps I did wrong to come, after all!"

"If you are not safe in the bosom of your family," said Theodore, "where, pray tell, might you be safe?"

Arabella left her husband's side and took Jonathan's arm.

"You shall have at least one protector and guardian, Brother."

Jonathan sipped his sherry and tried to ignore the tautness in his stomach. But under his breath he murmured, too softly for even Arabella to hear, "*lasciate ogni speranza, voi ch' entrate po.*" And then, to make amends, he smiled around him. "But we are not gathered for the sacrifice of *this* prodigal son, surely?"

"Do you offer yourself?" Martial demanded to know.

"Some of my friends in Washington, you know, rather thought I was doing just that, when I took on an abolitionist paper."

"And now we shall have the closest thing to an abolitionist President we are likely ever to have. Mr. Lincoln will win, I am sure of it."

"I trust you are wrong, Husband," Lydia said at once. "Mr. Lincoln is surely a vast improvement, but he is no abolitionist. And the country can just as surely do better. We have many better men."

"And women," Martial smiled.

"Indeed."

"There are, perhaps, better men here in this very room," Arabella affirmed. "But they are not, alas, likely to compete for the presidency."

Theodore cleared his throat and set down his glass.

"I knew I could count on you, my dear," he said quietly to his wife, "to set the stage for me." There was a decisiveness in his voice that compelled attention. He smoothed his vest over his mildly protuberant stomach. "I do have an announcement to make."

"You *will* be competing for the presidency, Uncle Theodore?"

"No, Michael. Exactly the opposite of that, for better or for worse. I sha'n't be competing for *anything* public, any longer."

There was a silence.

"You're leaving the Senate?" Martial exclaimed.

"I am." Theodore spoke with due solemnity. "I could not make the news public without first telling you, my family and my friends." He looked at their faces, carefully, as if trying to gauge their reactions. "How strange," he mused. "It was to Uncles Karl and Peter that I spoke, twelve years ago, before I became a candidate. And I shall go to the city, tomorrow, and tell them that I am ceasing to be a candidate. But it is to you, who are none of you in business, or in finance, that I wanted first to turn, now that I am leaving politics. I dare say there is a hidden moral in that, though I am not the man to dig it out."

"I am very sorry to hear it," Martial said slowly. "Are you quite decided?"

"Quite."

Martial shook his head.

"I am more pleased than sorry, Theodore," Jonathan declared. "You are quite right, after all. The wheels have spun, and the situation is not what it was. We may shortly be engaged in an internecine struggle of vast and bloody proportions."

Arabella shuddered.

"God forbid it."

"But we may," Lydia said quietly. "Where will you and Arabella live, brother?"

"Where we have lived until now. But perhaps more in this old house than we have hitherto, eh, Arabella?"

Arabella made a quiet face, which communicated nothing.

"It is rumored," Martial said, "that your colleague in the Senate, Theodore, I mean, that is, your New York colleague, Mr. Seward, will be asked to join Mr. Lincoln's cabinet. He is said to be the leading candidate for the post of Secretary of State."

"I think the rumors are well-founded. I should be very surprised, indeed, if they were not."

"Are you yourself—"Grace began, but Theodore cut her off with a laugh.

"My dear young lady, when I say I am leaving politics you must believe me. I am only forty-four years old; it is hardly retirement!"

"They will coax you back," Martial smiled.

Theodore banged lightly on a table.

"Never!"

"He has had almost twenty years of it, you know," Jonathan put in. "Six in the House, and now two full terms in the Senate."

"I shall be glad to have him back," Arabella said cheerfully. "The practice of law may be arduous, from time to time, but it will be nothing like so demanding as the Senate. And altogether quieter."

"I agree," Lydia said softly. "It is a good decision, brother Theodore. You and my sister Arabella will be all the happier for it."

"And that is, after all, the main thing, is it not? To be happy, these days, and to be in politics, are very close to mutually exclusive matters. For me, in truth, it has been increasingly plain that I was meant for a different life. Perhaps I might have been a lifelong politician, in some other age—but even then I do not think so. I intend to practice law, but not with any excess fervor." He smiled. "I have tried to practice politics in exactly that way. It does not seem to fit the times, I'm afraid."

"Have you informed Mr. Weed?" asked Martial.

Theodore spread his arms wide, an all-embracing gesture.

"I have informed no one." He dropped his arms, and smiled. "You, my dear family, are the first to hear. And then Uncles Karl and Peter. And then, in writing, the President of the Senate—for if I am not to stand for re-election, why should I stand in some more ambitious man's way? Governor Morgan will stand for re-election, this year. He will be elected, without any doubt. But by 1862, it would seem to me, he will be anxious to move on, if he is able, to the Senate. I could be of best service to him, I dare say, if I myself stayed on until then, and then bowed out in his favor, but I could not bring myself to do it. Not any more."

"Who would he appoint, were you to resign now?" asked Lydia.

"No one who would be a threat to his own ambitions, plainly," Martial put in.

"But someone who could stand for election this fall, and hope to prevail," said Jonathan. "But, of course, there is also Mr. Seward's seat, likely to come vacant in the spring. Not certain, but as you say, Theodore, likely.

"Mr. Morgan might confer with Mr. Lincoln; there are certainly others with whom he would confer, Mr. Weed among them. Mr. Weed is not such an ogre as, of late, people have maintained. And then there is your friend Mr. Greeley, Jonathan. He is something of a power in this state. And he is, as you surely know, much interested in public office for himself."

"Still?"

"Still, my dear Jonathan. The editor does not change his spots, nor ever will. Not that he will be chosen, no, I do not mean that. But he will need to be consulted."

"Will you make a suggestion to Governor Morgan?" Lydia wondered.

"Would you like me to, Sister?"

"If it is not to be a full-fledged political appointment—that is, if the person appointed ought in no more than two years to be obliging and step down for Governor Morgan himself, why not consider your brother Martial?"

"Lydia!"

She rose, her face a little flushed.

"Why not, Martial? You have traveled and spoken all up and down the state; your name is increasingly known. And what will Mr. Lincoln want, these next years, in the Senate? Precisely voices, and votes, like yours, Martial."

"Sister," said Theodore carefully, "I do not think it possible."

She turned rapidly toward him.

"And why not, pray? There are many things that have not seemed possible, and yet have of late been done. The election of Mr. Lincoln, half a dozen years ago, would have struck most knowledgeable men as laughable. Why, he could not defeat Mr. Douglas in Illinois, let alone win a national election. But he *will* win." She stared at Theodore. "Many things become possible, brother, when we conceive of them as possibilities."

"What Theodore means, Sister," Jonathan interposed, "is perhaps that a Senator cannot be a partisan appointment."

"Are not all Senators, and all members of the House, as well, partisanly appointed, and elected, and maintained? Are there, in truth, any non-partisans in our government, at any level?"

"Political partisans, yes. Our brother Johnson is not a partisan medical man, but he is very likely to be perceived, across the state, as an ideological partisan."

"At a time of imminent civil war?" Lydia demanded, standing almost at the center of a small half-circle—Theodore, Jonathan, and her husband around her. "What could be more ideologically partisan than killing your neighbor? And what could be more politically appropriate, pray, than an ideological Senator who would reflect and aid and strengthen that effort?"

"How bloodthirsty you are, Sister," Arabella murmured.

"We can hope that civil war will not be the path," Theodore said hurriedly. "There are men of good sense on both sides of the issue."

Lydia looked almost pityingly at him, but she did not reply.

"It would perhaps do no harm, Theodore," Jonathan finally said, speaking very carefully, "to broach the idea to the Governor. If, that is, our silent medical brother is prepared to be pilloried in your place?"

Martial was obliged to speak, at last.

"I am taken very much by surprise, believe me," he said a bit shakily. "I had not known that my dear wife was prepared to suggest this violent change in our domestic arrangements, and the domestic arrangements of our state, as well."

Theodore applauded.

"Spoken, dear fellow, like a true politician!" He laughed delightedly. "I do not need to hear more. Our Martial is willing!"

Jonathan blinked.

"Are you, Martial?"

"I don't know."

Arabella glided toward him and tapped his arm.

"My husband has spoken accurately; the infection has set in, and the patient will require some hard exposure before he is cured."

"Before," Theodore corrected, "he is elected."

"It hardly seems likely," Martial murmured.

"I agree," said Theodore. "But your dear wife has an uncanny knack for analysis, and she could just be right. I will sound the Governor, this next week, and let you know." He paused. "And you, Martial, you might well sound a few people, too. Mr. Greeley, for one. I will mention this to Uncles Karl and Peter, who have surely had business dealings with Mr. Morgan. He began as a commission merchant, you know, and became one of the great importers in the city. He is wealthy beyond counting, I am told. And he is a shrewd man, not reckless, but not above taking a flyer when the market seems right for it. He moves decisively, as you may have noted. He will make a good Senator, when he comes to it. If he can settle the truly ambitious with Mr. Seward's seat, in the spring, he may be willing to give you your place in the sun, Martial. You are not, after all, an undistinguished citizen of our state. You would have been immensely useful in the Senate, you know, to Mr. Sumner. Who knows how soon be might have returned to the wars, had a doctor been handy."

Lydia turned away, abruptly, but did not speak.

"Politics does seem like an infection, in this family," Grace said softly. "I had not expected it to bite you, too, Father."

"Well, I have been spoken for by my wife, and by my sister Arabella, and by my brother Theodore. But I do not think you have yet heard my voice, have you?"

"You have not said no," Grace answered gently, and Martial fussed with his suspenders.

"Well," he said, and that was all he said.

"I should like more sherry, if I may, Uncle Theodore," said Mark.

Sherry was poured, and consumed, and much more with it. And politics was abandoned, at least in their words.

As Theodore was heard to say to his wife, later that night when the house was still and the guests had left them, he had meant the day as a family gathering, not as a nominating convention.

She smiled at him, knowingly, and he did not protest farther.

29 August 1860

My very dearest Jonathan,

You will have to permit me the salutation. It has been earned, though it may not currently be appreciated.

I wonder if you know, truly know, how much I love you? You perhaps think of me, still, as "little Grace"—though I think you know that that time is behind us. But I can understand how difficult it is for you—I can <u>understand</u>, please believe me, though I cannot share your feelings. You have withdrawn yourself from me; I do not need to know why, and I am not asking you to explain anything to me. Not anything. I cannot, however, withdraw myself from you. You will smile, perhaps, but it is too late; I cannot ever love anyone else. "Bosh," you will say; I can almost hear *you saying it. But Jonathan, it can be bosh to you, and scripture to me. It is true. I will never love anyone else. And since you will not marry me, I will not marry anyone else. How could I, with my heart forever and solely yours?*

 Well, I am married, in another way, and I shall have to content myself with that. I could do a great deal worse. My mother could have been married in this same way, but she chose my father instead. I do not mean to criticize her; I certainly do not judge her, or regret her choice, either on her own behalf or on mine. I have had but two obsessions, in my entire life, as she also had two. She secured one, my father, and put everything else into second place. I have failed to secure you, and so I will put my dancing first, and second, and third. I must have a marriage of some sort—as surely all the proper people in the world would agree—and so I shall be married, happily and very busily, to my dancing.

 You will think me grandiose beyond my years. So be it. You will think me over-sure of myself: I expect to hear a great many such remarks, in the years left to me. Those who make such remarks will be totally in error, but totally in keeping with the usual perception of things. Mine is not that usual perception, Jonathan. You know that fully, because yours, too . . . well, let it go. I do not need to tell you about yourself, and I do not want to tell you about me. We have each to make our own choices. You have made yours, and since it is not to choose me, I must tell you what my choice will be. I have the will to accomplish it, though I could not be more aware than I already am how difficult it is going to be. My father will oppose this, I suspect—but that will be ironic, because it is by his doing that I have the means to do what I must do. God knows if I can do it well, but He knows, as surely you do, that I can do it, and that I <u>*will*</u>*.*

 Exactly how, I confess, I do not yet know. I will need to be terribly clever, and far more perceptive than I yet know how to be. I will need to watch for my chance, and I will need the courage to take it, to accept what opportunity may offer me. Like a child on a merry-go-round, I must be ready to snatch at the brass ring, and hold it tightly. I think I am likely to be ready, some day, when it comes—whether it take me far or near. I would hate to spend my life in some terribly distant place—though Aunt Arabella will tell you, probably, that I once suggested fleeing to Japan! Still, I am ready to go even that far, if it becomes necessary. Nor will it be a flight, if I go that far. Aunt Arabella can also tell you that I have said to her, oh, many times, that I do not need protection, that I am not a fearful female in need of a masculine shield. (I do not think that she is, either, but she has been obliged to pretend, and she more than half believes her own pretense, by now.) And love is a very different thing from protection.

 Well. I do not mean this to be a letter that you are required to acknowledge.

 Correspondence between us, now, is neither likely nor even useful. I do not mean that I am annoyed at you, dear Jonathan: I am not; I do not think I would ever be.

But neither do I wish to plague you—and certainly I do not wish to intrude where I am not entirely welcome.

We will see each other at such family gatherings as may take place. Someday, perhaps, you will fly in one direction and I in another. You are, I suspect, quite likely to marry. A dozen years from now, who knows? I might be Aunt Grace to a little Joan or Jonathan. I do not think I will mind, by then—though the thought is quite exquisitely painful to me, at the moment. I conjure it up, please believe me, to harden myself, not to afflict you.

But the best thing I can do to not afflict you, my dear, is, I think, to stop writing. I love you so terribly that it is painful far past, I think, your or anyone's understanding. But I do not quarrel; I only mourn.

And I will remain, forever,
your
Grace

"It was a momentous speech," Greeley affirmed, "though this time I did not have the exclusive printing of it."

"As you did, with the Cooper Union speech, I believe?"

"Indeed yes, Mrs. Johnson. Mr. Lincoln came to our offices, to read the galleys. And read them he did, with immense care and accuracy. He is a deeply serious man; that much is, I think, indisputable."

Lydia smiled. Jonathan did not speak.

"So you see," Greeley went on, "One can be defeated for the Senate and still go on to larger things. Though I do not expect your husband will try for the office Mr. Lincoln now occupies." He rambled back to his desk, fiddling with a gold watch chain that ran across his rumpled shirt. "I have had a certain experience with political rejection, Mr. Johnson. It is not pleasant. But neither is it destructive. To be denied that which one wants, which one thinks and knows to be proper and fitting, is nevertheless educational."

"I do not think my husband wanted education, Mr. Greeley."

Greeley chuckled and swung his gold chain.

"No, but there are some means of instruction, Mrs. Johnson, some pathways to knowledge, which can only be opened to us on their own terms. We cannot predict their illumination; we cannot even prepare the way."

"You are sounding more like Mr. Emerson all the time," Jonathan put in.

Greeley turned to him with a smile.

"Do you know what Mr. Emerson says of the *Tribune?* That we do the West's thinking for it, and at the bargain rate of two dollars a year!" He laughed his squeaking, trilled laugh. "The least I can do, Jonathan, is repay the compliment by borrowing Mr. Emerson's ideas. They are good ideas, even if, as he says, they are not his in the first place."

Lydia put the galleys of Lincoln's inaugural speech on a table.

"I do not find this momentous, Mr. Greeley."

"After all these years in which history has moved with painful slowness, often seeming not to move at all, it is moving very rapidly now, Mrs. Johnson. Very rapidly, indeed. And we shall soon enough know which of us is right and which wrong." He nodded slowly, thoughtfully. "It will be proven beyond any human doubt." He raised one hand dramatically, his voice starting to rise. "If the Union coheres, if Mr. Lincoln, now President Lincoln, can hold this nation together, history will have voted for him as surely as did all of us in this room."

"I do not vote, Mr. Greeley."

"I beg your pardon, Mrs. Johnson. It is a tribute to your force of intellect, and not any disrespect for your beauty, which leads me astray."

Lydia did not smile.

"Mr. Lincoln has extended, I believe, too fat an olive branch."

"Are you concerned that it might be accepted?" Greeley thumped his desk. "By God, no one will shirk from war, if I have anything to say about it, but it is peace and not war that I want. Do you want us to be fighting our cousins, Mrs. Johnson? What would you have had Mr. Lincoln say?"

"He would not have said what I would have had him say, Mr. Greeley."

"Do not fear. Events will move him. Were I a betting man, Mrs. Johnson, I would accept wagers on Mr. Lincoln's becoming, in the end, as staunch an abolitionist as—as you yourself!"

Lydia only smiled.

"It is an eventful time," Jonathan said.

Greeley suddenly looked at his watch and leaped out from behind his desk.

"Ah, you will excuse me! I must run; I am late."

And he hopped and bounced through the door and out.

"He will never change." Jonathan smiled. "He would be a terrible Senator. I have no doubt of that. But he is, I also believe, as good for the things he does do as anyone possibly could be. He is a very great editor. One sees that more and more clearly the longer one works near him. A much better editor than I could ever be."

"You are an editor of a rather different sort."

"I could not handle the *Tribune*."

"You do not have to."

"It is fortunate, Lydia. It is fortunate for the *Tribune*, most of all! All the same, I wish Greeley had not quarreled with Dana. That was too important a post. Greeley is always making excessively rapid decisions, and then having to live, catch-as-catch-can, with the consequences. He manages, I will admit. He manages well. But sometimes I wonder how!"

She sat looking across the room at him. The early spring sun was pale and almost seemed not to cast any shadows.

"You grow sadder and sadder," she finally said.

"Do I?"

"Can you deny it?" There was a silence. "You cannot, you see."

"I do not know how you can contemplate an actual civil war, a bloody fight between members of the same family." He shook his head. "I cannot contemplate it. We're, as it seems, inevitably approaching that. I am less and less able—not more and more, as the rest of the world seems to be—to accept such a conclusion."

"You do not say such things in print."

"It is not my place to say them in print."

"You are the editor of *The Weekly*."

"I am the servant of those who own and who fund *The Weekly*."

"Are you in disagreement with your editorial obligations, Jonathan?" He did not answer. "Do you wish to relinquish them?"

"I don't know."

"You are being introspective, brother! That must stop. You cannot afford to question yourself in quite that way. Nor can *The Weekly* afford to lose you. You are, in truth, as good an editor, for what *you* do, as is Mr. Greeley himself."

"Nonsense. But thank you for saying it. I do not know that I have had so very many compliments from you, Lydia."

"Do you require more?"

"I am mortal, and weak, and you are so fearfully good at what *you* do, my dear Sister, that any notice you deign to take of me is more than welcome!"

"Don't you remember—oh, so many years ago now, Jonathan—when I told you that I do not compliment, and I do not blame? I simply tell the truth."

He stared at her, wishing it were possible to say more.

"It is not so simple," he said at last.

"Only if you do not see clearly. I see very clearly. I cannot pretend to see more than a very few things, but what I am able to see I am able to envision without interference."

"You have rare gifts, Lydia. They are rarer than you know."

She stood up.

"You are about to flatter me, Jonathan. It is a tendency you display more frequently, of late. It augurs poorly for your own firmness of mind, I think. You cannot strengthen your sense of weakness by pretending that I am stronger than in truth I am."

"Is that what I have been doing?"

"It is, I believe, what you have been attempting to do. It is plain that you have not been successful. You could not be successful, Jonathan. Do not remain in this post if you do not wish to. But know yourself, first."

"Every heart vibrates to that iron string," he murmured, and she heard him.

"Is there a man wiser than Mr. Emerson?"

She stood in front of her chair, preparing, he thought, to leave, but lingering to challenge him, to quicken him. She did not realize, he was aware, what she quickened him to. He had no recollection of a woman more vital, more utterly captivating. He longed to throw himself on his knees in front of her and tell her what, for years, he had tried not even to think. But he knew he would not move, would not speak.

"Not me, certainly," he finally replied.

She came close to stamping her foot.

"You are excessively fripperous, Brother," she said coldly. "I think you had best be left to yourself for a bit."

"As punishment for my sins?"

She paused at the door.

"As a stimulus to greater virtue. You are capable of a great deal more than you know."

He did not turn to watch her leave. He was more virtuous than she suspected, but considerably less capable. He was, however, quite as saddened by events as she had said he was. He felt a growing sense of helpless misery and knew it would not be long, one way or another, before the dam broke, and he was moved—but to what, and to where, he did not yet know. For all his questioning, all his doubting, he did not know. He never knew anything until it had happened: for him, at least, knowledge and history seemed to be almost identical forces.

There was work to be done, work piled on his desk. He glanced quickly at it, then looked away. Did anything he accomplished, anything he wrote, now make any difference? He and his weekly publication had been whatever they had been, just as Mr. Lincoln had been what he had been. None of it mattered any more. "Those who nominated and elected me," Mr. Lincoln had said, speaking of his prior assurances to the South, assurances of non-interference with slavery in that part of the country, "did so with full knowledge that I had made this and many similar declarations, and had never recanted them." Yes, but surely Mr. Lincoln knew that nothing he had said, even nothing he believed, was as potent, now, as what was done, and not only by him. Events had swept too far out of any man's control. Events would follow one upon the other, tumbling like a long line of painted clowns at a circus, each apparently independent of the other, but in truth each wound and impelled by the same hidden, all-powerful spring.

Mr. Lincoln did not favor abolition, he did not want war. Did it matter? Not a bit, if the South thought he did, if the South continued to seize arsenals and forts, if the South continued to mobilize for a war that did not yet exist but that their very mobilization could bring swiftly into being. Jefferson Davis had already been inaugurated as president of something called the Confederacy. He had a presidential Cabinet, with some notable names. He had rifles in his hands, and he had aimed them at Mr. Lincoln, and he would surely fire. Would Mr. Lincoln not fire back? He would fire back. And what would follow? Who could predict anything, under such circumstances, except universal disaster, death, slaughter, and misery—and such a legacy of suffering that it would be a hundred years or more before anyone could be said to have "won"? What possible victory was there, in such a conflict?

And what place was there for *The Weekly*, and for Jonathan Bingham, in a world so rapidly exploding? Did he belong anywhere, on either side? He had never considered himself very much like his older brother, but Theodore had seen it coming, and had quietly withdrawn. This was a family trait, perhaps. Had there ever been a Bingham with a true martial spirit? Oh, cross a Bingham with something else, say a Johnson, and then it was possible, right enough. But the pure Bingham blood ran without heat. His father, now: the old man had been quite without heat—maybe that was why he had not gotten on well with his wife, Jonathan's mother, who had been all frustrated heat. They had neither of them possessed very much light; he smiled and nodded at the thought. His mother had been a Bingham only by marriage, to be sure. And what of Anne-Marie? There had been heat in her—and what had it come to? It had burned her into her grave.

This was not philosophy. It was sheer practicality. One was what one was. It was not up to Jonathan Bingham to change his clan—or his world. He had not come into the world to reform it; he was not the son of the engineer. But even that was less to the point than the stark, personal reality. He could not change himself: that was what it came down to. He was past thirty. He had been working at self-repair for over a dozen years; he had had a great deal of more than competent help, but the task was beyond him. He could not be different; he could only be what he was—however limited, however circumscribed, however weakened and defective that might be. The realization did not cheer him, but if he felt no better, at least he felt more sure. It would be time to act, soon, and he would need to be terribly sure. He would need to be ready. He could not have explained that to Lydia. He could not explain much to Lydia. He wished that, too, were different. It did not matter what he wished, as it had not mattered that Lydia's daughter wanted to marry him, and had said she would marry no one else if she could not, and was apparently thinking, now, of an emigration to Europe, probably to France, where the sort of life she felt was left to her, a wife dedicated to the dance, would perhaps be more possible. All that mattered, now and ever, was what was. It was, it had been, it would be.

"I have just been handed this telegram."

Jonathan took it, read it.

"Your informant is a reliable man?" he asked Greeley.

"Totally."

Jonathan looked down at the telegram. Confederate batteries had opened fire on the federal garrison, shut up these last weeks and months in Fort Sumter. It had been a four-month siege; federal ships, which even Buchanan had felt obliged to send, had been several times driven off by these same batteries. But there had been no true fighting, until now. The match box had not been opened; the tinder had not been lit. And now the shore batteries had begun what the telegram described as a heavy, continuous fire. Fort Sumter would not be able to hold out for very long: that was plain. But after the fort had surrendered? Buchanan had sent ships that bore no arms, with only stores and provisions. What would Lincoln do?"

"It will make a dandy front-page head," Greeley said cheerfully.

Jonathan looked up; the cheerfulness was assumed, for there were lines of anxiety already visible on Greeley's thin face. Jonathan handed back the telegram. "This is madness. I find it hard to believe. You are sure of your informant?"

Greeley simply nodded.

"Perhaps you would do well to await some official word?"

"And be beaten to the news by every other rag in town?"

Jonathan's sigh was more than an expression of weariness, of tension, of fear, of an intense sadness.

"It is pure insanity," he repeated.

Greeley waved the telegram about.

"It is pure fact, Jonathan. And you had better start getting used to it. And to facts, in general." Greeley moved toward the door, then came back. "Our lives may have seemed to be ruled by ideas, by notions and propositions and assumptions." He almost flung his arm, waving the telegram like a banner, like a starter's flag. "But now is a time of facts, and our job, yours and mine, will be to gather them and print them, not to help make them. There will be more than enough to keep us on the run, I can promise you."

"There will be war, a bloody war among neighbors and kinfolk, friend killing friend."

Greeley hopped and danced in place; the excitement began to register on his face, which turned first reddish, then chalk white.

"The war, my dear Jonathan, cannot be talked of in that way, in some vague, postulated futuristic tense. The war *is*, it has begun. The war, as I said, is a *fact*. And remember this, pray: we in the North did not fire the first shots. We held off, perhaps even too long. We wanted anything but war. But the war has been pressed upon us—and I can tell you something else, even at this point. We did not fire the first shots, but we all fire the last ones. For we will *win* this combat, by God!"

Jonathan did not look up, did not speak. He could sense Greeley hovering over his shoulder, expectant. It was as if Greeley had felt obliged to echo Lincoln's quite predictable proclamation of rebellion, and now felt obliged to wait for Jonathan's declaration, as well. Did each of them have to make a personal declaration of war? Greeley was no soldier, but neither was Jonathan. Would the North rise up in arms, as Greeley seemed to feel sure it would? Quite probably. But not Jonathan.

"Well," he finally said, his voice heavy, "that settles one difficulty." He turned and managed a smile, as he glanced up and met Greeley's overly bright glance. "It is clear *The Weekly* no longer requires my services. The deed is done."

Greeley's shock was apparent.

"*The Weekly* has never needed you more! Your country has never—"

Jonathan rose, putting his hand on the older man's bony shoulder.

"No, Mr. Greeley. The issue is joined, now. As you said, yourself, not a moment ago, it will be entirely in the hands of the generals. Guns and cannon will speak, and poets will need to be quiet." He made a wry face, then let his hand fall. "It has all been set in motion, and we could not stop it if we chose. Those fools in South Carolina, touching off their blasted cannon! They've touched off more than they know. It will be done, to paraphrase an ancient saying. And I *am* no longer needed. It would be my judgment, indeed, that *The Weekly* is not needed, not now—but that is not my decision to make. I merely venture an opinion, and only in private. My sister, and my uncles, and you, will decide that. And if you decide to maintain the publication, why, I have no doubt you will find someone suitably militant to run it. But not me. I am done, finished."

Greeley's face had turned wistful.

"And me?"

"Oh, you are very different. You are *always* needed! You and the *Tribune.* I dare say Mr. Lincoln would weep if you failed to support him. The public will need the information you can give them. They will need the advice and the wisdom you can offer them. They will need encouragement. You will have to contend with all sorts of mob fits—but I hardly need tell you: you have contended with virtually all of them already, in one form or another." He bent and ruffled the papers on his desk, idly shuffling them, as if they were cards on a gambler's table. "I wonder if there is anything left to hunt for, in California?" There was a strange silence. "I understand, from the pages of the *Tribune,* that there is gold to be found, up on Pike's Peak."

"We have so reported."

Jonathan turned and quickly embraced Greeley.

"I will ascend to its top, Mr. Greeley, and I will not come down until I am as laden with nuggets as a mule! Or else I will sit with a volume of Mr. Emerson's essays and commune with the oversoul. Surely it must dwell on Pike's Peak, if anywhere in our benighted land?"

"Are you serious?"

"Never more so."

"No one can stay up on a mountain. Nor is this the time to play at being a hermit. I wish to have you *here*, Jonathan. If I am necessary, so too are you." He jabbed at the air. "I know what I speak. And do you realize how much help you can be to me? Why, with Dana deserting the ship . . . ."

"I shall of course be obliged to descend from the mountain, in time. I quite agree: no one can stay at such heights for very long."

"And then?" Greeley shrilled, suddenly agitated in voice as well as in words. "What will you do then, eh?"

"I suppose, like most other mortals, I will go about my business—whatever that business chances to be."

Greeley thumped at the air, his face reddening.

"Treat it as a vacation, yes, and return here!"

"I think not."

"What are you *saying?*" Greeley hopped away from him, as if, like a painter, he could not find the proper perspective while standing so close. "You are talking foolishness, sheer tommy-rot."

Jonathan wished he could say, as in truth he felt, that most of the time tommy-rot was all he had ever talked.

"Pretend I am being bardic," he said as gently as he knew how. "That I am being gripped by a daemon, whirled helplessly in its invisible, invincible claws." He spread out his arms, as if invoking a muse. "All the poetry left in the country lies in the wilderness, now. I am simply journeying forth to seek it out."

Greeley sneered with vexation.

"You are still talking balderdash."

"Then let me just say that I am tired—tired of what I have seen, what I have known. I do not wish to be here. I wish to be somewhere else, somewhere different. There does not seem to me to be anything I can decently do, here. It is not a hasty decision, pray believe me. I have felt it, or something like it, coming upon me for a long time. And Lydia—Mrs. Johnson—she too has seen it coming. Do ask her."

Greeley sighed, his face clearing. He visibly accepted the decision, though he continued to protest.

"How much you could do, Jonathan, if you wished to!"

"The will is everything, isn't it? You have so much of it, I wish I could borrow only a small part. I have never had enough."

Greeley came closer, peering into Jonathan's face.

"You do not have to be alone, you know," he said warmly. "No man is utterly alone, and you do not need to maintain so hermetic a privacy. As, plainly, you have done in the past. Men can work together, you know. One can support his brother. It is not an idle premise; it has been tried, I have myself tried it."

Jonathan extended his hand.

"Goodbye, Horace Greeley."

Greeley's hand was faintly limp.

"Do you propose to start all over again, as if you were newly born? It does not work, Jonathan. I can assure you of that. That, too, has been attempted, and it does not work."

"Of course. I am not such an innocent as all that, I trust. I know that I am certain things, and can perhaps be others, and can never, not in this world, be still others."

"You're an infernally good editor!"

"Thank you, my friend. Perhaps that is what I will continue to be, out there." He spread his left arm. "It was you, was it not, who urged young men go to West? I shall follow your advice—and though what I am will remain the same, the location, at least, will be different. And perhaps other aspects, as well. I hope so."

Greeley reached out and clasped his arm.

"Is there something you're running from?"

Jonathan patted his hand.

"Mostly the one thing I cannot run from, as you have just so well said. That is, myself." Greeley released him. "But I can perhaps sneak up on myself, coming in out of the wilderness and the darkness of the desert. Maybe, you know, just maybe, I can catch that self of mine off guard, in that new world out there, and knock it off its infernal balance. That is what I need to do, in fact. I need to knock myself around. And I'm too well protected, here. There are too many people who care, too many people who protect this infernal self, who nourish and strengthen it. I dare say the Indians out there could tell me a thing or two about springing onto your self and beating it into submission!"

Greeley's face registered intense shock.

"Indians?"

"Or cowboys. Or buffalo. Don't mind the words. I don't know what I'm doing, plainly. I just know I am obliged to do it."

"You will be back," Greeley predicted. "Perhaps feet first, though I hope not. But you will be back."

"I shall have lost more than a bet, if I return. But who knows, eh? In ten years, perhaps I will come back and buy you out. Or beg for a meal. Or a job. I don't know." He lifted a finger and wagged it good humoredly. "And neither do you!"

"I know one thing," Greeley added, as he turned to leave, and Jonathan prepared to straighten his desk and ready it for his successor, if successor there was to be. "There'll be times, if you ever do get out West, when you'll wish you were back right here, right here in this office, dealing with old Horace Greeley instead of wolves and bears and Indians!" He shook his head, lingering for just a second. "Indians! Tommy-rot, Jonathan. The purest tommy-rot I have ever heard you speak."

Jonathan sat down at his desk and methodically began to order it. He did not feel quite so sure as he had made himself out to be. There would be many a slip between this cup and his lip. He was thirty years old, an effete literary man, a professional city dweller. He could ride a horse, more or less (though not without a saddle). He knew how to fire a gun. That was about the total of his usable skills. It was not much. What would a man like himself do, in that western wilderness? What could he offer, in exchange for his bread and board? How long would he last?

He focused on the papers in front of him. Details, everything was details. You overcame one set and then you had to deal with another. But details, like principles, could be dealt with. The only thing that was not amenable was, as ever, the self inside: *that* you could not bend and twist, you could not overcome. Well, even iron could be shaped, if the anvil were hard, and the fire hot, and the hammer heavy. If it turned out that he was too brittle to be shaped, he would crack, and then the ancient of days, the eternal blacksmith, would have to drop him back into the crucible, and melt him down, and start all over again. If that was how it had to be, that would be how it was. It was the trying that mattered, wasn't it, not the horse shoes or the nails or the wagon bolts you turned out?

Picture Credits

Page 5: The Bingham House may have looked something like this splendid example of a colonial/Federalist-style home, the Rockford House in Lancaster County, Pennsylvania. (Photo ca. 1930) Library of Congress Prints and Photographs Division, HABS PA-368-4. Public domain.

Page 135: Horace Greeley (Daguerreotype by Matthew B. Brady, ca. 1850). Library of Congress Prints and Photographs Division, LC-USZ62-110105. Public domain.

Page 229: Daniel Webster (Daguerreotype by Matthew B. Brady, ca. 1845). Library of Congress Prints and Photographs Division, LC-USZ62-110179 DLC. Public domain.

Page 230: This notion of what Theodore Bingham could have looked like is actually Bob Owen (Print of original Daguerreotype, ca. 1850). History Museum for Springfield-Greene County, 1992-56-30-10. Used with permission.

Page 345: Front doorway of Rockford House, Lancaster Co., Pa. (photo ca. 1930). Library of Congress Prints and Photographs Division, HABS PA-368-7. Public domain.

ABOUT THE AUTHOR

NATHAN P. RAFFEL

Known internationally as a poet, translator, literary critic, and editor, Burton Raffel (b. 1928) has published more than one hundred books over a long, distinguished career. From his father, who spoke Russian, Ukrainian, Polish, German, Spanish, Hebrew, and Yiddish, Raffel inherited a polyglot's sense of the "deep structure" of languages, a facility that has made him one of the great literary translators of his generation. Having received his J.D. from Yale in 1958, he followed temporarily in his lawyer-father's footsteps; however, Raffel has primarily lived the nomadic life of an academician, teaching in English, comparative literature, and creative writing programs in Brooklyn, Stony Brook, and Buffalo, New York; Austin, Texas; Makassar, Indonesia; Toronto, Ontario; Denver, Colorado; Haifa, Israel; and Lafayette, Louisiana.

A full-blooded Brooklyner, he has been happily transplanted to Louisiana, where he lives with his wife, Elizabeth, a designer and maker of jewelry. In rare moments when he is not writing, Raffel's conversation turns to old-school baseball, classic jazz, and opera.

The range of Raffel's publications can only be hinted at. His translations of *Beowulf* (New American Library, 1963; U Mass P, 1971) and *Sir Gawain and the Green Knight* (New American Library, 1970; Signet, 2001) remain magisterial, the standards by which any others are measured, as will become his Englishings of Balzac and Cervantes for Norton and of Chrétien, Rabelais, and Stendhal for Yale UP in the 1980s and 90s. In addition to several monographs on the art of translation, English prosody, and the development of Indonesian poetry, he has published volumes of his own poetry, including *Beethoven in Denver and Other Poems* (Conundrum, 1999). Recent work includes Raffel's magnificent verse translation of the great High Middle German epic, *Das Niebelungenlied* (Yale UP, 2006); his modernization of Chaucer's *Canterbury Tales* (Random House, 2008) and his annotated editions of Shakespeare (Yale UP, 2003 and onward) and Milton (Bantam, 1999) feed the scholar's mind while training the poet's ear. Forthcoming at the time of this writing, his Dante will be the jewel in a translator's crown.

Yankee Doric is his first published novel; it will not be his last.